02

208

GW00983091

METROPOLITAN BOROUGH OF WIRRAL

DEPARTMENT OF LEISURE SERVICES

LIBRARIES AND ARTS

WITHDRAWN FROM STOCK

£2.99

(3I)

Gift Aid Item

20 12583884 1227

The Bells of Agony

By the same author

The Voices of the Dead
Pattern for a Tapestry

AUTRAN DOURADO

The Bells of Agony

Translated from the Portuguese by
JOHN M. PARKER

PETER OWEN · LONDON

ISBN 0 7206 0681 0

Translated from the Portuguese *Os sinos da agonia*

All Rights Reserved. No part of this
publication may be reproduced in any
form of by any means without the prior
permission of the publishers.

130 1306

METROPOLITAN BOROUGH
OF WIRRAL
DEPT. OF LEISURE SERVICES
LIBRARIES AND ARTS DIVISION

SBN ACC.N.	0720606810	
LCC. COPY	0201	Y.P.
CLASS No.		

854134

PETER OWEN PUBLISHERS
73 Kenway Road Road London SW5 0RE

First published in Great Britain 1988
© Autran Dourado 1974
English translation © John M. Parker 1988

Photoset in Great Britain by
Ann Buchan (Typesetters), Shepperton
Printed by Billings of Worcester

Introduction

Published in 1974, *Os sinos da agonia (The Bells of Agony)* was written during what is generally agreed to have been the most repressive phase of the authoritarian government exercised by the military regime which seized power in Brazil in 1964. The book's publishers, fearing that it would be seen as an allegory of the contemporary situation, insisted on inserting an explanatory note which laid particular stress on the reworking of the Phaedra theme and the use of universal archetypes and myths. They declared the novel to be neither historical nor realist, its deliberate anachronisms pointing rather to an intention to create a synthesis, a symbolic vision of the economic decadence of Minas Gerais, one of Brazil's wealthiest states, during the eighteenth century. Dourado agreed to the inclusion of the note on condition that no alterations were made to the text, feeling, as he subsequently wrote in a private letter, that 'those who had eyes to see would see', adding – this was in 1981 – that *The Bells of Agony* illustrated how he felt about the despotic, authoritarian rule under which Brazil had suffered in colonial times, while its atemporal narrative was well suited to express his repugnance for the suffocating political climate of the 1970s. In those times, Brazilian writers had, as he put it, to speak in tortuous, highly baroque metaphors.

Baroque is an epithet which, despite its dangers as a critical term, comes to mind frequently in relation to Dourado's fiction, but perhaps nowhere more than in the present novel, the very title of which reflects the passionate, conflictual nature of the great baroque tragedies and paintings. In a much-quoted work on the baroque, Helmut Hatzfeld considers as typical conflicts the existential struggles between God and worldliness, the body and the soul, good and evil, while establishing a link between the baroque and the Counter-Reformation with its dramatic religiosity, for which the new lands of South America were to be of such vital importance. The same writer includes among the most serious baroque *motifs* reflections on time and eternity and the growth of death within life, and one can add further such concepts as life as a dream (compare Calderón's famous drama *La vida es sueño (Life's a Dream)* and life as theatre ('All the world's a stage . . .'; also another

Calderón play *El gran teatro del mundo* (The Great Theatre of the World). For another specialist, Warnke, the baroque hero is passive, his will manifesting itself in resisting temptation, his triumph residing in making himself a sacrifice, a sacrifice which, according to Hatzfeld, is both the result and the defeat of a great passion. In formal terms, writers stress paradox in literature, *chiaroscuro* in painting, and the *concertante* style in music; Hatzfeld mentions the use of dark rooms into which people come with lights, or women seen by the light of a candle. One should not forget, also, the ornamental side to the baroque, unfortunately responsible, as a result of certain excesses, for the pejorative sense often attributed to the term.

There are various reasons for insisting on the link with the baroque when writing about *The Bells of Agony*, not the least of them being the frequency of the author's conscious use of the term in a series of essays on creative writing, mainly his own. He talks, for instance, about being imbued with the 'tortured baroque spirit' of Minas Gerais and the 'gloom', or darkness, of the late eighteenth century, in the period of the Arcadic poets and the anti-Portuguese conspiracy known as the *inconfidência mineira* (the Minas treason of 1789). He has stated in an interview that the reader who knows Minas Gerais and is conversant with the absolutist tradition in Portugal and Brazil will be able to see the shadows of those poets and others involved in the complot, though neither they themselves nor their names will be found in the novel, which includes not a single date or historical figure. Nor are they necessary for us to feel the tension between the glories of the recent past, relived in the splendour and pageantry of the procession culminating in the mock execution, and the sense of decline brought about by the exhaustion of the apparently unending source of gold which, discovered in the 1690s, had given the Tridentine culture its baroque magnificence in the churches of Vila Rica and the constant festivities with their richly decorated allegorical floats and their firework displays. Such as those described in all their splendour in the *Triunfo Eucarístico* (Triumph of the Eucharist), of 1733, and the *Áureo Trono Episcopal* (Golden Throne of the Bishopric), of 1749, which, though alluded to only briefly in the novel, must have provided Dourado with a wealth of detailed information.

By the time of the second of these events, the installation of the bishop in the new diocesis of Mariana (still referred to as Vila do Carmo in the novel), the author of the panegyric is fully aware that the lavish celebrations in what he labels 'America's gold Emporium' are at odds with the real decadence of the province. Parallels can no doubt be sought in the short-lived 'Brazilian miracle' at the beginning of the

1970s and the rapid débâcle already under way when *The Bells of Agony* was being written. Or yet again, in more general terms, for the series of booms followed by crashes (sugar, gold, coffee, rubber) which has bedevilled the economic development of Brazil, for so long labelled as the sleeping giant. In the novel, the picture of the tropical paradise is tempered by old João Diogo's references to the harsh life led by the pioneering adventurers, known as *bandeirantes*, who opened up the country's vast interior and discovered the gold which made Vila Rica, in the eighteenth century, a city of one hundred thousand inhabitants, at a time when São Paulo possessed a mere ten thousand. Without resorting to lengthy descriptions, the novel succeeds in conveying the historical feeling of a whole century, in the development from the rough, unlettered macho trail-blazers to their wealthy town-dwelling sons, mixing with the best colonial society, sending their own children to complete their education in Portugal, from where they would return to occupy the most important positions in the Church and the legal establishment.

It is in this environment, but at a time when the new generation of colonial intellectuals had been infected with the bug of Enlightenment thinking, that Autran Dourado places the dramatis personae who are to offer us a new version of a classical tale, previously dramatized by, among others, Euripides (*Hippolytus*), Seneca (*Phaedra*) and Racine (*Phèdre*). According to the story recorded in mythology, Theseus had a son (Hippolytus) by an Amazon queen (Antiope or Hippolyta), whom he subsequently repudiated in favour of Phaedra, daughter of Minos and Pasiphaë, after killing the Minotaur and escaping from the labyrinth with the assistance of Minos's other daughter, Ariadne. Pasiphaë and her offspring are doomed to become crazed with love, in consequence of an oath of vengeance sworn against her father (Helios, the sun) by Aphrodite, and Phaedra conceives an incestuous passion for her stepson, Hippolytus. Being consecrated to Artemis, he has made a vow of chastity and therefore rejects Phaedra's advances, made during the absence of Theseus in the underworld. On his father's return, she accuses Hippolytus of having attempted to rape her; Theseus banishes him from Athens and he is killed when his horses, terrified by a sea monster (summoned up by Poseidon at Theseus's behest), overturn the chariot and drag him over the rocks. Phaedra reveals the truth and kills herself.

Dourado does not, of course, maintain the original names, any more than, for instance, did Eugene O'Neill in his Electra plays, but it is not difficult to identify his characters with their mythical forebears. In keeping with Brazilian reality, of the period as of the present, he has

7

covered the racial spectrum of white, black and mixed, all of them in the thrall of absolute political power. The bells toll not just for the individuals enmeshed in the novel's tragic web, but for a whole society, the country of unfulfilled promise, its moment of splendour more a theatrical show than a reality. In keeping with the conventions of tragic drama, the Brazilian writer has preserved the unities of time, space and action, while using the novelist's licence to broaden and deepen his canvas by the use of perspective. We are shown the events leading up to the tragic outcome from the viewpoint, successively, of the three main characters: Januario, Malvina and Gaspar. By taking the reader into the mind and feelings of these three, as they live and relive their experience, Dourado is able to create all the tension and density of dramatic immediacy for which the playwright can depend on his actors, as well as on the captive situation of the audience for the period of the performance. What is more, he succeeds in maintaining the pressure of the tragic atmosphere throughout the novel, partly, I think, because, as he himself has said, Malvina, his devil woman, is closer to the strong female characters of Sophocles than to her Phaedra siblings, a proximity suggested in the text by the presence of the oracular Tiresias, imported from the Theban trilogy.

Of the novelist's predecessors, Euripides gives the starkest version of the myth story, Seneca the most rhetorical – not, in any case, meant for the stage – Racine the most impassioned. Dourado includes them all among his intertexts, and the richness of the novel as a reading experience is enhanced by an awareness of the intertwining of its many strands, though, as the author remarked in an interview, *The Bells of Agony* can be read simply as a tale of forbidden love, a tableau of all-devouring passions and tragic destinies, set in Minas in olden days.

A brief word about the translation. Dourado has not attempted a pastiche of eighteenth-century Portuguese, just as he has made no pretence of imitating the speech of the Negro slave. He has, however, introduced certain archaisms, including terms for items of clothing which are no longer in use, in order to give a certain period flavour; for the same reason, and to make us aware of their status, the black characters are made to address their masters with long outdated forms. I have tried to convey the writer's intentions in both cases, just as I have refrained from correcting his deliberate transgressions of certain stylistic conventions. An explanation of the meanings of the names of places, churches and the like, for the most part left in their original form, will be found in the glossary.

JOHN M. PARKER

Glossary

Alto da Cruz: literally, hill of the cross.
Antonio Dias: presumably Antonio Dias Adorno, one of the early adventurers to visit the future mining country in search of precious stones.
atabaque(s):   an African drum of the type now used in samba, as seen in Rio de Janeiro carnival.
Boa Morte: literally, Good Death.
Cabeças: literally, heads; a part of the town of Vila Rica (q.v.).
cafuzo: hybrid offspring of Negro and Amerindian.
Caminho das Lajes: literally, paved way.
Caquende: name of a river near Sabará (q.v.).
Chacara do Manso: literally, mild man's homestead.
Chafariz dos Cavalos: literally, horses' watering-place.
Dias Bueno: the name combines both the Dias of Antonio Dias (q.v.) and the Bueno of one of great pioneering families.
Dom: title used by Portuguese and Brazilian aristocrats.
Fundos do Ouro Preto: literally, depths of Ouro Preto (q.v.).
Itacolomi: mountain overlooking Ouro Preto, discovered by Antonio Dias in 1698.
Jequitinhonha: town in the north-east of Minas Gerais.
Largo da Alegria: literally, Happiness Square.
Largo do Pelourinho: literally, Whipping-stock Square; *pelourinho* is also the name for the commemorative stone columns erected in Portuguese cities.
Morro de Santa Quiteria: literally, Santa Quiteria's Hill.
Ouro Preto: literally black gold; the modern name for Vila Rica.
Passagem: *see* Santo Antonio da Passagem.
paulista: person from stat of São Paulo.
Piratininga: the city of São Paulo was called São Paulo de Piratininga.
Ponte do Contrato: literally, bridge of the contract; Ponte was the name of one of the suburbs of Vila Rica.
Puri: Indian tribe occupying territory to north and west of Rio de Janeiro; also used for a half-breed Indian.
Ribeirão do Funil: literally, diamond field of the funnel (name of a river – the Funil)

Rio das Velhas: name of a river (literally, old women's river) in central Minas Gerais; was also the name of one of the three original administrative districts of the future province of Minas Gerais.

Rua Direita: name of street, literally, straight street.

Rua das Flores: name of street, literally, street of flowers.

Rua do Ouvidor: name of street, literally, judge's street.

Rua dos Paulistas: name of street, literally, street of the *paulistas* (q.v.).

Sabará: famous gold town, near Belo Horizonte.

San Cisco: Isidoro's shortened version of the next entry.

São Francisco: the São Francisco River, in the north-east of Minas Gerais.

São Vicente: at the time referred to in the novel, the name of a province which initially included the province of Rio de Janeiro. Hence the reference to Vicentine nobility.

Santo Antonio da Passagem: literally, Saint Anthony of the Passage.

Serro do Frio: literally, cold ridge; presumably the same as Serro Frio, one of the five administrative districts which made up the province of Minas Gerais.

surdo(s):   like the *atabaque* (q.v.), a drum now used in samba; also a military drum.

Taubaté: town in the state of São Paulo, which served as point of departure for many of the adventurers seeking gold in Minas. It was also the first administrative centre for the mining area, initially considered a mere adjunct to the then province of São Paulo.

Tejuco: or Tijuco; presumably the area near São João del-Rei, rather than the centre of the diamond mining (now Diamantina).

Terra Santa: literally, holy land.

Tripuí: name of a river in Minas Gerais, where gold was first discovered in 1691.

Vila do Carmo: original name of the town of Mariana, near Vila Rica (that is, Ouro Preto); important as the seat of the diocese.

Vila Rica: Vila Rica de Ouro Preto, now simply Ouro Preto, a historic town, one-time capital of the province of Minas and main centre of the gold business. As such it was also the cultural capital of Brazil in the eighteenth century, centre, among other things, of the Arcadic school of poets. The name Vila Rica was also used for one of the three original administrative districts, later five, which were to make up the province of Minas Gerais.

The Bells of Agony

This man was executed in effigy; the others went to the gallows. – J. Capistrano de Abreu, *Chapters of Colonial History*

Death in effigy, though a farce, had all the same consequences as death in person. It resulted in slavery and the infamy of the punishment as well as the confiscation of property. In no circumstance could the accused entertain any hope of pardon; and anyone could kill him without fear of criminal proceedings. – Diogo de Vasconcelos, *The Early History of Minas Gerais*

Of the 221 settlers or native-born Brazilians sentenced in the period 1711 to 1767, the following are *paulistas* by birth or adoption:
– . . . . . (auto-da-fé of 18 October 1726);
– . . . . . (auto-da-fé of 17 June 1731);
– . . . . . (auto-da-fé of 17 July 1731).
  The first, *deceased in gaol, was relaxed in statue*; the last, *relaxed in the flesh*; the other's sentence is not specified. – Alcântara Machado, *Life and Death of a Frontiersman*

Relax, tr. Latin relaxare . . .
. . . § – *obstinate and impenitent accused to the secular arm or secular justice*; (arch.) the surrendering of such by the Inquisition to the secular courts, after torturing and condemning them, so that the death penalty can be carried out. – *Dictionary of the Portuguese Language, compiled from the glossaries hitherto published, corrected and much enlarged by Antonio de Moraes Silva, native of Rio de Janeiro*

The Farce

From the heights of the Ouro Preto mountains, beyond the Chacara do Manso and to the left of the Terra Santa asylum, he could see Vila Rica, asleep, sprawled down the hillsides and valleys beneath him.

Don't ever come back, my son. You will never be able to see me again, said his father, and in those hard eyes, unyielding with stubbornness or in acceptance of fate, in that face burned by the mines' sun, in the creeks and the gold workings, Januario thought he saw (wanting to, straining his heart) in their depths the sparkle of a tear, a sign of grief.

His father's slow, heavy voice, cavernous, wrenched from deep inside him. What he said quite without reserve, embarrassment or shame, calling him my son, still swelled painfully within him, like waves, echoes, booming back from the mountains and ravines, chime upon chime, of a lead bell being rung in the far, far distance. Within him, in his memory, now, still, always.

The lead bells booming mournfully, backed up by the tenor bells picking up the sound waves half-way, the treble bells pealing joyfully, castrated, feminine bells, on sunny, diaphanous, strident mornings. Not now at night, before: on clear days held in his memory. Not now, with the measured beat, the drumming of the toads and the chirring of the crickets filling his ears. Long before, when he strained his ears, stretching them, trying to guess, to recognize, to hear what those bells were saying. Whether a death or a funeral procession, and from the number of chimes and tolls he could tell if it was a wealthy or needy brother, man, woman or child; if a mass said by a vicar or a bishop; if the dying person was in need of prayers and forgiveness in order to die properly. We must pray, my son, Andresa, his mother, told him. Because our turn may and will come. This at daytime, many years ago.

His father hardly ever said my son, just Januario. And he did not call him Father either in the others' presence, only when the two of them were alone. Even then he avoided it, the quiver in his voice might betray his emotion, his secret heartache. It had been always like that, even when his mother was alive.

Master Tomás, you fathered this child on me, now that I am dying look after him, don't leave him alone in the world, he could remember

Mamma Andresa saying (he a boy, she on her death-bed), shortly before she went to her rest in the silence of death.

Where was his mother now? He probed the shrouded folds of the night, his own silent waiting heart. Had she gone to the peaceful kingdom of the God they had imposed on her at birth, or to join her ancestral gods and relatives, surrounded by *atabaques* and *surdos* and mournful flutes?

His half-breed mother, the same copper colour as himself. People said she was Indian. The word sounded like an insult. Not to her, to him, because he confused it with something else. I'm not Indian, my mother was though, caught with a lasso, she said. I'm the child of a white man and a baptized Puri Indian girl. Himself half Puri before, now more and more. His mother a kept woman, as they put it. His father, Tomás Matias Cardoso, a rich man, almost a potentate, lived with his wife Joana Vicenzia and his four white children (they were not like him, they were born white), all married. His other offspring, of uncertain number, fathered on black slaves (not like him, not half Indian), were coloureds and mulattos, slaves too by law since his father was only likely to adopt them, acknowledge paternity and free them in his will, when he died.

Don't ever let them take you for a mulatto or a *cafuzo*, my son. You are quite dark at times. Don't let them, it can be dangerous, they might put you in irons. When I was born they wanted to register me as a *cafuza*. That way I would be a slave. My father had to be brave enough to come forward and say the child is mine, the child is mine by a native woman, protected by official seal, by the King's law. So his mother told him.

His father's tall house on the Morro de Santa Quiteria. From where he was he could make out, in the darkness, by the light of the moon, its roof-top. The house of Mistress Joana Vicenzia and her fair-skinned children. Mamma Andresa's house was over there, yonder, a hut over in Cabeças. When his mother died he went to live with his father in Santa Quiteria, in full view of Joana Vicenzia, under her white wings. In Mistress Joana Vicenzia's presence he did not call his father anything, not even Godfather. He was afraid of offending her, of hurting her. Joana Vicenzia was kind, a haze of kindness.

Hidden in the ruins of an abandoned mine, in the spurs of the Ouro Preto mountains, to the right of the Caminho das Lajes, protected by the branches of a fig tree, surrounded by ferns, pumpwood trees and iron-bearing rocks, he could see the sleeping town. The gentle murmur, the chilly night air impregnated with muffled sounds and soft odours.

Were it not for the milky light of the full moon, now high, small, completely round, in the sky (large and blood-coloured when it rose behind the black wall of the mountains; he had been there since before nightfall, the Negro Isidoro at his side, silent and withdrawn as always, his bloodshot eyes gleaming, saying only the occasional word, looking blacker still in the darkness and silence), the chalk-white light shining brilliantly on the cobble-stones, on the smooth polished flagstones, the moonlight with its pale gleam lighting the whitewashed houses, the solitary churches (Carmo Church on the Morro de Santa Quiteria, St Francis he could not see, Our Lady of the Conception of Antonio Dias, Pilar surrounded by tall houses, almost invisible, on the far side, in Ouro Preto, beyond Cabeças), Carmo Church, clearly outlined, the black roof-tops of the houses standing out against the powdery whiteness of the sky, where the tiny pale stars were fading. Were it not for this cold, neutral, indifferent, ghostly, still, moonlit whiteness – the gentle murmur borne on the night air, the silvery dust of the echoes, the glittering whisper: himself tiny and unprotected in his weakness and frailty (he felt as if he were already dead; am I not maybe really dead? he wondered), that world which was set and rounded like the slow, muffled waves of a great bell, that silent, majestically beautiful night, cloaked in a halo of mystery, in the sombre radiance, the estrangement in which he was lost, the night that sought to soften the sharpest thorns of his torment, his pain, his anguish. Were it not for all this, he would not be there now, observing the town which he could come no closer than the outskirts, but to which he was for ever bound, drawn towards it always, even when he was far away in the distant backlands where he vanished, to hide and be pursued. Drawn towards that house in the Rua Direita, towards that gate in the Rua das Flores by which he had so often entered in disguise, from which he had fled breathless the last time, a year earlier. His hands wet with sweat which he now wiped on his jacket. His hands soiled with dried blood, hard to get off when he washed his hands in the cold waters of the Caquende some days later, in his flight. He had hidden himself in a ditch on Hangman's Hill, as arranged with Isidoro. The black man there now, next to him, who was to go for him, so that they could make their way together, via mountain tracks and forest trails, to Sabará, where she was to join him later, when things had calmed down and been forgotten, so that the two of them, together with the two Negroes, the man and the woman, could make for the cattle lands and corrals, deep in the backlands of the São Francisco River, on whose banks lived her godmother, a widow of a powerful landowner, a woman of ostentation and wealth, as they had agreed and she did not come, that was a year ago. He sometimes got to thinking that even the godmother did not exist. Bound to that house and that woman, drawn to them like iron filings to a magnet. To that name, that house, that body, for ever.

Malvina, he said once more, softly, little more than a slight quiver of the lips moved by the hot breath of the syllables. Very softly, the black must not hear, not know what he was thinking. As if he could hide anything from Isidoro, who knew his whole secret, as if Isidoro did not notice and observe his faintest sigh and least gesture, like a dog there. Even in his sleep the black man seemed to see and hear everything. Occasionally he would try something, to see if Isidoro was on the alert. Just a murmur was enough, a stronger, deeper, more expressive exhalation, a short sigh, and there came that deep, hoarse voice common to Negroes who have endured the iron collar. Massa? Anything wrong, massa? Do you want anything, massa? Like that, repeated, chanted, hoarse, deep, in his faithful, affectionate singsong. The dark heavy voice like a heavy dark hand holding and supporting him. To hear that voice, the shadow that had followed him night and day during that nightmare year of remorse and grief, was enough to make him feel safe, to some extent even consoled. The same as if it was that other soft mestizo voice, the rhythmic whisper of his Indian mother's voice lulling him to sleep in the distant night of his childhood. The shadow following his steps. The gentle feet treading firmly, carefully, for fear of stepping on a dry branch or a snake, the rhythmic swaying gait behind him, that rhythm learned by Negroes from always being yoked together, shackled and bound to one another by heavy chains that fastened the iron collars together, so that they should not escape on the way back from the creeks and gold-diggings, from the gravel-beds. The feet behind him, those huge, broad, rough, hard feet, feet which had endured shackles and irons. How long had those feet, that hand with the soft white palm, deeply grooved by the lines of head, life and destiny, which even a blind gypsy could have read, and that thick, warm, singsong voice, the sorrowful echo of his own, how long had they followed him?

He could not remember, it had been so long. Night and day now eating and sleeping at his side, on the same mat, first in resting-places and shelters, then, for fear of his being killed, him particularly, since it was not a crime, in the mouths of abandoned mines in the hills and mountains, in riverside caves, together, forgetting (the long, painful companionship of two beings united by the same destiny) that one was the master, the other the slave. Him, a master, now? He looked at the coppery-brown backs of his hands and that year away from his white father's house seemed to have darkened them (the action of time and suffering) still more. Mamma Andresa's hands, the colour of old bronze. There in the dark, by the whitish light of the moon, he felt that the drop of white blood he had inherited from his father had deserted him, restoring him completely to the savage night of his race.

Redskin, they said when they wanted to insult him. And he would go for them like a jaguar, eyes full of fury, teeth bared, dagger ready to retaliate. Half-breed he would just about accept, he even felt some pride, though he had known early on that he was a bastard. What he would really like was to be white, the pale white colour of his brothers and sisters. Mistress Joana Vicenzia's children. Kind, she was kind, a haze of kindness. She accepted him at first as if she was ashamed, as if Januario was her bastard child, not her husband's. Godmother was what he called her. Like he called his father Godfather in front of the others, not in front of her, he was too shy. Once, in response to a somewhat furtive, timid caress, he came close to calling her Mother. The most he could manage was to kiss her hand. She let him, as if he were one of her own children. Then, with a sudden slight tremor, she pulled her hand away as if scalded, caught in a sinful act, something she was not allowed to do.

A redskin and a bastard, a love-child, the two open wounds in his soul. And the coarse word that to anyone else is no more than an obscenity, when said to him sounded like the most serious offence and demanded revenge. His mother had not been a whore, a bought woman, just his father's kept woman. He tried to justify her, and himself. Since he was very young, when he was still a child (how old would he be? fourteen at most), once he had got the point of his dagger at a man's chest in a flash because he had dared call him the two things he considered forbidden, because no one else dared say even the word redskin, they said Indian when he was close by. He had earned the reputation of being a spirited, dauntless, impudent half-breed.

He fingered the silver-wrought dagger, a present from his father, always stuck in the waistband of his breeches, ready to strike. Now the dagger was no longer used to attack, it was merely a defensive weapon. Since that night, a year ago, when the prison warder, as a result of a scheme hatched by his father, allowed him to escape from the King's prison. All the gold, influence and friendship his father must have used. Accused of a crime against the state. His last favour, last fatherly gesture. Don't ever come back, my son, was what he said. His father was not angry, he was not throwing him out, just speaking the truth, as he might have said it's raining or it's cold.

Isidoro, he said softly, though wanting the Negro to hear, hoping. Do you want anything, massa? No, nothing, I just wanted to see if you were asleep. I'm not sleeping, said the Negro. I'm not sleepy, I shan't sleep a wink. If you want to lie down a while, massa, you can sleep easy, I'll keep watch. As always, thought Januario. And he said, I can't get to sleep, my eyes are burning, I can't even close them. It's not surprising, said Isidoro. You haven't slept properly for days. Since you got it into your head to come back and die. You haven't slept either. Do you think I don't see? said Januario.

Isidoro waited a while before speaking again. His velvety eyes, their brownish whites streaked with blood, sometimes seemed to be turned inwards, searching for something forgotten in the past, lost in the darkness. Blacks don't need sleep, he said. No white man, nobody ever respected a black man's sleep. A black is an animal or worse. I'm mine trash, that's what white men say.

His father looked at him affectionately. Sober as he was, his father had a weakness for him. Maybe more than for his white children, he sometimes thought conceitedly. Was that before or after the present of the dagger? He could not remember, everything was so hazy, so much had happened, things were so quickly left behind in that year of absence. He saw everything at a distance, it was as if his father were talking not to him but to someone else, that someone who had died in the pantomime in the town square. His father's voice suddenly in his ears again. Januario, value this slave I am giving you highly. He is yours to keep. Isidoro is a crafty nigger, but he has only once tried to run away, he was caught not long after Passagem. Mine blacks are like that. Value my present highly. You know, it's a Sudan nigger I am giving you. I could give you the sort of slave that's given to look after women or children. An Angola, better still a Cabinda. Learn to value a Sudan nigger, Januario. They're sometimes mistrustful, though, and apt to run away, that they are.

In another vein of time's ore bed, submerged in the cavernous mists, another faceless voice: As if I would use a Sudan nigger for housework! Sudan niggers are for the mines, for the gold-diggings. The Sudan niggers' fame as gold-diggers, their nose for gold. They had truck with the devil, sorcerers they were. A Sudan's eyes could pick out a grain of the best-quality gold in a gravel deposit from a distance.

I'm not white, Isidoro, he said. I'm half-breed like my mother. Don't you see?

The Negro looked where his eyes had been absent, behind the velvet scales, in the dark depths of his memory, for a reply for Januario. He was looking for a deep-rooted, forgotten pain. He did everything possible to forget. Among useless mementoes. He was very fond of that boy.

So you're not white any more, massa? You don't want to be, you got sick of being white? It was your mother who was half-breed, half Indian. You are already two steps away from your Indian blood. But I'm not white! Januario insisted. When have you ever forgotten that you are not a white man and a master? Am I not here to remind you? Don't you have a slave, massa? You only said you would give me my freedom when you went your own way. So far, you haven't, I still hope you'll turn back. Then, I see now, what use would a letter of yours be, if you're dead, isn't that what they'll say? It's the same either way. If they catch me with a letter signed by you, I've had it, I shall be whipped to death strung up on a real gallows. That's a joke, massa, thinking you not a white man any more. Do you think you're a redskin? The Negro risked the forbidden word. Januario could do him no harm, he had the rifle now, primed, ready to fire, but something inside him (an ancestral fear, loyalty or bondage?) would prevent him firing should Januario attempt to beat him, he was sure.

Januario heard him without moving a single muscle. No inner turmoil, no hot blood rising in his breast, swelling his throat, making his eyes stand out. For the first time in his life the word redskin did not hurt like a slap in the face, it lost all its aggressive weight. The black had said that to test him. He is mad at me because I have come back, he thought. Because in the morning, when day breaks, after the sun disperses the mist, the one fluffy cloud that was the town, he was going to show himself before the soldiery in the square. They were waiting for him, since yesterday they had been scouring the town from end to end in startled gallops, hoofs churning up the ground, and the tramping of their boots, from the Vira-e-Sai to the farthermost pathway in Cabeças.

I can take anything today, he said in a slow resigned voice. Wasn't it to take anything that I came back? I can take being a redskin, I could even take being black if I were the colour of a mulatto. This year we have been together, stuck close to one another, oblivious of status, has related me to you.

Not me, said Isidoro, with a sudden anger unknown to Januario, who was so accustomed to the meekness that had been whipped into him since childhood. A meekness that Januario credited to the innate kindliness of his race, forgetting the stocks and the whips, the chains and the iron collars that beat them into submission. Related to me, a nigger? said Isidoro, opening his eyes wide, with a deep burst of laughter that seemed to come from way down inside him, shattering the silence of the night that was punctuated only by the bright chirr of the crickets and the monotonous drumming of the roads. Just because you are dirty? Just because you've been so close to my long-suffering nigger sweat? Isidoro went on.

And the black man came closer, now almost clinging to him. He smelt the black man's odour, rancid from not washing for days on end. Now he could smell, sickeningly, the disgusting stench he had got accustomed to and seemed not to notice any more, but which now suddenly offended his nose, turned his stomach. The black glistened with sweat in the darkness. His stink impregnated clothes, nose, memory. The smell that a thousand bars of soap, whether local or from Portugal, would not succeed in removing. How could he have forgotten what a black's fetid stench was like? First thing in the morning Isidoro was dusky. He grew brighter with the sun, at midday he was a lake of light and heat, a brilliant coal black. The beads of sweat oozed from his naked torso, trickled down his forehead and shiny face. How had he not been aware of the smell then and why had it only now become unendurable? Could it be fear that made the black man stink? Or the furious anger he suddenly noticed in Isidoro's bloodshot eyes?

He tries to draw away, Isidoro seems to notice, now he laughs softly. Isidoro's laugh could be taken as a sob. But Januario knew that he was really laughing, he never cried. He lifted his arm to his nose and tried to smell the odour of his own body. What if he also had the rank stench of his race, of his mother's race? You don't smell your own smell. The rank smell he sometimes smelled in Indian huts, even when they were not there, that rancid smell that impregnated everything. The same fetid stench he once smelled on his mother and tried to forget. Each race has its own smell, none of them is aware of its own smell, only of the others. Probably Isidoro, immersed in the cloud of his stench, in the stink of his own sweat, did not smell it and was only disgusted by his Indian odour which he himself could not detect at all. White men smell like rancid butter, so the Chinese said. So a Portuguese who had been in Macau once told him.

He turned his face the other way, tried to breathe the cold night air, the smell of vegetation, of the flowers that sprouted between the stones. He began to feel cold. At dawn, the sharp biting cold would make him wrap himself in the saddle-cloths and blankets, nestle into Isidoro's warmth, as he always did.

I came back to suffer the worst. He resumed the topic Isidoro wanted to avoid. I came back because I could no longer endure waiting for a killer's bullet. Any bullet can kill me without it being a crime. I came back because I want to choose my hour. I'm the one who'll choose when the time has come, not them. I am going to be in charge of my death.

Isidoro gave what looked like a smile, but he was not smiling. But massa, the real you has been dead for a long time. I saw them kill you in the square, didn't I tell you? I saw massa's body dangling in the air.

Yes, Isidoro might well be right. The one he had been was dead, he would have to take his death some other way, be someone else. But how, if he was bound by enchantment to that town, that house, that woman? He had come to meet his real death, for good. In the morning he would face the soldiers in the square.

What you must do, massa, is follow the advice I've been giving you, for us to get away from here and never come back to the Minas country. Disappear into the backlands, go as far as the headwaters of the San Cisco, or even farther. There we can change our names. I shall go on being your slave, don't fear. If you still have need of me, massa.

This was the Isidoro he knew, not that other who had momentarily showed beneath the glistening skin, the broad grin.

The black went on. What we can't do is keep on coming back here all the time, like birds caught in bird-lime.

Isidoro was maybe right. But a strange force held him, summoning him to the square. A powerful force pulled him towards the Rua Direita, to Malvina's side, Malvina's belly, her eyes, her hair, her tawny sex, the bird-lime. The bird cheeps as if it were crying, it goes against its will, struggling, into the snake's mouth, or so they say. Bird in the bird-lime, when he was a lad. Now he wanted to die at her feet, cursing her at the same time. He wanted her to see his body lying face down in the square, riddled with bullets, in a pool of blood. Those flashing eyes that laid him bare, holding him benumbed in their searching gaze. Her red hair, hair of fire like dark gold, the same gleaming rays. Born of the sun, born of fire. Born of something else, that's what she was, fury, insecurity, spuming hatred erupted inside him. Why hadn't she come, as they had arranged? Another man, of course. He remembered Malvina riding at the side of Gaspar Galvão. No, not him, jealousy begot doubt. Impossible, her stepson, that João Diogo Galvão's son.

João Diogo Galvão's name brought back the scream, his bloodstained hands, the dry blood he tried to wash off in the cold water of the river. He touched his pocket, the letter summoning him. She gave it to Isidoro herself, not Inacia the black woman. At least that was what Isidoro said. When Isidoro, in disguise, went to her at his command. Why was the town, which seemed to have forgotten him, suddenly put on the alert, with soldiers everywhere, scouring the town, sentries at the four corners of the square where he would try to enter next morning? Dragoons on sentry duty at the door in the Rua Direita and at the back gate in the Rua das Flores. It was Isidoro who saw them, came running back to tell him. When, as soon as they got to the summit of the Ouro Preto mountains, coming from the Ribeirão do Carmo area, he sent Isidoro to see Malvina and tell her that he had received her letter and had returned, as she asked. I couldn't, massa, the place is packed with soldiers everywhere. It's madness for you to try to go down there, massa. I ran away, I was terrified, they mean to kill me too. The soldiers are waiting, it's all they talk about. I saw some of them chatting at the Chafariz dos Cavalos, when I pretended to fetch water.

Something must have happened after she sent the letter, he thought. She just wasn't able to let me know. Somebody had seen him and gone to report it. How did they know that he was coming back, that he had arrived? Or perhaps the letter was false? No, Malvina wouldn't do such a thing. She had said that the danger was over and now the town was on guard. Although he doubted her in his mind, even cursed her for not having gone to him in Sabará as arranged, he could not believe Malvina capable of such treachery.

How did they find out, Isidoro? I don't know, said the Negro, there's always people ready to inform in the Minas country. Didn't we often have to get away from highways and resting-places because some curious cuss kept looking at us and recognized us? These people are just like that. There's a reward, massa. If they inform on you they get something, even if only thanks. A white man, or a nigger who wants his freedom. I have my doubts, Isidoro. There's no point being like that, massa. The best you can do is what I've been telling you, forget that woman, this accursed hell of a town. It's the only salvation. I can't, Isidoro, I'm prepared to put an end to everything. I can't live far away from here. I know I couldn't be the other man you have in mind, that you're seeing me as. I really am that someone else you saw dangling in the square. It's his ghost I'm going to give my body to. My body belongs to them, Isidoro. All they need is to bury me or scatter my bloody quarters to the four corners of the town, as an example. I'm not running away any more, Isidoro. You run away.

Isidoro said nothing, he began to fondle the gun barrel, toying with the firing mechanism which was not cocked though there was powder in the primer. So easy, if he wanted. The powder charge which he had to keep renewing, so that, when needed, it wouldn't jam because the powder was old. He'd seldom had to use it. A lot of niggers wanting their freedom. Never on people, only animals, hunting. So easy, if he wanted. A spark from the depths of the darkness threatened to detonate the gun. His hand trembled now, it wouldn't at the right moment. Easy, just had to want to. His only way of escaping. Old Nick tempting. He had thought of it a thousand times. No way out, he was lost, cornered. Only that way, his hand trembling, he could escape. He would be free of the death that awaited him, might even give him his freedom, as a reward. No, I don't want to think of it, he shouted noiselessly at the other voice that echoed inside him. That same voice that was unknown to him, that had spoken through his mouth when he said not me. Related to me, a nigger? His guffaw, bursting out, shattering.

Maybe massa was asleep. His voice shaking, his hand. No, he couldn't do it. The feeling was stronger than him. Instilled submissiveness, which the white men had stamped with red-hot irons on his mother, on the father he had never known. On him too, he recalled the scar on his back. He was gradually controlling himself. Sleep, it will do you good, said the old voice he knew, the voice that neither he nor massa were troubled by. The voice that said not me had gone from inside him, for good. His uneasiness and distress left him. His hands were steady again, not a tremor. Like his voice.

If it's because of the animals and of people, you can sleep in peace, I'll be prepared, on guard. We can't light a fire like in the woods, to scare off jaguars. It would be good, though, we could warm ourselves a bit. But I'll keep watch, massa, give yourself a rest. That's what the flint is here for. I'll set it up so's it's ready when needed.

No, I shan't sleep, Isidoro. I can stop thinking, my head is like a hornet's nest. The thing has got to finish today, I shall explode.

And after they were both silent for a while, Isidoro, why don't you go away? I've told you already you can go. It's a waste of time me trying to take off, massa. By myself I can't get anywhere, I don't have no way out. If you went with me, he said, now entirely oblivious of the other way, it'd be different. As your slave, in the cattle country, I still can. Once we change our names and stop thinking of coming back. By myself I'm lost, I can't do a thing. The first slave-hunter who sees me will lay hands on me. The first white who sees me will make me a slave again, I don't have a chance of taking off.

He stopped briefly, he expected Januario to say something. I don't believe in slave hide-outs any more, he said as if in answer to something Januario had said. The really big hide-outs seems they've finished. There's only a few stragglers holed up here and there in the woods, assaulting unwary travellers to get a bite to eat, just like I've often done for you, massa. Those times of liberated farmlands and abundance, won the hard way, fought for, not handed over on a platter, they ain't no more. The time when the white men faced great danger and were afraid, the councillors making a lot of noise, all worked up and shitting themselves with fear, seems it's gone, won't come back no more.

And Isidoro closed his eyes. Was he dreaming? Was he dreaming of the Zundu and Calaboca slave hide-outs? Had he sunk into the dream kingdom of Pai Ambrosio? Isidoro must be in his heaven, like the one the white men invented for him, inhabited by mulatto angels and creole Our Ladies. Pai Ambrosio clothed in a gold embroidered cloak, covered in jewels, sitting on his silver throne. His blue cloak, the same cloak that clothed Our Lady of the Rosary of the Negroes.

I can only escape with you, massa. I'm doomed to slavery. The Negro went on with his litany, trying to persuade him to set aside the sinister idea of going to his death in the square. I'm doomed to be a slave. Either yours or some other white man's. I'm used to you, massa, I like you a lot. (It was the first time he had spoken that way.) Me, I haven't got what it needs to be a runaway, it's a hard life, that. I don't have no more strength, my spirit has left me. I ran away once, didn't I? Have you forgotten the letter they branded on my skin, on your father's orders, in the blacks' prison, in the gaolhouse? They forced the red-hot iron on me, sizzling on my skin, the pain.

The raised scar, a small snake in the shape of an F. Januario wanted to pass his hand over that letter of fire. That was what they did with runaway blacks. There were people who thought they should cut the ankle tendon so that the black could never run away again.

What for? Isidoro went on. Sooner or later they would end up finding me. Don't you remember, massa, that heap of niggers' ears strung up on a vine rope, dripping blood and brine? As an example, for white hunters, whites who beat your forebears like they did mine, to receive the reward for their great feat. The council chamber all decked out, the councillors bowing and scraping to the big white chief, who was their lord as well. You don't remember, ʌnassa, you must have been a little boy. The Captain-General in his finest regalia, covered in gold braid, in his richest uniform, drooling with satisfaction.

And after a brief pause, as if in answer to another suggestion that Januario had not made, only if it was a big hide-out, one like Ambrosio's, where people can make a stand. . . . A really huge stronghold, the size of my people, big enough to hold every nigger there is. . . . A stronghold just like the kingdom of heaven that white men promise us for when we die. . . .

Isidoro fell silent. His eyes, which were now open, had a more velvety glimmer, fish scales glinting, caught by a ray of light. His eyes shone with stars like the Virgin Mary's mantle. A brilliant light, shining from within. Isidoro was drifting in a dream cloud, shining through.

You can keep the gun and the casket of jewels she gave me, said Januario. With the jewels you can buy your freedom. Tomorrow I shall go unarmed, I would like to go naked as I was when my mother bore me, Januario said. The gun I accept, said the Negro, it has its uses. But what use are those jewels to me, those pieces of silver and gold, those little stones? Have you forgotten the time I went to sell one in exchange for a gourd of flour? A jewel is only worth anything in a white man's hand or in the ear and round the neck of a nigger woman a white man's going to get with child, if he's taken a fancy to her. If you went with me to the backlands, massa, like I said, and we changed our names, they'd be of use to us there all right. You could sell them yourself, massa. With me by myself these pieces of gold and silver would be my doom. When you go away, massa, and I'm alone, you know what I'm going to do? I'm going to take hold of the whole lot and throw them down there in the river, to make the saying come true – come from water, gone with water.

Ay, said Januario, you're probably right. And he began to think that those cut stones, those silver pieces, all that gold, were worthless. It was all worth just the same as the freedom letter the black had refused. Because he could no longer even sign his name. When Isidoro told him, with his few words, what the pantomime in the square had been like, the gallows made ready, that puppet theatre, he wanted to laugh. If he could have imagined what his life would be like from then on, hiding in the woods, keeping away from the roads, hungry, thieving, sticking to remote pathways and clearings, he would have wept.

At his command, Isidoro had returned to the town to seek out Malvina and find out what was happening, why she had not come.

From very early, just like now, scarcely had dawn broken and the cocks lined up on their roosts to challenge each other and summon the day (no cock has crowed yet, today; it is still early – that is to say, the night is still dark), the streets came to life full of dragoons and people carrying arms, hired troops and even enlisted men.

Unlike now, when the soldiers were frowning and solemn, and armed dragoons galloped, nervous and watchful, up and down streets and slopes (the horses' hoofs glinted and sparked on the cobble-stones and guttural shouts echoed from side to side when units of soldiers crossed and exchanged news or warnings), riding uphill and downhill, from one hamlet to another, from the Alto da Cruz and Padre Faria to Fundos do Ouro Preto, Cabeças, their eyes keen and alert (the horses panted and whinnied, tired by the hills and slopes, their coats wet, gleaming with sweat), the regular soldiers' and the enlisted men's eyes sharp and sparkling, on the look-out, waiting for Januario, should he be brave enough to come and give himself up at last.

Unlike now, the town had started the day embellished, sparkling with banners and shouts.

Since the previous day, men in groups of three had been moving about the streets and byways, in formal dress, their brightly coloured uniforms ironed and starched, straps and belts shined, gold braid and trimmings gleaming, badges and weapons polished for the next day's ceremony, which was meant to be impressive. From time to time they stopped in a public square or on a corner, and a throng of curious people would immediately jam together, although the inhabitants here and from the neighbouring areas, for one, two or more leagues around, starting from the cross, knew what was going to happen the next day.

And they would bang out a thunderous roll, with rhythmic beats, first slow and solemn, then in a flurry, on their drums, large and small, which were adorned with red and blue ribbons.

When more people had gathered, one of the men would solemnly unroll a long document and make public the proclamation with the decree signed by His Excellency the Governor and Captain-General of the Province of Minas. Copies of the same, in the same large, embellished hand, so that it could be read and understood even by people who were only acquainted with printed letters, were nailed on the cross and on the church doors.

So that no one could say he was ignorant of the decision of the all-powerful Captain-General. Because tomorrow he wanted the streets and squares, particularly the square in front of the palace, where the cross was with the pillar marking the town's foundation, full of people for the great puppet pantomime which he meant to be real, notable and memorable.

Lest any be in doubt as to the retribution, abhorrence and thunderous power of the King's Majesty, always magnanimous on fitting occasions or when the people are worthy; the King's Majesty who is far distant but who is valorous and stalwart and always present in the person of his Ministers; the King's Majesty saddened and heavy of heart because one of his beloved vassals, whom His Royal Majesty much prized, even that he once did write a letter in his Own Hand, wherein he acknowledged his services and offered favours, a friend who perished at the hand of an assassin, a vile crime which was the signal or token for yet another act of sedition and mutiny, such as do infest this treasonous and conspiring land of Minas; lest any malign his Sovereign even in thought, as is said in the Psalms of the Holy Scriptures; wherefore his memory be for ever repudiated and abominated as vile, treacherous, pernicious, disloyal, and spat upon and cleansed with salt; as an example and admonishment for perpetuity; and so shall be salted the house where the knave first saw the light of day; so that all who read this edict or who hear it proclaimed shall be assured that he whose name is mentioned with loathing and is cursèd shall be hanged until he is dead on the gallows raised for that purpose in the most public place; in the form of an effigy, statue or doll, in that he be absent and fugitive from the arm of the Secular Law, as of the Canonical Law, which execrates and abominates those accused of crimes against the sovereign in His Majesty's Ordinances; the accused being proclaimed dead for the civil record, therefore his possessions may be seized by whomsoever may want them; and likewise his real body, if found, its pursuit being desirable, may suffer destruction for ever by bullet, dagger, sword, cutlass, hands or any lethal weapon,

26

without his slayer be so much as accused of a criminal act, rather he shall be most worthy and deserving of His Majesty's esteem and of his generous favours, as of those of his delegates and ministers; and of receiving praise from righteous public figures and men of standing, and even from the ordinary people, in whatever manner and ceremony as considered best shall be determined, ordained and proclaimed in this edict, which shall be affixed in the most visible places and made public by proclamation at street junctions and corners, and squares and public places, &c.

All this articled, paragraphed, with flourishes and serifs and other formalities, as was required – that is to say, demanded, by Ordinance of His Royal Majesty, in high-flown, ornate, lofty, stilted, bombastic language. Just hearing it left them all open-mouthed and pop-eyed: with fear, awe or wonder. All of it read over and over again in a monotonous singsong voice, once the beribboned drums and snare-drums were silent, by the criers who toured the town. Where they stopped longest in concert was in Alegria and Pelourinho Squares, the latter so-called because the stone pillar bearing the town's coat of arms was first placed there, the second pillar being the one that now stood in the main square.

And all day long, even after nightfall, the shades of night as they say, when the bells at Carmo Church and the city gaol struck their nine unhurried chimes as a signal for prayers, sleep and silence, the criers hastened up and down streets, back and forth over bridges, past fountains, to the farthest city limits, proclaiming the great, gloomy solemnity, the joyful entertainment that everyone was waiting for, when their fear of the royal command left them for a few moments, the women and children mainly because the men never considered themselves safe and free from the powerful and implacable arm of the King (they were always guilty of something: adulterating some gold or silver, slipping some glittering stones past the sharp, unsleeping eye of the Royal Treasury and smuggling them out through the cattle lands, a few mortal sins, cases of incest, sodomy and adultery, or even venal ones, which could be redeemed just by paying for masses, giving alms or buying indulgences, but it is best to be on one's guard, because scheming and feuding is our main occupation, pastime and business here in Minas), everyone's eyes, though, worried and glistening with the agony of waiting.

And early next morning the town decked out in festive attire as if it were a day of splendid gaiety and not of a macabre pantomime and condemnation, the troops armed with the customary powder and twelve bullets, their sabres polished with carborundum, glinting in the morning sun which had by now completely overcome the early morning mists and shone brilliantly on the square, on the white walls of the houses and churches and against the blue of a clear day with just a few floating scraps of cloud, the soldiers covered the town's main points, divided in squads and platoons, waiting for the procession bringing the condemned man to go past so that they could follow it and join the main body of troops in ceremonial dress in the square.

All along the route it was to follow, the windows and balconies of the houses were adorned with flowers and hung with gorgeous red damask quilts and embroidered lace-trimmed table-cloths, as if that cortège were a splendid Corpus Christi procession instead of being the escort for a ceremony which the Captain-General wanted to be a showy, mournful warning. Wanted it to frighten the people of Minas and make his authority still more feared and respected, to the advantage and glory of His Royal Majesty.

The cortège was to be long and lengthy, starting out from Cabeças, going past São José and Pilar, and ending up in the square. They had never raised a gallows in the square before, the hangings ordered by the court in Bahia were carried out in the usual place, on Hangman's Hill, where few people went because as a rule those being executed were blacks or unimportant criminals. But the Captain-General wanted this different punishment to be carried out in a striking manner that would be out of the ordinary too. It was being whispered that the Captain-General felt his position was under threat, so many were the acts of plunder committed on his own behalf rather than for the Crown, and meant to use this to strengthen his position with the King and prepare the people, through fear and power, for the tax levy that was expected to follow.

It was a huge gallows, made out of brauna wood, with fifteen steps, specially built to the Captain-General's own design and measurements, so it was said. Any criminal could be executied on it, however strong and bulky he might be, not just a straw doll meant to look like the accused Januario Cardoso, escaped from the arm of the King's justice.

In the square, their backs towards the scaffold, facing the fortified palace which was decorated with pennants and flags bearing the arms of the realm and the Captain-General's insignia, the troops chosen to guard the gallows had taken up a triangular formation. The apex of the triangle pointed to the palace, from where the Captain-General himself would witness the ceremony and command the exemplary hanging. A line of sentries, their weapons primed and loaded, was strung out along the front of the palace, linking the sentry-boxes.

From very early, almost before daylight, crowds of people thronged the streets, lanes and alleys on their way to the square, where they herded together and fought for the best places. People from opposite ends of the town, from Antonio Dias and from the Ouro Preto settlement, long-standing rivals, fraternized briefly, forgetting their old quarrels which they would renew at nightfall, when there would be a right old brawl; from the Padre Faria district, from Fundos and Cabeças; from Cachoeira do Campo and from Passagem; even from Vila do Carmo, from way over, people had come to see the Grand Guignol spectacle, the singular hanging in effigy, which the Captain-General was putting on for the edification of those turbulent, unruly, rebellious Minas folk. In the evening there would be illuminations and fires, by which time everyone would obviously be wrought up and people would commit all sort of sins in the frenzied excitement of blood, sex and drink.

They argued and fought over the best places, in the streets and squares through which the funeral procession was to pass, as well as in the main square where the great pantomime farce was to take place. Everyone wanted to see, no one could miss the great event which the news-sheet would afterwards record. Despite an order that the stores should stay closed, many people had stocked up with spirits and baccy the day before, and the drink was running freely, drunk straight from the bottle, accompanied by burps and stinking breath. And those who were already high, the drink having gone to their heads, were already laughing in the stupefying cloud of drunkenness and looking forward to the Grand Guignol, the fantastic puppet theatre. There were chronic drunkards, hookworm and dropsy sufferers, with their swellings and wetting, emancipated blacks, mulattos and native-born Negroes, dirty poor whites, stinking humanity.

Occasionally, soldiers with swords unsheathed would go rushing past and the tipsier ones in the crowd would move aside noisily, cheering the King and the Captain-General, scared to death of the horses' hoofs and of the sword and sabre blades. Jests and news were swapped, the coarsest obscenities were uttered. Dark-skinned mulatto women had their bottoms felt, displaying all their gleaming white teeth in excited laughs and hysterical squeals, their hard, full breasts, with nipples the size of olives, completely uncovered. Vivacious, sensual Negresses, in brightly coloured dresses and shawls, covered in gold bracelets, braids, chains and necklaces, with powdered hair, loop ear-rings, beads glinting in the sun, had their plump arms pinched. It was a revel for nigger boys and offduty housemaids, for whores and mine overseers, for freed blacks and poor whites, for mulattos and mestizos, *cafuzos*, cross-breeds of sambos and mestizos, Guarani Indians. That mishmash of hot-blooded, highly excited people who would spread the Gallic disease

29

and the pox. A great feast of races and trades, wild, infernal, utterly tropical.

The inhabitants of the two-storey houses in the Rua Direita and the main square, people of quality or presumption, brought their stools close to the decorated windows and balconies hung with brocades and damasks, with fringed silken quilts, and amused themselves watching that tatterdemalion rabble while they chatted animatedly and nervously with their guests. They were mostly women and children, because the burghers and the nobles of long standing in the King's roll, as they liked to boast, falsely or not, were more fearful and would only come to the fore when the Captain-General appeared on the palace's main balcony or came down into the square, whichever he did, so that they should be seen and their loyalty to His Most Faithful Majesty in Lisbon not be put in doubt for a single moment. The men in their best doublets, breeches and dress coats, with white wigs. The women in their tall turbans, low-necked velvet or taffeta dresses with gold embroidery, covered in pearls, large and small, in coral, in solid gold bracelets, wearing rings sparkling with jewels, chokers, ear-rings, brooches. Hennaed, rouged, powdered, lurid.

From time to time a squad of dragoons had to use their swords and their horses's hoofs to push back the riff-raff, which was getting wilder and more restless all the time, in order to keep the entrances and the centre of the square clear, those were their orders. The impatience was now general and the babel of voices grew louder, with outbursts of shouting every time someone claimed to have glimpsed the procession down below, appearing round the bend in the Rua Direita.

All impatience, the cortège in fact only began to move off at nine o'clock, with the slow pace of a funeral procession, keeping time with the church bells all tolling the burial knell.

Opening the cortège was a squadron of ten soldiers in elegant dolmans, mounted on horses with colourful, gold-fringed saddle-cloths, polished worked leather and brass harness, gleaming stirrups and bridles, muskets slung across their chests, swords carried in their right hands, reins held firm and high. The animals panted, neighed and kicked out, unnerved by the uproar of voices and the crowds, the rockets that were beginning to be fired up on the hilltops, the debris from the repeater rockets.

After the soldiers, at the very front, came the crucifer in his dress cassock with its lace-trimmed surplice, holding aloft the great silver cross. After him, another priest, casting the fragrant smoke of the incense in the thurible over the people as a blessing. As the crucifer passed, the people bowed their heads, removed their hats and crossed themselves and knelt in customary contrition. Praised be Our Lord Jesus Christ, shouted some. May His name be ever praised, came the reply. From the wealthiest houses they even called out cheers to Our Lord the King.

Next came the office-bearers and chapters of the religious guilds in their purple, scarlet, blue, brown or black surplices. At the head of each, its own priest in his richest vestments, praying aloud, blessing the faithful at their windows, cursing the infamous criminal. Anathema to the infidel conspirator, they said aloud, exaggerating, in ringing tones and emphatic pitch. And slowly they passed by, dragging their feet and sandals and shoes and boots as they did in funeral processions, the guilds of Carmo, St Francis of Assisi, Grace and Favours, of Rosario, Pilar and the Almshouse. They walked sedately and in silence, their rosaries in their hands, heads bowed, mute and pious in their fear and devotion.

The lengthy procession wound mournfully up the steep streets.

Also included as the town council with its banner, the arms of Vila Rica embroidered in gold. The councillors in their gowns with ruff collars in the style demanded by the ceremony, unlike the guild members in their surplices, were pompous and swaggering, their heads uplifted in haughty gaze. And the glittering procession continued with the chief magistrate, judges and notaries in their finest cloaks with garish silk stripes, their woollen dress coats with gold-embroidered collars, shiny silk waistcoats, plumed hats under their arms, powdered heads, lofty brows sweating profusely, silk stockings stretched tight to outline the legs, precious buckles on their shoes, gloved hands grasping the handles of rapiers and staffs of office in a hieratic gesture.

They were all men of wealth whose passing silenced the excited, disrespectful riff-raff. So willed the Law, so wished the King.

And finally, what everyone was waiting for; the cart pulled by three teams of slaves, painted a scandalous red, made specially for that day. The Captain-General had had time and fastidiousness to neglect nothing. As with the actual design of the gallows. On the cart, seated on a high chair of state, so that it could be bound and better keep its balance, and not fall with the jerking of the wheels on the cobble-stones, was a huge straw figure, the size of a man, which they had taken the macabre care to dress in a penitent's robe. On the doll's neck, the hangman's noose, its end held by the Negro Mulungu, in striped breeches made of local cloth, his naked torso black and shiny with sweat, as if he had smeared himself with grease. The Negro was genial and majestic, famous hangman that he was, distributing glances and smiles. He had never been so important as this in his life. A shutter was part opened, a shock of mulatto hair appeared. A whistle and the shout Mulungu you devil, which exasperated him. But the black man was like the tree of the same name,[1] he pretended not to hear. He went on smiling, his mouth open wide, huge teeth gleaming white.

The black was the only person who succeeded in laughing. The expected entertainment, the noisy festivity, was not materializing. On either side of the cart walked three priests, their hands crossed on their breasts, reciting psalms, saying prayers, comforting the sufferer. All a pretence, in imitation of a real exemplary sacrifice. When the cart passed by them, the people all choked back their laughter and fell silent. Though they thought it to themselves, no one had the courage to say that the Captain-General was taking his fantasy too far. Only later, in lampoons and letters in verse.

After the cart more armed men, to prevent the disorder usual in tail-ends of processions where the people swarmed and crowded together.

When the cart came into the square, a long oh! of amazement and consternation was heard. Although everyone expected a straw figure, apparently deep inside they wanted the penitent himself to appear there in person, in the flesh. The oh! was gradually hushed until it faded away in the now lake-like silence of the sun-drenched square.

The Captain-General finally appeared on the palace's central balcony and the eyes of the crowd and of the people in the houses were turned towards the palace. His dress uniform glittered, criss-crossed with baldrics, covered with decorations and gilt trappings. In the eyes of the courtiers and in the tortuous language of the golden throne panegyrists[2] he was the New Sun of America in person. That, at least, was how he must have felt, such was the radiance of his face, of his modestly lowered, yet glowing eyes; he must be feeling very happy in his glory.

Amid utter silence there appeared a black horse with silver caparisoned harness, velvet saddle-cloth, its mane braided and adorned with bells and multicoloured ribbons. It was the colonel of the dragoons who was to command the ceremony. With his stiffest and most soldierly bearing, fierce countenance becoming a Portuguese officer, all decked out in gold and medals, his sword erect, he made his way at a measured trot, his body rising and falling in the saddle, to the Captain-General's

[1] In Brazilian Portuguese the word *mulungu* means 'coralbean tree'.
[2] The 'golden throne panegyrists' were the poets who celebrated, in the ornate baroque style, the installation of the newly appointed Bishop of Mariana. Some of their efforts were included in the description of the event published with the name of *Áureo Trono Á Episcopal* (see Introduction).

balcony. In a loud voice he respectfully asked permission of His Excellency the Lord Governor and Captain-General of the Captaincy of Minas to commence the ceremony. He returned to the squad of soldiers who had taken up position opposite the gallows and began to shout orders, which he accompanied with broad flourishes of his sword.

Up on the gallows stage, on his platform, Mulungu the black man looked down haughtily on the square full of people and the soldiers in the strictest military formation, as majestic and haughty as the puppet-master Captain-General on his balcony decorated with old gold brocade. In the sun, motionless and glistening with sweat, without the slightest movement or tremor of his muscles, chest thrown out, head uplifted, his hands holding the end of the noose, Mulungu looked like a gigantic statue coated in tar. So stately and solemn (the clinking of the sabres and swords, the sparks from the horseshoes striking the paving-stones, the brilliance of the chevrons, banners, insignias and uniforms, the long-awaited and feared appearance of the Captain-General on the balcony, added further to the solemnity of the moment), emerging from the gloom of an old print, that no one, no overbold or tipsy young nigger had the courage to whistle and shout you devil Mulungu. In the eyes of that fear-stricken crowd he really was a power of darkness.

A lieutenant ascended the stairs up to the gallows, pausing at each step, and said something to Mulungu. So close to his ear and in so low a whisper as if he were afraid that, in the bell-glass silence of that sea of heads, the whole square might hear him, even the caparisoned and flamboyant Captain-General. The black man did not understand; the lieutenant, as he turned away, seeing the surprise in his eyes, had to go back and repeat it in his ear. From his laugh, it seemed Mulungu now understood. Without a word, the lieutenant turned to the priest at his side, silently indicating that it was his turn to speak. The lieutenant descended the steps more quickly. Only the priest and the hangman remained up there; the silence grew.

And the priest, with his resonant Holy Week voice, as if he were celebrating the office of Tenebrae, began to recite the Creed. The speech in plainsong, his voice in the same rhythm, the same crescendos and fading of the phrasing, the same pauses and silences to which he was so accustomed. It was as if he were waiting for the condemned man's answer.

As the dirge finished, the last note echoed on like a stone in the still dark water of a well. The silence that followed was shot through with the sparkling brillance of bees buzzing in the air.

At an upward thrust of the sword from the colonel in command on his statuesque horse, the two rows of drums decorated with fluttering, many-coloured ribbons, lined up opposite the platoon that surrounded the gallows, began a thunderous roll, in frenzied, rumbling, unbroken, deafening, funereal and unending beats. . . .

Isidoro went on saying what he had seen. With the aid of imagination and memory, Januario tried to re-create the whole scene which the black man, in his ignorance, could scarcely describe. He pieced together everything he knew and had been told about sacrifices and sorcery, going back to the lilting, bewitching voice of Mamma Andresa, the blacks in his father's slave-quarters, and later the lessons recited in chorus with the headmaster at the Boa Morte seminary, in Vila do Carmo, where he was sent afterwards. He remembered hangings he had seen and others that had been described to him. Of the sufferings and death agonies. Of the slaves shackled by the ankles to a long chain, doing forced labour in the streets, the painful clank of the irons. The blacks whipped amid tears, howls, blood, piss and sweat, on the whipping-post. The judges, councillors and priests with their stately ceremonial gait. The soldiers and lieutenants and captains and colonels and captains-general in their splendid uniforms, sashes and decorations, on special formal occasions. The priests, monsignors, canons and bishops in their black, purple or scarlet cassocks, white surplices trimmed with embroidery and lace and fringes, at high mass with the smell of incense, candles melting drip upon drip in the flames. The crescendos and diminuendos, the resonant, plaintive notes of the organ echoing on and on in the naves of the churches, the doleful chant.

With this mixture of dream and experience, Januario recalled what his eyes had not seen, his heart not felt. Everything that the black man was trying, in his impotent lack of words, to communicate to him. As if he were painting a picture of his own death; and indeed it was, he felt it. Anticipating the feeling of his neck being wrenched with the weight of the hangman jumping on his back. And suddenly, in a flash, he saw:

That same Mulungu pushed the condemned man off the scaffold. The body stretched tight with a thud, the rope fastened to the beam, and swung from side to side, twisting with a pendular movement, the legs, with nothing under them, hanging loosely, in one leap the hangman was astride the victim's shoulders, riding him, to make his death easier, or maybe just to amuse himself, one can't be sure. It was said it was to shorten the sacrifice, out of sheer pity and compassion. Just as out of sheer pity and compassion, earlier, in the gaol, he no doubt asked the condemned man's forgiveness, it was the custom, so they said. Just as out of sheer pity and compassion the judges and ministers . . .

. . . When suddenly, at a fresh, even more energetic thrust of his sword, from the saddle of his horse, which was as black and shiny as Mulungu the Negro, from his horse decked out with stitched leather and gleaming white silver and bells and ribbons in its braided mane and in its tail which was like long, loose, woman's hair, the commander ordered the drums to cease their hysterical funeral rhythm.

Contrary to expectation, Mulungu the hangman did not push the body off the scaffold and ride it; on the contrary, he pulled the rope back vigorously and the straw figure was suspended high up by one of the pulleys.

And as if this operatic finale to the great farce so painstakingly arranged by the Captain-General were not enough, it was followed by the political apotheosis with which he ensured, for himself and for the King he served, the continuation of the crimes, the thefts and murders; the burning and pillaging; the extermination of races, which were even condemned by many priests, who benefited indirectly from their enslavement, from their pulpits inlaid with soapstone; the perpetual plundering and misery, the hypocrisy and bullying; the tyranny of arms in the service of an empire and a faith which were supposed to be for ever blazoned wide in verse;[3] an obscure, feared, baroque, beloved and absolute colonial power before which they were all powerless.

Indifferent to the silence of those dirty, sweaty heads and bodies, to that nauseating mixture of smells and races, sufferings and miseries, addressing himself only to the lined-up troops, the same lieutenant appeared once more and began to read the Captain-General's terse, uncompromising speech to his subordinates, to the rich men and the people of Minas.

What did the speech say? In his dark silence now, in his night of waiting, the night that enveloped him in its softness, sounds of crickets and frogs and dog barks and hoofs of horses trotting on the stones down below, like soft echoing waves of a great bell rung by celestial hosts in the far distance, between waking and sleep, life and death, immersed in his grievous passion, Januario could not reconstruct it. No doubt what such speeches always said, he was thinking to himself, not knowing if he was just remembering or beginning to dream.

The flint prepared, Januario half asleep, Isidoro moved a little way off, massa was snoring already. If we take a doll, say a fetish figure, and do all sorts of bad things to it, imagining and saying that the figure is a person we desire much evil to, if we prick it or pierce it with a knife or a dagger, even if the person is far away he starts to writhe and suffer, to bleed and

[3] The reference is to a passage in Camões's famous epic poem *The Lusiad,* which celebrated the Portuguese discoveries and has since been used, particularly by the Salazar regime, as a justification for Portuguese colonialism.

die, just like the doll. That was what they said in the magic they taught Isidoro to do. The doll like massa hanging up there on the gallows, the muffled beat of the drums. Even at a distance, massa must have felt the thump on the gullet, the spasms in the body and the legs, when Mulungu the Negro jerked the big doll the Captain-General ordered to be hanged. Massa was dead, it was a question of when. Only his body to be handed over, his soul already pierced, massa dead. No, it seemed more like he was snoring. Or was it just an impression, he was dying, not sleeping? He'd given up trying to understand that young massa they'd given him to when massa was little more than fifteen. Be clever but the right way, Massa Tomás kept telling him when he fetched him from the mines and gave him as a present to his half Indian son. That was funny master wanting to be an Indian altogether now. I accept being a savage, I would even accept being black, was what he'd said.

Black was what *he* was. Massa had no idea what it was to be black. The neck-irons, the stocks, the whips. The pain, the endless suffering. He raised his hand instinctively to his shoulder, without even noticing he felt the scar of the letter. Be clever, nigger. Don't go trying to run away, because I'll catch you whatever it takes. I'll go after you to the ends of the earth, nigger. Massa Tomás could be hard, hadn't he felt that hardness on his shoulder? Be clever, serve Januario well and when it's over either he or I will give you your freedom. Funny Massa Tomás was, he didn't want just service he wanted affection. At first he refused, he couldn't altogether forget his idea of running away. Fear and the memory of his previous failure made him give it up. He served more because he had to serve, he obeyed. Wasn't it the destiny of his race to serve and obey? Afterwards he started to get fond of that strong, broad-shouldered half-breed, with the hard, straight, thick black hair of a Puri Indian. Half Indian, that's what he was. His mother was half Puri, the daughter of a white father and an Indian slave girl, a neophyte they called them. They liked to have things clear. So's nobody would confuse a half-breed Indian with a black or a mulatto. They sometimes baptized half-breed Indians as sambos or mulattos, just so's to have the mark of slavery in writing. Many priests do that, or so they said. Worse is nigger, Indian gets away with it. Weren't there lots of São Paulo people who made a thing of having Indian blood, from a long way back? But they only said that when they were very white, when they ran no risk of being taken for Indians or niggers. Black is worse. I would even accept being black, was what he said. There was something in what he said. Looking back in time, he could see. As if with all that time, the two of them together all the time, each a shadow of the other, in the skin of the other, massa had grown darker; at times he really looked like an Indian, not a half-breed

Indian, which was what he was. He got to liking massa. So much that he couldn't ever remember when he started serving him out of affection, instead of fear and duty. Godfather, Januario said one day in front of the others, don't lock up Isidoro in the slave-quarters at night any more, he doesn't need to be locked up, he won't run away, I promise you. His father gave him a long look as if to say watch what you're doing. Then he looked deep into Isidoro's eyes. Isidoro hid his thoughts as best he could, pretending. Racial wisdom, learned under the whip. So's old Tomás would never know what he was thinking. Showing what he was thinking was the same as admitting he was weak, a coward, without strength. His strength was silence, that dark heavy silence in the presence of white men. The old man must never know. He had to rely on his bastard son, on his certainty. For Isidoro to let the old man know was the same as accepting bondage for good. He still had a lot of grief, a lot of pain, hidden inside. If he could, the thought was beginning to take shape. He gave up, better to think of something else. Not now, it was before that he put aside the idea. Now he was free, he could go where he wanted. So he used to think before now. He laughed softly when he thought that he was free, now. He had never been so trapped, never so captive as he was now. Maybe more trapped, more manacled, more of a slave than when he had the chain on his feet, the infernal neck-iron tugging his neck, biting into the flesh. Because before, he could still run away, not now. Now, alone, without massa, he couldn't even get away in the wilds where the cattle were, way out by the San Cisco. There would always be some white man to enslave him and fasten the iron ring to his feet, the iron collar on his neck. Or capture him to receive the reward from his former owner. The bounty-hunters, armed soldiers, terrifying assassins. It wasn't only massa, anyone could kill him too. It wasn't a crime to kill someone who was already dead, that was what they said in the proclamations that were hurriedly made in the squares and at crossroads. He felt strangely one with massa, hand in glove, more than ever. So much so, he took the other's death on himself. Like a decree of fate. If it was not a crime before to kill a nigger. Unless the owner reclaimed the lost piece of property. Now less than ever. Together for ever, he was thinking.

There was only one way to be free, to buy his freedom, that way. He didn't want to think about it, he couldn't. He mustn't, that was the truth. The thought was stronger than him, than all the devotion of a Negro retainer. Not noticing what he was doing, his hands started to think for him, to act for him.

When he noticed, he had his carbine pointing at Januario's chest. It only needed one shot, like that, point-blank. A bit afraid of Januario, the way he could spring like a cat. Not now, now he can't do anything, asleep surely. He was quicker than massa now. He stopped suddenly, shaking his head vigorously, saying no no, trying to reject it, trying to get rid of the thought which his hands were weaving again. No, he said almost aloud to the persuasive voice echoing inside him. That unknown voice coming from fathomless depths. Shaking hands, he couldn't do it. So easy, if you want, the same ancient voice said again, angrily, darkly. No, I just can't, he resisted. He had become very attached to that boy. Half Indian, he was. He never beat him. Not even when he shouted at him. White men are born evil. White man's kindness is all invention, lip service. Like white man's religion. So's they don't need to use iron and chains. A stronger bondage, the sinister voice went on, and his hand lifted again to take aim. Massa in his sights, it was easy. If they give you your freedom, even if you buy it you have to thank them. Was he asleep? What if he was only dozing, his eyes watchful even from way off? If massa suspected, guessed what he was thinking, what his hands were thinking and doing for him, he was lost. Not him, Januario. Then he'd have to do it, there was no other way. The carbine was loaded now, easy. Better talk to massa again, see if he could make him change his mind, he went on, trying to use his arguments, the plan he had thought over so much, to silence the other voice, the other voice that was stronger than him. The other voice that came from his people, from the other side, from across the sea. So easy, a twitch of the hand would be enough.

Massa, he almost shouted, like when we try to utter a shout down in the dungeon of an agonizing dream, our voice strangled in our throat. So as to wake from that nightmare that was stronger than his bondage, his loyalty.

Deep in heavy sleep, Januario grunted something. The way a dog growls and barks in its dreams. Massa! he repeated, more firmly this time. He too needed to wake up. To stop that other voice, that other, nocturnal self dominating him, taking control of his hands, the weapon at the ready. What? said Januario, clearly now, coming round. Did you say something? No, nothing, said the Negro. I only wanted to help you wake from your nightmare, massa. You were so restless, in the torment of your dream. Was I dreaming? Did I say anything in my sleep? asked Januario. He did not at all remember having gone to sleep, so gently had he slipped from dozing through the silent wall of deep sleep. Another self within him stayed watchful and unsleeping. A self that could never sleep. So unsleeping that a mere name, spoken by the black man, had woken him. Did you shout? he asked, to find out how deeply he had been asleep. No, the Negro lied, calm now, his phantom had returned to the other side, to where it had come from.

Maybe he was dreaming after all? Not now, then, that time which he couldn't remember. Before, when he remembered what Isidoro once told him. The scene he had to create with all the strength of his imagination and experience, the black man had so few words, he could barely understand the absurd dream the other was telling him. That sticky mixture of dreams, memories and nightmares. The scene in the square was before his eyes yet again. The scene which he had always to reconstruct, meticulously, with fantastic attention to detail like an old usurer weighing out gold. That wealth of something actually seen, a real occurrence, then recollected in tranquillity, when the tiniest, most insignificant details stand out in hard, bright, sharp relief, and one recollects for all time everything that one was not aware of seeing at the time, that one did not notice. The world, beings, things were being noted down in miniature by the mind's eye. For afterwards. The whole scene that now kept coming back to him in his dreams and he at times doubted if he had actually heard from Isidoro, if Isidoro ever did tell him anything. As if he had seen it himself, in the square. And it had not all been a dream that was repeated over and over, like the repeated bars of a melody that sticks in the mind. The dream in which he was now immersed, even when awake. An endless succession of boxes, one inside the other. As if he himself were his own dream, the dream of someone who urgently needed to wake up. As if suddenly, with God's help, he could wake up, and he imagined himself restored to his father, to his home, and none of that business of João Diogo, of blood and hanging, even of Malvina, of that nightmare life of waiting and anguish, none of it had happened, it was no more than a macabre fantasy, a sudden flash of lightning in the sky the first time he saw Malvina.

The first time he saw Malvina on her horse, by the side of Gaspar on his roan. Who was that apparition, that woman he had never seen before, of whom he had heard nothing? No, she was not local, she could not be anyone local. There was no one like her in the town, no one who dressed as she did. Those presumptuous, aristocratic airs, the immodesty of her gestures, the way of riding and of looking. He looked at her, observed her at length, and he could never take his eyes off that flaming hair and that body swaying to the rhythm of the horse's ambling gait.

He followed her at a distance, pretending that he happened to be going in the same direction. Though he had turned back suddenly the moment he saw her. She had seen him too, had noticed him. Their eyes met, she even stopped her horse. The other rider had to turn round in order to find out why she had halted. Gaspar looked at him in astonishment, with an inquiring look in his eyes, as if to ask what impudence was that to stare at his companion, to the point of making her stop her horse. Januario thought the other might come and demand an apology. He was not a fighting man, quite the reverse. But being a hunter, he was certainly a good shot. His hand, accustomed to this sort of encounter, gripped the whip handle, he felt his pistol with his elbow. He waited for the other to make a move.

Who is he? he heard her ask. Nobody, some half-breed, said Gaspar, unable to hide his anger. Because he knew him, Januario had even exchanged a few words with him some time in the past. Come along, said Gaspar, calling her. She followed him.

That Gaspar Parente Galvão, with his refined manners, wealthy, a gentleman and a hunter, always away in the forests with his armed niggers, his virginity a laughing matter in that town full of womanizers and whoremongers, those sowers of wild oats.

Forgetting the momentary annoyance of the interruption caused by Januario, there they went, the two of them, the reins slack, taking care only not to wander off the track. Gaspar seemed to be paying her a great deal of attention, though he occasionally lowered his head, as if to avoid looking at her for too long.

Who was she? From the moment he saw her, he was unable to tear his eyes away from that woman, from that Arab horse. He followed her on his horse, pretending he was going in the same direction, taking care it should not look like provocation. The two of them stopped just ahead of him and he hid in a thicket at the side of the track. Then he could see her better, even hear her silvery, crystal-clear voice. Silver and coral the choker at her neck. Not now, there, on horseback, but afterwards. When she was dressed differently, her shoulders bare, the generous *décolletée* of her lace-trimmed dress, her breasts resting on the tight bodice, rising and falling (the scent of basilicon and benjamin afterwards, he tried to single it out, the fragrance lingering in his nostrils, he smelt it again now in the dark, in the cold scented breath of the wind, flooding the least fibres of his body, of his memory, when he came near to her, when he lost himself in her), her firm, snowy breasts, with soft, scented skin – even at this distance he could feel it and in his imagination, timidly, fondle them, often in his dreams he fondled and kissed them – which she barely covered, quite the reverse – in her vanity she displayed them provocatively, lowering the lacy curtain of her mantilla so that they could all let their eyes swim in that snowy whiteness, in that misty sensuality, and sink in the fragrance of her curling coppery hair, which fell in calculated disorder over her round shoulders, the same freckled whiteness and roundness as her breasts. The coral and silver choker glittering and strangling the whiteness of her neck, which was softly transmuted into shoulders, bosom and breasts, as soft also was the continuation of the rounded line of the chin, all of her a harmony of curves and scents. All provocation and sensuality, an invitation to the despair of dream hours, of burning nights, endlessly cursed and desired in torment, a foretaste of death and happiness. Her face too was round, her eyes large and full, with a permanent glow which stayed on in the air even when she closed them or went away, like the sound of a bell echoing on in the air. Her mouth was small but full, she kept moistening her lips with the tip of a pink tongue which flickered between her well-shaped, white, shining teeth (pearls, he said, in the language of that exaggerated poetic tradition of shepherds and shepherdesses, nymphs, woods and meadows; nacre, whose white brilliance simulates the rainbow which secretes itself in the glassy delicacy of the shells, he went on in the exaggeration which attributes heat to the coldness of white things), and that slender nose, its cheeky tip, its nostrils opening and closing daintily with the scented heat of her quickened breathing when she was on fire (now he thought, as all the despair of love tinged with colour and warmth that first cold, white apparition, on her distant cloud, Malvina on her Arab horse), her fiery-red eyebrows, the same harmonious curve, arched. . . .

That fair-skinned woman with her sun-bright hair, black hat well back on her head, blue velvet riding-jacket, tight-fitting, filled out by the solid bulge of her breasts which were corseted beneath and which rose and fell with the rhythm of her breathing, her left hand holding the reins in a stately and graceful manner, her right hand toying with the silver whip in the folds of her riding-habit, sitting erect, making a perfect statue with her horse, artfully provocative as befitted one who knew herself to be beautiful, admired, desired, her head turning this way and that with a grace which, after long practice and calculation, becomes part of the natural beauty of a person's movements, she was a very goddess of the hunt, he told himself in a mythology of half-forgotten verses. How she grew in her dazzling whiteness, before the darkness and humiliated pain of his bastard half-breed eyes. He was tiny before so much sun, beauty and power, he began to think, pierced by light, dwarfed, a target, reduced to an insignificance which his sense of his illegitimacy and mixed blood dwarfed further still, while magnifying her and elevating her in the loftiness, pride and nobility which he from then on began to associate with her.

He had never seen a woman like her, even in dreams. He never thought she could exist. No, she could not be local. From which palaces, from which courts, from which enchanted forests, brought by which winged beings, in the folds of which winds, in which dream's white, snowy breezes, from where had that woman come? he kept asking himself over and over again, when she gave a clear, high-pitched shout (it could almost be a laugh, he thought in his humiliation), whipped the horse smartly, galloped off and disappeared round the dusty bend in the track.

He began to hear the clatter of hurried hoofbeats coming across the night air. In the silence of the night, punctuated only by the glimmer of crickets with their endless, monotonous song and by the drum-like croaking of the frogs, the horses sounded very close, but he knew they were far off, on their way to the square already. Even so he instinctively shrank into the thickest shadow of the fig tree, whose leaves a cold gentle breeze was beginning to rustle. The dry, aggravating rustle of silks and taffetas, when she undressed and threw off her clothes, which even so far off, in the depths of time, he could still sense in his nostrils, on his fingertips. . . .

They're far away, massa, said the Negro, seeing how he crept into the darkest patch of the fig tree's shadow. So accustomed was he to hiding from the sound of hoofs, on the trails and tracks, on the paths along which they had been travelling for so long. The tinkle of the decorated lead mare's bells, the distant shout of the drover pulling a string of pack of mules loaded with saddle-frames and saddle-bags, was enough to send them looking for shelter in the nearest thicket, crouching so as not to be seen. The life of fugitives and robbers, suffering hunger, those worthless jewels and gold.

Januario wrapped himself in the blanket and covered his arms and legs with the thick sheepskin saddle-cloth, the night was getting cold. Do you want a drop of rum, massa? asked the Negro, feeling the cold. As Januario was slow to answer, he added it's a drop of the best, massa, warms the cockles of the heart. Januario pulled the corn-cob stopper out with his teeth and poured the spirit hot down his throat. That good feeling, the warmth. He handed the bottle to Isidoro, who wiped the neck with his hand before raising it to his mouth. Tightening his lips in a half-smile, Januario thought what a strange life it was. Now it was the black man, his slave, who wiped the bottle he had drunk from. Before it was the reverse. In their misfortune the two had become equal and in the darkness one couldn't tell which was the black and which the master.

It was past midnight already, he knew that from the leisurely strokes of the gaol-bell that had rung a long time before. The moon, small and round, was indifferent, cold and too far away above their heads. A bat plunged downwards, then up again, its dark shadow silhouetted in the moonlight as it made off in blind and rapid flight. In his cold, dry nose the prickling caused by the dust which he barely saw, merely sensed, in the dry thicket from which the bat had flown.

Once the uncomfortable prickling had ceased he could feel the air chilling his nostrils when he filled his chest with air, warming them when he emptied it, trying to see the whitish steam of his breath in the cold, clear, pure air.

Down below, the valley was hidden by the mist which grew thicker as it followed the course of the Tripuí from its source in the mountains, close to where he was, joining its waters to those of the Caquende to form the Ribeirão do Funil at the foot of the valley, a wide stream which went on to swell other rivers, winding between hills and mountains with majestic peaks, serrated crests of stone standing out in the silvery gleam of the moonlight. Now, with the town enveloped in shimmering, whitish clouds, he could see only the bulbous towers of Carmo Church on the hilltop, their spires outlined in the white moonlight. In a short while the mist would also swallow up the soaring, glittering white towers, their light inward too, the moonlight casting a silver sheen on the clouds round about them, which, looking like a mysterious floating shadow, made them ethereal, fantastic and unreal.

The town cloaked in mist, the moon tinging the blanket of white down with silver, it was to this dream town that he was returning once more. A thousand times in dreams and moonlight, not there and now but overlooking other villages, towns and hamlets, on paths and trails, in resting-places and huts, he was always returning to this town. Like a destination he could not stay away from, a destiny from which he could not escape. Like the plan which an idle, terrible god had mapped out for him long before he was born, before the beginning of time, since all eternity, as a challenge to him and to his impotent rage (as he had done to many others since early antiquity) to break out of his magic circle (impossible, no use trying), and from behind a static, dreadful smile of stone, with no apparent meaning, deliberately open to all manner of interpretations and veiled conjectures, had said this is what I have reserved for this loathsome creature which I would nevertheless love if he prostrated himself at my feet (a sacrifice of no use to me or to him) with his incenses, lambs and blood offerings. Chained to that town, that street, that house, that woman of fire for ever in his heart, suffocating him. He kept returning, always; this time was the last, so he hoped.

Don't ever return, my boy, said his father and he was always returning. This time for good, he knew it. Next morning, his father, if he had the courage and if they let him, would be able to have his body brought from the square. Tired of running away, he was coming back.

In the prison, when the gaoler let him escape. His father told him to put out the lamp and like that, in the dark, shrouded in the smell of soot and oil, the quiet low voice, in that deep hoarse tone induced by darkness, was more like a thick shadow which he heard because he could not see it.

In the small secret room where the gaoler took him so that father and son could talk properly, well away from the other prisoners and the soldiers. You have to be quick, Senhor Tomás, don't lose me my job and my head, I have got a family to look after, you know. His father said nothing to start with, he did not want to speak in front of a stranger, what he had to say was very special and dangerous, although he and the gaoler had linked their interests and destinies through corruption and fraud. Now, from straining hard, he could see his father's shadow as a thicker patch of darkness, he knew he was there more by his silence than because of his voice. In his nose, still, as well as the smell of soot and oil from the now extinguished lamp, the odour of the tallow candle that someone before them had lit and snuffed, leaving the stump. Quickly, Senhor Tomás, I'm beginning to regret what I'm doing, said the gaoler, his white Portuguese voice a mixture of greed and obsequiousness. And in justification, no amount of gold can pay for the service I am rendering you, Senhor Tomás. Enough, said his father, furious at the oily subservience he had bought. Have you not had your part? You have never seen and never will see as much gold as I have given you, because you are not worth it. I'll give it back, Senhor Tomás, I'm having second thoughts, the man kept repeating, lies, because he was not going to give back anything. Come on, man, stop annoying me, said his father, now seeking retaliation for the act he had been obliged to commit to save his son. The worst about types like you is that we have to put up not just with your presence but with your smell too! He said it with intent to offend, knowing that the man, on account of the gold he had received, could neither back out nor answer back.

And his father stopped talking, to see if the gaoler would understand his silence. A tap on the yoke and the donkey understands. I'm going, Senhor Tomás, said the man, understanding, in a resentful shaky voice. The fear and compunction he claimed to be feeling were real, only they sounded false because he could not back out. Keep your conversation short, Senhor Tomás, while I go and see to filing some of the bars to make it look more like Senhor Januario escaped. It has to be now, Senhor Tomás, for the holy love of God. While the prisoners are asleep and the warders busy with a task I've given them. The man wanted to go, he had understood, but he was so nervous he could not stop talking.

And much as he wanted to stop, he went on talking in his heavy Portuguese accent, with a nervous, worried stammer brought on by his fear and anxiety. Januario's father broke the silence that had been meant to show the gaoler that he should stop talking and go. If you keep on talking like a rattle, how am I going to be able to be quick? Excuse me, Senhor Tomás, I'm going, said the gaoler, bowing with that obsequiousness which corrupt guards know how to put on. He finally went away and left the two of them alone.

When the two were alone, his father's silence was harder, heavier and darker. A silence that was a mixture of hatred and recrimination on the point of exploding, from being so long in check. The hatred and recrimination with which he attempted to disguise the affection he felt for that half-Indian son of his. Afterwards, at the end, he would be overcome, when he said don't ever come back, my son. You will never be able to see me again. His voice trembling with the emotion of saying my son, at the moment of a farewell which he knew was truly for good. When the two were quite alone, he who had always avoided calling him Son, particularly in the presence of others.

Shortly before bringing his father to see him, the gaoler told him what was going on and the plan that they had agreed in order to let him escape. He knew of nothing, only suspected that something different was happening, because the others would not speak to him and sought to move away when he went near them, dragging his clanking chains. Why? Was he not a criminal like them? Did he not have the same shackles on his wrists, the same fetters on his feet? Or was his a different crime, had something that had occurred come to the ears of those prisoners who knew everything despite being segregated from the town?

In a short while I shall bring your father to speak to you, said the gaoler with that intimate manner conferred by corruption, the money received, when he took him to the secret room. Afterwards you escape, sir, he went on in the formal manner he knew was lost for ever once he had received his payment. But, for the love of God, forget me. If they find out that I was the one who let you get away, I'm lost. Your crime is much more serious than I thought. If I knew it was so serious, I would not have agreed. When Senhor Tomás made things right with me, I thought your crime was a different one. I've only discovered what your crime is now that I have received the order for tomorrow. Tomorrow you are supposed to go to the military prison. . . .

The military prison, the crime of treason. Januario did not understand the gaoler's contradictory speech. What was he talking about? What more serious crime was that? Why the military prison? Someone had denounced him, was what the gaoler said. That much he knew, or suspected. In his despair and isolation he even suspected Malvina, she had not gone to meet him in Sabará. A woman capable of every sort of, any crime. They went and arrested him in the agreed place, known only to the two of them and the Negro Isidoro. But Isidoro, though a nigger, was not capable of such a thing. Accused of theft, the missing jewel-case, which she had given him and he later offered to Isidoro for the black man to run away, was proof of the crime. Of theft, he was aware of the accusation. But what new and more terrible crime was the gaoler talking about?

I know I am being accused of theft, he said. It is about that they are going to hear me tomorrow, is it not? I did not steal anything, said Januario, for something to say. If only it were just theft that you are accused of, said the man, attempting a laugh at Januario's ingenuousness. And to his bewilderment began to talk rapidly, giving a proper explanation of everything that was happening. Januario could not understand, it was all too strange, too absurd, none of it was true. Official inquiry, the Captain-General had ordered an official inquiry. The orders were strict, other people were being arrested at that very moment. Who engineered it all? The infernal scheme from which he would be unable to escape. Once the lever had been pulled, setting the first wheel in motion, no one would be able to halt that diabolical machine. He was too puny in the face of the stratagem mounted against him. However absurd the accusation, everything fitted together so perfectly, fitted him like a glove. No one would believe anything he said, his personal truth. He himself felt powerless, found it difficult to believe he had not been the creator of the devilish scheme they were now seeking to charge him with. The Captain-General himself had taken the step of ordering an official inquiry, tomorrow he was to be heard, the orders were strict. There would be torture, confrontations with witnesses.

That was when he learned the truth. He had been arrested for theft, which was not true, the truth was different, but he could never tell it. And even if he did, how could he prove it, if only he and Malvina knew about everything? No one could suspect Malvina of anything, no one knew what had happened between the two of them. Except Isidoro, but what use was the evidence of a nigger, his own slave at that?

He had been thinking of this unceasingly since he was arrested a week before, but failed to find an explanation that could satisfy not only his judges but himself. And now along came the gaoler with an even greater absurdity, he found it difficult to believe that anyone could think it up. But looked at from a distance, in the cold logic of such well-co-ordinated facts, it seemed more probable even to him than the truth which he alone knew. His own truth at times seemed the more absurd, instead of the newly invented one.

It must be today, I have already received orders, said the gaoler, when he told him the plan for his escape that had been agreed with his father.

I've already received orders from above to transfer you to the military prison. There neither I nor anyone else can do anything for you, even if Senhor Tomás had the largest fortune in the land. Military prison, Januario began to think, assailed by a suffocating fear which he had never experienced even in dreams.

And he learned the truth. He had initially been arrested as a common criminal, that was what they told him. That was why he was in the municipal prison. But things had become complicated, clues had started to add up and become facts which could easily be proved with torture and confrontations with witnesses. The wealthy João Diogo Galvão was too important to the Captain-General and to the King. Military prison, he thought again in fear. Neither I nor anyone else will be able to do anything, the man said.

It all made sense, he started to think again in the same vicious circle. The pieces fitted together perfectly. Only his own truth failed to make sense. His crime was a different one, not the one he had committed, that was what the gaoler was now telling him. The absurdity overwhelmed him, his mind was blank. Next day, under duress, under torture, he would tell them whatever they wanted. His blood would merely be proof of what was already known. They found me out, discovered everything, even what I never dreamed of, he told himself, overcome by the absurdity. He was himself beginning to believe he was guilty of the crime of which they now accused him.

As a prisoner of the King, nobody can do a thing for you. The voice of the gaoler, scared on account of what he was going to do, now he could not back out, on pain of being accused and involved in the plot. His father must have spent a great amount of ready money. The service I'm doing Senhor Tomás is worth a fortune, the man repeated again and again. And those words which he was going to hear, terrible enough in themselves, became still blacker due to his impotence and lack of prestige, in relation to the absurd plot of which he was now being accused. They had received information about what was being planned. Mutiny, was what the gaoler said. Leader of a mutiny. He would have to say who was the leader of the mutiny. No one would believe it was him, a simple half-breed. He was only the cat's-paw, his murderous act had been the warning, the agreed signal for the mutiny to take over Minas. He would have to say the name of the leader, of all who were involved in the conspiracy against the King. João Diogo was one of the town's leading citizens, a friend of the Captain-General and the King, to whom he had rendered the highest services, from the time when he cleaned up the bandit-infested rivers. Who on many occasions had offered a force of armed Negroes, even whites, and Indian archers, when it reached his ear that the King and the Captain-General were in need. When they destroyed the great slave hide-outs. The names, tell us the names. You'll have to tell us, so tell us now. And now he, Januario, did not know which names, he would not be able to accuse anybody. Nonsense, the judges would speak the names, he would have only to confirm, to add his imagination to the facts they told him. To satisfy the fury of the Captain-General and of the King's men he would invent. He felt capable of the feat. He could already see the irons on his flesh, the fire for the torture. He would tell everything, even what he neither did nor thought of doing. In his fear and dread he wished he knew something, that he had heard something from someone, that he could imagine a reasonable plot. Even in the knowledge that the crime of lese-majesty (crime of indictable treason against the King's person, was what the gaoler told him, neither of them really understanding what the words meant, but knowing they were dreadful) was punishable by the gallows, he would confess, such was the terror inspired in him by torture suffered in anticipation. Rather death, he thought. He saw death as a liberation from torture. No, not the pain, he would not bear it, he repeated to himself.

What on earth have you done, Januario? It was not the gaoler now, but his father talking to him. What a mess you've got yourself in! I can't do anything for you except this. You will escape and never be able to come back here.

But I didn't steal anything, said Januario, trying in vain to explain to his father. He already felt guilty of whatever crimes they might choose to accuse him of. That is not what they say, said his father, looking him searchingly in the eyes, straining to discover in their depths some sign that would allow him to believe in his innocence. His father's voice was deeper and hoarser than usual. The father he had always thought so powerful was now as puny as him. All I can do for you is what I am doing, he said. I shouldn't even be doing this, sheer madness. Why did I come here? I shouldn't have come. I could do what I'm doing, but I shouldn't have come. His father seemed to be talking to someone else. They might involve me, think that I am in some plot against the Captain-General, against the King. . . . His father was talking to himself, to someone invisible. I didn't steal anything, Father, he almost shouted. I had no need to steal, Father, he said, trying to bring his father back to reality. He had never seen him with such fear in his eyes.

It is not what they are saying, was all his father could keep repeating. They say you stole more as a blind, the thing is much worse. It was revenge and retaliation, the signal for an uprising. João Diogo was the first, your companions now know what to do. Conspiracy, mutiny, uprising, schemes I do not understand, that I am even afraid to understand. I who have never doubted, never talked to anyone about the rightness of what the Captain-General or the King's ministers do!

His father spoke partly to him, partly to someone invisible, seeking to justify himself for a crime he had not so much as been accused of. He felt sorry for his father, for what he was going through on his account. Your companions have abandoned you now, my boy. The Captain-General has devised a terrible machine, no one will have the courage to stick his neck out.

What companions, Father? he started to say, but gave up, he could see it was useless, not even his own father would believe what he said, his truth had no value, counterfeit money. The town is all up in arms, the whole captaincy, his father went on. A crime against the King, lese-majesty, that's what they are saying. Everything is a crime against the King. Everywhere you go you bump into a soldier. It will be difficult for you to escape. And if you do escape, the only way not to die is by never coming back again. They can put a price on your head, you have to get away from here. Even if you are far away, they can judge, even condemn, you. Even hang you in pretence, in effigy as they say. But it is just as valid. They have often done it in the past, they do it now and will go on doing it. It's the King's law, the King's arm is very long and very strong, it will always be after you. Only if you disappear from here. Anyone can kill you, it is not a crime.

His father stopped talking, he hoped to see in his son something to deny the certainty he now felt that the boy was guilty. And since Januario said nothing and he could not discover in his eyes the denial in which he did not really believe, he went on. I am giving you what I can, it's all I have for now. I've already spent everything else I had to buy your escape. Value it, my son. In any case, you will never again be the man you are, the man you were. If you want to stay alive, if you are clever as I hope you are. . . .

His father's voice was gruffer now and more sombre. He believed he detected a hint of a tear in it, of those tears he never saw his father shed.

Even though he knew for certain that his father would not believe what he was going to tell him, he needed to speak. He thought of telling him everything that had happened between himself and Malvina, up to the end, the most private things, his most secret thoughts. Father, he went on, without much conviction, not the least bit sure that the old man would believe what he was going to say, Father, none of this is true, it's all invented, crazy ideas the Captain-General and his people have thought up. I didn't do any of that. I'm mixed up with a woman, with Malvina. Dona Malvina, he said, noticing his father's astonishment.

What? What story is this you're inventing? You've started lying now, have you? You're trying to tell me that you dishonoured someone else's house just so that I'll believe you're not guilty of a crime against the King? You are finished, Januario. Even if I believed what you're telling me, even so you would be done for. A half-breed son of mine just had to go and dishonour me . . .

Useless, absolutely useless to try and convince his father. Neither his father nor anyone else knew about his affair with Malvina. His visits to João Diogo's house took place late at night, in secret and heavily disguised, by the back door, in the Rua das Flores. If he could not convince his father how would he manage to persuade the others?

And his father, who had heard what he had merely thought, said even if you could convince me, if you could tell me the truth, who on earth could persuade the Captain-General, the judges, the whole town? Tell me that, Januario. These things, once they start, nobody can stop them any more. It's like a cart on a steep slope. Nobody can. Not even the Captain-General, nobody. You are finished, my son. Except if you don't come back. Don't ever come back.

Januario said nothing, he was too puny for what was happening to him. Not even the Captain-General, his father said. He was right. His father knew the Minas country, the law, the arm of the King's law. The Captain-General's men would make him confess whatever they saw fit. The Captain-General himself, the Viceroy too, they vied with one another in their zealous concern for the King's business. They were crazy for a scapegoat, to serve as an example. They needed a victim, to make it easier for them to collect the gold tax. When they got round to the unpaid taxes, that would be it. That was what his father said and it all followed on and made sense. Much more credible than his own truth, he recognized weakly; his father was altogether right.

Isidoro gave him the bottle again. The spirit was sharp going down, rasping his throat, burning his empty stomach. As if he had a sore place in the pit of his stomach. He squirmed with pain, where he felt emptiness. Do you want a piece of bread? said the Negro. It's from yesterday, massa, from those drovers. Even being yesterday's, it's good to have something to line your belly, it's not good to go on drinking on an empty stomach. And he passed him the bread. Januario bit a piece off and began to chew. It was hard and dry, the taste of old mouldy bread tightening his throat, making the inside of his nose smart. He chewed the hard dry lump, couldn't swallow it and spat it out.

The effect of the drink, the mist in his eyes. A mist that came from inside, the town now sunk deep in fog. Even the spires of the Carmo Church towers had disappeared, covered in a blanket of mist. He himself cloaked in a whitish cloud. The cold that the drink drove away with its pleasant warmth. When he stirred his head went round and round. A dizzy feeling, the world turning round with him. The machinery of the world going round,[4] nobody could stop it any more. You're finished, on a steep slope. Nobody, caught up in a hell, among pulleys and cogwheels. The great mouth that would devour him. Dead, I'm probably dead, he told himself. Maybe life is just dying, only we don't know, we think we're dreaming. And only afterwards he would find his life, when he was dead. He didn't think that way, in order, more of a diffuse feeling that he had died and had been in hell for a long time already. The hell he had been living in for a year, with its devils and nightmares. Malvina, João Diogo and his father were shades from the depths of hell. They came from the mists, from the other side, just to torment him. Even Isidoro, though he could make out the brownish-white of his eyes, there next to him, gave him the feeling that he didn't exist: another shade from his memory, a shape from the mists of a dream. Dead, in hell. The same diffuse feeling that he had been dreaming, sunk deep in the heavy black pit of a great dream. Those higgledy-piggledy dreams, coming from inside one another like a multitude of empty boxes. As he dreamed, the absurd feeling that he was part of someone else's dream. He had to come back. But I'm not dreaming, I'm dead, he told himself again. Dead, in hell. His suffering made him feel as though he were alive, he was merely dreaming. And in hell or in his dream his movements had that illusion of speed increasing steadily, frighteningly, until it became unbearable, like echoes reverberating in the great bell of a dream, in endless ravines, he thought he would go mad.

But he knew he was not sleeping. When he was asleep it was different, he was fully aware of his sleeping and waking states. That cataleptic feeling, the tingling in his limbs, that he was asleep, when he was really awake. Thus for several days he had not succeeded in succumbing to a heavy, complete sleep, total annihilation, provisional death. He longed for that death which would reunite him, but contradictorily he did not want to sleep. The fancy that when asleep he was a prey to all manner of perils. The magical fancy that when awake he could dominate the world, all beings and all things: nothing would happen unless he wished it.

[4] A multiple allusion and deliberate anachronism serving to link different historical periods. The expression originates in a Camões poem, was used in the baroque period to refer to the uncontrollable nature of man's life situation, and was fittingly taken up and used as the title of a poem by Brazil's great modern poet, Carlos Drummond de Andrade (1903–87), like Dourado from Minas Gerais.

Fatigue made him drowsy, he did not so much feel sleepy. He was not asleep, everything was strange and unclear. Wakeful, yet as if he were sleeping; things lost their hardness of outline, were blurred and fuzzy, existed in a misty dream-state. When he was asleep he seemed to be living with complete lucidity and clarity, like day. Everything was transparent and pure, things regained their edges and solidity. He was able to see the world as a perfect whole, its smallest details, nothing escaped him. Not a shadow, not a movement. He knew then that he was asleep. Because in that utter clarity, bathed by a strong, white, harsh and blinding light, he felt a thump in his chest, a shudder and jerk in his limbs – and knew that he was asleep, he had just been dreaming.

In this confused and cataleptic, lucid and lunar, white and silver state, beings and events lost their temporal and sequential reality, things that had actually happened merged with those still to come, came and went with the monotonous, disturbing fatality of repeated dreams. That gluey mixture of dream and reality in which past, present and future were of the same colour and intensity.

He had thought and dreamed so much about his return to the town (the meeting with Malvina, their first words, those first pregnant silences; then himself facing the soldiers in the square, his own death) that his dreams acquired the intensity and cold lucidity of real events. In the future, when they actually had to happen (he in the square, the soldiers supplied with the prescribed bullets, the clink of the ramrods in the musket barrels, the order to take aim; fire, the commander shouted, and he fell in a blaze of exploding powder, his body riddled with bullets: though dead he could hear the solders' remarks), if they did not happen as he had imagined a thousand times, he was likely to think that they were not really happening, that he was simply dreaming. All this foggy mixture of past and future, and even the feeling of the present (the tingling sensation, the pain in his limbs and in his weary chest), made him giddy: his head began to spin, he thought he was going to faint.

Like that first time, not long ago, Malvina on her Arab, at the side of her stepson. The jealousy he felt now, as if it had just happened or was still to come. The scene was so clear, as if he had dreamed or imagined it, it had not happened, might still happen.

And that was how he had seen, saw or would still see Malvina in her splendid sedan-chair, with two liveried Negroes, on her way to Pilar Church for the Governor's installation.

Malvina's hand had opened the damask curtain, her long smooth fingers suggestive of a caress he felt in anticipation, and she had opened her mantilla, revealing herself altogether: the splendour of her firm, snowy, velvety breasts, shining at a distance.

And she had smiled, she smiled at him now, he was certain she would smile at him once more, my God. And he had seen those fragrant breasts which he would afterwards fondle and kiss and bite. He saw the small, full mouth, the lips moistened by that adorable and lovable habit of putting the tip of her tongue between her teeth. He would see the large, round, shining blue eyes sparkling, smiling at him. And he had seen her hair piled up high, interwoven with pearls, the hairs glittering. And he saw her round shoulders, all of her a single rounded harmony of myriads of gleams and perfumes – even from a distance he could see and smell them, and in addition the small spot near the dimple in her face. All of her a promise of endless happiness and voluptuousness, a tenser and intenser pleasure than he had ever experienced or ever would. When it went on too long and was stretched to its utmost, like the string of a musical instrument, he thought his breast and his soul would suddenly burst in absolute anguish, as if it were possible to draw out the pain of pleasure to the point of death.

Blinded by passion, he was destroying himself, he followed her openly, not caring whether people noticed his foolhardiness in pursuing a married woman in the street. Now he knew that she was the wife of João Diogo Galvão, from São Paulo (of the Vicentine nobility, they said, with typical *paulista* veneration), from that whitewashed nobility, like mangoes ripened by being wrapped in paper or placed in the bottom of a drawer, from São Vicente, or rather from Taubaté, where he had gone himself to fetch her (with his accumulated wealth, plus his promises) to put an end to his widowed state. João Diogo was more than twice her age. Ugly, wrinkled and old; she was beautiful and young, inordinately and exceptionally young and beautiful.

Januario was out of his depth and was capable of the wildest follies just to see her, to smell and breathe the breath of her presence, to be near her. For her he had done, would do, anything.

With the curtains of the sedan-chair now wide open, Malvina actually put her head and the upper part of her body outside so that he could see her in the fullness of her power, and possess her with his eyes. It was manifest in the fiery gleam in her eyes: she wanted to be possessed and overpowered, destroyed. She showed herself without the least discretion, for him alone.

And as the chair now moved on more quickly, she went so far as to turn round, following him with her eyes as she was carried farther away by the hurried pace of the blacks accelerating on the steep slope. He smiled at her and she gave him a long smile (with her eyes, her mouth, even with the covert glow of her skin) and he was to such an extent possessed and possessed her, that he lost his last scrap of decorum and fear of being seen and, bowing low, took off his hat to her.

When he looked up again, he saw that she prolonged the smile which would continue to vibrate in the air, quivering like the soft waves of a church bell; even when she was far away, grievously separated from him, Malvina answered his gesture with a gallantry of her own. As if they were in a hall all lit up by a thousand candles, not caring that they might be observed. No one saw, he was absolutely sure no one knew a thing, whence the surprise in his father's eyes, the impossibility of proving his innocence. And she made thus with her fan, opening it wide in a half-circle, as if, instead of being the chaste wife of a vigilant and jealous old man, she were a courtesan, a dancer or an actress.

Then he realized that she was ready for him. Now it was a question of sooner or later, of a thousand and one ruses so that they could meet and speak to one another. He knew how difficult these things were, impossible even in his mestizo eyes, but that they would happen.

Now at the window of the mansion, with her hair let down for the casual ease of a drowsy afternoon. If she had lost the brilliance and luxury of her Sunday clothes, which raised her to the moonlit window of a high baronial tower, she had gained the languid warmth of intimacy – the good, fragrant, unhurried warmth with its thousand promises.

They looked at one another once more, she smiled again, this time a still more lingering smile, so insistent and troubled that he had to lower his eyes. Almost standing in the stirrups, he threw the flower to her. Without a care for anyone who might be watching, she raised herself, like a playful, clever cat, catching the flower in the air, and hid it in her bosom. No one saw, no one ever saw, if they had seen it would be easy to prove. Because afterwards the two of them took more care, their communication was afterwards carried on not in the symbolic language of flowers, but through Isidoro and Inacia, Malvina's black maid, who fetched and carried their notes and letters. Until the notes and letters were no longer enough, and the two started to meet at night, when he sneaked in, heavily cloaked, by the entrance in the Rua das Flores, at an agreed hour, which became habitual.

Malvina springing out of her silks and taffetas, tusser and shot silks, cambrics and hollands, naked, no longer protected by her petals, like a rose opening at night, yet smaller and more beautiful like that, letting her hair fall completely loose – at close quarters it was even glossier and more fragrant, and it crackled.

Naked in bed, her frenzied abandon. Without the least fear that her husband, in the next room, their bedroom, might wake, find her missing and go looking for her armed with dagger and pistol, ready to kill her; he would have to defend her. So he imagined it. She apparently wanting to be surprised: her shouts, the violence of her love-making, going on and on, like a she-cat on the roof-top. The fire never dying down, always wanting more, posturing to provoke him, a she-cat and a queen.

That wild woman in bed. Her red hair, a woman of fire. That red-haired woman of fire whom he did not deserve when he compared his dark, almost Indian, mestizo skin and his bastardy to Malvina's white skin and her nobility, of pure blood, as they said. She did it all just to destroy him, so that he would kill and die for it, now he could see it clearly.

And completely naked, with none of that false modesty, with its myriad little shrieks, that he was accustomed to in the women he knew. Even her pubic hair, the same tawny colour of old gold, seemed to gleam sombrely in the semi-darkness which was lit only by a small oil-lamp in the prayer-niche. Even when she was lying down or reclining her breasts always looked firm and high. And above all, that warm, penetrating perfume (he smelt it just now) summoning him.

Sweating and shuddering, with passionate ahs and sighs which he attempted to stifle with his mouth, so as not to wake João Diogo Galvão, the two made love, abandoning themselves to one another in the struggle of two bodies with every pore aflame, then sank back exhausted, afterwards, in a lake of silence, and both, now weary and still, almost melted with the languidness of limbs, breast and satisfied belly. Until it all started again, over and over. Because that way she was binding him and killing him.

Out of the mist which was dispersing in the morning sunlight, the Corpus Christi procession started to move off. Now, night suddenly became bright day and the sun shone intensely. Strange, the procession was very like the glittering parade which the Captain-General had arranged for his execution. The same people and guilds, except that there were no saints and litters, no triumphal floats with figures representing winds and planets, in the hanging procession, apart from the priests and the crucifer. When Mulungu appeared all black and shiny, as if he had been smeared with tar, a bronze statue, majestic.

It was a procession such as he could not remember ever having seen. One like this I only saw when I was a kid and saw the Eucharistic Triumph,[5] in the thirties it was, recalled a very thin, old, old man, from under his white hair and from behind his puffy, lacklustre eyes,

[5] The Triunfo Eucarísto (see Introduction) relates nothing more than the transfer of the divine sacrament from one to another of Vila Rica's many churches, describing with a wealth of baroque detail the fantastically rich and ornate attire and theatrical appearance of the characters who lead the procession.

showering spittle from his shrivelled mouth. He knew the old man very well, only now, desperately though he racked his brains, appealing to his memory, the name would not come to him. What was the importance of a name? But he tried anxiously to remember. The old man must be confused, soft in the head, his recollections muddled. He could not have been a young boy in the thirties, otherwise he would not be so old now. the old man got older and older until he was all wrinkled up. Januario tried to count up on his fingers, to see if the old man could have been a boy in the thirties.

Suddenly he lost interest in the old man, he gave a sigh of relief.

Now he was watching the procession from a distance, his eyes filled with wonder. The crucifer raising the silver Christ aloft, everyone kneeling and making the sign of the cross as it went by. Mulungu, his chest naked and shiny. What was Mulungu the black man doing there? No, it was not a dream, he knew that, in spite of the diaphanous clarity, the brightness of things. He tried to put Mulungu's presence down to his tired mind, to his state of mental confusion. It was not something Isidoro had told him either, none of it had yet happened: his arrest in Sabará, his escape from prison, the conversation with the gaoler, the farewell scene with his father. His death in effigy was still to take place in the square, he would see that from the brownish whites of Isidoro's bloodshot eyes.

Mulungu disappeared back to the mists, the dark depths from where he had come. It really was a Corpus Christi procession, he was absolutely sure of that now. He could see the mouth, the grey-white face of the old man who had compared this procession to the festivities of the Eucharistic Triumph. The shrivelled toothless mouth, with just two large front teeth, opening and closing as if he were chewing, his reedy voice like a broken bamboo flute. The broken flute had been before, when he was still listening to what the old man was saying. Not now.

The streets festooned with arches covered with inscriptions and emblems. Along came the floats and the dances and the masks and the religious guilds. The Christians and Infidels in military attire, gorgeous uniforms and turbans with jewelled brooches the size of coins, gleaming silver swords and daggers accompanying the rhythm of the dancing and music. The musicians' floats, their instruments and voices. The pilgrims and nymphs, the angels and seraphim, dressed in all the colours of the rainbow, their wings of white velvety feathers, glittering with stars and precious stones. The youngsters: the pages and the black buglers and pipers, with their gold epaulettes, frogs, braid, buckles and buttons. The allegories of Orient and Occident, of the Moon and the Sun, the Spring decked with flowers. And the wonderful creation invented to

56

represent the Seven Planets, Fame, the Four Winds. Surrounded by pages and nymphs, there they all were, from Mercury to Vesper, from Venus to Saturn. North, South, East and West. All dressed in tragic style. And their heads crowned with feathers, cockades and chignons trimmed with red ribbons. And the valuable horses, not a jade among them. The Arabs, the roans, the sorrels and the bays, their coats all brushed and shiny, their manes and tails braided and adorned with a variety of ribbons, bells and jingles polished until they shone like gold. The saddle-cloths trimmed with gold, the saddles of velvet, the bits, stirrups and surcingles of silver. A glittering, resplendent feast of gold and wealth.

And there came all the religious guilds, that of the Coloureds of St Joseph's Chapel, those of All Souls and St Michael, from that of Conceição de Antonio Dias to those of Our Lady of the Rosary of the Black People, of Pilar do Ouro Preto, of Grace and Favours, in their best, finely woven tunics with silks, ribbons and sashes, with their insignia and their patrons' emblems embroidered in gold thread on the coloured, fringed damask banners. In perfect order and with great respect, the flip-flop of their boots and sandals in the silence and devotion, according to the degree and importance of each, from the ruling members of Carmo and St Francis to the lowest brothers of Rosário of the Black People and of Grace and Favours. Bearing their staffs, torch-holders and highly polished silver crosses. With their image litters lined with silk, brocade and damask, with fanciful scrolls of gilt carving, on which the saints, the patron of each one's devotion, shone in their silver lace mantles, covered in stars and crescent moons embroidered in gems and sparkling glass beads.

And the priests with their vestments as gleaming and richly embroidered as the saints' cloaks. The thuribles of fragrant incense, the incense boats. They looked like noble wise kings bearing gold, frankincense and myrrh to the Christ child. The fabulous pantomime, the great occasion.

Farther back, the Captain-General in his lavish, brilliant uniform, with his decorations, sashes and epaulettes, surrounded by the military and literary nobility, the town council, the regiment of dragoons. And finally the Holy Sacrament beneath the crimson canopy, in a jewelled golden monstrance.

He saw it all clearly and exactly, as if each thing were separate and apart, instead of mixed and mingling together, a grey blur. With a lucid, sharp, unmoving eye like a watchmaker taking apart and putting together a complicated mechanism. He saw it once more, viewed it afresh.

Suddenly his eyes fell on the showy, ridiculous figure of João Diogo Galvão, right next to the Captain-General, who called him his friend, recipient of a letter written in the King's own hand. And he kept looking at him, like a tailor or a seamstress dressing him for the occasion.

What João Diogo had turned into! A fop, a courtier! He was a different man, another João Diogo Galvão. No longer the severe dress of a former councillor. Now he wore a tailcoat of bottle-green velvet with gilt edging. A green satin waistcoat, of a lighter green than his tailcoat, with a white flower pattern. A large bow at his neck, its ends falling in contrived disorder. Brocade breeches, pearl silk stockings, cordovan leather shoes, elegant silver buckles. His cocked hat, with its metal clasps, carried under his arm as a sign of respect in the presence of the Captain-General and the Sacrament. He was now a refined and courteous man. His shirt-cuffs were of soft frilled lace.

A different man, another João Diogo Galvão. What Malvina had turned him into! All for love of Malvina, to attract her. That was how she wanted him. In place of the old rawhide belt (he remembered seeing João Diogo for the first time when he, Januario, was a boy) a velvet baldric. The old broad-sword, or cutlass, which had cut through masses of scrub, hacked out many a path, lopped off the ears of many runaway slaves and the heads of many Indians (like his swashbuckling father, from Taubaté, one of the first to reach the Tripuí after the gold finds), had been exchanged for a silver-cupped foil, of no use other than to complete the fine figure. Instead of his wild, unkempt hair, a powdered wig, its pigtail secured by a pleated grosgrain bow. Above all, a very white, pomaded, closely shaven face, coated (horror of horrors!) with powder, had taken the place of the aggressive, pioneer's beard of previous times. Just as his home, since he had moved to the tall house in the Rua Direita, with its tracery balconies, was no longer a stronghold in the Padre Faria district, with armed slaves and assassins – the house of a warlord, as they called them – so he himself was different. My God, what a scandalous thing! They had turned the old paladin into a fop of a courtier. He was disgusted by old João Diogo, not yet altogether accustomed to his new role, awkward in his new clothes. And the worst thing was that no one laughed, they all seemed not even to notice, maybe even thinking he looked attractive. The sort of showy attractiveness the ordinary people like. Was he perhaps the only one, because of his seething, concentrated hatred, to notice? Was it just him, because of Malvina?

Then suddenly all eyes were seen to turn in the Captain-General's direction. Not so much the Captain-General, in fact, but João Diogo Galvão next to him. The old man broke into a sort of tottering dance step. They turned to look at him, as if they could see, beneath the powder on his face, now sticky with sweat, running into a paste, his waxen pallor. Something was wrong with him, João Diogo couldn't be feeling well. His legs started to give way, his body swayed and he fell sprawling to the ground. The men around him, the Captain-General included, bent over him (that had a most useful effect, afterwards, for his policies) to help open his tailcoat, unbutton his waistcoat and his sweat-soaked shirt.

The procession came to a halt. The Captain-General called out something to the men in his vicinity. The Captain-General's golden chaise, which always followed him at a certain distance in case of necessity, was brought. All this added greatly to his grandeur, and he already so grand by birth and possessions, with his father's and forebears' names inscribed in the King's books, as they said in their feather-brained courtly flattery. Borne on willing shoulders, the old man was lain in the chaise, which set off noisily, hoofs and horseshoes ringing out and kicking up sparks, in a blaze of gold and sunlight.

Shielding the candle's flame with her hand, minding the light as if it were an egg or gold dust in the trays of a scale, so that it should not be doused by the agitated breath of a hasty utterance, Malvina repreated once again the plan they had been hatching. '*They* had been' is a manner of speaking, in reality it was all Malvina's idea, she was the one who devised it.

At first he did not want to, he always suggested another way. Why don't we go away without any of this, if you really love me? We'll go away, no one will find us, he said, trying to dissuade her, to see if he could persuade Malvina just to go away with him. No, she said, João Diogo will come after us with his armed men, he will follow us to the end of the earth. You don't know João Diogo, his power. In any case, why spend our lives running away, in a different place every day, with nowhere safe to stay? No, Januario, the life you're offering me doesn't suit me. Am I a gypsy going from camp to camp, the Virgin Mary with St Joseph fleeing on a donkey? I hope Our Lady will forgive the comparison, but I wasn't made to be for ever fleeing on an ass's back. Don't you tell me you love me, that you would do anything for me?

She was probably right. She was a real lady, accustomed to the easy calm of wealth, she could by no means live the life he was suggesting. He had to do what she wanted, he could no longer live without her. The day he did not see Malvina was a day of doglike sadness, of fierce disconsolate despair. Now he wanted Malvina all for himself. The mere idea of João Diogo, or even Gaspar, living near her, drove him wild. Lately their meetings, which were becoming riskier and more dangerous, were getting difficult, if not impossible, to arrange and less frequent. Not tonight, she would send word, by means of Inacia or Isidoro. Nor tomorrow. I don't know when we can meet. From her who loves you to the lord of her heart, she wrote in hope, kindling the flame of his passion, and embroidered her signature with flowery arabesques. Or else, always refining to the point of preciosity the close of her letters and notes, which he kept in his bosom like scapularies: from this prisoner in her tower, sighing for her lord, Malvina. She was gnashing her teeth and breathing hard.

And he was desperate at being unable to see her, unable to hold her in his arms and possess her. At times it seemed she was making things difficult in order to force him into a decision. João Diogo is sick, he doesn't want me to leave his side for a single moment, he hardly sleeps, keeps waking up all night long, she said, and the mere mention of her husband's name made Januario crazy with jealousy. She did not go so far as to write Gaspar's name, even avoided mentioning it in speech. But if she did not dare so much, she no longer spoke – as she did at first – of 'the old man', she made a point of using the name João Diogo, just to goad him, he felt sure, at bottom. Malvina was well versed in guile.

You won't have to do hardly a thing, she repeated. All we need do is wake him suddenly. He'll be startled, seeing us together, he'll faint. He'll very likely die even, without us, you, needing to do anything more, she hissed sinuously, slippery. He's very old, weak and sick, he keeps fainting, with a shock I promise you he'll likely die, she said, to and fro, circling, weaving, trimming, like an embroideress. You haven't seen him, you haven't heard? she asked suddenly, surprised, daintily, coquettishly. And she sparkled; he was so stunned he thought she even gave off a sweet fragrance. He could not live without Malvina any more. That day of the procession, when they carried him home, why he didn't die then I do not know, she went on, amassing reasons, pursuing a zigzag course. He nearly didn't regain consciousness, I thought we wouldn't need to do anything, Malvina lisped softly yet again, girlishly. And not just her mouth spoke, but her eyes too, the sway of her body, the buzzing flutter of a bee, the graceful dance of her gestures.

You'll hardly have to do a thing, she was saying now, yet again, the hand with which she shielded the flame trembling slightly. He could see the huge shadow projected on the white wall by her pale, transparent hand. It was a momentary tremor, more of a desire on his part to see it, for Malvina to weaken, so that they should not need to do what they really had to do. A momentary tremor, he was the one who trembled more. A choking sensation in the pit of his stomach, the fear of not being strong enough when the time came. Suddenly, he who was so strong, who had faced worse situations, who had already knifed more than one in fights and duels, without any fear, now he trembled at the idea of facing a sleeping old man. The sleeping, unprotected body gave him a strange fear. And in his distress, in the dark, by the candle's flickering light, he could visualize a white, defenceless body, dangerously defenceless, terrible in its silence.

She was stronger than him he could see that. Maybe because she was the one who had plotted everything. And if he only faints, doesn't die, threatens to regain his senses, then what would they do? In that case we, you, because you're stronger, will have to do something. And before his fearful eyes, as if to reassure him: there won't be any blood, all you need do is choke him with the pillow. If he doesn't die, when he tries to come round. And now she was able to say it all, in that soft manner; nothing surprised him any more.

What was all that for though, why have to wake him? thought Januario, reasoning logically. Though his fear and distress would be stronger in the presence of the sleeping body. Just choking him with the pillow would be enough. No, came her cunning rejoinder, the less trace we leave the better, they will never find out how it happened. Because no one knows about us, except Isidoro and Inacia. They will know that we killed the old man, he said. Of course not, she said, they too will think he died in his sleep, we'll arrange his body afterwards.

He felt small, smaller than her. A sense of shame at being used as a cat's-paw for such a feminine plan. He preferred fighting, then he was in command, he was master of his own movements. No fighting, she said, guessing his train of thought. If they find out that you killed him, we're lost, the two of us, his death will be of no use.

How could she be so cold, how had she thought it all out? You take the casket, go and wait for me in Sabará, said Malvina. When the danger is over and nobody suspects any more, I shall invent a visit to my godmother out near the São Francisco. Once the danger is over, we can even come back, if you want, without people noticing. Nobody will suspect a thing, nobody knows about the two of us.

Very complicated that idea of the casket, of going to Sabará. What was it all for, if nobody knew anything? He should be able to stay here, nobody knew a thing. She was smarter, always found a way of persuading him. Because here, my sweet, you will want to see me, me too, it will be noticed, everything might go wrong. When everything is over, if you don't want to live here, we can go into the wilds of the São Francisco. With the wealth he will leave me, we shall be able to live an easy life, just the two of us, without having to do everything in haste and in secret. We could even get married, on second thoughts it would be better.

There were times when he felt a touch of disgust towards her, because of the cold way she thought out all these things. Towards himself too. But he did his best to forget, and agreed.

Come, she said, pulling him by the hand. Without the hand to shield it the candle's flame flickered as they walked down the corridor. Their two shadows on the wall were huge, hers much bigger than his. He followed her obediently, a boy being pulled along by his mother. His hand was moist, Malvina's cold. And cold and moist was the taste of the kiss she gave him before they left the room at the back of the house where they used to meet. Before, her mouth was warm and moist, with a warm scent. Now, when she kissed him, it was just cold and moist. It was his hand that was sweating. How could she be so sure of herself, so cool? he thought with awe, fearful of Malvina. That trick of moistening her lips with the tip of her tongue, which so excited him, took on a dreadful significance, making his heart beat more quickly in his throat.

And what if he could free himself of that hand, which was merely cold, he thought, feeling tiny. Malvina's hand held him fast, it was no longer that languid, plump, soft womanly hand that enchanted him so much; it was acquiring a rigidity, a strength it did not have before. He decided to give in, the best idea was to surrender to the strength she had suddenly acquired.

It was she too who turned the key in the lock. She had taken care of everything, of the smallest details, even of locking the old man in. She pushed the door open, it gave a dry, rusty creak. The mere creak of the door might wake the old man. But the noise was not that loud, it was the silence and his agony that made it unbearable. Treading softly, they entered the room, which was suddenly lit up by the light of the candle. In the bed, with its fine, transparent curtains pulled back and held at each corner by a broad ribbon, the old man moved about in search of a comfortable position, like a sleeping dog, as if just his body had become aware of the light and of their presence in the room. Once more Januario felt the impression of effeminacy the old man had made on him that time in the procession. Skinny as he was, in his white embroidered night-shirt, with its soft, pleated lace cuffs, João Diogo looked more like a coy old woman dreaming of heavenly angels.

What she has brought her husband to, he thought quickly, not realizing that it was not she who had changed him, but he who had changed because of her, in order to charm her. Just as he himself was doing what he did not really want to do: being obedient, passive, womanish.

In the silence and his agony, his heart racing in his throat, scarcely daring to breathe, things acquired a life they did not have before. And he saw everything absolutely clearly, and slowly. Nothing escaped him, as if not just the sleeping old man, but even the objects around him were threatening him. And how the bed itself was like the powdered, waxed old fop in the procession. Slender, delicate bedposts, everything filleted, the headboard with the same white fillet forming wreaths, leaves and flowers surrounding the inscription LOVE BROUGHT US TOGETHER.

He saw everything, the minutest things, and everything threatened him. The clean, wrinkled face, the slack mouth part open with his snores and noisy breathing, the dry, dull, dishevelled hair, like the wigs on purple images in their niches, he really did look like a decrepit old woman. Were it not for the anguish constricting his chest, and his fear, João Diogo would have seemed as ludicrous to him as on the other occasion. But he could not even control his face muscles, which were twitching. In his anguish and fear, mesmerized by the silk bed-curtains, by that body sunk in the straw mattress which creaked (just as the door did) at the old man's slightest snoring movement, he saw the body turn over and the right hand hang down outside the bed. That dark, skinny, wrinkled hand, covered in thick veins and blotches, standing out from the lean white arm, the tendons skin-deep, so prominent they were like cords, it did not seem to belong to that arm, it acquired a life of its own, it was an animal.

He took his eyes away from the old man buried in sheets and embroidered pillow-slips and ran them over the room. The floor with its wide boards, the white walls, the panelled ceiling, the dresser filleted like the bed, the crimped leather chest with the initials J.D.G. Odd how his interest was engaged by these small, unimportant things which suddenly acquired special significance, life and shadow, sap and omens. He felt a thud in his breast when he saw in a corner the old wide-mouthed carbine which must have belonged to João Diogo's father, surely no longer in use, kept just as a souvenir.

Why did he concern himself, let his gaze linger on those trifles? Perhaps so as not to bother himself with the old man's body itself, buried under lace and embroidery, his heavy disturbing snores. With what he would actually have to do. Malvina let go his hand and moved a short distance away from him. Malvina's eyes were suddenly no longer blue, they were growing darker. With a harsh gleam which simply showed her anxiousness to have the whole thing done quickly, it was taking so long! He was trying to hold his breath or to breathe in time with the old man's snores, as if he were trying to control his sleep from a distance, by magic,

63

so that the old man could only wake up when he allowed him to. Paralysed by the silk bed-curtains, by the dark, skinny hand, he could scarcely move.

His eyes rested on the slippers and, close to the hanging hand, as if the old man were trying, unconsciously, in his sleep, to reach it, on the long-barrelled, chased silver pistol. The pistol glittered. Still the same man who was unable to sleep without a weapon by him, defenceless, exposed, as if, despite the calm and peaceful life he now led, he could not do without his pistol, as if he were assailed by misgivings and nocturnal fears. She had not mentioned that pistol, the thought occurred to him. He was unarmed, he suddenly remembered, how crazy and careless he was. But the old man went on snoring, at the slightest suspicious movement he could easily subdue him in one leap.

He looked again at Malvina, silently asking her about the pistol, which was surely loaded and cocked. But she only said anxiously (with her mouth or with her eyes?) come on, quickly. He understood what she meant, what she said. Quickly must mean now, they had no time to lose.

And he moved towards the bed, he would put his foot on the pistol, should the old man wake up suddenly. He did not take more than two steps, Malvina was by his side again, reaching for his hand. He saw, not with his eyes, which were fixed on the body which now twisted as if sensing their presence in the room, but with his hand, that she was handing him something. He felt the hardness of the handle, the cold of the blade, she handed him a dagger. She was prepared, he was not, his instinct suddenly warned him. She had told him nothing about the pistol or the dagger. The old man moved again and his fingertips (his arm was now completely outside the bedclothes) almost touched the pistol. What if the old man was not asleep, was just pretending, to see if he could reach the pistol without being noticed?

Before he could reach the pistol with his foot, Malvina cried out. He turned towards her, and before he was aware of it, João was sitting up in bed, the weapon in his hand. There was a sort of smile in the old man's eyes and on his slack mouth. The pistol pointed at her, at him.

He's going to shoot now, thought Januario's cat body quickly, ready to spring so as to stop the weapon going off.

And what was just a suspicion before became a certainty: the old man was laughing malevolently, masterful behind his weapon. His mouth began to move and he said you redskin! to Januario; and you whore! to Malvina.

But Malvina was quicker than him, she did what neither of them expected, she blew out the candle. The bedroom in darkness, Januario threw himself full length on the floor. A flash, a bang. The old man had pressed the trigger. Now he's done for, thought Januario, his mind working faster, near the bed. With one bound he was on top of the old man and held him down. And he was shouting, not knowing why, he was shouting, an Indian throttling a jaguar.

Once the old man's body was subdued he plunged the dagger deep into the hard, skinny chest, feeling the resistance first of the bone, then of the soft straw of the mattress. One, two, three, he lost count of the blows, striking at random. A fury, he felt a furious power in his grinding teeth. The old man moaned once, twice, three times. Then he was silent and moved no more. Even so Januario continued to hold him, as if he feared there was some life left.

Come on, said Malvina, and only then did he realize that she was alive, and that the pistol shot could have wounded her. Come on, she said, and he followed her voice, groping in the dark until he found the hand that felt for him. This way, she said; she knew the house blindfold and did not need a light.

They crossed the corridor, where it was lighter, in the direction of the lighted room from which they had come. In the glow of the candle he could see that she was livid. With fear, he asked. No, she said, but there was a tremor in her voice, an impatient haste. It was not fear but something worse, she did not know what it was and he it was who was trembling.

Now go, quickly, now! she almost shouted. Jump from the window. Someone may come along the corridor, our shouting must have been heard. The casket, don't forget the casket!

And without thinking how high it was, he leaped from the window. He fell on to a small roof and slid down to the ground. He fell on his feet, running for the gate. Then he thought he heard a shot behind him, in the house. Then another, this time he was sure. What if the old man was not yet dead, had the lives of a cat? He opened the gate, and only then did he look back. The figure of Malvina stood out in the lighted rectangle of the window. She was shouting something over and over again.

Daughter of the Sun, of the Light

I

When João Diogo Galvão decided to remarry, he made an unusual and magnanimous gesture: he asked his son's opinion on the rightness and wisdom of what he was about to do. He told him about his chosen one. A very nice São Paulo girl, belonging to the São Vicente nobility, he made a point of adding. From one of the best families in Piratininga. And swelling his voice, which no longer shocked his son, so many and so fast were the transformations the old man was undergoing, from his clothes to his more careful and elegant gestures, his refined manners, swelling his voice he said a Dias Bueno! Aristocrats, with lineage and coat of arms, with their name inscribed in the royal registers.

It was this he was in need of, he said modestly. And his voice swelled again, as if he were ashamed of his modesty and meant his voice to make up for the weakness of confessing his lack of lineage. Because he was not without gold and property, and he had position. It is true that he had received the Habit of Christ, albeit petitioned, on his personal merit, and his father's. I am considered a friend of the King, he went on; and the Captain-General received him at his pleasure, even heard his advice on matters of state. When they decided to put an end to the danger of the slave hide-outs, he was the main one they approached. In the town council, if he opened his mouth, they said amen immediately,.

Gaspar heard him with apparent lack of attention, his eyes on the window, a half-smile on his lips.

Everything that we have, his father went on, was won by me and by your grandfather, God rest his soul. Everything achieved with might and main, at the cost of much blood and peril. Everything I own was sweated for. Behind us there is nothing, just wilderness, desert. Our lineage, if that's what we can call it, really starts with me.

Because old Valentim Amaro Galvão, João Diogo's father, mingled with the half-breeds, sleeping in rough shelters with Indians and blacks, never slept in a soft bed. Like him, in the early days, when the two of them crossed those desert backlands, all the way from Taubaté to the Tripuí River. Blue-blooded, as they say; born in the purple, the saying goes; pure-bred nobility, that was what she would bring to their house.

And as Gaspar looked at him inquiringly, he said your hands are clean, Gaspar, not like mine. As for your grandfather's, the less said the better.

Grandfather Valentim had even killed white men, because untamed Indians hardly counted, he killed Indians just for amusement, thought Gaspar. Afterwards, he obtained a royal pardon for his crime against a white man. The King always pardoned him, he needed his services for capturing Indians and for working the mines.

Gaspar stayed silent, lost in thought, his eyes on the ground. He was amused by his father's new way of talking, but he was unsmiling, his brow creased with concern. It was not only in his clothes and manners that his father was different now. Gaspar was a model of respect and reverence. His eyes, which he was wont to keep lowered, were dreamy, pure and pensive. With their long lashes and dark brilliance which made women sigh in vain. In front of his father and in the company of women, particularly if they kept looking at him, he would blush.

And now he did not know if his father was merely fulfilling a new obligation or if he really did wish to know what he thought about such a personal matter. So he listened in silence, and pondered. Which was, in any case, his nature. A man of few words and short speeches, he liked listening more than talking: he let other people finish first and then said a few deliberate and carefully chosen words.

Maybe the old man really was seeking his advice. But then, in view of the enthusiasm in his voice and of the fiery sparkle that shone again in his tired old eyes, lighting up that face of his, burned dark by the sun (he remembered) of many deserts and gold-digs, the dark tan he now tried to conceal by means of powders and creams, adding a fresh layer every day, Gaspar held back: better to see what the old man was getting at.

There was an explanation for Gaspar's half-smile – his father was now blinking like an artful lad who had just played some trick or been given a pat on the head. He had been suspicious of the old man's journeys to and from Taubaté, leaving his mines and farms to be managed by agents and overseers, since his son cared little for such things. Gaspar was always off in the forests with two or three black riflemen, hunting big game. When he was in the town he kept to himself, locked in his library.

At first, before the mischievous remarks he began to hear, he thought his father was visiting old relatives. João Diogo was also from Taubaté, from where Antonio Dias set out to discover the gold-mines, he was even slightly related to him. He had come as a child with his father,

Grandpa Valentim Amaro Galvão, in search of the apparently endless Tripuí gold, recently prospected and excavated, which promised to last a lifetime, so much so that nobody gave a thought to planting crops. His mother didn't want her husband to take João Diogo. The boy has barely gone twelve, she said. He's a big boy, a man already, I don't want a sissy for a son, said Valentim, as Gaspar's father liked to tell him. Because of the dangers involved in going deep into the backlands, clearing the land and capturing Indians, guided only by the instinct of half-tamed Indians and impudent half-breeds, and by the lure of diamonds. The unreliable, overgrown trails and paths, infested with dangers – fevers, wild animals and Botocudo Indians, renowned for their savagery and gluttony, who watched from a distance as the first diamond-pans appeared in the streams and came down on them with arrows and clubs. Such were the tales they invented.

As his father was still given to womanizing and boasted of his adventures (hot-blooded people, they said of him and of the late Valentim), not being particular regarding race or age, quite the contrary, actually preferring tender young black and mulatto girls, Gaspar did not at first give much importance to those absences of his, month after month. The old satyr is still sunk in the mire of the flesh, he said with some distaste. One more kept black or mulatto girl, half-breed or Indian, or less, would not add excessively to the already long list of old João Diogo's sins, he now said to himself with a shrug of his shoulders, resigned to his father's incorrigible ways. Which was not the case when Gaspar was younger and his mother was still alive, when he discovered the existence of yet another bastard, one of the many natural children his father spawned and scattered about those woods and backlands and would later be certain to be named and given a share in his will and its codicils. As the fortune was large, Gaspar attached little importance to those future benefits; he was sure the greater part would come to him, the only legitimate heir of the great man of wealth João Diogo Galvão now was. The natural children, if born as slaves, would get as their share little more than their freedom. What disturbed him most and, despite his apparent present indifference, upset him, was his father's restless lechery, his father as a seducer of young virgins and other men's slaves. One day the old man would be waylaid and shot, or so they said. Above and beyond all this, Gaspar was chaste. Pure by vocation and by oath, it was said.

His father went on talking. Gaspar listened in silence, disapproval in his eyes, which were now turned towards the open window, winging their way to the blue sky.

Malvina is her name, said his father. A pretty, nice-sounding name, don't you think? Just by saying her name I seem to see her person. What a beauty, Gaspar! You'll see!

Not before I have to, thought Gaspar. When she arrived he would no longer be there. He would go to Serro do Frio, to some houses they had there, and stay there for a year, if not more. That would give the old boy time, he did not want to witness lovers' talk, doting leers. How disagreeable all that would be. But he already knew it would be difficult and useless to go against his father. Even if he had the courage.

She was very pretty and clever, said his father. She could read and write, the two of them could become good friends, they would have much to talk about. She would be good company for his son, who was becoming so unsociable and solitary that it worried him. . . .

And after a pause, oblivious of his son, his thoughts far away in Taubaté, he said she's a real beauty! I've never seen such a beauty!

Was his father about to be improper? He lowered his eyes to see if that way his father would tone down the bells of his joyfulness.

A beauty, he kept on repeating. A redhead, her hair, her face seemed to gleam. A pair of sparkling blue eyes like two heavenly beads, two drops of light, two stars come down from above. . . .

It was too much, an effrontery! His father must be soft in the head. At his age to talk like that in his son's presence. Without modesty, and he had always respected him. Gaspar was thinking of his dead mother, of course. For her he had taken his oath of chastity for life, when she died and he had to come back from Portugal, where he was studying, without even seeing her in her coffin, surrounded by flowers and ribbons, for the last time. His father's words seemed to him to offend and soil his mother's memory. His mother who was the very opposite of everything João Diogo was saying, with her calm, severe beauty, all gentleness, her generous snow-white soul, heaven's own whiteness and purity. His father was now offending his mother's memory.

You don't need to overdo things, Father, he cut in pointedly. His father was caught on the raw by the sharp remark and glared at him. Gaspar knew how best to confront his father: he lowered his eyes and said no more, letting his silence hang heavy.

João Diogo controlled himself, clearing his throat noisily by way of an answer. He was weird, that son of his! Pure, a virgin! A disgrace! In a line of womanizers and profligates, his chastity was almost an affront, a blot on the family name. For all his slight appearance, his courteousness and the foreign manners acquired at the Jesuit College in Coimbra, where he had studied music with the best teachers in Portugal, and from sojourns at the courts of France, Tuscany, Venice, Naples and Rome, for one who had had everything of the best, Gaspar was a spirited fellow, with a taste for hunting and for the dangers of tangled forests, and had put aside the foppish clothes and manners João Diogo was now beginning to use in his old age. Otherwise he might even think his son was effeminate. No, Gaspar was no effeminate. He's just pure and chaste, he consoled himself.

Although Gaspar had never talked to him about it, João Diogo found it hard to get used to his son being as he was. He wanted to initiate him, the way old Valentim had initiated him, in the harsh ways of the backlands, to know everything about life. So that the others, seeing him go by, would say there goes a true son of the grandee João Giogo Galvão, of memorable renown. Despite all his respect and reverence, Gaspar seemed not to like his company. There was only the respect and reverence to console him. His son went as red as beetroot and lowered his eyes every time he tried to tell him about his past adventures, his love affairs. Before he gave up trying to guide him in life's ways. Best to leave well alone, was what he said then.

Not now. Now he said are you finding fault with my words, with what I've been saying? No, Father, of course not, said Gaspar. And after a longer silence, it's just that I thought, out of respect for my mother, you should spare me this lover's talk, which would sound better in the mouth of a dandified young fop.

He saw his father's neck thicken, the veins swell, his face grow fiery red, the rage about to explode. Then the sudden pallor; he would have a fit. He did not want to quarrel with his father, he respected him. Let the old man do whatever came into his head. For that matter he ought not even to listen to him, it was against the customs, no father did that. Before the old man exploded with rage or fainted, he said don't be offended, Father, forgive me. My voice spurted straight from my heart, out of my great love and devotion for my late blessed mother.

It was too much for him, the old man could scarce regain his composure. He tried reciting the credo to himself, it always helped to cool his blood. Though irrascible by nature, he had learned to control himself with his son, whose learning and intellect he respected. It had not been for nothing that he had sent him abroad. He was only sorry that Gaspar had not completed his law course in Coimbra. After Ana Jacinta's death, he had not wanted to return to Portugal. He could be an important man in the district, but was not. He lived alone, either out hunting or shut away in his room. His father knew the reputation he had for being eccentric and odd. The townspeople laughed about his purity and chastity. But they continued to respect him. Because Gaspar, though not a rowdy, was a good shot. That was some consolation. Another was the reason why he had not completed his studies. A noble heart, the devotion he claimed to have for his mother. Yet he could see that was not the main cause of the respect in which he held his son. Since childhood Gaspar had been sensible and reserved, an aura of respect had always emanated and radiated from his person. As if he never had the need to raise his voice and shout in order to be heard.

Although he did not understand his son's heart (he was like his mother, there was no one with a character like his in João Diogo's family), while wanting him to be a worthy successor to his name and wealth, hot-blooded and fiery, which was what was needed most in those treacherous, cut-throat Minas lands, those backlands full of animals and Indians, those hamlets, mine-workings and farms full of rebellious, devious blacks, who could only be broken by whippings and floggings, despite all this he respected him and, after he had given up trying to set him on the right path and accepted God's design, he loved him with all his heart. Now was no time to throw away a relationship which had cost many retreats and blandishments to become good and harmonious.

I understand you, my son, he now said, speaking calmly and slowly. He had no studies, indeed he had no letters at all, it being as much as he could do to scribble his name. All in all, he was really a man of the old school, he said, barely concealed by present-day fashions. Underneath those clothes he was still a frontiersman. Like his father, Valentim, an old Christian, God rest his soul. But he understood his son's feelings, at least he tried his best to. What he could not make out was what his late wife had to do with it all. His Ana Jacinta whom he had always worshipped and whom he had never allowed to want for a thing, the Lord keep her. Your late mother is in heaven, my son, in God's glory, he said. What she wants is soul's ease, she's not bothering about our earthly business. Leave her in peace, pray for her.

It was the voice of paternal authority, Gaspar could do nothing but obey. Yes, Father, you are probably right. But that's the way I am, it is my character, I cannot be different. I was born this way and so I shall die. You have to take an axe to a twisted bough, is that not what you always say, Father?

No, he did not want to straighten his son out with an axe. He only wanted Gaspar to understand him, he did not mean to upset him. That was why he listened to what he had to say.

But he needed to. He talked gently now, and there was a touch of tenderness in his voice. He needed to let the mother's soul be in repose, otherwise she would not find peace in God's bosom, among the flock of saints and angels. He had had countless masses said for her. Even in his will, which he was going to make before his marriage, she would have masses for more than a century, for as long as the memory and gratitude of men lasted and the mice did not eat the papers in the notary's office.

The old Gaspar, a colonial well read in French books, formerly given to culture and ideas, to poetry and music, and who, suddenly, on the death of his mother, had thrown everything up to return to Minas and adopt his present rough ways and clothes, bearded, wild and unsociable, the old Gaspar half smiled, an ironical smile, at his father's naive belief. Father, please do not be offended by what I am going to say, but masses get you nowhere. Spoken or chanted, with a vicar or a bishop. What matters is the heart.

Again João Diogo's face darkened, the blood rose to his head. Don't be offended again, Father, please forgive me. If you feel I should not say what I think, Father, we ought not continue. In truth you had no need to hear me at all, all that was necessary was to let me know your pleasure. You know that your wishes are law, sir, I kiss your hand here and now as a sign of respect.

The old man calmed down again, that son of his was very clever and adroit. A pity he had not wanted to finish university, he could be a justice by now. But clever and adroit as he was, he was in danger. That talk, those books. Just to know another language, to own a library without being a priest or a man of law, was very dangerous. He knew that his son was occasionally rather outspoken, that he had some strange ideas. When he once said, in the presence of the Captain-General and him friendly and kindly pretending he had not heard, that he actually considered it an honour to be a colonial, it had distressed him. He said even worse things to his father, about government. Sheer madness, best forgotten. Which was what he had done, as he now remembered.

My son, I have something to say to you, listen to my advice, he said. They were the words of one who loved him and who would suffer a great deal if anything bad happened to him, times were dangerous. He must never talk like that. Not even think aloud, walls have ears, he should always remember that. What Gaspar had said about mass, that it was the heart that counted, could be his undoing. It had the ring of Luther or Calvin, one of Satan's servants. Tongues were loose, the Captain-General was his friend, but he would never forgive him if he discovered his son was a heretic, had dealings with the devil's conceit. They were Satan's ideas, had the Jesuit Fathers never told him that? Even though the Captain-General, because of him, being very close and privy with him, did not want to, if anyone were to go and tell him that Gaspar doubted the faith, and therefore the King, he would have to act. He knew his son did not think that way any more, but these satanic ideas were in the air, they were mists that came with the ships. The Captain-General was a kind-hearted but dutiful man, he fulfilled his obligations. And so, for all his power and prestige, he would not be able to do anything for him.

I know, Father, I shall say no more, I thank you, said Gaspar. In any case he had ceased to think as he once had, when he was living among fops in the academies in Portugal. When he saw that colonials and white Portuguese were all of the same ilk. When they indulged in enlightened talk, they were thinking only of themselves and of feathering their own nest. In these lands of Minas, peopled by blacks, mulattos and mestizo Indians, one had to think the way they did and leave all those others to one side. . . . They were the ones who had to take charge, all this land was theirs. And then he no longer believed in idle talk, mere wittiness, an accomplishment for priests and slave-owning men of law.

João Diogo went livid as he listened, terror painted on his face. Thank goodness his son spent his time alone in the woods and had no particular white friend, no one must hear him.

And it was unreasonable for me to have slaves and think the way I did. . . . Gaspar did not go on, it was quite absurd for his father, too difficult for him to understand! Better keep quiet. Father, forgive me once more this loose tongue of mine, he said. But I go for so long without talking that I lose control when I do talk. As far as these matters are concerned, though, you need not worry, Father.

That was what I expected to hear from you, said his father, recovering himself. It is very dangerous, my son, it will not do. Always remember – walls have ears.

Now an embarrassing silence began to hang between father and son. In the silence, the room suddenly grew cold and dark. As if a thousand noiseless, weaving spiders had closed off the blue window.

You can continue, Father, said Gaspar after a time. Tell me more about the lady of your choice.

He was sure now that his father would not go on any more about the beauties and solaces of his future stepmother.

She is not quite a lady, my son. She is not what you are thinking. She is not a young girl any more, but there is nothing matronly about her. She is twenty years old, younger than you.

Gaspar had an odd feeling inside, a silent horror assailed him. Father, he said, you will have to forgive me once more, for the last time, but I have to ask you a few things. First of all, are you asking my opinion just for the sake of asking, to pass the time away, because you want to tell someone about the woman you have chosen, or do you actually want to hear my opinion?

Speak, my son, said the old man, controlling himself yet again. Talking to that son of his was like drawing one's finger along a razor's edge. When one asks a question, one wants an answer, he said. If one just wants to hear one's own voice, one talks into the wind and waits for the echo. If he had asked it was because he wanted to know.

Gaspar thought carefully, weighing his words one at a time before speaking. Although he said he wanted an answer, his father was not likely to let him speak his mind, it was not his habit. Father, have you thought about one aspect? Have you given any thought to the age difference? You are at least three times the girl's age.

João Diogo suddenly sagged. All the youth and gaiety, all the warmth and light had disappeared. Now he looked an old man, almost humbled, his real age. I know what you are trying to say, what's behind your words, he said, getting hold of himself. The one who will have to forgive now, if a father needs to beg his son's pardon, is you. I know you do not like me talking about my own things, my mannish business, in your hearing. I have not said anything for a long time. I've been beating about the bush when I have talked to you, have you not noticed? But now I am going to have my say, you can wash your ears afterwards if you wish. Time has hardly caught up with me, my son. I don't have the same fire as I used to, of course, but no woman I've gone with has complained. Never, not a single one so far. Some are even full of praise and gratitude. And it's not because of my money, either. It will be a good while yet before anyone tells me I am worn out. Well now, since I've known Malvina, my ardour seems to have returned. I have become my old self again! I will be difficult for anyone to jeer at me!

Gaspar's mind whirled, his face burned. Eyes on the ground, he did not dare look his father in the face. He was not going to say anything to upset him, let him do what he thought best. The way he always did, as was usual, according to the habit his father had wanted to break.

Father, you must do as you please. Forget what I said. If things are as you say, I really think you should get married. It is better than being around on heat, open to some trickery or wickedness. Get married, Father, it's the best thing you can do.

Now old João Diogo smiled with satisfaction. He had heard what he wanted, now that was the son who was so dear to his heart. And to show that he was pleased, he even allowed himself a friendly word of advice, father to son. Gaspar should not be so attached to his mother's memory, out of remorse, just because he did not arrive in time to see her before the funeral. Though she was weakly (after you are born she was never very healthy, he said), no one could guess that she would die just then. If he had suspected that she was any worse than usual, he would have sent for him. Even so, there was the sea between them. Even if he had sent for him, he would never have arrived in time. Remorse is cured by covering it over with soil, was what he said.

It was no use. His son had always been like that. Do you remember when your sister Leonor died, he asked, and noticed that his son shuddered. Gaspar cultivated the dead, he did not forget easily. When his sister died, he was seven and she nine. It was the same when Leonor died. To tear Gaspar away from the coffin was a business. To get Leonor out of his mind was a struggle, the boy could think of nothing else, of his sister cold and hard, her hands crossed over her white dress, in the flower-filled coffin, an angel going up to heaven.

While his father talked on, he looked away towards the window, the clear blue sky. It was as if he was not listening. His father was used to it, he would stay like that but he was listening. Just his strange, eccentric character. He had inherited that mannerism from his mother.

What if the same had happened to Gaspar as happened to him, he asked. He was out fighting tooth and nail over some claims belonging to his father, in infected streams out Serra do Frio way. Thanks to a mistake in a message given by a runner, who passed it on to someone else by word of mouth, his father thought he had died. Old Valentim got such a shock that he died there and then. He had those sudden fits of weakness towards the end of his life, like me, said João Diogo.

He too had felt guilty about that death. Because he could have dictated a letter to someone telling his father what had happened. He did not, and it was as if, contrary to his intention, his silence had killed his father. But he realized that he must be strong. I had to have the strength of old Valentim, God keep him, he said. That was what he would do if he were in Gaspar's place: he would try to forget. He too had suffered terribly, he loved his father very much. But he got on with things and stopped thinking about it. Only once in a while, like now, he remembered.

My son, he said, we should never go against God's will. We should let the dead rest in peace. To suffer for others is common charity, but to distil one's grief, to drag out one's suffering, is to doubt God's sense of fitness, it is an insult to God's aim.

That was more or less what Inacia, Malvina's maid, who heard and knew everything, told her mistress. That was the story as Malvina pieced it together, adding a certain amount of fantasy to the conversations she later had with the townsfolk, with João Diogo and even with Gaspar himself.

Malvina did not pay much attention when she first heard the name of João Diogo Galvão. He was no doubt one more of that infinite number of plainsmen who turned up in Taubaté, on their way back from Minas, pretending to more wealth than they really had. Afterwards they proved to be nothing short of paupers, all they had for wealth being just two farthings to rub together.

What her father wanted was one of those renowned gold and diamond magnates to marry his daughters to and thereby gild his shabby, faded family arms, which were showing signs of ruin since he was obliged to move from São Paulo to the town of Taubaté, after his bad luck in putting most of his wealth into the bands of adventurers constantly leaving for the Minas Gerais country. Like so many others, before and after him, as soon as the first news of the gold-fields began to arrive.

Malvina paid little attention because she knew that the first to leave home so as to save her father's much proclaimed house and lineage, with its roots in the old royal books, should be Mariana. Mariana was the eldest, she was approaching thirty-five, which caused her parents to despair of the black future of an old maid in an impoverished noble family.

Not that Mariana was ugly, quite the reverse – she was really quite pretty, but with a vapid, maudlin prettiness, though she was lively enough in other ways. It was simply that her suitors were dark-skinned coloureds or even impudent mulattos, who concealed their colour with a great deal of powder and paint, and boasted fame and wealth in Minas Gerais. The pedigree whites were impoverished like themselves, so that if their father were not careful, instead of saving his lineage, he would end up losing it altogether. After making inquiries and sending messengers, doing sums and discovering the wealth and possession they boasted of having in the Minas lands (old Dom João Quebedo, though well on in years, his hair white with old age, was very shrewd and quick in these matters), it turned out that the suitors had nothing to their name, all they had was swagger and noise.

All the ones who had appeared till then were no more than paupers, saucy ragamuffins, if not picaroons. Exactly like the gaudy, unsuitable clothes they wore in order to parade a dandyism which, without experience and knowledge of the rules, was the object of much laughter and scorn among the local girls.

With noblemen of that sort, of lineage and caste, her father had long ceased to trouble himself. To bring no wealth and spread poverty is sheer folly, the wise old man would say every time one of them came to see him. Afterwards they stopped coming, they got to know better – the illustrious Dom João Quebedo Dias Bueno was as poor and as down in the field as they themselves. As could be seen from the single-storey house where he lived in the town and even more from his ruined farmhouse. In other words, all lords together, tarred with the same brush.

Not that Malvina was all that disinterested or obedient, and that she passively accepted the order of precedence established by her father, at her mother's subtle promptings. But her mother had lost much of her power after that indiscretion, when her husband was away in Portugal seeking the protection of relatives with influence in the royal household, which resulted in the birth of her much loved and unhappy Donguinho, a source of shame and sadness to the whole family and even a contributory reason for their move to the country estate and subsequently, due to the lack of labour and capital to get things moving, to the town of Taubaté. Dom João Quebedo had accepted that accursed Donguinho and eventually, out of generosity and a good deal of charity, conceded his Vicentina a pardon she never deserved, then or later, in her mature years, for ever flushed and inflamed, intemperate in her behaviour, in the vicinity of any male. If her mother previously ordered and ruled, now she did no more than hint and prompt; it was her husband who was in charge and took the decisions. Dom João Quebedo had always been a benign, noble gentleman, who forgave his wife's weakness if only because he was sickly and had never attended her wants with the desired regularity. He too had his youthful peccadilloes, but he took advantage of that aberrant and painful birth to take the reins of command away from his wife. That was many years ago, thirty to be precise, which was Donguinho's present age.

Malvina, then, was not so disinterested and obedient. She was a spirited, strong-willed girl, as strong-willed, lively and artful as her mother had been in her youth. In addition to the knowledge that she was much younger and prettier than Mariana, she trusted her charms and attractions, and the infallible power of her machinations. True enough, heer patron saints were very strong, they helped a great deal, but she put her trust in her own strength and destiny.

Thus, though only twenty, Malvina was a patient weaver, next to her Mariana was no more than a shadow. When the deceivers gave up and the real good suitor appeared, she would know how to proceed. Malvina had her mother's cleverness and cunning, but also her father's ambition, which in him was undermined only by his noble, lackadaisical amiability.

While in her the same calm, lackadaisical amiability was only apparent, a light veneer. In reality she was her mother's spitting image, as the saying goes, she had the same beauty and presence, the magical power which Dona Vicentina had in her youth. So they said, and Malvina smiled a mischievous, knowing smile. She put her faith in the quiet, calculating virtues she had inherited from her father, not allowing herself to be swept along by her mother's rashness and come to grief. When the time came, she would know what to do. And so she smiled, and waited patiently.

Through people he trusted completely in Minas, which was desperate now that the gold and gleaming stones were growing scarce in the gravel of the river-beds, curbing the noisy, extravagant happiness, Dom João Quebedo made inquiries about that João Diogo Galvão who had been introduced to him. The plainsman had spoken to him about his real intentions and asked if he might visit him and meet his family. Go back to Minas, sir, back to your houses, said Dom João Quebedo. I shall see to finding out, from the sources you have given me, about your virtues and worthiness. When you come back we shall see.

João Diogo nodded in agreement, his whole appearance was that of a serious, reliable man. But Dom João Quebedo, who was well versed in life's deceits and trickery, said, mainly to test his man, it is settled then: if all goes well with my inquiries, the girl is the first-born, called Mariana.

João Diogo grunted his assent and Dom João Quebedo added: his daughter, beyond her family name and breeding, her virtues and good appearance, her manners and accomplishments (she could actually read and write, which is not to be despised, he said), had little to give. I have no need, said João Diogo, you, sir, do not yet know who I am. The young lady, Mariana, if after the inquiries you are going to have made, you accept me as your son-in-law, sir, I shall take her to Minas with just the clothes she has on her back. As for jewels and gifts, beautiful things and the rest I shall be the one to cover her body.

Dom João Quebedo flushed, a violent spasm shook him inwardly. Though poor and reduced in status, his family pride was still keen and fervent in his heart. His face burned and João Diogo could sense his shame and humiliation. Even if he was as rich as he said, without exaggerating, which impressed him greatly, the man was coarse and rude, despite the false front and the clothes he now wore in order to create a good impression. He would not let him visit until he was quite sure that his daughters, Malvina in particular, who was very agreeable, would not lose their heads and ruin everything. First he would need to know the truth about this stranger and his, by him, much-proclaimed wealth. Discretion is the better part of valour, he said to himself.

A peasant, a clod, still stinking like a Negro or an Indian, I'll be bound, so his pride and lineage whispered to him. But he was mindful of his need, of his noble house, with its capital back in Portugal, of which he was so proud. He thought of his family, of his wife and daughters; of the idiot Donguinho, his pain, humiliation and shame, which he would have to endure his whole life, until someone (when the boy was loose in the meadows and woods at the farm: covering mares if he got out of his windowless, locked and bolted room; foaming, wetting himself all down his legs, in a fury) or he himself, one day when he was particularly desperate, killed him. He thought of his town house, where he previously only came for special occasions, now a permanent home, with no more than six Angola slaves to serve and ensure the upkeep. He thought of his lands, now worthless; of his estate, called Ribeirinha, left abandoned, the bush reclaiming the lost land, previously won by hard graft, the farmhouse itself crumbling in ruins. He remembered how formerly, in times of plenty, Ribeirinha estate was a prize, a flourishing garden; he remembered his quince trees, his fruit-preserving, the two thousand and more cases of quince and guava preserve he sent to Bahia; his pear trees, his vines, his fig trees; his sugar-cane (he could even feel on his skin an imaginary breeze from the old sugar plantation), the boilers and stills; the hundreds of slaves toiling away; the smell of the pastures, cowpats in the corrals, the good warm smell in his nose, from afar, when he was lazing on the veranda, just watching; his many stud-bulls, the cows with calf, the heifers prancing and mooing in the grey-blue air of the late afternoon. All of this had to come back, by God! He badly needed to be happy and contented. And in his imagination the farm and the fields became green again.

And farther in the distance, like an echo heard in a dream, the music of violas and lutes, of spinets and harps and melodious flutes, in the houses of relatives in Portugal, on the occasions when he went there. Fuming with hatred, he remembered his ungracious kinsfolk, with all their prestige in the King's presence, and how they abandoned him when he most needed their help to recover the vast sums that had melted away in those ill-fated ventures he had gone into with the bands of pioneers, not actively, only lending capital, when all he wanted was a recommendation to the Captain-General of Minas which would win him some contracts and allow him to move, perhaps to Vila Rica and later to the court in Lisbon. The old man was dreaming. The old man was raving.

He thought of his painful neediness, his privations. He thought of his rank and shield, his lineage and coat of arms, which his humilated nobility still trumpeted, and felt a lump in his throat, tears in his eyes.

He thought especially of his present poverty and set aside his pride.

Because he misunderstood what João Diogo Galvão had said. He was confused and flustered, partly deaf in his right ear, and in his humiliation he understood the verb *cover* in its most vulgar sense: Donguinho loose in the pastures, on the farm, after the mares. It was only later he learned that it was Vicentina who, out of love and her weakness for the bastard, let him out. Now, with the keys in his pocket, Donguinho's howls did not bother him so much, except when he could not sleep at night.

Dom João Quebedo was so absent, so engrossed in his dark broodings, that João Diogo thought his mind was wandering in senile decay and that not only was he not listening but, with such a far-away look in his eyes, had even forgotten he was there. Dom João Quebedo, did you hear me? he said, pulling him by the sleeve of his threadbare coat, which was clean though faded and much repaired. The old man looked after himself, that one could see. He took great pains to keep up his old-style noble appearance, his snow-white beard was perfumed, which was not now the custom, the plainsman noticed, having himself shaved off his beard to be in the fashion and impress the young ladies, now that he meant to marry into the nobility.

João Diogo had to pull the old man's sleeve again. What? said Dom João Quebedo, suddenly coming back from the misty horizons of his broodings. Did you say something? he said. If you did, forgive me not hearing, I am rather deaf, it is age.

Dom João Quebedo Dias Bueno had such noble manners and speech that João Diogo, slightly intimidated, said no, it is of no great matter, you have heard the main part. Because all of that, all that courtesy, those manners, charmed him. He tried to keep the old man's image firmly in his mind, so as to copy it afterwards, back in Minas, when he was at the Captain-General's palace or residences. Except for the beard, which he would not grow again. He was not so old after all. His beard also reminded him of the old days with the bands of rough adventurers, when he himself led his blacks and tame Indians, and his gunslingers, up river in search of the gold-diggings under the blazing sun.

Do not take offence, sir, I do not mean to be inconsiderate, Dom João Quebedo said again. He now had a very good impression of the man. If there was wealth behind him, then the family tree and coat of arms were saved, his whole life would be rebuilt like pastures and plantations turning green again after the rains. Yet again he could imagine the good smell of molasses in the vats and boilers, as he lazed in a hammock. And sunk in the obsession common in the crazed and the nostalgic, he once again caught in the air the good smell of sweet grass and of the steaming dung in the pastures and corrals.

Our Lady of the Conception, I need all this badly, he asked silently. Do not let me die without having it all again, he begged in prayer. I will pay for masses, I will have the altar carvings painted in gold, I will have a chapel built on the estate. Maybe it would be better for him to leave it all behind and go to Minas with his son-in-law, to that much acclaimed Vila Rica. He gave yet another dreary sigh. Yes, he would go to Minas. With his son-in-law's prestige he would win contracts, he would prosper once more.

And Donguinho? A thorn pricking inside him. A way would be found. . . .

It is agreed then, we shall settle matters when I return, said João Diogo, seeing the old man in a stupor, just not coming to his senses. With your leave, sir, I shall be on my way. . . .

When the first news about the suitor arrived, the excitement nearly killed old Dom João Quebedo. Once over the crazy dreams that impoverished nobles have, he made the usual allowances, he knew that the alluvial wealth of Minas was in decline, the millionaires were few and far between. He assumed João Diogo Galvão was merely well off and privy to the Captain-General and Governor of Minas. Though given to moments of absent-mindedness due to age, Dom João Quebedo was not yet in his dotage. But he nearly died.

Vicentina, Mariana, Malvina, come here and listen, he shouted, forgetting his manners. His wife and daughters thought something very serious had happened, Dom João Quebedo had gone off his head.

What is it, for goodness' sake? said Dona Vicentina in alarm, at the same time sending a slave to fetch a strong cup of holly tea.

The old man slumped down on a stool, while his daughters fanned him. Prostrate, livid, in a cold sweat.

The man is a potentate, he began, when he got his breath back. A potentate with a great retinue, rich in arms, silver and gold, precious stones. He even has an army of a thousand black riflemen, Indian bowmen, just like in the old times. His house is a real fortress, they informed me. Mariana, keep your ears open, listen.

And he spoke haltingly, constantly short of breath and needing to be fanned.

The one who listened most carefully, however, was Malvina. Her eyes glowed, they sparkled. Yes, she thought, none of your fortress, your thousand and black riflemen, blacks only as servants. A tall house, a house with a panelled ceiling, not like their lath-and-wattle house. All painted to absolute perfection. In the best street. And the gold and silver plate, the expensive jewels and clothes, the silks and velvets, cambrics and linens, damasks and brocades. She saw herself at the mirror already, her hair all combed up high, the feathers, the sparkling jewels, her coiffure adorned with threaded pearls. Malvina, like the old man, was letting her imagination run wild.

Seeing her youngest daughter's eyes, Dona Vicentina said it is not for you, Malvina. It is Mariana's turn, that was what your father arranged.

Mariana, who had not missed the gleam in her sister's eyes, was already weeping. Go on, you dolt, get a move on! said her mother, giving her a push and making ready to speak.

That is what I arranged, said the old man, recovering his breath and his command of the situation, and giving his wife a severe look. This familiar semaphore let her know that Dom João Quebedo had silently reminded her of her bastard Donguinho. Have you perchance forgotten, madam? he seemed to be saying. Dona Vicentina kept silent.

But I didn't say a word, said Malvina, feigning astonishment. She would have to be careful. My eyes betrayed me, she thought rapidly. And in an instant, with the most innocent face imaginable, her eyes blurred over, she was the very picture of a reserved, obedient daughter.

I know it is Mariana's turn, I am not going to betray my sister, she said, and Mariana checked her tears. Even their mother, who was as quick and artful as Malvina, believed what she said. And to undo the bad impression she had carelessly allowed to show in her eyes, Malvina went on: He must be at least three times my age, he could be my grandfather. Despite his clean-shaven face and the powders and creams, you can see that, she said, giving herself away again. She was having an unfortunate day, letting herself be carried away by the novelty and her excitement. She promised herself it should never happen again.

How do you know that, miss? said her father with an imperious look. Come, Father, I saw you from behind the shutter when you were talking to him, she said, and her father felt relieved.

Everything was prepared and made ready for when João Diogo Galvão returned. Dresses and coats cleaned and starched, everything well ironed. The house all bustle. Even the black slaves who worked out of doors to ensure the upkeep of the family were set to cleaning. And everything, though their poverty was ill concealed (being poor is hell, thought Malvina, with sorrow in her eyes and mortification in her heart), was clean.

They no longer had furnishings and silverware, their misfortune had taken everything. What counts is nobility, my dear, said Dona Vicentina to Mariana, as she adjusted her best dress, which had escaped the moths by being kept with great care in the chest in her parents' bedroom. Because the potentate João Diogo Galvão must have a good impression.

And he did. Except that everything was quite different from the way it was intended.

When João Diogo entered that single-storeyed, street-facing house, a poor man's house in Sunday attire, they only showed him Mariana. Malvina had locked herself in her room, saying she was not going to spoil anyone's party, she would only appear later and even then only if summoned. Which put an end completely to the clouds of mistrust that continued to darken the blue sky of Dona Vicentina's fantasies.

In fact, Malvina did only come when she was summoned, a week later. Because João Diogo might find it odd, thought her father. Particularly he might think that it was not only the accursed Donguinho who was always locked up.

João Diogo already knew about Donguinho. All the locks in the world cannot for long hide a madman in the family. Or a beauty. Though he was a taciturn person, who had no truck with loose talk, he learned about Donguinho's dangerous insanity and Malvina's youthful beauty. He asked about her. Not that he was particularly interested in Malvina, he was pledged to Mariana and she was more suited to him, he himself thought, on account of her age. But what about the other daughter, Dom João Quebedo? he said.

And Malvina appeared. It was as if the sun had come into the room, they all thought, stupefied. She was so gorgeous. The swish of her silk dress, the handsome coiffure, the coy elegance of the blue grosgrain ribbon.

Where did the sly miss find that dress? her mother must have thought as her castle in the air crumbled before her eyes. Forward girl, her father surely thought. And the gleaming red of her hair, the glow in her eyes, the halo of light that seemed to encircle her, thought João Diogo Galvão, dazzled.

And she smiled at him as she curtsied. She offered him her fingertips, which he felt for hesitantly. Her pertness was such that she did not immediately withdraw her hand, only when he released it.

But everything about her was right. I find her altogether charming, João Diogo said to himself, oblivious of his pledge to Dom João Quebedo. A shepherdess, one of those beautiful enchanting shepherdesses in the lyrics and odes which the Captain-General like to hear recited in his mansions. That was the comparison that occurred to João Diogo. Not that he cared for lyrics and odes, but he had heard enough of them. And him even dropping off during the soirées and poetry entertainments at the palace.

From the plainsman's eyes, from the tremulous chill of his hands and the pallor of his face, the noble Malvina Dias Bueno realized that she had triumphed.

From then on everything happened in a rush. Mariana's tears, her mother's screams, her father's seizures were of no avail. Malvina said nothing, they had to guess what she was contriving. They had their suspicions. She merely smiled, which drove the family to despair.

Also of no avail was her father's conversation with João Diogo Galvão, when he told him that if he was going to marry anyone in his family, that someone would be Malvina. João Diogo had made up his mind, and when he made up his mind any attempt to make him change it was a pure waste of time. That was what Dom João Quebedo told his wife when he informed her that he was obliged to give Malvina's hand in marriage. And then, there was no point refusing, the man was a potentate, he was perfectly capable of abducting the girl. And for us it would be like biting off one's nose to spite one's face, said he to Dona Vicentina sententiously, by way of an excuse. Not that he needed one: they both thought the same way.

3

No, she would not stay for long in that squat, uncomfortable, single-storey house, which was as bare as a pauper. Tired of being poor, she scarcely remembered the bounteous days of her father's largesse, when she was a young girl and actually fingered a spinet he had sent from Portugal for Mariana, at the Ribeirinha estate, deep in the country. A plain house, but a solid one, a proper fortress, a citadel, as her father said, and he was not exaggerating. No, out of the question, was Malvina's first thought when she set foot in João Diogo Galvão's house, in the Padre Faria quarter of Vila Rica.

The house was like a ranch or farmhouse, with little in the way of furniture or appurtenances, empty of everything that Malvina's powerful, fertile imagination dreamed of. Everything for which she had been obliged to do what she did to Mariana and her family (she consoled herself that only she would be able to save her parents and the family tree, Mariana being too silly), not in self-sacrifice (though the thought crossed her mind when she saw João Diogo in his night-shirt, in their marriage bed), but because she wanted wholeheartedly to marry a man past his middle years, of elderly appearance, old enough to be her grandfather.

A spacious house, certainly, but sparsely furnished with clumsy, badly finished, unadorned pieces of furniture, which almost disappeared in the vast expanse of drawing-rooms, bedchambers and vestibules. A large house, neat and airy, but lacking silver tableware and cutlery, crystal glasses and carafes, porcelain dinner and tea services. If he had any, they were hidden away in secret chests or buried, kept as capital rather than for use.

The greatest luxury (luxury no, comfort, Malvina corrected herself) which João Diogo allowed himself were tin plates and bowls, enamel mugs and glass bottles for water, otherwise empty wine flagons or pot-bellied clay pitchers. That's fine for the kitchen, for the slaves, said Malvina.

Even so, lately, when he began to enjoy greater access to the Captain-General's confidence, he had started changing a good deal. Since he decided to remarry, he began to take more care of his person and, though lacking knowledge on the subject and being shy of asking advice, stocked his dressing-table with brushes and combs, scissors and feathers, devices for spraying, pots of creams, implements with a thousand and one uses, which he barely guessed at, going so ungratefully far (that was what Inacia, the maid Malvina chose, told her. Though Inacia, herself black, sided more with the whites than with the blacks, and with missy, as she started calling her, whom she revered in particular – so she said, since she gave her linen and jewels, and the promise of subsequent freedom, which she cared little about now that she was so well off, no longer confined to the slave-quarters, but living in the main house, close to her mistress), so ungratefully far as to swap his old black barber (Inacia said it more in fear than in pity, for missy might do the same to her) for a new one, purchased at a good price, skilled in the trade, well versed in the arts of dandyism.

João Diogo's big house looked more like a poor farmer's house, thought Malvina a little sceptically, linking in a single image the two houses in which she had lived until then, the country house and the town house. But her scepticism evaporated when she saw the number of blacks in the slave-quarters at the bottom of the garden. That profusion of slaves and overseers and half-breed gunslingers toing and froing from the farms and gold-diggings, and the many mines her husband owned not only in Vila Rica, but also in Vila do Carmo, Serro do Frio and even in Tejuco. This too she learned from Inacia, who was tireless and alert in her search for news. Malvina sang and danced with glee, she even planted a kiss on Inacia's gleaming face, which completely won over the Negress, who, for her part, was putting aside some small savings for later.

In short, João Diogo's house was lacking in everything. At least for Malvina's aristocratic taste, as she saw it.

No, just imagine going on living there, she thought, when she had only been married a month, now that she was aided and well served by Inacia, who immediately set about keeping the other maids well away from her, moving them to the kitchen and the slave-quarters. By decision of Malvina, to whom João Diogo immediately handed over the management of his dwelling house, Inacia was in charge of the black house-servants.

No, that was all very well in former times, in the days of your father, who was a captain and man of valour, she said to João Diogo, aware of his weak points. Not for you (by the end of the first week she addressed him simply as you, she wasn't going to spend her whole life addressing her husband as mister and sir); not for him, a man who was privy to the Captain-General, who had a controlling voice in the affairs of the district. Not for my darling husband, said she coquettishly, at which João Diogo melted completely, his eyes overflowing with gentleness, so great was his passion for his wife.

And she, who was versed in cunning, said with a tactful smile, my love, let me adjust your bow. It will take a bit of effort, but you shall become the best-dressed man in these parts. Enough to be the envy of the Captain-General and the Chief Justice. And she gave him a beautiful smile, while she freshened the lace pleats of João Diogo's embroidered shirt. And she gave him a light peck on the cheek that got him all excited. He was in his underpants, for he now allowed himself to be at ease with Malvina, something that had never happened with his first wife, and he ventured a more audacious caress, which was politely but firmly rejected. Tonight we'll do it, when we come back from the party, she said.

Although at first he was somewhat taken aback by Malvina's cleverly suggestive, even loose language, which he was accustomed to hear only from whores and wanton mulatto women, he now found it amusing. This manner of speech stirred glowing pleasures and urgent flames in his old heart. So, instead of sulking, he smiled, looking forward to the delights promised on their return, though he knew that he was always dead tired when they came back from those evening entertainments, being unaccustomed to late nights, he was a man for hard work and fighting, he did not have strength for other things. Even so he made the effort, so as not to disappoint his wife; even at some risk for his heart, as his older, more prudent side warned him.

But Malvina knew just how to measure her remedies and potions. Be careful, missy, don't show you want it, Inacia told her impudently; now they were so thick, she moved a step forward, a degree closer, every day. And so, by turns flighty, when he was discouraged and forlorn, and

86

skittish as a frightened dove, when he got too excited, she led him along as she chose. Because Malvina was afraid he might think she was a woman of experience and not a virgin. An unnecessary fear: João Diogo Galvão knew his virgins and maidens like nobody's business, he was as experienced in pastoral delights as she was in provocation.

And so for the first few months the two of them were very happy and contented. He more than her, it is true – a young woman had other needs as well. Not that he was a lame duck, he allowed himself to say one day, and she laughed aloud, affectedly but pleasantly, taking care with her tone so that the old man would not be surprised, when he explained to her what lame duck meant.

During those months there was only one matter that caused Malvina much concern. This was because her family, especially Dom João Quebedo and her mother, was very insistent in wanting to come and stay with the happy couple. Mariana had resigned herself and with the aid of her godmother she had retired to a retreat in Itu, where she lived in the silence and peace of the Lord. The presence of her family would mean the loss of everything that she had contrived with endurance and with such attention to detail, everything she had patiently planned for her own greater glory and profit. She too badly needed to be happy, she said, echoing her father. More than him, her mother and Mariana, who had made the best of the old days of plenty.

And Dona Vicentina wrote her the most pathetic, pleading letters. She spoke of hard-heartedness, called her heartless daughter. With such sadness, her father was on his death-bed, would probably die without seeing her, his darling daughter; why did she not come to his assistance and send for him? Despite his nobility and his family tree, his high conceit and coat of arms, Dom João Quebedo could find no one to give him credit, their daughter's ingratitude was there for all to see, something they could not hide. So wrote her mother, the flourished writing of her letters stained with tears shed at will.

Malvina did not send for them mainly on account of her mother. Of her and Donguinho. Not her father. Dom João Quebedo, despite his cleverness and greed, was very old, nothing he might do would spoil João Diogo Galvão's reputation. Donguinho would ruin everything. And his loving mother would never abandon her beloved bastard. Malvina knew that, her mother had a big heart.

This was what she told her husband, cautiously revealing the family secrets, when he saw her tearfully reading the letters that arrived continuously from Taubaté. Malvina wept the most heartfelt tears, wiping them on the prettiest little flower-embroidered cambric handkerchiefs that might have been sent from heaven.

João Diogo was saddened, those tears spoiled his love. He was getting on in years, he did not have much time to lose. Accursed degenerate family, he muttered between his teeth, out of his wife's hearing. And he agreed with Malvina's thoughtful reasoning, even praised her judgement and good sense. That was the sort of wife he needed. But neither the Captain-General nor anyone else in Minas could learn of the existence of mad Donguinho and Dona Vicentina. Dona Vicentina had been so brazen as to give him some fiery, sinful looks when he took leave of her. Fearing the incestuous promise in Dona Vicentina's eyes, he turned away, bowing his head. In his confused state of mind and in view of the low value he placed on human life, a relic of earlier days, he even imagined having the furious Donguinho killed when his mother let him loose in the field. To get rid of that nightmare which threatened to disturb the blue sky of his domestic peace.

The two of them talked about all this while they discussed the best way to help the Dias Buenos without putting at risk the growing fame of João Diogo Galvão, who was the beginning, not the end, of a line.

And they decided that the best way would be to give Dom João Quebedo Dias Bueno what he needed to put his life in order, the Ribeirinha estate, and restore the town house in Taubaté for feast days and other special occasions. Her father was very sensitive to words, he would take offence for no reason at all, was what Malvina said, and João Diogo corrected what he had dictated, so that she wrote 'lend' instead of 'give', though it was clear between the lines that it was for good. Give or lend the necessary, not to restore or increase the former splendour, which João Diogo could never discover whether it was real or wishful thinking, but for the old nobleman to enjoy a better life. The more so since Dom João Quebedo had neither age nor strength now to expand property and wealth.

All this as long as none of them set foot in Vila Rica, João Diogo was careful to add, and his wife wrote. Malvina was not in the slightest upset, it was what she wanted, and gladly. She found some flowery, refined, ingenious, mannered, very lofty turns of phrase to set down in writing what João Diogo said in his blunt manner. She thought the same, but not for a moment would she dare think aloud in her husband's presence, so exalted were her sentiments.

She said these things in her letters with great skill and perfection, in a fine copperplate. She was afraid that her father, knowing that all the blame lay with his wife and Donguinho, might unleash his old fury, thereby intensified, not on Dona Vicentina but on the bastard lunatic. Basically she loved that half-brother of hers, thorn in her flesh and blight of her life. Beneath his filth and his madness, Donguinho was strong and beautiful; meek and gentle at times, with pure blue eyes, when they were able to cope with him on his better days. Because Dom João Quebedo might feel tempted to kill him, he had often actually sworn to do so in former times, and from behind doors she would hear her father threaten her mother. Old age calmed him down, but the feeling might return. She therefore took pains with her letters, her carefully chosen words, the niceties of sentiment.

And so, with great assurance and cleverness, she did everything to conquer her husband and obtain what she wanted. She put all her skill into her caresses and purred like a she-cat, she now went naked in his presence. But that he liked it so much and it made him feel so good, he might have found it odd; but he did not, not now. To get what she wanted most, a costly double-storey house on the Rua Direita, near the square, the palace and Carmo Church.

And she got it. João Diogo no longer denied her anything. His wife's slightest whim was a command he attended with pleasure, he did not count the cost. His great wealth and fortune seemed to be endless. He did not trouble even to think about it. If the gold grew scarce in the streams and river-beds, on the mountain slopes and the gravel of the foothills, and if the prosperity of the mines country was declining, he, with special favour from above and receiving his share along with those closest to the palace and, through them, cunningly, with the Captain-General himself, was now obtaining good contracts in the diamond country and land grants of many leagues in the São Francisco hinterland, where the pastures were good and the cattle, of the best quality, from the best stud-bulls and pedigree cows ever seen, from distant lands across the seas, mooed peacefully in the hot sun, herded by reliable blacks and half-breeds.

João Diogo bought an unfinished house on the Rua Direita and set to work, himself overseeing the masons and blacks, completing and furbishing it. Inspired and aided by his wife, he was no longer ashamed or afraid of being rich. He squandered, so they said, and he, self-assured, secure in his wealth and property, and in the Captain-General's favour, laughed and donned his finery, he and his wife playing a most amusing game, pretending to be nabobs and potentates from the Indies.

When he was finished, the floors of wooden boards set flush, well planed and smoothed, panelled ceilings, costly paintings, balconies with wrought-iron grilles decorated with João Diogo Galvão's initials and crystal fir-cones, glass windows, the rest was left to Malvina, who took charge of the furnishings and decorations. And as a reward for all João Diogo's sacrifice, she had carved on the bed-head the inscription LOVE

UNITED US, surrounded by flowers and garlands. She insisted and dwelt on it, he did not want the inscription, he considered it rather soppy, more suitable for young people, but then these things were all part of the new fashions. There is a time and a place for all things.

João Diogo was really the happiest and most loved man on earth. As he counted his beads during mass in Carmo Church, all corseted and dandified but full of piety, he never tired of giving thanks to God, to Our Lady of the Conception, Our Lady of Carmo, to the image of St Quiteria in the old chapel, to all the saints and angels, for the happiness he had received in his old age. All that was too much for his age, enough, he said, almost bursting. And if he did not ask the heavenly powers and his own private saint to increase his share of love and happiness, it was for fear that he might not bear it. His heart was flabby now, he sometimes suffered from cold sweats, strange feelings, dizziness and fainting fits. And such as his fear of losing Malvina's love and his horror of disrespect, saints being very suspicious, that he never once went so far as to utter the prayer he kept hidden in the depths of his soul – a few more years without loss of sexual power. He feared divine punishment, the gods are very envious and jealous, at times terrible, they might suspect his secret.

Before a year was out the happy couple was living in the house in the Rua Direita.

The tableware, chandeliers and plate, the brocades and damasks, the carpets and curtaining, the bed-hangings, the bed and table linen, all the other household linen, all this was left to Malvina's care. I leave it to your discretion, was how João Diogo put it, even his vocabulary was improved. Only one thing he would not allow her to touch: his late father's carbine. The carbine was to stay in a corner of their bedroom, in full view, as a memento of yesteryear, he said, with particular attention to the expression. That carbine had an involved and fabulous history, Malvina would scarcely believe it, she could not appreciate these things. Of when Valentim Amaro Galvão, on one of his first sorties in to the backlands of Minas Gerais, after the discovery of gold in Ribeirão do Carmo and Tripuí, the better to arm himself, was obliged to exchange all the gold he had striven might and main to obtain for that carbine which was to serve him so well in forests and ambushes. The value of gold was as low, contradictorily, in those tumultuous times, as the value of weapons was high.

That mob of armed blacks and half-breed fighting men, of faithful field-workers, who filled the slave-quarters in the Padre Faria district, Malvina made a point of sending them to her husband's diggings, to Tejuco and to the cattle lands, where they would be more useful. This was the judicious reason she gave her husband. He agreed, once again praising her good sense and judgement, virtues rare in so young a woman. She only wanted the household blacks, those gentle, strong smiling Angolan slaves, who were so docile and obedient – the result of many beatings, it is true, Inacia, for instance, was an Angolan from Cabinda. Her husband could keep those renowned and troublesome Sudanese blacks, as long as they were sent far away, she had no need of their sort. That was how she reasoned it and told him, and once again she was obeyed.

Only in one other thing was she not obeyed. That João Diogo should get rid of the silver pistol which he kept ready primed by his bedside for any necessity. Though he was now carefree and jovial, he was afraid of attacks and reprisals. No one gets so rich with impunity, or so it seemed an inquisitorial spark, hidden in his conscience, kept telling him and he did his best not to give an ear to it, but there was no way. He did not tell his wife that. A Lazzarino, from across the seas, was what he said, in praise of the weapon, to justify it, since these origins were so important for his noble wife.

On the other hand, he gave her a sedan-chair with two trained black servants, in livery, all braid and trimmings. It was a beauty of a chair, so costly and gilded, the inside lined with damask. And without her having asked him for anything, quite the reverse – she was all generosity, large-hearted, and he repaid all her affection and endearments with the liberality of his wealthy heart, covering her with gold, silver and coral jewels, with stones and cameos, peridots and filigrees, all those beautiful things that charm female hearts.

And finally it occurred to Malvina to ask for a spinet. Not only to add lustre and animation to the parties and soirées she would give, but so that she could practise. When she was a girl, in the times of plenty, she had had the beginnings of a musical education, then everything went wrong. She also asked for and was given a music teacher, a freed mulatto who knew his clefs and staves. He not only played the spinet, but was also good on the flute.

When Malvina, who had a good ear and was studious, and was making good progress with her lessons, played some gavottes and sarabands, and even some parts of a sonata suitable for beginners, with Master Estêvão on the flute, filling the house with cheerful sound, João Diogo Galvão lay back in his high-backed chair and listened in rapture.

One day he suddenly thought about his neglected son Gaspar, who had been away so long, he did not know whereabouts in his domains he was, where in the wilds, in which of his houses. Happiness does not allow painful memories, was more or less what he told himself by way of an excuse. Not that he had to find excuses for anything, Gaspar was a well of ingratitude, he went on, seeking more comfort for his spirit.

Malvina, it will be splendid when Gaspar is back, he said. She could not remember if it was the second or third time João Diogo had mentioned his son. She was not interested, she did not want to hear about competition for her husband's esteem and liberality. From conversations with women friends and Inacia's abundant information, she knew already what Gaspar was like, but revealed not the slightest interest in him.

He plays the flute very well, he learned in Portugal when he was studying other subjects, João Diogo went on. He never played again after his mother died. He was always shut away with his books, not now so much, he is more often off in the woods, hunting and enjoying himself. He is a bit odd, but he is a good soul, you shall see. I do not know why he has not put in an appearance yet, he will turn up any moment, to meet his stepmother, he said jokingly. Very likely, seeing that you play so well, he will take heart and be like he was before. No, I cannot play properly yet, she said modestly. It does not matter, Master Gaspar is probably out of practice, stiff fingers, short of wind, said the mulatto, sticking his nose where it was not invited. It would make me very happy, said João Diogo. He is an odd fellow, but he has a good heart, he takes after his mother in matters of feeling. Very good and sensitive, he has always been the same since he was a boy. When his sister died . . .

Really, asked Malvina, interrupting him, feigning surprise and unconcern, though now she actually was interested. Gaspar was certainly a strange man. His father had been married for a year and he had not even deigned to come and see her. But if he was as sensitive as his father said, he must have a soul like her own. If he liked books, he must know those poems about nymphs and shepherdesses, lyres and pan-pipes, which she now found so enchanting at the soirées and academy receptions. If he played the flute and liked music, he must be a kindred spirit, she thought, winging away to the blue-rimmed mountain crests, quite the musician already.

Because she was beginning to tire of the lonely afternoons, when her husband was away visiting his mine-workings. Her soul went soaring away to distant mountains. The clean green fields, the sonorous crystal-clear streams, the purest sweetest springs, the shady foliage of the groves, which she read about in the odes and the lyrics, the sonnets and the fables, the eclogues and romances, the ditties and cantatas.

4

In fact Gaspar kept to the promise he had made himself. Only a year after his father had taken up residence, with his newly wealthy and aristocratic Malvina, in the new house in the Rua Direita, did he make his appearance. Even then João Diogo had to send strongly worded messages, though they never reached him, he travelled so deep in those woods, in dense brush and far-off rivers. As if Gaspar, scenting his father's messengers from a distance, avoided well-known trails, preferring almost impenetrable tracks known only to his Indian guide and his armed slave. Always staying in the woods, always running away.

It was going too far, it looked very much like an intentional insult to his father and particularly to his stepmother, whom he did not even know. So said the message his father sent with the many couriers dispatched to Serro do Frio, Tejuco, the banks of the Velhas and São Francisco rivers, the cattle lands. Messages which kept on missing him.

And João Diogo was furious because he did not know where that odd, crazy son of his was hiding himself. But he told his wife that Gaspar was his heart's joy and the hope of his old age. He overdid the description of his feelings, though they were genuine. All to excuse himself and his son. Malvina might have doubts.

And Gaspar, always of changeable disposition, evasive and moody, continued to cover league upon league of ground. Out of sight for days and months. Yet always in his father's mine-workings, farms, woods and land grants. So vast, by now, were the domains of the potentate João Diogo Galvão. Always running away, running away not only from his father and his stepmother, but from something else, something he could not define. He was so uneasy and distressed.

He himself certainly could find no way of explaining what was happening to him. It was as if the same anguish and hallucination, the same despair and fever he had suffered when his sister died, when he received the news of his mother's death but was unable to say his last farewell to her corpse when it went to burial, as if all the turmoil to which his sensitive heart was susceptible had come back.

This was what João Diogo told Malvina, to try and justify Gaspar's cult of the dead and his vow to abjure love. They were the fruit of a very noble and generous spirit, he told his wife. He knew that she prized those proofs of sensibility.

She liked all this, but João Diogo could not restrain his anger and pain at not being obeyed. His despair at not even finding him, wandering about the pathways of his princely world.

From time to time he had news of his son. Someone had seen him way beyond the Sinkhole, in the dangerous lands of the Botocudos. João Diogo sent men to the area. When the messenger, accompanied by fearsome blacks and half-breeds, got there, there would be new, completely different information: Gaspar had been seen in dense woods in the Velhas river valley, going in the direction of the São Francisco.

And since these searches were fruitless and fanciful suggestions were being made, exciting the imaginations, creating dream and fable, which detracted greatly from the power expected of an old potentate, João Diogo got ready to reassemble his men, as in the old times when they flushed out the infested streams and rivers, the days of the wars with the slave settlements, and set off on the trail of the rebellious son who had fled the reach of his arm and his word of command.

All this excited not only the imagination of the common people, but that of Malvina, too, she being more given to dreaming. Those conflicting stories and tales, of lost trails in the backlands and in the river valleys, together with the fame of a soul disturbed by the dead, and the greatness of a pure heart, of which her husband had told her, began to fill Malvina's monotonous days, her dull depressing afternoons, as she stretched herself like a purring she-cat trying to wake up. In the half-light her blue eyes flashed, her charms increased. She looked more beautiful than ever, João Diogo noticed, and his love increased still further.

And she, for amusement, so that the searches and fanciful stories would not stop, becoming more and more exciting and impossible, feigned greater sorrow, sincere resentment, that her beloved husband's son had not the slightest interest in meeting her. It is so, João Diogo, it seems to me your son did not approve of our marriage, she said. And he, yes he did. And if he does not approve even more now, he will do, he replied firmly, in a solemn voice. And beneath his elegant clothes, his powders and outer casing, the brave, valorous João Diogo Galvão, of feared and awesome renown, was reborn.

And João Diogo changed his clothes, donned the fustian and leathers required in the woods and backland plains, pulled on his boots and spurs, equipped himself with stores and munitions, and was setting off at the head of his best-armed blacks and battle-hardened half-breeds, when one of the messengers he had sent to the four corners of that God-forsaken expanse returned with the good news that he had not only set eyes on Gaspar, but had spoken to him: Gaspar was on his way back, in obedience to his father.

What is this supposed to mean? said João Diogo, his eyes red with hate, when he was face to face with his son. Was this sneaking off an affront to me? Do you disapprove of my choice? Have you an criticism to make of your stepmother's reputation? And the questions were harsh, more like recriminations and outpourings of hatred than inquiries wanting answers.

No, Father, said Gaspar, I simply did not know that you had need of me, he said gravely, and João Diogo looked into his mournful eyes for some sign of untruth that would allow him to assert his authority and justice. When the first messenger who caught up with me gave me your message, I came at once, sir. As fast as I could. I nearly killed the horses I changed at the rest-posts all the way, he said and his father believed him, he was so dirty and tired-looking, exhausted really.

Go and get cleaned up, said his father. And do not appear in Malvina's presence looking like this. She would get a very bad impression of you. And, turning to Inacia, the Negress, who was listening and watching everything pop-eyed, he said, you, nigger girl, don't stand there like a scarecrow, move! Go inside and see to a bath quickly and a change of good clothes for your young master.

Inacia saw to things, quickly, blinking with excitement, with a great deal of bustle. Then went to tell everything to her darling mistress, who was nervous and anxious for the news. The return of her stepson had become more than a question of honour for her husband: by now she was beginning to feel humiliated, despised even. And she laughed with satisfaction, triumphant once more, when Inacia gave her account of the news, in her own exaggerated fashion.

Gaspar did not immediately come down to the drawing-room to meet his father's wife, the famous gentlewoman from Piratininga, from one of the best families, belonging to the Vicentine nobility, as his father said so long ago. He recalled that painful old conversation. Laughing a little to himself, he was so tired he could not move his face muscles, his voice was faint. If he had never taken seriously the conceit of the Portuguese aristocrats, who detested him so when he was over there, addressing him scornfully as a colonial, a word which he, like others, transformed into a motive for pride, he was not going to be impressed by the Vicentine nobility. He was going to get a good rest, then he would come down, he told his father, slumping heavily on to the soft bed he had not seen for so long. And he fell into the deep peace of an exhausted sleep, into the torpor of oblivion.

João Diogo carefully closed the door, counselling silence. Everybody on tiptoe, not a word, said Inacia to the blacks under her authority, mistress's orders. It'll be the whip for anybody who disturbs my young master's sleep, she said affectedly to the underlings in the kitchen and slave-quarters.

His father, too, came on tiptoe, carefully, to look at him. He was suspicious, he wanted to be sure. He was afraid his son was a rebel and that he would have to take a decision. Despite everything, old resentments (Gaspar was not like him and old Valentim), he had great love and respect for that son of his. He opened the door softly, taking great care for it not to creak. He stood some way off looking at the sleeping body, sprawled out with fatigue, listening to the tired, noisy, laborious breathing. And when on the second day, he saw that Gaspar was sleeping more peacefully, he came closer to the bed, for a closer inspection, holding his breath for fear that it might wake him. Gaspar really was in need of a good rest, he might even be ill. He was sorry, he had judged his son unjustly. Disrespectful and rebellious he was not; odd, eccentric, no more than that. And seeing him asleep he was quite sure that Gaspar loved and respected him. And he looked at him from a distance not just with his eyes but with the fingers of his imagination, as if he were stroking him: his tousled hair, his thick beard, his long eyelashes, the fair skin he had inherited from his mother, even fairer because of the contrast with his gleaming black hair. Just like his mother, so pure and gentle. And that purity which previously enraged him, now made him feel a pleasant warmth in his breast, a lump in his throat, a moistness in his eyes. A sleeping child, that is what he was. The same child who had so offended his masculinity and roughness in earlier days now moved him to compassion. Caused him some remorse for having tried to bring him up in accordance with his and old Valentim Amaro Galvão's rules and customs, when they were not suited to his son's character, which was effeminate judged by the old prejudice of a hardened plainsman. He felt sorry, his eyes kept on watering. And alone, with no one to see him, tears fell from his eyes.

This was what he condescended to tell Malvina. He was a different man now, he took to this sheepish business of telling his wife everything. Not at all, João Diogo, there is nothing wrong with tears, she said. And he, though a little dubious, agreed. It's just that I have not got used to all these noble manners, he said. It is a matter of time, my love, she said. You have changed a great deal, you progress by the day. There are times when I think that you are not so much as the shadow of that brute who wooed me in Taubaté. So she said, and it pleased and sweetened her husband's temper, though João Diogo himself, while agreeing, knew that it was she who had wooed him. They are very noble sentiments, Malvina went on, which simply set you apart from these backlands brutes. All right, he said, still dubious, but do not tell anyone.

Fiddlesticks, João Diogo, it is of no importance! And though he really felt he was being unmanly, which wounded the dignity of his old self, he continued to educate his heart in his old age.

Malvina herself, when she was having her music lessons, tried to play softly. None of those boring scales, she asked Master Estêvão for some short sonata pieces. She shut the drawing-room door, and when her teacher waxed enthusiastic in his instructions and on the flute, she would say quiet, softly, very softly. Not to wake my stepson who has arrived and is weary from his journey. And though she wanted her sweet music and no other noise to wake him, she played very softly and asked her teacher to be quieter. The distant, muffled notes of the spinet, not that conceited mulatto musician's flashy flute; her soft sweet music was supposed to wake up her stepson. And Malvina soared on the wings of thought, as she liked to say. Soft music, just as it should be for a sleeping child. Now he slept like an angel in heaven.

This was how she put it to herself in her frustrated maternal desires. Nor did she want problems and disagreements with Gaspar. What she wanted most, now, was to keep all that luxury and abundance, the great position, her husband's love, and add the respect and friendship of her stepson. Her husband's contentment was her happiness, he showered her with more presents and costly objects by the day. And then, she told herself, she would gain a great deal from judicious conversations with someone so well brought up, educated in Portugal, as they said of Gaspar. They would be good for her mind, they would complete the education which had been interrupted by the downfull of her *paulista* family, itself so different from most others, in which the daughters were not even allowed to learn to read.

But he is a strange one, they say he abandoned all those gentle pursuits, another voice whispered to her. Love and music, to throw himself like a brute into big game hunting, monkeys, panthers and cunning stags. Surrounded by savages, who stank and were fearsome even at a distance.

She would change things, cleverness she did not lack, she thought firmly, in answer to the uncomfortable voice. Just as she gained the passionate love of João Diogo, changing him for the better, in her opinion, so too she would win the friendship and respect of his son.

And then the pleasant times of old would return to that house. Like in the days of the late Ana Jacinta, which the slaves still talked about. For whom Gaspar used to play his flute and recite poetry, so Inacia told her. Dona Ana Jacinta, who, though unable to read, loved her son so much and had so sharp an ear and so gentle a heart that she understood it all. Floating in the snowy clouds of the distant blue sky, which came together and dispersed with the wind. It was no longer Dona Ana Jacinta who was there. Less still Malvina, galloping on the wings of the wind. Sitting there, with her fingers held in suspense, dreamy-eyed, alone in the dusk-filled drawing-room, was a two-headed figure – or rather, a fusion of the two, of Malvina and Ana Jacinta. A liquid, ethereal, winged creature who could already hear the purest notes of a flute and the most beautiful poems from Parnassus that her contaminated imagination dreamed of inventing.

And when, on the very day of Gaspar's return, she realized that Master Estêvão was not behaving in accordance with the silence and piety required by the fine house, she made the excuse of not feeling well and the next day she sent him away, saying she would let him know when she felt better.

Left alone she practised diligently on the spinet. She was only sorry that her fingers had not the skill and agility of her thoughts. If, as was happening nearly all the time, it chanced that one of the town's thousand bells began to ring for mass or eventide, good tidings or death, she only begged God and her favourite Our Lady not to let anyone be dying. She could not bear the mere idea that those interminable, sad, tormenting bells which sometimes tolled for a death all day long (they only stopped when the dying person gave up the ghost), those accursed bells and not the music made by her fingers (rather than by her as yet clumsy fingers, by her heart) should wake up Gaspar.

She was feeling so good and motherly. She really did now want to give João Diogo the peace and love he deserved. And give Gaspar a tranquil, peaceful home where he would find the repose, the purity and the serenity that his tormented spirit so longed for.

And your son Gaspar, she eventually asked him, no longer able to bear it. Has he not slept enough, rested enough?

João Diogo looked at her with a mixture of contentment for her interest and some surprise at the irritation and sharpness in Malvina's voice when she asked the second question. No, he said, I have been to see him. I have spoken to him a number of times. Not much, it is true, but we have talked. He is so tired that even his voice is weak, a mere whisper. I had to strain my ears to hear what he was saying. He has no head for anything, he cannot concentrate on a book for more than a few lines, or so he says. Just talking exhausts Gaspar. That is what he told me, poor boy.

Malvina asked in alarm if he might not perhaps be ill. João Diogo shook his head. Might he not need a doctor? she asked. There is a very good one here now, he attended the Captain-General once. So I was told, she added, seeing a hint of suspicion in her husband's eyes.

João Diogo stayed silent, he was giving careful thought to what his wife had said. No, he is not ill, he complains of nothing, except for tiredness. But that is no normal tiredness, said his wife artfully. It is quite common, he said. That is because you do not know these wild backlands, and you do not know Gaspar either, and how delicate he is. He was not made for that sort of life, I think he would be better off with his books, at a lawyer's desk, than hunting and roaming the woods. That is why I sent him to study back home in Portugal. But he got other ideas, he is stubborn and pig-headed, he did not want to go on studying after his mother died. I now think that, if he does not overdo things, a spell in the woods occasionally would do him good. This time he went too far, that is the reason he is like this.

But might he not have fallen ill? Malvina came back to her idea. Might he not have caught one of those malignant fevers in those infested rivers? No, said João Diogo, there is no sign of fever in his eyes or his face. I already thought of that. Once I was suspicious, I felt his forehead, he actually laughed. He has no fever, he is not ill.

Malvina's maternal heart would not rest, she was determined to help. If he is not ill, then maybe what he needs is a woman's care. I could help, she offered.

João Diogo laughed outright, almost guffawed. You have never seen Gaspar, you do not even know about him, he said. Gaspar has never allowed any woman to enter his bedroom, except his mother when she was alive. He does not like women. And seeing in Malvina's eyes what he himself had often wondered with sadness, he added: That is not what I mean, nobody thinks that about him. They know how good a shot and a swordsman he is. He is not merely feared, everybody now respects my manly son. Apart from his character, which is not like mine, he takes after his mother's family, he made a promise to the Holy Virgin when his mother died.

But what on earth sort of promise is that? she said. Heaven knows, I cannot follow the reasoning of his promise, said João Diogo. I gave up trying to understand. If it were not to marry, said Malvina, I could understand the reason for the promise. Even without knowing in exchange for what he made the promise to the Virgin. There are people who do not get married, who do not wish to settle down. But to abandon life in the town, everything that is good and beautiful, people like himself and you, when he could live in close relations with the palace, so gifted they say he is. . . . That is what I cannot begin to understand. Who can imagine living out in the wilds and jungles unnecessarily, risking one's life. And always running away, running away from something or other.

Gloomy and withdrawn (his wife had resurrected old doubts), now accustomed to his son's ways, João Diogo said nothing, put a stop to the conversation at that point. Unless he no longer heard what his wife was saying, his eyes resting on Malvina's hands on the keyboard, the music his arrival had interrupted. Those hands which were delicate yet firm, plump and tender, well shaped and fragrant, the soft fair skin, slightly freckled because she was a redhead. An indoor flower, fit for palaces and drawing-rooms, he was thinking bizarrely, while he smiled to himself remembering his wife's exaggerated care protecting herself from the sun, she who had the same flame-coloured hair. She, daughter of light and sun, he thought tenderly. She had every reason, with a skin that was so white and soft, just the afternoon heat was dangerous. And he recalled Malvina's vanity and care with her beauty, her baths and beauty treatment. In other times, he would have thought badly of her. Recalled how he had been surprised by her behaviour in bed, her flaming nakedness, calmly at ease, in the early months of their marriage, now his passion and delight. How he too now looked after himself and preened himself. Such were the customs, and there was nothing to be done about it.

Are you not listening to me? she said, annoyed at talking at thin air, he was obviously nodding off. I am, he lied. I was just pondering on all these things you have been telling me. And do you not think I am right? she said. You are, my dear. It is just that I have learned one cannot try to change a person's real character, only the outer shell. If one really tries, with care, one can, she said, remembering João Diogo's own case. Who would imagine the man he used to be even listening to such talk?

With the stick, in childhood, he thought, remembering himself, his own feeling of defeat. One does not beat a man, said another of his masculine rules. You can kill him, but not beat him. A slave is the only one you change with whippings and beatings. And if he does not change, he holds his tongue. Even then there are some that become runaways and you have to finish them off with sword or gun.

But anyway, what is it you really want, my dear? he said, cutting short his own thinking aloud, he might annoy his wife. I want to know if he has anyone to look after him, she said, feigning a sulk she was far from feeling, merely baulked in her mother-not-yet-to-be's most secret desire. He has, said he, he has his black servant, a special, reliable nigger, who sees to his every want, like his shadow. Well now, a male nigger! she said. A woman understands these things. Even if she were a black woman, there are times when what is really needed is the tireless care of a white woman, who knows these things of body and heart. Well now, a peasant! she said, forgetting the hands and generous heart of

Inacia, to whom she now surrendered herself unreservedly. What if I were to go and try to help?

If he meant to cross or annoy her, he would have laughed. Just imagine, a woman in Gaspar's room! That was funny, enough to make one laugh. But he said, my love, don't upset yourself by trying. I shall not let you upset yourself, you had enough with your own family. It's not me, he is the one who will not for one moment allow you in his room. When a woman, married or unmarried, comes close to him, Gaspar seems to change, he even trembles. If one is forward enough to touch even his hand, he turns as red as the reddest flower.

If that's the way it is, she said, pouting; he pretended not to notice. The best we can do is wait, he said. If by tomorrow Gaspar gives no sign of intending to appear, I shall have a weightier talk with him. Then you can try what you have in mind.

I do not want to do it for myself, she said, putting things straight. If I want to, it is because you are gloomy and concerned, and you have hardly anything to say.

Backing away like a cat, she stopped. It is sometimes as if I no longer exist, she started, trying one of her last resources, but João Diogo said firmly, in his old voice: tomorrow; and she saw there would be no point in continuing.

5

Gaspar came out of his room. Malvina was in the drawing-room, near the window, when he appeared at the corridor door. He did not come in immediately, and his eyes ran attentively all around, from the floorboards to the panelled ceiling. He seemed to be interested in the graceful pictures, the subjects of which, the four seasons, had been her own choice. Standing close to the curtain, Malvina sought to conceal herself, that way she could see him without being seen.

And he continued making his round of the furniture, the carpets, the damasks, the crystal chandelier. She was pleased, the chandelier with its fifty lamps was her pride. Would he like it? Did he approve her work, the great changes she had made in João Diogo's life? Yes, he was sure to. If he was a refined man, who had lived not only in Lisbon but in other capitals where life is always better. Those marvellous lands, those fantastic kingdoms which did not seem real. She would love to live far away from there! From those backward people. They were always criticizing everything she did, her behaviour, her clothes, her manners. They gave her no rest, they spoke ill of her behind her back, she knew, did Inacia not tell her? Yes, a different life. She had been born for a different life. An aristocrat, with a family tree and coat of arms, as her father liked to say. She was not like those common people who got rich from one day to the next, from the river water.

She was so interested in seeing whether he approved her work that she was unable to notice what her husband's son was like. Conceited and self-interested as she was, she would be enormously sad if he did not approve. Something told her he might not be enjoying it. Was it not because he disliked that pompous life in Lisbon and the way they tried to imitate it in the palace and in the best houses in Vila Rica that he left the town and hid himself in the woods, with people so different from himself? No, that was not why. It was to be alone, she said. To flee from remorse and sadness. Since his mother died. A refined spirit suffers a great deal with that sort of thing. It was like that when his sister (what was her name? Oh yes, Leonor) died. No, it was not the towns and the refinements of art and of the spirit that he was avoiding. He was running away from dark thoughts, he was a tormented spirit. She would know how to treat him. With her sunny disposition, all sweetness and light. She could see herself changing him. She would turn him back into what he was before. She saw herself so much that she forgot to see him.

Now he was in the centre of the room. Though robust, he had refined manners, a light measured step, though not the mincing step of a beau. It is hunting and roaming the woods that has made him like that, but you can see he is not one of those brutes. A refinement of gestures, neither deliberate nor overdone. In the posture that was part of his body, light from within things. Nothing in him seemed laboured, everything natural. His postures and gestures were not effeminate – something else to which she could not give a name. Not even in the Captain-General, who was of the best Portuguese nobility, formed in the government of the Indies and in the King's embassies, did she see such manners. That was what nobles should be like. The Captain-General was sometimes rather brutal and coarse, he did not control his tongue and his hands. Once he even. . . .

He did not wear fashionable clothes. The clothes which João Diogo wore so clumsily. He was not dressed the way he was when he arrived. Those riding clothes, and him all dirty and unkempt, what a sight. Different. A topcoat and waistcoat of severe cut, no edgings, embroidery or lace. Good-quality cloth, but not bright colours. No ornaments, no gilt or silver. And those cordovan leather boots that no one wore nowadays. As if he were going riding, but he was not wearing a riding outfit. He was the opposite of everything she considered attractive in a man. If he were to go to palace receptions like that, they would laugh at him. They would not, in fact, his person and appearance inspired such respect. But he would be disapproved of, criticized. Those cutting tongues. In any case he would not go to the palace and to the houses of the rich. He did not need to be a dandy, a beau. Instead of criticizing him, she was full of praise for his overall appearance. She had never seen anyone like him. A man from other times. Not from the other times she used to imagine, before, from other times. Out of the books she read, the town women did not read. It was not the custom for women to read. Even less to discuss what they read with men, in lengthy intercourse. Even at receptions, at the palace. It does not look good, for a married woman. Backward, gossipy people, overnight nobility. If, instead of Piratininga, she thought about Portugal. Or about the invented countries of her fantasies. The heroes in books, which she then (before) clothed in different garments and different colours. Now they should be like him. So noble and courteous, with upright passionate hearts. She was carried away by what she read, the poems she heard, now floating on metres and rhythms.

He walked over to the spinet, pulled back the damask cloth. Now he was directly facing her. So much so, she was afraid of being seen. She did not want to be seen, not yet. Her heart was thumping wildly, that figure of a man. His face was very pale and white for someone who spent his time in the woods and streams. He must protect himself with those big hats, otherwise he would be darker. The part of his face not covered by beard was very white. Maybe it is not that, maybe he was consumptive. Motherly again, she wanted to look after him, if he was consumptive. He was not, his father would have said something. One does not always know. The whiteness of china, her fingers already touching it. Once more she was oblivious of her maternal feelings. Not just whiteness, light. A halo of light, of enchantment, about him. The silvery splendour of saints. Not only about his head, his whole person. He shone.

And she was enchanted, she had never seen anyone like that, she kept on repeating. And his beard (men's faces now were always close-shaven and powdered, she was beginning to think that these fashions were not very suitable for men), a beard which he had trimmed in his room (did he put perfume on it, benjamin?), a thick, black, glossy beard. His hair, which was glossy too, simply caught up at the back with a black grosgrain ribbon. She could not see his eyes properly. No doubt as shiny black as certain agates. His eyes were bent over the keyboard of the open spinet, his fingers stroked the keys which she had so often thumped desperately in her learner's anguish. She wanted to learn quickly, she had no time to lose. As black and shiny as his hair. Two damsons. No, two black onyxes,

103

she corrected herself, preciously. She was already embellishing and imaging.

And his hands tanned by the backlands sun. He was white, one could see that. She saw from his face, before. Very white, pale. Delicate, was what they had told her. More than they had told her. Tanned, but without the roughness of hands accustomed to tilling the soil, working the rivers or handling weapons. They must be soft, his fingers used to caressing silk, fur or ermine. How did he manage that delicate softness? A hand with long slender fingers, she imagined the pink nails.

Suddenly he hit a key, a D. The sound vibrated in the air with a sustained volume, louder than it really was. Now a C which he struck, with a rounded, drawn-out sound. A firm E. He was picking notes at random. Isolated sounds, no chord yet, she thought remembering her first music lesson. She played like that when she was a girl, trying to imitate Mariana, who could play already. Later she too began to learn. Then everything came to an end, gone with the wind, swallowed up. The chords, now she could play very well. At least so she thought. She dismissed that crafty mulatto for a few days. He was like a child pressing the keys to see what sound they would make. When he should know, so his father said. But he said that it was the flute his son played well. From music, of course. You could see he was no player by ear. Anyone who plays the flute well must occasionally have been accompanied on the spinet, he knows where the notes are. And he knew about instruments, he nodded his approval of the quality of the spinet. She said, to him, just in thought – from Portugal. Made in Lisbon, Master Estêvão said for her, stretching his lips tight, the pretentious mulatto. Priceless, I have never seen such a beauty, her teacher exaggerated his praise. You have another jewel in the house. More than a jewel. The first time he saw the spinet. But he did not have to say anything, he (not the mulatto) must be well acquainted with these costly refinements, the delights of well-endowed spirits. Of wealthy spirits, music and poetry. She was riding on the wings of fancy again, on the legendary gryphon, into the distant heavens.

Then she was brought back to the hardness of things, to the harsh light of day. He had eventually struck a chord, waking her. Badly struck, even to her ear. He is out of practice. So much so that he himself noticed, frowned and screwed up his eyes. As if he had broken something, a mirror for instance. And he struck the chord again. Now his face was calmer, almost cheerful and pleased. At least in the grave, sober repose we associate with someone who is sure of things and knows he has done a thing properly. The same chord again. For her at least it was perfect. He thought so too. From that chord a melody could be born. A sonata, an aria, a heavenly thing.

But something happened to him. Maybe some painful memory, feeling of remorse. My Lady of the Conception, I promise all the candles for your altar for a year. Do not let, do not, for anything in this world, let him have made a promise never to play again. It happened, now he had really broken the most precious mirror. Because he ran his hand angrily over the keyboard, from end to end. With such a crash, dozens of startled doves suddenly flapping noisily around the room, the blast of a carbine. She shuddered so.

And shocked and trembling though she was, she managed to walk towards him, seize his arm and commandingly say no! A no which to him must have sounded as loud as the rush of sound that woke her from her lethargy and spellbound delight. And he shook his arm (unintentionally, as she realized later, in her room, when she could not stop remembering), stepping sharply aside. A boy terrified by the rolling rumble of those thunderclaps resounding in the distance, loud and deep, worlds crashing. When the lightning flashed in the mountains and cleft the heavens on stormy nights. This she realized afterwards when she was remembering the incident in her room – in the pale, muzzy hour.

And she did not let go of his arm, there was no way she would let it go. Not because she did not want to, her fingers were rigid. And he, only now coming back to himself, saw her for the first time. His eyes were startled and wild.

Yes, he had wild eyes that were at odds with the rest of his refined, moderate, thoughtful, courteous temperament. She did not think this in words. Nor in her head, her heart or her belly. In some part of her which she was quite unable to locate: inside and outside of her, above and below her. Not only before but after it happened, while it was happening. As if a sombre, premonitory person, ubiquitous in time and space, thought for her, in her, beyond her.

(He was a chaste man and a wild man, he looked at her like a startled wild animal. The words came afterwards in her room. Even in her room, she did not know where the words had come from. Nothing like this had ever happened to her.)

You, she said in a softer voice. And he, still unable to speak, white like ivory that has just been scraped. Don't do that, she went on, more in control. And he, only now seeming to become aware of the flesh and blood presence by his side, began to get his colour back. In an instant, as quickly as it all happened, he blushed. She had never seen anyone as red as that. Could it be because of her presence, because of her woman's hand still holding his arm (her fingers no longer rigid, but because she wanted to), she wondered, as she realized later in her room.

Now it was not his whole body that shuddered. Only his hand trembled, when he, firmly but delicately, removed her hand.

And he still said nothing, perhaps unable to. He moved away from her, went over to the window. Though he had his back turned more or less towards her, she saw that he wiped his hand over his face, from his forehead to the tip of his beard, with exaggerated force, as if he wished to tear off a mask that was stuck to his face. Something was suffocating him and perhaps by tearing off the mask he would be able to breathe. It was not the well-known gesture of someone wiping the sweat from his face.

For a long time, a few moments, he stayed like that. Looking at his back she could see that his chest was rising and falling with the panting of his laboured breathing. Short of breath, his heart too weak for so strong an emotion.

She was miles ahead of him, she had controlled herself long before. I just have to wait, she said patiently to herself. And she waited.

When Gaspar turned round he was a different person, almost the same person as earlier. Only very pale, not a drop of blood in his face.

And she saw him full figure, saw beauty such as she had never seen in a man. She found the words, suddenly discovered the meaning of all his human secret. Which she herself before and she was sure that no one else before her had succeeded in discovering, nor never would, of that she was sure. She alone, unless (which was impossible) they suddenly felt the sudden and overwhelming power of so much beauty.

Yes, what made him a being white and pure, chaste and elusive, different, whom the more vulgar and obscene at first called a queer, and later regretted, because in reality (she saw it in his wild eyes) he was not, was his beauty. Not the ordinary beauty one sees in women and even in some men; a different beauty, a beauty which did not exist before on earth. Maybe the innocent, terrible beauty of the angels, she fantasized. The pure, immaculate angels which come dangerously close to sin, she went on, by now immersed in thick mists.

Forgive me all this, he said. You see I thought I was alone. And seeing that her gaze lingered on his hands, trembling as always, which he had almost stretched out to her when he spoke, palms up as if ready to catch something very delicate and light which might fall from heaven – he took them away quickly, protecting them from her gaze. But none of this (all his modesty and shyness) offended or hurt her, rather it enchanted her.

The sound of his voice and the harmonious fullness of his speech had the same spellbinding beauty. Everything about him was pure, sonorous, poetic, dreamy and bucolic, she was already starting to think in that precious rhetoric which, from hearing it so often, she repeated and confused.

Gaspar's eyes rested on hers, penetrated her to the soul, piercing her with light, turmoil and pain. Now they were softer, but still wild. The wildness in his eyes was for good, she perceived, transfixed, trembling all over. And it was her turn to blush. She went pale afterwards, as if she were fainting very slowly, for the duration of that look. And she felt her whole self trembling and burning inside, in a conflagration of agony. Wounded, pierced, lost, she thought in a last effort to recover her senses. This never happened to me before, I shall never break free of him, she kept thinking, afterwards, in her room.

But she was still a strong woman, self-assured. She managed to gather together her fleeting strength and rise to the surface. And as she rose, it was her turn to give him a long, slow, almost masculine look. So strong and powerful were her eyes now.

Gaspar seemed unable to endure her gaze. He bowed his head reverently, not daring to hold out his hand. With your leave, madam, he said, turning away.

Thus she could not so much as guess at what the effect had been on him.

6

From that day forth everything happened in a crescendo in Malvina's life. From the first look that pierced her with turmoil and pain, plunging her into the darkness which she, child of joy, life and light, did not know (that was why she felt lost, for ever crushed and dwarfed, and only succeeded at great cost in rising to the surface, where she was able to refurbish her weapons and move to the attack); since that meeting in the drawing-room the changes which began to take place in Malvina escaped her control completely.

A new woman had been born at that moment, she thought, believing she was someone else. If she had seen herself from outside or from deeper inside, she would have seen that she was the same artful, cunning, dominating, wilful Malvina as always. The Malvina she sometimes got to looking at through the eyes of her father, her mother and Mariana, before, and now through Inacia's, making her say (the Negress herself did not dare, she could not yet say) missy's in league with the devil. Trembling in spite of herself, fearful of what she was saying, she called upon the darkness for a pact. Outwardly she crossed and cursed herself. Get thee gone, Satan! Save me, My Lady of the

Conception! She wanted so badly to be happy! Unwittingly she repeated the words of her father and mother.

The same Malvina, the same strong, triumphant woman as always. The difference was in her passion and suffering, but passion and suffering are added things in the soul, they do not change anyone's essence – they only silence and overwhelm one. She was like that as a girl, the seed of what she is and was. Simply, until recently, although all her family's humiliated poverty and aristocratic decadence had cut short the splendid, happy life she considered, by right of birth and heavenly favour, naturally hers, she had not really known suffering and pain. At least so she suddenly realized. All the humiliations and poverty she had experienced merely served to give her strength, hatred and cunning; to be the woman she became.

Yes, she suffered. From that day on, she began to suffer and to bleed. She burned in her silent, impossible, sinful love. She knew herself that her passion was sinful and had no possible sequel. She condemned her incest severely and punished herself. After all he was her husband's son.

And because she suffered, she went the gamut of her doubts and contradictions, in the ambivalence of love and emotion. Though she was in the depths of darkness, she allowed herself, consciously and lucidly, to be devoured by an invincible fate which she had to obey. But she was sincere in her confused prayers. That Our Lady of the Conception should protect her and forgive her in anticipation.

She who had never felt guilt (on the contrary, she was always justifying herself, always finding reasons to explain everything she did or was doing), now mulled over old wrongs and feelings of remorse, of which at the time she was really unaware. Ah, heaven has taken revenge on me, she said in her despair and anguish, in her agony. For what she had done to Mariana. Though influenced by her mother and appearing meekly to obey the plans and wishes of her father, Mariana already silently loved that promised Diogo, closer in years to her than he was to Malvina.

And she begged forgiveness, now she badly needed heaven's favour and clemency. She remembered her father's suffering, the despair of his last days, not being able to be with her; his death. There was the consolation of knowing that she had not left him destitute: João Diogo provided for the recovery of the estate. If her father dreamed idly of abundance, power and glory, the gilding of his family coat, her mother was like her: she only wanted playful, carefree happiness, life's pleasures, the delights of the flesh and the heart. But her mother consoled herself easily, she had the gift of shallowness and forgetfulness. And she particularly remembered Donguinho. She remembered Donguinho with a special tenderness, her eyes moist with grief and repentance. Despite his filth and his madness, Donguinho was beautiful, pure and strong. His muscles and his bellows reminded her of the gods. Of the three, he was the one whose dreams were most innocent. All he wanted was green pastures, the blue sky of early evening; the warm, moist, panting smell of the mares; the warm dung and the green grass of the pastures and corrals. He was the only one who did not annoy her, who did not have even the understanding necessary consciously to annoy her.

For this reason she was now even more repentant and begged forgiveness. For the death of her father and Donguinho. Her father died of sadness and old age. Donguinho, on the other hand, was killed in a clever ambush: when, no longer satisfied with the freedom his mother lovingly allowed him, he began to climb over the fences of other people's pastures and corrals. Her mother, free at last, after the settlement of the possessions she was to receive, went away with a rogue to Portugal, where so far she was enjoying a life of plenty and happiness.

It all happened so quickly, at the time she gave it little thought. It was as if it only happened at that moment, when recalled in bitterness and in the absence of forgiveness. Formerly mistress of the sighs and chemistry of the emotions, now she wept uncontrolled tears in the sleepless nights she began to have. Everything that had happened to her family happened all over again.

And she punished herself, saying that what was happening to her with Gaspar was her fault, she was paying old debts. It was happening because she had allowed it to happen. Even in her grief and repentance, she thought herself omnipotent, thought she could dominate and govern everything. Always the same Malvina, nothing changed.

Because she wanted clemency and forgiveness, she began to understand and forgive. So she understood and forgave her father's ambition; so she understood and forgave her mother's sins and the disgrace which had resulted in Donguinho; so she understood and forgave Donguinho's own insanity, which she had no reason to forgive. So severe before, not any more.

Still full of joy and light (she was begotten of the sun, of the light), in her eagerness to understand and explain, she attributed everything to the forces of night and death. It was the forces of darkness that turned against her, it was the magical, implacable power of darkness that was intent on crushing her.

Her passion for Gaspar knew no bounds, mentally she overcame them all. She merely lacked the strength and courage, sufficient audacity to confess it. Yet. Neither to him nor to Inacia. Not to anyone.

She used all her resources and cunning. But she was now a fearful woman, the slightest thing startled her, everything made her suffer. A woman who allowed herself to be overwhelmed by passion, she who had never loved. And she ate herself away and burned, let herself be consumed by it. Night and day her impossible love gave her no rest. A love she must not speak of. Which she must not for one moment allow him to suspect and learn about.

Though very different from his father, Gaspar loved and respected him. My husband's son, she kept saying over and over. Why not someone else? Why him precisely? She could hope for nothing, she hoped impossibly. And that same figure she saw herself as through Inacia's borrowed eyes whispered to her, insinuating and mysterious: no man is chaste, every woman seduces and lets herself be seduced. Sin is the mark of man, since time immemorial. She had only to try.

She then began to play the most intricate and dangerous of games. Often she believed she was close to the abyss. One more step and all might be lost. She meant to have everything, she did not want to lose. She was a divided self, a cockleshell in the raging waters of a river which the current might bear away.

Contrary to what she expected, Gaspar did not avoid her the next day. Nor on the following days. Quite the reverse, he began to seek her company, appearing in the drawing-room the moment she played the first notes on the spinet, however softly.

And he talked a great deal. She, previously so talkative, now had her tongue tied, her shrinking heart in the palm of her hand. Gaspar was always respectful and sensible, his conversation always as gentle and harmonious as his voice the first time she heard it. He told her some of his adventures, once he even laughed.

And these conversations lulled her into day-dreams, in the warm, soft mists of fantasy; they oppressed her solitary nights.

She wanted more and more. Wanted more, knowing that she could not desire him even secretly. Gaspar was chaste and pure, he respected his father. He did not offer the smallest light of hope, no sign of any other desire beyond that of sublime family intercourse. By inevitability and choice so solitary before, now he sat close to her as if by the edge of a calm, smooth, cloudless lake – the tranquil breeze of gentle thoughts on his brow. She had taken the place of his mother, he was his father's beloved son. Malvina was rambling.

João Diogo was full of praise for his wife's attitude. Malvina, I am so happy, he is a different person, he said when he noticed the changes in his son. He was not the same any more. Still serious, it is true, but so kind and good. He could see that Gaspar was happy. It was all due to her. It almost reminded him of the times when he sat whole afternoons talking to his mother. He did not go out, certainly, but he did not avoid him any more, nor her, though she was a woman. He was so afraid that things would not be like that!

Why should he run away? she said, pretending to laugh. He did not notice how forced her laugh was, he was too happy to notice. Am I by any chance an animal? she said. Do I bite? No, my love, said João Diogo. It was just that he was so afraid the two of them would not get on. Not a night passed but he thanked God for all the good she had done him. There was no better wife than her, he would never find one. Now then, behave! she said, pushing him away. Gaspar might come in suddenly and see. Not on my account, on his. He is so pure, so shy, so good!

João Diogo's happiness reached a peak when he heard the first sounds of the flute coming from Gaspar's room. At first softly. He is afraid of being heard, he thought. As if he was doing his lessons. He did not need to, he played so well. Afterwards more at ease, he had stopped exercising. Now João Diogo, from the distance of the couple's bedroom, could hear a whole piece of music. It was angelic, celestial music. Going out into the corridor, he came across Malvina listening enraptured at Gaspar's door. She shuddered when she saw her husband. What a shock you gave me! she said afterwards, concerned. When they remarked on the incident. He was so happy he did not notice how his wife trembled. She raised her finger to her lips, requesting silence. Nothing could disturb Gaspar. Most likely he, who was so shy, if he suspected he was being watched, would even throw his flute away and never play again. That was what they told one another silently.

She leaned against the wall. With her hands crossed on her breast, her eyes closed and her lips parted, she could scarcely breathe – the emotion was too strong. It was dangerous, what she had done, she accused herself afterwards. But João Diogo always looked at her with the utmost devotion and love. She was as pure and fine as his son, he told her later. How could a person be so fine? How could music have the sort of effect it had on her? He, who always went to sleep during the musical sessions at the Captain-General's soirées, could not understand. Even with me, when I play? she asked artfully, pretending to sulk, when she saw how close João Diogo sat to the spinet when she was playing. My love, in your case it is not for the music, it is for yourself, he said. Just to be close to you makes me drool with happiness. And as he was most insistent this time with the pressure of his caress, she left him. She even returned it with a light kiss on his powdered face.

In view of what her husband told her she saw that she was not in danger. Nevertheless she was cautious, she was afraid that her voice or her eyes might betray her. One day, he, being jealous, might suspect what was happening, what she was thinking. As if her most secret and dangerous thoughts might be visible in her eyes, her voice, her slightest gestures.

Advancing step by step, more self-assured and surer of the ground she was treading, Malvina allowed herself some, for her present state, rather daring behaviour. Apropos of everything and nothing, she spoke Gaspar's name several times. She divagated, invented subjects. Just for the pleasure, the enjoyment, the satisfaction of pronouncing it. Her heart throbbed in her chest, in her throat. She looked at João Diogo's face, his eyes were clear, he saw nothing unusual. He does not know nor could he know, she breathed with relief. She was winning.

Only one thing João Diogo noticed, that she was changed. She was not the same in bed as before, she did not give herself the way she used to. And as he mentioned it to her, she said, my darling, I have been feeling tired. . . . At times I feel like giving up my music lessons and dismissing Master Estêvão, she said, testing the ground. Certainly not, he said. I still want to see you and Gaspar playing together, one of those, what are they called? Sonatas, she said. That's it, playing a sonata for me. So now you want a duo, she risked asking archly. Are you so fond of music? No, he said, it is to see the two of you happy. It would do his father's and husband's heart so much good. She shuddered, a rock broke away from the mountain and rolled down the slope.

She could not go on like that, withholding herself night after night, feigning tiredness, headaches, indisposition and other discomforts. One day, involuntarily, when she yielded to one of João Diogo's pressing desires and reproduced an old pleasure she no longer felt (he must not suspect, she made every effort with her writhing and her sighs), she noticed in his wrinkled face some of his son's features. She had never noticed before, they always said Gaspar was extremely like his mother, he was her altogether. He was like his father too, he was a younger, improved João Diogo: the roughness of his features softened by the beauty and refinement of a fine soul. João Diogo when a young man, though coarse, rough and hardened, must have been just like his son. Her desire to see that was so great that she saw what was not possible to see. She somehow invented a young, handsome João Diogo. Still not the son's terrible, angelical beauty, but no longer the ugliness that had increased since she met Gaspar. She even attained the same pleasure as before, when Gaspar did not yet exist in her life.

And having reached the climax, she became once more the old Malvina, and perfected her skills. João Diogo was gratefully happy. He could die like that, he said. So strong were the pleasure, the joy and the happiness that convulsed his sick heart. And with the joy that once more shone in his eyes, seeming to remove the cataract and the dullness of age, she saw in them the eyes of Gaspar. The same flashing, violent brilliance, the same wild look as always (not in surprise or astonishment as she had thought), which contrasted with the fineness and purity of Gaspar's person.

These minute discoveries grew out of all proportion with her desire, exciting and magnifying still further her abandon and her wantonness. She held João Diogo's head tightly in both hands, plunging into his fire, into the fatal depths, the danger of those glistening waters. And when João Diogo's wrinkled mouth sought hers, she held back: she wanted his eyes, only his eyes, his eyes for always.

In her delirium and her dream, she was afraid only of giving herself away. Of letting slip the name kept in her heart, repeated restlessly – Gaspar! Gaspar! Getting closer and perilously closer to the thick woods and currents. And she stopped only when João Diogo, worn out, said, enough, now it's me who is tired, I might die. The last lucid spark in his heart warned him the world would collapse.

After the storms, the lightning flashing and the thunder rumbling, when the sky cleared and was all limpid blue again, she would fall into the depths of sadness and prostration. Confused, agitated. She felt that she had already committed every sin. To which she herself answered not yet, Gaspar knows nothing, he will never know. She no longer dared pronounce the name of her protective saint, for fear of offending her. To ask forgiveness and say never again, for fear of not being able. She was dazed and divided, a thousand voices screamed within her.

And she began to play this same subtle, dangerous game with Gaspar. Alone in her meditations saying she did not want to, at the time wanting. She would go to the point where he might notice. Then she would stop, would go no further. The next day she would go a little further, by now wanting him, in the most secret corner of his heart, to know. To know and to stifle it, not to allow so much as a glimmer in his dark, sombre eyes to show he knew. She could tell him with her eyes, beneath the scales of her words; by word of mouth she could not. Only if he, one day feeling the same love and the same sin, were to say. . . . Malvina was going crazy, for the first time in her life she was in love, she burned, aflame with passion.

Master Estêvão came in the mornings, gave her her lesson and went away. Gaspar never appeared when he was there. When Master Estêvão asked her about the young man they said played so wonderfully (I want to see this treasure and contest a duet with him), she said jealously no, you know how he is. But you could at least have a word with him, said her teacher. I already have, he does not want to, she lied.

The afternoon was when Gaspar appeared in the drawing-room. In the morning, at the long dining-table (he at one end, his father at the other, she in the middle) the two spoke very little. Only phrases suited to the occasion. Do you want this? Or that? Are the beans to your taste? Do you want more meat? Or general topics: how it was cold or hot, how the day was dry or rainy. It was father and son who talked. João Diogo, who seldom went now to his vast domains, asked Gaspar, who had been there lately, how things were going with his workings in the Serro do Frio, his contracts in Tejuco, the oxen and the pastures in the cattle lands. They were quiet, slow conversations, father and son now got on well together. Forgetting the afternoons and the nights, Malvina smiled contentedly, peace reigned in that house. She was the architect of all this harmony and happiness. At least that was what João Diogo said, praising highly his wife's talents and character. Even to people in the street he did not conceal his satisfaction. He went so far as to mention it to the Captain-General.

When Gaspar appeared in the afternoon, it was a sun coming suddenly into the room, putting to flight the sad shadows. She did not turn round yet, but slightly lowered the volume of the chords (would he notice? she wondered), she knew that Gaspar had entered the room. And he approached (her fingers carefully picking out the chords, seeming more skilful than they really were), he was in the middle of the room. Gaspar now close to her. Were it not for the spinet, she would even be able to hear his soft warm breath. Without turning round, she said is that you, Gaspar? Her heart leaping, quivering, heavy with desire. So good, so deep, that pleasure hidden in the shadows. Yes, it is me, go on, he said. She played on without turning round, prolonging as far as, as long as possible, the warm, silent proximity, the mere presence. You are getting on, you are playing well, he told her. Then Malvina turned round and stopped playing. You have turned liar now, have you? She strove to control the tone of her still tremulous voice. And she laughed, to gain time, to see if there was any trace in him of the emotion she felt. Nothing, neutral and cold. His eyes were just soft and sad.

After a time they started to play together (he on the flute, she on the spinet), short pieces, sonatas, pavanes, even some tarantellas. Gaspar at first said no. Malvina, seeing that he really wanted to (it was not for nothing that he practised in his room), insisted.

Despite her emotion, or even because of it, she played better with accompaniment than by herself; she played with more warmth and emotion. Gaspar corrected her in some passages and she certainly learned more quickly than with that insufferable Master Estêvão.

Again, he would say patiently. With you it is much better, I learn much quicker, she said. But carry on with Master Estêvão, he knows his trade, he said, perhaps sensing Malvina's thought. I know very little about the spinet, he went on modestly. I think you know a great deal, said Malvina. He smiled with pride.

Here, Gaspar pointed to the place in the score. Let us repeat it until we get it right. They repeated it.

Once Malvina was nervous and inattentive, she did not know why she was unable to conceal the despair in her eyes and her voice – that endless anguish which tormented her. When he repeated here, she felt Gaspar's arm brush her shoulder, very close to her neck. Gaspar continued to point at the place in the score for longer than was necessary, longer than she expected. To stop him getting away, Malvina moved very slowly closer, until she felt Gaspar's body against hers. Here? she said. Move your hand for me to see.

And trembling she took hold of his hand for the first time. It was cold at first, then warm; soft but firm. The temptation was too strong, her heart thudding pell-mell, she thought she was going to faint. Later, alone in the solitude of her room, she went over that moment a thousand times. To engrave it on her mind to be able to remember and dream of it later. In her dream she went further and prolonged the scene, inventing what did not happen. Afterwards she remembered what she had invented, it was as if it had happened. She did not want ever to forget the smallest moments, gestures and sounds. An ear, a heart in its normal state, would never hear them. She did.

And he was taking longer than he should, than she was entitled to.

Gaspar was not brusque as Malvina expected and feared. Nor did he recoil, he just went a little redder. Then, in an instant, before they could both notice and say passionately, the two of us, eh?, he recuperated and recovered his lost equilibrium and security. From a silent hint in his eyes Malvina understood that she was to let go of his hand and that it must never be repeated. She thought it strange, between mother and son there should not be such concerns and fears, a part of her insisted. That was how Gaspar must visualize her: not as a passionate, ardent woman, but as someone who was in place of his mother. Because she could not see in him anything more than friendship and respect. After all she was his father's wife, Malvina acknowledged, humiliated, with hatred.

A strange man her husband's son, she thought sometimes. When there was nothing strange about him, as she herself admitted. She wavered, going from one extreme to another of her doubts and ruminations.

Despite her suffering, she enjoyed those afternoons enormously. If she did not go further it was for caution: fear that he would realize and escape her for good. Her heart hoped, it always does. For this reason she was cautious, she controlled the future part of her dream, the part that had not yet happened. Those afternoons ought to last for all eternity.

Like the evenings, by the light of the candelabrum, his face bent over the book, as he read her an eclogue, a lyric, an elegy. The nuances of light and shade, of colours and half-tones, extending from old ivory to the newest ivory, the small blue vein throbbing in his forehead, his luminous pallor, everything grew in size in the candle-light. With wide staring eyes she saw and stored everything for always, for afterwards.

She believed they were experiencing the loftiest moments of spirituality and beauty. They were chosen, privileged beings, favoured by the gods. And they were no longer in Vila Rica: she projected herself in space and time, travelling to other places. First Lisbon, then other, more refined and cultured kingdoms. Tuscany, Naples, France, Venice, those dream worlds she knew through his eyes. And she could see herself in an opera house lighted by a thousand chandeliers sparkling with sounds and reflections.

You are playing so well, he said once more. What about our calling the old man to hear our duet? Another rock broke away from the mountain peak, so deep and strong was the beat of Malvina's heart. Without their knowing it, João Diogo was listening in rapture behind the door.

They called his father. Malvina then realized that she could not nurture any hope. If Gaspar had any feeling for her, it was the affection that should exist between a son and his father's wife. Seated comfortably on the sofa, João Diogo was now fast asleep. He must be having pleasant dreams, he was smiling. He was very happy.

Look at the old man fast asleep. Look at him snoring, he said and laughed. Gaspar too was happy. The times of yore had returned, Malvina realized with some sorrow. Only she was unhappy now.

And she began to make use of word-play, of unfinished, ambiguous sentences, of hidden meanings, with their labyrinths and snares. With meticulous care, like someone putting together the delicate mechanism of a clock or working with gunpowder, she calculated her every utterance, the most insigificant words. Through them, beneath them, in their folds and inflexions, she spoke all that was hidden in her heart. It was what she thought, she could never be sure if he received her tender, desperate semaphore. Always cautious, however: he might understand consciously and make off.

One day Malvina asked him point blank why he was opposed to love. Gaspar looked at her for a while. She could not divine if his look was one of surprise, of shyness at find himself suddenly unmasked. If he was annoyed by having such private territory invaded. If it was merely astonishment in the face of so absurd a question.

After a heavy silence he answered by asking who had told her that. No, I am not against love, he said, looking her straight in the eyes. There was nothing in Gaspar's eyes to suggest that he meant to say something just to her. It was an ordinary sentence, an assertion like any other. But the enamoured heart thought: if he is not against, he is likely to become for. Underneath his words there might be a mysterious message, to be deciphered. Yes, perhaps. He was such a reserved, sorrowful man, he had known much grief. A man trained in the art of hiding his sufferings. She forgot that he used to grow pale in the presence of women. Before, she thought. For some time now he had stopped being awkward in her presence. Always at ease, even silence did not weigh heavy now. So calm, sweet and slow-moving were their afternoons now.

I am against, it's true, he started to say and she thought he is going to confide. But Gaspar did not go on. Because he did not know what to say? Because he regretted having started to confide? Assuredly he would prefer to talk of other matters, of vague, airy things, in accord with his temperament.

Is it a promise to the Virgin? she asked. What promise? he said. Not to marry, she said. When your mother died. Is that what they told you? said Gaspar. They discuss my life too much. Because they do not understand me. And she said it was your father that told me. Probably I did say it once, he said. Perhaps to get rid of some girl they were trying to foist upon me. And as she was working up courage to put another dangerous question, he said I probably did make some such promise and then forgot about it. And when she laughed, he went on: but as you see, at bottom I didn't forget, I am fulfilling the promise. I have not married. And he began to finger the first notes of an octave on the flute. No, she said, gently taking the flute from him. Later, now we are going to talk.

Now it was Malvina who talked, Gaspar only listened. Occasionally he smiled with unbelief. And passionately, calmly, dangerously and cautiously, she spoke the tenderest words a heart learns from love. He should love, he could not refuse love. It was against nature, against God's wishes. And realizing that she sometimes came too close to the quicksands, she amended. You should find a girl (she would not say marry, never, she thought), someone of about the same age, who can understand you. Someone with the same tastes as you. Someone to care for you. The companion your heart deserves. In reality she was saying – me.

Even while amending, she was being very daring. But Gaspar gave no sign of understanding, he said playfully and my promise to the Virgin?

And she said, in a very intimate manner, you silly boy, a promise can be annulled. The Church is a mother, not a stepmother, there is a way for everything. So there is, he said, laughing openly for the first time. It is not a stepmother, and from his eyes she could tell that he was teasing her: she was his stepmother.

And there was no end to these conversations. The enthusiastic praises of love became more and more daring and insinuating. But she was always careful and calculating, she did not wish to take too many risks. One piece of carelessness could ruin everything. She never went beyond the limit permitted by her fear of losing him. And she went on trying if even without words, saying without talking, without speaking through her eyes, from her soul to his, via the invisible paths of love, she could convince him of the secret which she kept intimately and in silence.

He did not understand, he was blind and deaf. Maybe he is pretending and playing the game, said her private demon, inciting her to break that ice, to move that cold unfeeling soul, that hard passive heart.

7

When she advised her husband to make the journey to the São Francisco backlands, Malvina did not have a very clear idea of what would or could happen. Later, when she tried to remember, she was unable to discover the exact moment when the first seed surfaced of the plot which began to grow inside her until it suffocated her and she no longer knew what to do. Unable to halt the headlong machination, to stop herself.

Sometimes she thought that it had all stemmed from her desire to be as long as possible with Gaspar. She was no longer satisfied with those warm tranquil afternoons, the two of them alone together, so splendid; she wanted the evenings as well. In the evening her husband was in the drawing-room, snoozing. João Diogo even snored, his mouth open, at times he drooled. Those snores, that spittle, that body sprawled on the couch spoiled the moments of what she believed to be the loftiest spirituality. They disturbed the wonderful world of poetry and music, the delightful intimacy of two kindred souls. Her ardent imagination soaked and inflated everything.

It was very easy to believe that her desire was honest and pure. So far these things were only taking place inside her. She was never sure that Gaspar suspected the meaning of her subtle, silent messages and semaphore signals. She herself suspected that the root of it all must be deeper. She kept digging deeper, to see if she could find it. What if it had been that first look? A thought that was as imperceptible and stealthy as the exact moment of conception.

All of a sudden she began to talk to João Diogo about his business affairs. She wanted to know how things were with the cattle and the pastures in the backlands. He did not suspect that she wanted him far away. Even Inacia, who was always inquisitive and alert, did not suspect anything. She concealed things so well, she was on the razor's edge.

You are getting very interested in my farms and my cattle, he said laughing. Everything Malvina said he found amusing. She was a plaything, an excellent entertainment, to cheer him up. To tell the truth, I am very concerned about your property, she said. And he, opening his eyes wide, asked her why. It's not just fancy, she said, you shall see.

She had reasons for her fears. João Diogo, who with old age became alarmed more easily, asked her to speak straight out, he did not like riddles. In fact he believed in women's instinct for some things, their premonitory eye for disasters and ruins. He started with surprise, frowned and grunted. Something was not right.

Malvina knew João Diogo better than anyone, she knew how to deal with him. Now she could speak, she would be heard with attention. She told him of her concerns. He needed to give more care to his lands and his cattle in the backlands. Was he not aware that the gold was drying up, that the streams no longer yielded what they used to, that everyone was getting poor? That the era of Minas was at an end? And she mentioned cases with which he was familiar.

João Diogo was pop-eyed with amazement. Where had his wife been and found so much savvy? He had grown used to seeing Malvina merely in terms of beauty and love, he would never have imagined that she took notice of what was happening. Your salvation is in the cattle and the land, she said. Forget the gold and the shiny stones, which were my father's perdition and will be the perdition of Minas. With his fine nose for these things, he already knew, but he had just not given the matter more attention, other people's troubles were best forgotten. When he saw that the gold was starting to dry up, he set about increasing his domains out towards the São Francisco, now he had the best cattle of any of them. Secure in his wealth, he did not bother to keep an eye on the others. But Malvina's words alarmed him, stirred him deep down. Salvation, my love? Where did you get that idea? he asked, trying to find out just how much she knew. I am very well off, I don't know what to do with so much wealth.

His heart was now always apprehensive and once he had been reminded he was alarmed by the words salvation, perdition of Minas, he saw she was right. And he suddenly remembered that everybody was falling into debt, selling and hiding things, not like it used to be, now everybody was in arrears with the King. The fear of the tax levy terrified them and kept them awake at night. A disaster in his cattle lands could bring ruin on his possessions accumulated with sweated toil. So he told Malvina afterwards, when he yielded.

Now, however, he did not want to give the impression of being altogether convinced. But, my love, who told you all this? Someone at the palace? The Captain-General? I know, she said, self-assured, and noticed that the Captain-General's name acquired a different intonation. João Diogo was so suspicious and jealous of the attentions, the looks and speeches with which the Captain-General had started to besiege her, and which she, freely and conceitedly, permitted. Once João Diogo actually revealed his suspicion, but seeing the astonishment and innocence in her eyes, he merely looked stern and told her be careful, my love, don't give the Captain-General any encouragement, he likes to get off with married ladies.

I know because I know, she said once again. It has nothing to do with the Captain-General. I have been hearing a good deal of cross-talk, of lamentations and fear in the air. Just like before, I was just a girl but I recall what happened to my father. And note that at that time there was plenty of gold. Why don't you talk to Gaspar? Has Gaspar said anything about it to you? he asked and she replied he mentioned it, you know how he is. He is like you, he thinks I shouldn't know about these things. But he should have told me, said João Diogo angrily.

Malvina had already talked to Gaspar about their property in the cattle country. He told her it was rather abandoned, but the backlands are like that, who could look after it all? Malvina tearfully told him the story of her father's bankruptcy. No one imagined that could happen to them and it did. She succeeded in convincing Gaspar of the danger they were courting. Now she was doing the same to her husband.

I shall have a serious talk to him, said João Diogo. To which she replied take care, my love, you don't want to spoil all the work we have had to get Gaspar to stay here. He might go away again and never come back!

João Diogo saw that she was right once again. He would need to talk very carefully to his son. He would see. That's right, my love, very carefully, she said, and to tempt him further asked why he did not send Gaspar. Her heart was thumping wildly, he might accept the advice. I'm afraid of you all alone in those woods, she said. He was not a youngster any more to be doing these things, something might happen to him, she said, feeling a deeper thud. For the first time the idea came into her mind, clearly, that there was a possibility of João Diogo dying. She quickly pushed the idea away. Very green, it needed to mature. Only much later did she allow herself to think openly about it, without horror or fear.

Why don't you take Gaspar with you? she said, certain of a refusal. It would actually be a way of starting to hand over to him the control of what would one day be his.

João Diogo would never accept. First, so as not to show weakness, secondly, not to leave her all alone – now that the alarming shadow of the Captain-General had fallen over his life.

Come, wife, I'm still man enough to look after my own! I don't need a son for such things. As long as I live I shall be the one to see to my affairs. I am still man enough to face any backlands, me and my niggers and half-breeds, he said sharply, and she realized she had won. He would not fight with his son, Gaspar was in no danger of going; there was no way the two of them would go together.

Some weeks later João Diogo left.

During the time João Diogo was away, Malvina lived her happiest moments. She did not apparently advance any further than she had already – she was happy in a different fashion. A tense happiness, at times it was painful, the pleasure she experienced was so deep. Only those who have experienced the subtleties of secret feelings and emotions, the perils of sinful passions, could understand what she was experiencing. So thought Malvina, increasingly desperate. As well as her nobility of birth she created for herself an aristocracy of suffering hearts.

She was happy and knew pain. Exaggerating, she went so far as to compare herself to a nigger, to a dog. She suffered so much. But she preferred suffering to ceasing to be happy. Though she suffered, she thought she was happy. For this reason she did not advance beyond the point she had already reached. She was even more cautious than before. In her emotions, however, she plumbed ever greater depths.

It was Gaspar who talked more now. Malvina lowered her eyes when he looked at her. She was afraid to stare at him, her heart might betray her. She opened wide her ears and listened. The pleasure was so deep she frequently ceased to pay attention to what he was saying and simply enjoyed the music of his voice. She opened completely and soaked up that voice, those gestures, that presence, those black eyes. Dry, greedy soil, though shady. Even without looking she could feel Gaspar's eyes rest upon her. Malvina felt them as a soft, sensual caress. She felt herself loved, let herself be loved in secret. She imagined his eyes were not only melancholy and dreamy: passionate and burning. She stretched out her face, her neck, her bosom, towards him. So close at times, she could even feel the warmth of his breath. Her breasts heaved and burned when she proffered them: for his eyes to rest lightly on them. Like the gentle, warm, moist pressure of a pair of lips. Too close, dangerously close. Cautious though she was, she was getting closer to danger.

During those moments of ecstasy she would close her eyes. In simple grievous agony, with parted lips, she waited hopefully. She had no right to hope, but she did. She did not know just what she hoped for, she simply hoped. She did not know that happiness and love hurt so much. She was reduced to a little ball of fur and shudders, of pain. Tiny and tensely contained, a single nucleus on which sensations all converged. Deeper and deeper by the day. Afterwards she enjoyed them bit by bit as she reviewed them in silent recollection. Recollection not just of the past but of the future too. So far had she advanced to what would and could happen. Into her absurd, fanciful recollection of the future she worked fine precious threads. Her nervous hands, like agile, calculating spiders, wove the filmiest and sheerest of close-fitting fabrics. She curled up inside them in her attempt to overcome the solitude of her cold, empty bed.

Reviewing the secretly accumulated emotions became fused with the absurd recollection of the future. Past and future were a single recollection, food for the present. She could no longer distinguish what she had experienced from what she had dreamed.

And she rolled about in the darkness of the empty bedroom, soaked in sweat and anguish. Her whole body hurt, a bundle of nerves and pain. The night hours passed, the monster grew frighteningly in the mists of the darkness. She believed she was possessed by a thousand demons. Her mother's curse weighed upon her.

Suddenly, black with dirt, hair unkempt, she would be running howling in the fields, her hair and her mane licked by the cold night wind. The night grew smaller, she was on the hacienda on those blue afternoons. She was no longer Malvina, but a monstrous, androginous creature galloping the fields and heathland of the late afternoon. It was Donguinho alive again who was coming, lovingly, to become fused with her. He was affectionately inviting her into the endless darkness, into his eternal, madman's night.

Only when the fantasy woven by the spiders in the darkness approached the red and black jaws of the monstrosities did the very anguish of her dream awake her. Bathed in sweat, paralysed by blank terror, she realized it had been a nightmare, that it was not the cold lucidity of her feverish, sleepless imagination. Her heart beat wildly, more out of control than when she dangerously opened herself in offering to Gaspar's eyes.

She lit the candle and stripped in order to dry herself. Naked, by the flickering light of the candle, her skin was livid, bluish, she was covered all over with painful weals. She rubbed her body vigorously to try and remove the slime of the nightmare.

After a time, still quivering, but almost recovered, when she saw she was completely awake, she went to the window to breathe the cold night air. She snuffed out the candle, afraid of being seen by one of the overseers in the slave-quarters, the niggers were locked in already. She thought of calling Inacia, but she was afraid. The sky was deep and starry, the stars cold and hard, distant, out of reach. The sticky mist had passed, she was returning to the cold lucidity of a world which really existed.

Feeling all right again, she put on a fresh night-dress. The cold, starched, fragrant softness of the cloth – the same good feeling of the starry night. The world really existed: it was hard, cold and good.

She was tempted by daytime fantasies, less dangerous than the leaden mists of her nightmares. She went out into the corridor. Dousing the candle, she went barefoot. If surprised by anyone she might give the impression of a sleepwalker. One should not waken sleepwalkers, they do not remember afterwards.

And barefoot on the hard, dry floor, she glided along, groping in the dark. Until her toes found the cold limewashed wall. Then the first door, the second. Finally Gaspar's door. Her fingers stroked the thick boards which separated her from him: from his sleep, from his cold darkness. She stroked the door in a caress, her fingers trying to reach him from a distance, touch his white, silky skin, his rough black beard. And she tried to hear his nocturnal breathing through the door, his calm, sound sleep. Such was her desire (her face against the door, her ear touching the wood) that she thought she could hear. Large tears fell from her eyes, running down her face. She swallowed back her sobs, not a moan or a sigh. She was so submerged in her amorous despair, she probably did not herself realize she was crying.

Everything was going on right down inside her. She never dared try the lock, to see if he left his door unlocked. It was just fantasy and recollection of the future, afterwards. As if it had all really happened.

As if she was being followed, she came running back to her room. She collapsed on to the bed. Her eyes big with fear and darkness, she started thinking. She had to put a stop to it, find a way out of her desperate solitude.

In the darkness of her empty room, a seed in the moist darkness of the earth, there began to grow and take shape the desire that João Diogo might, should die. That was why she had sent him off to those distant backlands. It was not for her to confess her impossible love. Even in her delirium, she was sure that Gaspar would not allow her so much as to speak the first word of her love.

She was now thinking without evasions or equivocations of João Diogo's death. She really wanted it with all her heart. If she did not ask her heavenly godmother it was for fear that the saint would punish her when she heard from her lips what she had already seen in her heart. She was quite conscious of the sin which she neither wanted nor could any longer flee.

The death of her husband would remove the parental tie. It would no longer be a sin, she thought. Gaspar would not reject her, he would accept her love. She had confidence in her own arts and charms, in her secret cunning, in her hidden power of persuasion. Used to being on the precipice of fantasy, she believed she saw the Church giving its blessing to the new couple. Briefs of annulment were easy to get. . . .

She dreamed that João Diogo died pierced by an arrow or a bullet. She saw him dying slowly, he had been so unwell recently. But dreams like these, in which everything happened without her moving a straw, soon came to an end. Much sooner than she expected, João Diogo returned.

8

João Diogo returned, everything turned out altogether different from the way she had imagined.

The first few days she was still hopeful. He had come back jaded and exhausted, showing signs of being ill. Almost as tired and weary as his son when he returned from his voluntary exile. Less, certainly. Despite his age, João Diogo did not have his son's delicate, sickly nature. Hardened by life in the outback, the air and sun, he had reserves, hidden strength, which Malvina could not begin to suspect. A man from another era, so they said.

In a short while he was well again, on his feet again. But he was no longer the same man as before, one could see that. Though they had not finished him, the cattle country, the miles and miles, and the life to which he was no longer accustomed, had shaken him a good deal. But it was not a fatal malady, it was the sort that can last a lifetime. Just a complaint of old age, she realized to her despair. Aches and tantrums, grumbles and gripes. Listless, turning up his nose at everything. She would have to put up with all that for ever.

Even his feeling faint or pressing his hands to his chest, to indicate excruciating pain, which she initially found so encouraging, became quite meaningless as danger signals, being quite banal; she no longer attached any importance to such things. When he complained, she shrugged her shoulders and sighed with annoyance. It's just smelly wind, she told herself prosaically, discouraged.

Even João Diogo's fire and sexual demands, formerly weekly, started to get less frequent. Without his asking, she would rid herself of her clothes, springing stark naked out of her last pieces of linen. White and gleaming, smooth and sinuous, she would slip under the bedclothes and snuggle like a purring cat into his flaccid, unresponsive flesh. Not that she wanted it or was burning with desire, it was more a matter of tempting him. He might lose his senses for once and all, for ever. No, dear, I'm feeling very poorly today, he would say. With hatred and resentment, she would eventually give up. He was a living corpse, a dead weight. He would not die. And she hated herself for what she had done: she had sent a still vigorous old man off to the backlands and in return received a useless old ruin.

Her anguish and despair grew by the day. Suffocated, seeing no way out, she was even more afraid of not controlling herself, of ruining everything. To make matters worse, Gaspar's behaviour was much colder and more distant, although he did not leave the house and they were together every afternoon and evening.

And those moments which were formerly so good turned into a lengthy, silent, endless torment. She could not even scream.

There was nothing she could do, she repeated over and over again. What was happening to him? she began to wonder. Languid, cold, indifferent. Maybe after all what they said about him was true. It was not normal, that indifference to women, particularly to her. A sin against nature. But she ended by saying no, he was not a pansy, he was worse – cold and neutral.

If she began by believing that his refusal was a promise to the Virgin, after their companionship and their long conversations, she could see it was not true. She had never seen him go to church, let alone pray. In religious matters, if he was not against (as João Diogo once remarked to her unhappily), he was as cold and indifferent as in love. God could punish him, a part of her threatened. For his indifference in matters not of faith, but of love.

If it was not a promise, if he was not a pansy, what was it then? Purity and chastity, an eternally unblemished soul? She was ironic and resentful. Hurt in her female dignity, she realized that her beauty, her arts and charms were to no avail with Gaspar. She would destroy and corrupt him! she then muttered. Corrupt that beauty and that chastity which were so an insult to her vanity and pride. Her hatred grew, destroy him, perhaps, Donguinho.

Because she began to want him desperately. In any manner, wholly and immediately. Without veils, masks and subterfuges. She was no longer satisfied with the arts and nuances, the subtle, innocent, solitary pleasure of fusing her recollection of the past with her recollection of the future. She wanted the present, now, immediately. She could not bear to wait any longer. Even if she had to kill or to die.

And she began to believe that the resuscitated Donguinho, the enraged, insatiable Donguinho, had returned to take over her soul, her woman's body. Not just in dreams, he was the same Donguinho in the daytime. More terrible and threatening than when she was asleep. And this Donguinho with sharp, reddish eyes, burning, leering, avid eyes, meant to soil all purity and chastity, to possess him. It was an androginous creature, a fabulous monster. She eventually ceased to see herself as a woman, a human being: an untamed stallion, a snorting beast, she wanted to impregnate and destroy. In her despair, she was afraid of slipping for ever into the insanity that plunged Donguinho into the mists and darkness.

She realized she could not go on like that. She needed to confide, to seek someone's help, confess herself. No one can live like that so alone and in such torment. Silence stifles and destroys, silence is the desert, the hell of love. So she seemed to think and say. She had overstretched her silence, her suffering, her love.

It was then she remembered Inacia, forgotten all this time, Inacia, her salvation.

She closeted herself with the Negress and, before she spoke, begged a thousand times absolute silence, it was a mortal secret. She gave her a gold chain, a medallion the size of a doubloon, gold ear-rings, all the best carat. Goodness, missy, you don't have to, said the Negress, putting away the jewels. She promised her her freedom, appealed to her devotion, to her friendship. In tears, she embraced and kissed the Negress. Inacia stroked her head and dried her tears, as if she were a child. She rested her head on Inacia's warm, ample bosom and from her very depths gave vent to the most heartfelt sighs and moans. All that impetuous, poisonous torrent, concealed and stifled for so long, burst its banks. Malvina had found the tender bosom, the shelter and protection she had always lacked.

There then, missy, said Inacia. Calm yourself first, before you talk, you shouldn't talk like that. If after you've done crying, you don't want to say any more, don't. If the crying is enough, you don't have to say anything. I shall understand your silence, my young madam. But, if you do talk, don't be afraid, open your heart. I promise before God, before Our Lady of the Rosary of Black People, that I will forget. If I can't help. You never know I may be able to help, darling missy.

Inacia, I am in love, she said, after she wept all her tears. And more than her tears, it was just saying it that relieved her tense soul, relaxed her body and her heart. The feeling of relief, like squeezing a boil, was so good and great! Now at last she was herself again: the cloud lifted and she could breathe again. All just madness and fantasy, the dark night was over. The sun burst into the bedrooms and corridors, she was once more the child of light. Donguinho left quickly and melted away for ever into the peace of his everlasting blue sky.

And all she could say was I am in love, Inacia, I am madly in love! She told her she had been on fire and consuming herself for a long time, there were times when she thought she would go mad. She was no longer her own mistress, she was so much in love and suffered so much. She had never been in love before, she did not know what love was. But it was an impossible love, Inacia. What could they do?

Her eyes open wide, Inacia was in her element. She spoke. She had known for a long time that missy was in love and was no longer her own mistress. Could she not see, did she not have eyes and heart to see? But she had never plucked up courage to leave her corner, she knew her place. When called, she came; she didn't call her, she stayed put. She was waiting for when missy herself would feel the need to speak out. Now she had said she was in love, she only needed to say was the lucky man who deserved so much love? You don't know, Inacia? You never suspected, never wondered? She looked the Negress straight in her brown eyes. No, Inacia did not know. Malvina had been stronger, cleverer, more skilful at concealing her feelings that she thought herself capable. Neither Inacia, nor João Diogo, not even Gaspar himself, knew of her delirious love. She still had time to draw back, to change her mind. She was relieved, the boil was squeezed, she could even say nothing.

Although she said the opposite, Inacia was burning with curiosity. She so wanted to help! Missy could count on her, for her she was capable of the most awful things. Missy was so good, Inacia so devoted. Before she knew missy, she was a nobody, a nigger with nobody on her side. Is it anyone I know? she asked. At the palace? She had once been by the door and heard the master making a jealous scene. The Captain-General? she suggested.

If only it were, Inacia! God grant it were the Captain-General! And she nearly smiled at Inacia's ingenuousness, satisfied with herself, with her arts of concealment. With the Captain-General there would be no danger, she need only say the word. The Captain-General was infatuated with her, he had actually declared his love to her. If she wanted, she need only crook her finger, he would come and lick her feet like a puppy dog. Like that she would have not the slightest fear of João Diogo: if he found out, there was nothing he could do. After all, the Captain-General was the Captain-General.

Who is this fortunate wretch? said Inacia, unable to contain herself. I don't know if I should, if I have the courage to say, said Malvina. Might it not be better if I say nothing? She knew she was sly, she was trying to get Inacia to commit herself still further. And what is worse, while I won't say he despises me, most probably does not even know I am madly in love with him. Haven't you told him, missy? No. Haven't you even let him suspect? No, I couldn't. When we're in love, even without wanting to, we show it. No, so far I am my own mistress, that has not happened. I can't, it would be madness to let him find out. But who is this mystery man then? Missy, why can't you, maybe not tell him, but at least show him? I don't think I should tell you, it is a great sin for me, Inacia. Tell me, missy, you can tell me.

I shall not say his name, I do not have the courage, you shall say it. Me? said Inacia. Yes, you. He is not from the palace, you know him very well, You know him all too well, you are always seeing him.

And Inacia's eyes began to open, round and wide, shining with amazement. She had guessed, she knew whose name missy was going to speak. You see him all the time, you saw him just now, said Malvina. No, missy! said the Negress in horror. Master Gaspar! Forgive me for telling you, said Malvina, hugging her. I just had to tell somebody. You promised to say nothing. If you can't help me, just keep quiet, I know what I am going to do.

And seeing the desperate look in Malvina's eyes (it could be an indication that she was going to kill herself), she said forgive me, missy, I just never would have guessed. Even though I am a bit forward sometimes, I know there are some things we can't do. Don't say anything yet, let me finish. We need to keep a hand on things, not let them happen. Put a break on runaway thoughts, if we just think, we can do anything.

Malvina was crying again. I shouldn't have told you, you'll not forgive me, not even you, you'll never forgive me, she said. That's not it, missy, it was just I expected anybody except Massa Gaspar. White man taught me we have to keep an eye on sin, there are some sins we cannot do. Let's see if we can do something to make missy forget.

Forget? said Malvina, almost screaming. But I don't want to forget!

The Negress could not be her ruin, nor was she going to ruin herself. For now, she said. While we see what can be done.

And by turns retreating and manoeuvring, advancing and defending, they began to examine what they could do together.

Very little, the best was to wait. Not do anything yet. Wait, is that not what hunters do? Is he not fond of hunting? They had to set the trap and wait. With the gun always primed though. When the game was off its guard, fire! At least go on the same as up to now. Not let Gaspar see, nor João Diogo suspect. If she had endured it all alone until now, with the two of them it would be easier. It was a question of time. Maybe before long God would decide to summon João Diogo. No, Malvina had thought of that, God would not summon him so soon. Maybe, the two of them started, neither of them having the courage to say what Malvina had often thought and Inacia was just thinking for the first time. In the council of the gods he was condemned. João Diogo must die.

Do you want my advice, missy? asked Inacia. Do you want the opinion of a nigger woman who has sinned more than enough? I know men, missy. Niggers, you will say. But inside black and white are the same mouldy bread. And, forgive me mentioning it, but I've slept with plenty of whites, plenty took a fancy to me. I'm not only used to slave-quarters and hovels, I've been in many white men's and gentlemen's bedrooms.

And seeing there was no outrage at talk which she herself considered wanton, she relished the promiscuity and began to give her idea. Missy was young, there was no one as beautiful and desired as she was. It would be easy for her to seduce some other man. No, not a Captain-General. But what if I am not able to love any other man? said Malvina. You will, missy, we always can. Afterwards we sometimes find we love more, much better.

Malvina should find another man altogether different, in every way, from Gaspar. A strong, fearless man with a ready courage. A man without tremors and purity, a women's man. A man who could sweep her off her feet and subdue her. A man who would awaken ambition and jealousy in Gaspar's cold, sleeping heart. A man who would do anything for her, she would not need to do a thing. A man just like her inside, of her ilk. A rough, determined man, everything Gaspar could never be. In sum, a man ready to kill and to die.

The final touch of paint Inacia added to the man's portrait was not the same as Malvina saw. What she said was not the same as Malvina's tormented heart conjectured. Another seed fell on the ready soil, she saw at once, she did not need time to discover. And within her the seed was already swelling and growing, within her the tree bloomed.

9

The idea of riding to Vila do Carmo was another of Malvina's whims. At least so it seemed to João Diogo Galvão, who was accustomed to satisfying her smallest desire. This time, however, he resisted a while before giving in. But, my love, he said, my health isn't good enough for me to go with you. After that long journey you dreamed up for me. I'm not complaining, I mention it merely to show that I deny you nothing. But this time think again. After that long journey I scarcely have strength for anything. Let me get better and then we shall go. She said no, pouting her lips and rolling up her eyes in vexation. You have nothing to do out there, said João Diogo. She continued with her no and her pouting, she knew her husband. He insisted in his arguments. And then, in any case, you won't stand up to it, he went on. Why not? she asked. Have you forgotten I lived on a ranch and used to ride my father's horses? It isn't that, Malvina, it's because you are not used to it any more, you haven't ridden for a long time.... It's a good many miles for someone who doesn't ride regularly. Even if you only go as far as Santo Antonio da Passagem, which is quite close, that would already be too much for you, you would come back exhausted. No I would not, she said firmly. When João Diogo started with explanations, the battle was half won. But I am tired and knocked out, I can't go with you, he said, falling back on his state of health. Then I shall go alone, she said wilfully.

João Diogo only looked at Malvina, he said nothing, did not even grunt. In other times he was different, he would not admit disrespect, his will was absolute. Even for someone as adorable and delectable as his darling wife. These days he was so changed he did not seem the same: she had tamed him excessively. The solution was to agree, otherwise he would have to put up with a sour face for days on end. Which eventually made him sore: she was an innocent, purring little creature and he could not bear to see her suffer. Even though the suffering was for something insignificant. It might spoil her charm and beauty, which were now his only joy in life.

Not alone, the very idea! Only if Gaspar goes with you, he said, finally giving in. Actually, he still believed that his son, because of his promise, would not like to be seen out of doors with his wife. Though she was his stepmother and he greatly respected her. She who had been a blessing from heaven, bringing Gaspar back to the bosom of the family.

But this was exactly what Malvina wanted. While he was half-way there, she was already half-way back. She had already spoken to Gaspar, who had disagreed. Are you afraid of going about with me in the town? she asked, provoking him. People will not say anything, after all I am your stepmother. With irony, not knowing whether or not he had understood what she meant. For the first time in many months Gaspar appeared to blush and she felt very happy. At least he was reacting, which was a good sign. That's not it, he said, it is just that I do not want, do not like to go about the town, to see these people, and she said they would not see anybody, they would go through the woods, was he not very fond of woods and animals? He could even show her all those things he was so proud of. But you will not stand up to it, said Gaspar, presaging his father's words. She did not pout, it did not work with that one, she said that if she could not stand it they would come back from Passagem.

When his father spoke to him, Gaspar had no choice but give in. A few days later he had his roan saddled and a very docile, well-mannered horse for her. Although Malvina had said she was an experienced horsewoman, in previous times. He laughed, he was not very convinced.

Malvina dressed for the event. She was so elegant and pretty in her blue jacket, with a black silk hat perched high on her head. Resplendent and beautiful, lace and embroidered silks on her blouse and cuffs, twirling a chased silver riding-crop which slapped against the folds of her riding-habit. He went so far as to ask her jestingly if she was going to some party. Yes, she said, greatly daring. Once she had made up her mind she kept moving forward, although Inacia had urged caution. We are going to waltz together all night, without changing partners, and she saw that he blushed more than the first time. She was almost happy again.

By this time the two of them were riding slowly towards Passagem, chatting. He was describing what the woods and brush thereabouts were like when the first *paulistas* came up against the Tripuí River.

It was just then that a horseman came towards them from the other direction. At first she did not pay much attention. Instinctively she slowed her pace, the man's mount might be a mare and could excite her Arab. She did not have as much confidence in her wrist and her reins as she tried to show.

The man reined his horse in abruptly and sat staring at her. Very slowly and boldly, his eyes alight and sparkling, in amazement at the apparition. She felt his eyes touch her, so virile was the mestizo. And fearless, for he took not the slightest notice of Gaspar. In a way it was an affront. Now she wanted men who were impertinent, such was the image she and Inacia had carved and incarnated. That mestizo scored a direct hit. In her memory of the future she saw herself hooking him. And the man looked more and more like the picture the two of them had concocted. That was the virile sort of man she needed.

And less in response to the insistent, almost brazen look that was irresistibly fastened on her, than out of provocation, she returned him a strong, full, sultry, unflinching look. She felt victorious again after so long. The stranger lowered his eyes.

Who is it? she asked, and Gaspar replied sharply that it was just some half-breed. Come on, he said. He was in a hurry to go, she noticed. As she also noticed, she was sure, that the half-breed was following them. Her, that is! She could feel his eyes burning the back of her neck. She was afraid, something might happen. Not now, it must not, she did not want it. The half-breed cut through the wood and was waiting in a thicket farther ahead. Gaspar probably did not see, but she did. Just to look at her, she felt flattered. She stopped again. She was displaying herself brazenly, she wanted to be seen.

She laughed without reason, gave a shout, applied the whip to her horse. Off at a wild gallop, mad, completely thunderstruck, happy. The wild gallop, Gaspar trying to catch up with her. She letting herself fall off dangerously. And that marvellous thing, a forward vision of everything she wanted, happening. Slightly dazed, she took advantage to pretend she was fainting. He came, sprang from his horse before it came to a halt. He supported her, held her against him, very close together. Anything might happen. In reality nothing happened, just wishful thinking.

And the half-breed no longer gave her a moment's peace, she was happy to notice. Where she went, the half-breed would be there watching her. He was daring, was not ashamed of staring at her in front of everybody. Just like the first time. An insultingly virile look, he knew his strength. A look that whetted the exacerbated, hot female part of her. More! her eyes pleaded, provoking him. She lured him on, backing away when he advanced too far. A fearless, restless man; if she gave him the chance, he was capable of accosting her in the street in front of everybody, even in front of João Diogo. Though aware of the danger, she now smiled at him; the most open, joyful and shining eyes she could make. More! said her swiftly beating heart.

When she went out in her chair, she offered herself to him in looks and smiles, protractedly. He prowled around the mansion. Every time she went to the window, she would see him lounging against the house opposite, always presumptuous. She asked who he was. Inacia had already noticed, she said he was Januario, the half-Indian son of Tomás Matias Cardoso. That's our man, she said, confiding completely in Inacia. But it didn't have to be a half-breed, a bastard, said Inacia, nigger though she was. He probably won't do for what we want. Massa Gaspar won't take no notice, he might even be disgusted. He's the one, said Malvina, by now imagining another plan, quite different from the one she had worked out with her maid. It had to be him, only he would have the courage. No other before him.

So that Januario should be in no further doubt, she once made a point of returning his compliment. She was ready for him, was what she meant. Another time, she was at the balcony, he, on horseback, tossed her a flower. She caught the flower and put it in her bosom. But the silent language of flowers was not enough and he threw her his first note with a stone. She replied by means of Inacia. Inacia was trying to protect her, they were risking too much.

From then on it was all a logical, natural sequence of events. Their first meeting. Experienced and cunning, Inacia brought him one night to the back room, the keys to which she now kept. She was a watchdog.

The first time Malvina was still afraid. Quivering and restrained, unable to control her racing heart, she surrendered herself to those strong burning arms which crushed her. The reckless womanizer's frenzy took her quite by surprise, after being used to João Diogo's limp, lukewarm embraces.

Then a second and a third time, she ceased to worry herself and she abandoned herself completely. Relying on Inacia's cleverness, on her watchful, doglike eyes. Gold could not pay her.

And now, when João Diogo was fast asleep and the light went out under Gaspar's door, Inacia would go and fetch Januario at the gate in the Rua das Flores. Every night that frenzied, agonizing abandon. The intrepid half-breed pitted himself against her she-cat's cunning: her feline tension – outwardly tame, inwardly wild. Her shuddering spasms all arched like a cat, with the howls of a she-cat.

And she then went beyond limits, she overcame the last barriers. She was all body and controlled frenzy. And the two of them, she in particular, rolled in ecstasy and delirium.

Not that Malvina had forgotten Gaspar. By some diabolical cunning, her spirit moulded itself to everything. She did everything to preserve that refined part of her soul that Januario would never satisfy. And just as previously she saw the shadow of Gaspar in the eyes of João Diogo, she only attained the rhythm which her heart and her body demanded when she saw: Januario was outwardly what Gaspar was inside. Those wild eyes did not deceive.

And she fused the two in one figure: Januario and Gaspar complemented one another, they were one person. And her recollection of the past and her recollection of the future, all of her recollection, came together in the present that was that body. In it they materialized. When she abandoned herself to Januario, she no longer knew which of the two possessed her. In reality it was she who possessed them both at the same time, at the same time impregnating and bearing them.

But this perilous, happy fusion did not last long. It could not, her soul desired calm idyllic pastures, crystal streams and groves of trees, purity, chastity. Music and poetry, the gentle breeze of the blue-tinged late afternoon. Januario (that body) could give her none of that. Gaspar was not merely the wild eyes: he was a divine being for whom her soul yearned and adorned itself. For whom she lost her soul.

And she came back to the plan of which Inacia only knew a part. Once the first steps were taken and everything arranged, she went into action. It was a matter of days. Though wild and fearless, Januario was a midget compared to her. She would do with him exactly as she wanted. More easily than with poor João Diogo. Child's play compared with Gaspar's elusive soul.

But she did not know everything. Her recollection of the future could not foresee and record everything. So, that still distant night, when they stole along the corridor, she ahead of Januario, towards João Diogo's bedroom. She recalled her husband's habitual seizures and fainting fits, the pistol by the bedside, the dagger hidden in the folds of her dress, the other pistol which she was carrying under her jacket. Trembling with the effort she was making to control herself, her hand shielded the candle's wavering flame. She only knew to a certain extent what was going to happen.

ACT THREE

The Destiny of the Past

1

His father's coffin, the four crackling candlesticks. The body covered from head to foot with a purple damask cloth. Even so it was possible to see the damp patches. The colour did not show, being absorbed by the embroidered material and the variations of hue. Then they saw some patches of blood or liquid start to ooze through his waistcoat. The blows had been many, the patches were small at first, just here and there, tiny rosebuds which began to join together until they were transformed into horrible patches of dark, bruised blood, the purple blood of boils. That was why they chose the purple damask. Even on his green velvet tailcoat a large stain appeared, looking like another decoration. Next to the Order of Christ with which they decided to adorn his sunken chest, giving it that solemn splendour for which the deceased had recently shown such a liking, when he attended festivities and processions.

On the tailcoat it was still possible to disguise the stain by changing the position of the insignia of the Order of Christ; on the waistcoat, no. They only brought the damask table-cloth when the body was already in the drawing-room and the stains became too glaring. A glossy, light-green satin waistcoat embroidered with branches and flowers. The waistcoat he liked best when he walked in the Corpus Christi procession. So said the new slave barber. The old man bought him for a good price, that slave. When he began to groom himself, changing his appearance, he wanted to be a dandy. That hard, rough man becoming a dandy, a fop at his age. What would happen next? Yet it happened. Poor Father, letting things get to that point. Lately he had gone soft in the head, so folk said. At times he thought so too, the occasional puerility. He was not, not then. His real decline only began after he returned from that distant journey. She thought that up, he did not know why, she always had plenty of reasons. He himself had been convinced. Because until then his father was still in good condition for his age, he still made a show of vigour. He was going to remarry. What did his son think? he asked. That painful conversation seemed more distant in time that it really was. Because of everything that had happened. Suddenly things began to happen so quickly, in no time at all they belonged to the past beyond the hills, dead times. Even things from a month ago had the colours, sounds and mustiness of old things. It was so difficult to remember, to unearth the very beginning of it all. Now he remembered that painful conversation. The bragging, the claims of virility, the feats, the professed sexual prowess. None of them has ever complained so far, said his father. A slaver of satisfaction on his slack, wrinkled mouth. The hired mulatto women, the famous young virgins he was so fond of. Old satyr, he said now, remembering, trying to go back to being that Gaspar of old. He was no longer the same, so much had happened so quickly. Suddenly he began to feel ashamed of the poor figure he had cut with his father, his violent reaction to the bragging, to what his father liked to call his sexual prowess. Because of my great love and devotion for my late revered mother. What does your late revered mother have to do with this? said his father. At the time he did not feel ashamed, but so much had happened. The old man's self-proclaimed sexual prowess, when he was still capable. All over, the candleholders, the coffin, the purple damask.

It was the Negro barber, all bowing and scraping and rolling eyes, sighs and feigned tears, who washed and arranged the body. Why did you not dress him in his councillor's black tailcoat and waistcoat? he asked, and the Negro said it would not be suitable, the old man would not want it, he hated black clothes, lately he wanted to have only bright colours. He once told me, the Negro was going to continue. He did not go on, he saw the displeasure in his face. Then he wanted to tell him about the body, how many knife wounds. He stopped him. What an unpleasant black his father had got himself! He had had enough with the previous night's dose, that he had been obliged to see. When he was woken by shouts of thief, thief. Malvina was shouting like a mad thing, in an exaggerated manner that was unlike her. She was unable to speak, she was shaking and choking. Afterwards she fainted in Inacia's arms. He did think of making a move to support her, but lacked the courage. He did not want to know how many knife wounds, it pained and sickened him. The nigger's shiny mouth, his grimaces, obsequiousness. He did not let the Negro speak. He did not want to see the naked body, all nakedness horrified him. All the more dead nakedness, he thought with disgust. They told him he ought to, it was a sort of ceremony, he ought to witness it. Not me! he said in horror. He imagined the naked whiteness, the hairs and the groin, the slack genitals. His father's body pierced by goodness knows how many dagger blows. Brutal! It was brutal! the men were saying, the room was full. Must have been a redskin, they're not **human beings. Redskin? How did they know? It was the nigger woman** who saw it and told, someone said. He did not ask. Yes, the nigger woman, the maid. He did not like Inacia. It would be her. Always listening at doors, eyes alert in the drawing-room, a shadow in the corridors. He shouted at her once and the woman made off. Now, when she saw him, she vanished in thin air. There was nothing he could do, she was very close to his stepmother, he thought, the first time he saw Inacia all self-assured. Well, you should see the deceased being washed, said someone else, not the barber this time. It was not the barber who said it the first time, he was getting confused. It had been an old man, he remembered now. Being a respectable, well-dressed old man, he had asked why. To remember afterwards, the old man said. To feel more hate in the hour of revenge, of punishment. He must have put on an expression of displeasure, the old man moved away muttering these young men nowadays. Revenge? For what? If it was a robbery. Malvina shouted thief, thief. Even if it were not, why revenge? For honour, he seemed to hear his father say. Even for honour. These young men nowadays! Let it pass. Honour! Probably his father. . . . He did not continue.

He only went to see the body when it was dressed and ready for the drawing-room. When he saw his father, he went white and dumb with horror, he backed away trembling. The death-mask was not enough, he thought emphatically. Far better the waxen pallor, the skin's ivory hue. The clothes he could just about allow to pass, but not that. Take that off, clean his face, he shouted, when he saw his father's ghastly white face. But he was so fond of it! said the Negro. Who had this done? Was it the mistress by any chance? No, the widow only wants to see the body in the drawing-room, someone said. They were all talking, it was all so confused. The Negro waiting wide-eyed. Well, clean it off, then, I am ordering you! I'm giving the orders here, he said, to his own astonishment, he had suddenly taken his father's place. He had taken his father's place, but not just now. He was horrified even more than when he saw that white face, he closed his eyes. Ghastly his father's face, like a theatrical mask. The white pomade, the carmine on his slack lips. It sickened him when the old man was alive, so much the more now he was dead. His face is to be his own, he said, now directing the finale of the macabre pantomime. Just as he was, he said. As he should be. Like he was before Mother died; he felt a pain deep down. Before. He did not go on, he was not going to follow that dangerous path now. He gave further orders, then turned away and went to his own room.

He only made his appearance in the drawing-room later, after the bier had been set up and the candles lit. The candles crackled as if someone had thrown salt on the flames. The melted wax ran soft and thick, hardening half-way down the candle. Shapes sculpted in wax, candy figures. When he was a boy, in church, he would sit day-dreaming for ages trying to decide what they looked like – animals or people? He used to lie down in the grass, too, watching the dance of the clouds, the patterns and shapes which the wind formed and scattered. Once he saw Leonor in her white dress, just like her, all that was missing was her laugh. Just like the last time. He wanted so much to see her. When she died.

He had been in his room for a long time, his father alone in the crowded drawing-room. Without him, he meant without her. She had no doubt come before him and gone back to her room. One at a time, better that way. The two of them together, never, only when the cortège was about to leave. The rules, he had to respect them. To avoid. They might see. Certain things. Start thinking.

The bells began ringing again. As committee member and benefactor of a religious guild his father had the right to special chimes. One, two, he counted. Two chimes repeated three times, with intervals between each knell. First the treble bells, then the tenor bells. Finally, the lead bells. What toll was it? Must be the one his father had a right to, the passing bell. In all the churches. At intervals, until the coffin left. All day long. All the churches will be tolling the passing bell. Captain-General's orders, someone said. An honour for him. For whom? For his father, of course. Dead, the tolling and the pomp were of no use to him. Alive, he would enjoy it, he enjoyed that sort of thing. Better so, better the passing bell. What was really awful was when they tolled for the dying. Sometimes, all day long, the chimes drawn out, it got on one's nerves, one after another. Thank goodness his father had not had a long agony. Him dying slowly would have been horrible. Her.

She had been already and had retired. Supported by the other women, who were moved by her terrible grief. That was his first thought when, even not meaning to, he looked for her near the bier, in the midst of groups which formed and drifted into corners, near the curtains, on to the balconies. He had not seen her again since that night, she screamed and he had to go to her assistance. He did not spend the night in his father's room, neither did she. She was quite shattered, that was what they said. After all the thing happened near her. She saw, it was she who screamed thief, thief. Poor thing, she is suffering so much, they said. Bloodstained, her night-dress was bloodstained, with marks of gunpowder, she had not gone to the trouble of putting a cloak over it. Brutal, it was brutal! Brutal when he ran his hand violently over the spinet keys. The spinet was no longer there. Instead they had brought more chairs for the visitors, there would still be more to come. One of the town's leading citizens, his father. He will have a great funeral, said someone. He could see from the sample, the drawing-room was full. If it was like that so early, later on it would be like an ant-hill. A swarm of people coming in and out, whispering. If they spoke loud, someone said lower and the voices subsided once more to a muffled lisping. People, he did not know why, weeping. When they were not even relatives. They came and embraced him, with sorrowful faces. A great man, a great loss. People already praying, *ora pro nobis*. Later it would be unbearable. He felt like running away, getting away from it all. No, madness. What they might think, what they might say. He would have to stay by his father the whole time, he had already been a long time in his own room. When she had no doubt been by the coffin, the body already covered by the damask cloth. The whole time, would he be able to go through with it? Him and his frailty, that cursed delicate soul of his, he was afraid he would not stand it. What if he were to feign or even let himself faint. He would be carried to his room, he would be excused. No, people would talk. Womanish behaviour, it would look bad in a man of his age. Only his father, recently. But recently his father had been very unwell. He often thought that he . . .

He would have to stay until the end. He had never been to a funeral again, but he knew what it was like. As if he did not remember. That gloomy, showy cult of the dead. He also revered the dead but in his own way, in private and with refinement, his alone. The dead, his two deaths. Only one, he did not see the other. He grieved in vain. Alone in Portugal, he had wept. He wanted to keep the pure beautiful image of his mother for ever. As he kept his sister's, stationary in time, immutable. His alone, for always. Because his mother being alive when he was in Portugal, distance had dissolved her features, it was difficult to recover her. Death fixed the features, it froze them in wax.

My God, now they've brought flowers, huge vases of flowers. The flowers, the wax. They were covering the damask cloth with flowers, no doubt the stains. That warm smell of molten wax mingling with the penetrating, sickly sweet smell of the flowers. That other time, twenty years ago. Then he liked the smell, it was actually nice to smell, at the time. At the time, not afterwards, when he remembered it afterwards he felt sick. After that he could not stand the smell of flowers and molten wax together. Each by itself was all right, together he could not stand it. Flowers he still liked, they did not immediately bring back those linked memories. Even when they made him go to church, he would not sit near the altars, because of the smell, the sick feeling. For others it probably was not a bad smell, just for him. Somewhere between a dog's stench and the smell of something gone rotten. The smell did not come from

139

the candles or the flowers. Or perhaps the candles and the flowers were intended to mask another, more penetrating and permanent smell, the smell of the corpse? The smell came neither from the flowers nor from the molten wax, he kept repeating over and over. The smell was right inside his nose. Came from inside him, like an illness. He had only to remember and there was the smell. At times so strong they could notice. He moved away when the smell was stronger. He began to get cold sweats. What if he were ill? Perhaps that was what purulent rhinitis was like. He had never seen it, just thinking about it made him feel sick. An unbearable rotten smell, so they said. Even the sufferer could not stand it. The anguish, the cold sweat and the smell were getting worse, he would not be able to endure it.

Something? Do you want something? Are you feeling all right? a woman said. Only then, when the woman spoke, did he come round, the feeling of anguish improved. The smell was not really as unbearable as he thought. When he imagined himself close to a coffin again, like now. Now, close to his dead father. He had to bear it, the smell was not as strong as he thought. He just had to avoid breathing deeply, think of other things. A case of getting used to it, forgetting. Yes, he could endure it, he could not go away. What would they say? Those people talked so much. After all it was his father, he was the one who had to take care of everything. Now, afterwards. He took a handkerchief from his pocket and wiped the sweat from his face. Feeling better now, asked the same woman, in a kind, concerned voice. Yes, he was. He was much better in fact, he was overcoming the anguish. When he felt the anguish, the smell because nauseous, unbearable. He had to overcome the anguish once and for all. At once, now. He closed his eyes and felt himself. He existed, he sighed with relief; the smell was going away.

The odd thing is that he liked the smell. At the time, before, not now. At the time, twenty years ago, Leonor. She was beautiful and cold, white, diaphanous. All white, the coffin lined with silk, the lace, the garland of flowers on her head. Her black hair, as black as his, as Mother's. They were very alike. Nine years old, he seven. He could not leave Leonor, they were going to take her away for ever. No more Leonor, the two of them never together again on blue afternoons. The same wax and ivory colour. Ivory more in her case. A new, bluish ivory, hard and smooth. When he touched Leonor's forehead with his hand. He thought he would not be able to bear it, like now with the smell. The first time he touched the cold, hard flesh, the bluish ivory of Leonor's face, he did it fearfully. Then again, when he saw that nothing happened. He did not know what would happen, he was afraid, what might happen. When he saw that nothing happened, he actually liked stroking the cold, hard, ivory-blue skin. Then they came and pulled him away from his sister. Then they took her away. Then no more, only memory.

Slaves came into the drawing-room and began to move back the furniture, making a space in the middle of the room. What were they doing? Why did they not do it before? As they did with the spinet. He could not make out what they were doing. Then he saw, when they put in place the white linen table-cloth, all lace almost, it was so trimmed and embroidered. They still had the cloth, one of the Negresses who was more attached to his mother must have remembered. The cloth was his mother's, he had sent it to her from Portugal. She so wanted a table-cloth like that. The finest there is, for special days, she said. There were seldom special days in the old house in Padre Faria. His father did not bother, he did not remember, he was a man of few needs, at that time. She, too, hardly asked for anything, she was not a woman of whims and desires. Submissive, almost absent, shut away in her prayers, immersed in her tranquillity. A pale, diaphanous figure. So purely and piously beautiful, her beauty was the sort which pacified the heart. After her, no other. All dangerous, diabolical. After my mother's death I can love no other woman, was what he said when he received the news. He who had never loved any woman, never allowed any woman's fingers to touch him. And he laughed to himself, a bitter, ironical laugh. One should not say I shall drink not of that water. He had not drunk, so far nothing had happened. Or had it? No. Strange how things alarm us before they have happened. Hence fear, anguish. The devil is not as ugly as he is made out. The devil's words, wiles of temptation. Before a thing happens is worst. Hadn't it been like that just now, with the smell of molten wax and flowers? Now he did not even notice, he was quite used to it. He only noticed now again, when he thought about it. Better not think about it, his anguish might come back again.

The cloth on the table. The two chased silver candlesticks must have been heavy and valuable. They had not been his mother's, that was obvious. The other's work, undoubtedly. He did not remember seeing them before. His father's house in the Rua Direita was a show of wealth, after his second marriage. The huge crucifix, the trunk and the arms of the cross imitating wood. The grievously agonizing body, the drooping head. Pain incarnate: on the forehead with its crown of thorns and on the body pierced by spears, ruby droplets emulating blood. It was not of damask, but of the whitest, purest linen, the sheet in which they wound the martyred body. His father had not been sacrificed, the comparison was madness. Unless he, or she. Of linen, the best linen. I want very little, said his mother when he asked what she wanted from Portugal,

141

when he took his leave. Like his father, formerly, more so than his father. Of few, hardly any needs. She asked for nothing and received little. Deep remorse for what he had not done. Even though she did not ask, he should have done more. Afterwards his father's life changed completely and he gave everything. She was the one who had helped to scrape and save in less plentiful times. Now this mansion in the Rua Direita, right on the square. His mother would never have thought of this, he realized again, he had forgotten so long. Remorse for having forgotten. In any case, bring me a linen table-cloth, she said. The best Galician. And, reproaching herself for having a special wish: it can be ordinary cambric. But I really would like a linen one, if you can. It will probably be used on the day of my death. Always thinking of death, his mother. He thought then, again now. Come on, don't think such things, Mother! I shall not see you again, Son, something tells me. Always imagining herself at death's door, sickly she was. Always ill, suffering, he paid little attention. He should have, at least then he would not have gone away. He paid no attention, so he did not notice. And his eyes filled with tears now, though he made an effort not to cry. They must be thinking the moist eyes are on account of Father. It was used for her, the cloth. One of the black servants who was closer to her, now a kitchen skivvy, hid it afterwards. So that the other. Jealous mistress, the other might use it. No other woman lays a hand on a dead mistress's things. The fear of those black slaves, the evil eye. Him too. Eyes penetrate things, impregnate them, leave a presence. Afterwards no one can touch them, dangerous. Now a kitchen skivvy, when Inacia took over, the other woman.

Speak of temptation and the Evil One appears. One must not speak. Missy sent me to ask for your orders, sir. Inacia came and said. How he wanted things. What things? he asked. She did not know. When the time comes, later, we shall see, he said. He did not know about these things. You can go back to your mistress. So she was asking for his orders? She wanted a yoke? A woman to be mounted, was she? He laughed to himself again, the tears disappeared. She was playing the meek one, she wanted to be subdued. The yoke, the order. Him in his father's place. What he had always feared was happening. It will not happen, he said, cutting short the thought which began to slip between the cracks and which he pushed away once more into the pitch darkness. Things were happening.

Strange how things alarm us before they happen, he thought once more. Calm and cool now, his eyes no longer tearful, merely sad. Those dreamy eyes, women liked to tell him he had. They annoyed him so much, when they were forward. No one ever touched him, his pledge of purity. Not to the saints, those people's nonsense. To his mother. A comedy that business they invented about a promise to the Virgin. He let them, it was better, more of a way of protecting himself. She herself asked him one day about the promise. What promise? he said, laughingly he thought. Then. He protected himself with the promise, the Virgin was a good shield. He who wanted them at a distance. Women, the viper-like undulation, wriggling, they hissed. He wanted nothing to do with women, he knew not woman. Medea, wife of Aegeus. He wanted to be master of arts, the company's college. Condemns all women, Medea. How did the poem go? Seneca, how could he? Master of Christians and counsellor to Nero. Virtue and the lions, the bloody genitals. He wanted nothing to do with women and they pursued him. The promise was to some extent a shield. With some it actually whetted the appetite, an attraction. Sin was born with the first woman, he remembered the spiritual exercises. Ignatius, the company. Another woman, the Virgin, stamped on sin, redeeming. The sleepless nights, the imaginary hair shirts biting into the flesh. I a sinner do confess myself. A vocation for almighty God, would he be? He would not, he was not. Her naked, white feet. Barefooted she trod on the head, Sibylline, they would not leave him. That white foot, its fleshy colour. He crossed himself, begged forgiveness in nights of penance. For his filthy heart, he suffered. He suffered and they pursued him. He was the magnet, he attracted them. His irresistible charm. He did not want it, they insisted. He attracted them on sight. Unintentionally, his mere presence. His smell, even before he arrived they could sense it. When he walked into a room. Even now they did not tear their eyes away from him, he had to bow his head. They all turned to look at him. Even the men, when he was a boy. He shrank away, ran away. A pure one at heart, despite his penitential accusations. In view of his old ideas he wanted not to be, but he was. Before, formerly. Now he suddenly felt filthy again. Step on my head, My Lady of the Conception! he begged in those sour nights of pain and remorse. He did not know why, he had done nothing. Nothing happened before, now. How things alarm us before they occur!

Like that since a boy. Pretty thing, they said. He got angry, pretty was being a girl. His father's doubts caused him such pain. He wanted his son to be strong, ferocious. Like himself, like, further back, Valentim Amaro Galvão. He did not succeed, his father. He felt himself that he was delicate. He made a superhuman effort to overcome it. That was why he devoted himself to hunting, to the wilds. To big game hunting when he came back from Portugal. It was also a way of getting away from the town, people were such a nuisance. His father was pleased, he felt rewarded. He wanted to be alone, like now, they would not let him. All the time someone would come and greet him, embrace him. Even the women, he pushed them away, gently but firmly. Unpleasant embraces. He was a good hunter, no one was a better shot. With bow and arrow, even his domesticated Indians, his bowmen. How much had it all cost him? Because he knew he was delicate and fragile. He wished he were not like that, wished he had a different soul, a different body, to be different.

When a boy, the women said he was pretty. A girl, and they tried to stroke his head. He strank in horror from those hands, those fingers, those hot, sinful lips. The mere touch of those hands made him shudder. Only his mother was allowed to stroke his head, he felt nothing. Nothing horrifying and terrible – instead a blue, nice, gentle feeling. A deep, drawn-out pleasure, he wanted to stretch it out for ever, it should never end. A feeling of purity, the desire to be like that all his life. That could not, should not come to an end. The tears he wept in secret. He did not want to show, could not show he was crying, not in front of his father. When he grew to manhood, he said goodbye to his mother and went to Portugal. A linen cloth, embroidered in lace, was all she asked for. Something tells me I shall never see you again. A choking pain, a premonition – he was never to see her again. People impregnate, leave a little of themselves in the things, in the places they were in. That was why he returned. If he did not like Portugal anyway, his mother's death gave him one more reason to return. When he was away from home, he imagined he would be able to find her in the things her fingers had caressed. When he returned, the empty house, painfully empty. A cold wind had swept away his mother's presence, dry leaves. Things were sad, cold and mute, opaque and hard. Even her things. His mother had vanished into thin air, mist dispersed by the wind as soon as the morning sunlight. The patterns formed by the clouds dancing, solidifying, fading away.

The sky was blue, clear, not a cloud floating, at that hour of the morning. He could see from the window opposite. He lowered his eyes and sat looking at his own hands, not wanting to look at the others, the slight tremor of his hands. They might think he did not care about his father's death. So far they had not seen him shed a tear. Forgetting that just a while before his eyes had filled with tears. He was not crying, a man does not cry. His father frowning at him. When they took Leonor's body. Leonor too was allowed to stroke his head, his face. She closed his eyes, the two of them children lying down (the clouds floating) in the grass. Keep your eyes closed and wait, something will happen, she said. He foolishly waited for ages. Like that, with his eyes closed, it seemed to be longer. Can I open them? Not yet. It was hard. And he could tell she was laughing, he enjoyed it, still did not open his eyes. Then he felt her softly coming closer, the nice warmth of her breath. She kissed his closed eyelids and he felt the pleasant moistness of her warm lips. And they laughed now, the two of them were laughing together.

Girls he could endure, liked them even. Before, no. Leonor was enough for him. Now, a grown man. When they saw him in the street they came after him. Even now there is one, a bit older, looking at me, I can see. They waved to him, blew kisses and he liked that, smiled his thanks. In Coimbra, when he left the house to go to the Faculty of Theology, there was always one waiting for him at a window. She would be about five years old and lived in the house next to his. He just smiled at her. Fear, other people might get ideas. Men watched not only over their wives, but their daughters too. Someone might. Following their own sinful thoughts. His little neighbour, a bit like Leonor. And always dressed in white too, so pure, diaphanous. His mother, Leonor. One day the girl's mother came to the window and saw him. From then on he had no respite, those pleasant mornings came to an end. The girl's mother began to cast some heavy, hot, sticky looks, which made suggestions to him. Pretending she was just keeping her daughter company, the woman waved to him. Offering herself, mysterious, artful. All the same, always that hell. He started to walk down instead of up the street, that way avoiding the woman at the window. So those delightful mornings came to an end.

The bells again. Too far away, he could not tell which church. Only when it was Carmo Church, right next door. Like that all day long. They did not bother him, but what was it all for? His father enjoyed it, he would like to know he was being given all those honours. He could not hear, deaf for ever, dead, his father. Seen from the side, the body covered by the damask cloth was the gentle profile of an old mountain range. He could imagine the relief outline: the head, the nose, the crossed hands, the feet. A soft saw edge, the mountain ridge. The feet were the highest mountain. Shoed, surely, the silver-buckled shoes, he did not remember whether he had seen them in the bedroom, when the body was brought into the drawing-room. Body present. Someone said there will be a mass with body present. Requiem mass, they were giving his father all the honours. He deserved them, a great potentate, a magnate, was what they were saying.

And the priest came in his finest, silky, lace-trimmed vestments. The boy with the censer, the good-smelling smoke from the incense. The smoke hung, penetrating, in the air. And that nice smell, one of his best memories, drove still further away the sickening mixture of candle and flowers – occasionally it came back, if he remembered.

The priest greeted him and asked permission to commence. Yes, you may, when you wish. Suddenly master of the house, in his father's place. His father would certainly approve, lately he always wanted to have him standing in for him in business matters, he was taking care of everything that would be his. After he fell ill, not before. After he came back more infirm, not before. Suddenly he remembered, he had forgotten. A moment, wait a moment, he said, calling the priest. Someone go inside and find out if the widow wishes to be present. He said widow, not wanting to say stepmother or Malvina. His father would approve, he himself, Gaspar, did not. Approve what? He did not know, something hurting. He in his father's place. But was that not what his father wanted? he told himself, consoling himself.

While they were away, an uncomfortable silence weighed between himself and the priest. The prest felt the discomfort first and began to speak, to console him. He should have faith and trust in God, in the Virgin Mary. He merely nodded. Our Lady of the Conception stepping on the snake. Or was it not Our Lady of the Conception? The priest asked if he would not be taking communion. No, and noting the expression in the priest's eyes, he said I am not prepared.

Someone came to say that Mistress Malvina had eventually managed to go to sleep, she was dead tired and the women who were attending her thought it would be better for her not to come, at least not now. He thought so too, but said nothing. You may begin, Reverend, he said, creating a vast distance between him and the priest.

Now they were all praying, even the men, rosaries in their hands, counting beads. They beat their breasts and mumbled the words of the prayers. He did no more than follow, mechanically, what the others were doing: kneeling if they did, standing up when they did. He did not pray but crossed himself clumsily. He lowered his head at the right moments, when the mass-boy's bell rang. Everyone was looking at him, it disturbed him.

Throughout the spoken mass his thoughts were flying far away. From time to time the priest's Latin rose above the lisping monotone of the waves of voices. And every so often those snatches, which he mentally translated, started to cause him pain. Not the sentences exactly, certain words. Words which acted as springs, carrying his thoughts with them. Macabre and terrible words. If those people knew what they meant, they would have different expressions on their faces instead of that falsely pious contrition. He got annoyed with the others. Because he was beginning to get annoyed with himself. Those words were addressed particularly to him. When they spoke of sin and death.

He went back to thinking about his father dressed like that. In his mind the figure of his father was more unpleasant than just now, in the bedroom. In the bedroom he had at least had them remove the white mask of powder, pomade and rouge. Now he could do nothing. The bloodstains were beginning to show. They were linking one to another and forming a single dark patch. And that dark, moist patch was growing; he felt his head spinning.

He sat on the nearest chair. With his eyes closed the stain seemed to grow still larger. Until it covered the waistcoat completely, while the bottle-green of the tailcoat, growing steadily darker, was now the damp, heavy green of old soiled leaves. Impossible to avoid, weak as he was he no longer had the strength or the self-control. Impossible to avoid the repeated dream he began to have after those afternoons: she at the spinet, he on the flute. Those afternoons, he never thought they could happen and they did, and he enjoyed them so much. Those afternoons, nothing actually happened except for the music. Nothing happened, he said, trying to ward off the first colours, the dark chords of the dream. His heavy heart did not confirm what his mouth said. And the dream came nearer, though far off he could tell when it was coming, before he could still make it stop. Not now, thinking he might faint. It would be horrible, all those people around him. Frail, delicate, he accused himself. It was coming nearer, now he could see his father's bedroom door open wide, the man did not even touch it. That dream was somehow a premonition of everything that happened. The door wide open, the man he was behind stood motionless in the doorway. And he saw his father alone in the empty double bed, she was not there. The figure of his father, white and frightening. His head and torso raised up on the pillows. His night-shirt all lacy, he was swamped in lace and embroidery. And his face, unlike it always was, very white and painted, his lips a dark carmine, almost purple. Why did he paint his face to go to bed, was the question he asked himself. Actually his father did not paint his face to go to bed, that was what was strange, he knew that. And instead of the man moving towards his father, it was the bed that came sliding towards him, as if the floor were slanting, and came to a halt a yard away from him. Then the man moved to the attack and sprang on to the bed, the black arm struck several knife-blows in succession. Not a scream from his father: at the first blow the carmine mouth opened and the tongue was purple, the shout choked in his throat. The scream stuck, suffocated, purple – inside him, Gaspar. When, with an effort he did not think possible in the dream, he managed to produce the scream, he would wake up. The same strangled scream now, like a piece of hard bread stuck in his throat, he was choking. He had to scream, to wake up. Yet he was afraid of letting out the scream, the arm which shot out of the

147

man's body (the hand was no longer black, but all too familiar) was his own. The scream held fast, he would wake up if he screamed. But he could not scream there, all those people. He could not see their faces, their eyes, but he knew they were all looking at him. If he screamed he would be done for. He would scream.

At that moment a heavy hand grasped him by the shoulder and pulled him backwards, preventing him falling. The hand woke him up, returning his body to the drawing-room and the light of day, to the fresh air, to life. No, he did not scream, he realized with relief. If he had screamed they would all be looking towards him – in silent reproach. The strong, real, kind, protective hand. Desire to kiss the hand that had saved him. And he began to feel cold all over his body, as if he were feverish, he might start trembling, his teeth start chattering. The sweat oozed cold on his forehead, his shirt was soaked, greasy, sticky.

The man by his side leaned forward, his lips almost pressed to his ear and said all right, are you feeling all right? You are so white, and you are sweating a great deal. Do you want to go outside? I will help you. No, I am all right, it will go away, he said. They all turned towards him. He straightened up, gathering his last strength. After a few terrible moments, people started to turn back towards the altar. Now he was alone, safe. He placed his hand over the hand on his shoulder. He thought, but did not say, God bless you. He did not believe any longer. He said nothing, the pressure of his hand on the protective hand said it for him. Because the man removed his. He was all right now, he knew. The anguish had gone away again, the dream evaporated.

And as he returned from his anguish, safe from the torment, cool and lucid, alive, his lips mentally uttered a prayer. So intimately, so secret and timid, would even his immediate neighbour, if he were paying attention, see so much as the slight tremor of his lips, notice his laborious breathing? He who no longer prayed, who had even forgotten. He said the first prayer his mother taught him. The simplest prayer, the one that lived on and reappeared in the hour of torment. He prayed, silently begged, implored the unknown powers, the divinities hidden for so long beneath the soul's ground, not to abandon him. Afterwards they could destroy him, not at that moment. He begged for strength to hold out, he who gave others a feeling of serenity, security and strength of spirit in so delicate and fragile a body. He whom men feared (their laugh did not overcome their fear, it stopped short, in confusion) and women sought, captivated at the first glance by his beauty and serenity. And he cursed the fragile, angelic beauty that was his perdition. And he begged to be deformed by wrinkles, white hair and ugliness. So as not to be a source of temptation, so as not to be tempted any more.

And that silent prayer, unearthed from the dark depths, long since forgotten, restored his lost tranquillity. Now he was sure that it would not happen again. And his eyes filled with tears. The tears ran gently down his face. So great was his joy at being free of the dream, the sticky, choking feeling: it no longer mattered if he wept. Wept freely, he never wept like that. A child seeks the safety of its mother's bosom and abandons himself to the weakness of tears. He was clean and forlorn, protected and happy.

And he said again how things alarm us before they happen. Now he was strong, whole, transparent. He was ready to take on his allotted role. And the certainty that he was strong in his fragility, that his soul had found in tears its lost balance, made him noble and illuminated. And the light which came from within him must show in his face and his eyes, like a radiance of gleaming polished silver around the image of a saint. He radiated a luminous epiphany. A feeling of peace and beauty, gentleness without end. As if his skin possessed an inner light and radiated serene tenderness.

And they turned towards him, mainly the women, touched by that tenderness and beauty, touched by light. And there was no impure sentiment in them: everything was peace, enchanted tranquillity. Touched by light, they enveloped him in a halo of affection and love; they too began to weep. And their weeping was gentle and good, made only of tears. No scream, no sigh, no despair, no torment. They wept in silence. And for the first time since the distant days of his childhood, the same unconstrained feeling of beauty and love without sin. Love was good, it flooded the heart with harmony, serenity and light.

And the tenderness which hovered in the air – a gentle, soft, fragrant breath – spread to them all. It was as if all of them, in one voice, in sweet harmony, eyelids slowly closing under the sweet weight of sleep, were no longer praying: they were singing a hymn of glory in the nave of heaven.

He took a deep breath. The smell of flowers and molten wax no longer sickened him, he felt a pleasure old and new. That same pleasure of twenty years ago, Leonor. And his memories of his sister were good and tender, pure and gentle, like the eyes of those women.

Nothing could happen. But like a spark hidden beneath the ashes of a brazier or a seed in damp earth tilled for years by solitude and anguish, the fear remained still in his hardened soul: it could happen. He once more diverted his thoughts from the old course. He was not weeping any more, he was a strong man, his father would be proud. Thy sins shall be forgiven thee, said an ancient voice, he would never know whose it was – he neither remembered nor wished to remember. Enough were the peace, the promise. Even transitory.

When the mass was over, someone came to tell him that the Captain-General had arrived. He knew the part he would have to play. Having overcome his anguish, he felt stronger and was sure he would easily endure the Captain-General's presence.

He went to greet him at the door, it was his duty. Welcome to this house, he was in his father's place.

With the bright colours (red and yellow) of his uniform, which was embellished with braid and tassels, sashes and insignia, enamel and precious stones, the Captain-General glittered, out of place in the atmosphere of mourning. But he was the Captain-General and Governor of the Minas, he dressed in his finest ceremonial uniform as an act of homage to the worthy subject. But these gilt epaulettes, the embroidered trimmings in gold, silver and silk, the bright sash, the martial bearing in which he took pompous pride on any occasion, did not this time cause Gaspar any discomfort, the slightest shudder. He found it natural, his father deserved it all. The showy visit was an act of homage, his father would have enjoyed it. Everything as it should be.

The presence of the Captain-General caused a great stir in the drawing-room. The courtiers and the leading citizens and their wives, who till then had been scattered in small groups in murmured conversations (men on one side, women on the other), opened up in one huge smile. Forgetting that the main thing in the room was the body of João Diogo Galvão, they all turned towards the King's representative with smiles and cackles, winks and grimaces. And the women, even the apparently most virtuous, allowed themselves tender, promising looks in the direction of that short, stocky figure which aspired to be elegant and resplendent. Such, at least, was the Captain-General's opinion of himself and they, male and female, in their eagerness to please, confirmed it. The women are the worst, thought the old Gaspar. The Captain-General was given to flattery and philandering, and his furtive, covert love-affairs were whispered around, so they put on their best appearance.

The tender, fraternal communion vanished into thin air, the spell was broken. The old hatred choked his breast once more. It was not the Captain-General, it was the women; they are all just one thing. And mentally he lumped them all together in one obscenity.

After some time in silence before the body of the potentate João Diogo Galvão, his head bowed and his eyes almost closed, as if in prayer, he said that Gaspar should be proud of his father. A most worthy man, the King considered him a friend. A great loss for me and for Portugal. Though knowing it was all false (the King barely knew his father by hearsay, very likely he did not even remember his name, the famous letter from the King was a paid address to a loyal and distant servant), Gaspar, clothed in the new figure he had made himself, to be in all ways a worthy son and successor of João Diogo Galvão, said Your Excellency knows, my father nurtured a filial devotion towards the King.

The Captain-General smiled with contentment. He had always had his suspicions of Gaspar – one of those educated colonials who returned to America full of dangerous ideas; in fact he felt an undisguisable scorn for him. Gaspar knew it, but now he had to behave himself. We shall get on well, my boy, said the Captain-General. Allow me to address you like that, out of the great esteem I had your father. I hope to have the honour to deserve the same esteem from Your Excellency, said Gaspar, somewhat embarrassed by his new figure. All his father's wealth and power, acquired with such toil, was not going to come to nothing, as a result of weakness and pride. Suddenly, like a repentant prodigal son, he discovered: it was his duty, he was carrying it out. If Your Excellency will be so kind, in one of your letters to Portugal, you may assure His Majesty that he has in the son of João Diogo Galvão the same loyal, devoted vassal, he said solemnly and awkwardly, unused to courtly language. It was a ridiculous comedy he was performing, but he pursued his intention – from then on he would be a different man. Whatever the cost, at any price. He would take a wife, if necessary. In this part he felt no anguish, he thought himself protected. Even when she arrived. She was stronger and cleverer than he; he knew it.

The Captain-General called him on to one of the balconies, he wished to have a word with him in private. He signalled to his entourage, they understood that the conversation was private. Well trained, they moved away; with ears pricked, but some way off.

The Captain-General said he already knew who the murderer was. A certain Januario, a half-breed bastard. One of that rabble of mestizo loafers and bastards that infest these lands of Minas! Did he know him? he asked. Yes, not well, but he knew him. By name and by sight. A son of Tomás Matias Cardoso, a half-Indian son. But his father is a conscientious, honest man, said the Captain-General. Tomás Matias Cardoso appeared embarrassed, covered in shame, he did not know what to do. That was what he said, when he called him to ask about his son, as soon as they found out. How did you find out so quickly? said Gaspar, adding if Your Excellency will allow me the presumption of asking. Dona Malvina's maidservant, Inacia her name is, told us. Her again, always her, thought Gaspar. She saw him when he jumped, said the Captain-General. Everyone knows him, he is a noted vagabond. Dona Malvina, whom I shall see this afternoon, can confirm it. She does not know the man's name, she does not know him, but if she sees him, she will probably recognize him. At least that was what the maidservant said.

Gaspar remembered that bastard half-breed, of ill repute and tough appearance. One of those lecherous, bastard half-breeds he absolutely loathed. That time when the two of them were on the way to Vila do Carmo. The insolence of stopping right in front of Malvina, his insulting stare. He nearly did something, he should have. Who is it? she asked. Some half-breed, he remembered saying. What made her interested? His audacity, of course. Flattered, like any woman. The Captain-General was right, those mestizos were a rabble. As a chaste man he loathed shameless people like that, brought up among low women, a mere look soiled one. He should have done something, he was armed. Afterwards he forgot all about the encounter, now he remembered it again. Was Malvina likely to remember it? She remembered, of course. No, she probably did not, she received attention from so many men, he said furiously. To surrender to her beauty was an obligation, she no doubt thought. Like they did before the King, the Captain-General. Compulsory homage. When she passed by, they all turned to look, he often saw it. At the palace, the Captain-General with his reputation. . . .

The Captain-General continued, Gaspar listened politely. His father would like to see that new son of his. You can be assured, sir, that the criminal will receive from me an exemplary punishment! That is entirely my wish, said Gaspar. Whatever Your Excellency thinks best.

No, there was no doubt, he was the one, said the Captain-General. Everything pointed to him. His own father, an honest man, said that his son did not sleep at home. These bastard sons soil a good name, said the Captain-General angrily. My men are on his trail, they saw which direction he went. And for theft! Poor Tomás Matias!

Do you believe it was theft, Your Excellency? Could there not be another motive? asked Gaspar. Because Tomás Matias Cardoso was a wealthy man, his son, though illegitimate, lived with him, was pampered, and boasted of his position and wealth. That had occurred to me, said the Captain-General. You mean an act of revenge, sir? Yes, said Gaspar. It is possible, I have thought of that too, said the Captain-General. Because of the many services he rendered to the King. An act of revenge, or maybe something worse? The Captain-General's eyes shone. A signal for something else, said the Captain-General.

In an instant Gaspar divined the Captain-General's lightning idea, the treadmill of his rumination.

But what about the casket he stole? said the Captain-General, after a ponderous silence. He was not asking Gaspar, it was more a habit of thought. Casket, asked Gaspar, and the Captain-General said yes, has

Dona Malvina not mentioned it? Nor the maidservant? No, he had not seen her since the night of the crime and the maid told him nothing. Yes, he supposed so, she shouted thief. You are right, said the Captain-General, it may be a well-arranged plan, to divert attention from the real motive. . . . Or maybe a signal? I favour the signal, for something bigger. . . .

The Captain-General was working fast. We shall soon see, he said, my men are after him. I have sent a regiment of dragoons in the direction they said he took. There is no escape, I think he will be here by tomorrow. If we catch him, we shall force him to confess. We shall see, you have given me a good idea, sir, I applaud and thank you, he said, although Gaspar had said nothing, merely asked a question. The Captain-General was concocting something.

The Captain-General was naturally thinking about the tax levy, and of being in good odour at court. Gaspar preferred the idea of revenge. His father was a powerful man, formerly a hard man. In the clean-up of the infested rivers and in the war against the slave settlements he had been merciless. My wish is to thank you, Your Excellency, for all your interest on my father's behalf, all you have done. From the tolling of the bells by the guilds to the dragoons at the door of the house. You are welcome, said the Captain-General. I am doing no more than my obligation, after all your father was a friend of the King. Yes, that is true, said Gaspar, acting his new part perfectly. Concerning dragoons, said the Captain-General, not as a homage but for protection and as a precaution, would you mind giving hospitality for a few days to a lieutenant if I send one? I will choose one myself, one who has my confidence, a man of refinement and manners, and respectful, because of Dona Malvina. No, indeed I thank you, said Gaspar, and his words were sincere, he had no desire to be alone again with Malvina.

Either divining his thought, or because he was thinking about her too, the Captain-General suddenly asked after Malvina. A suspicious interest, a hint of lechery, in his glittering, blinking eyes. Anything was possible with that Captain-General, he thought uncertainly. I will send someone for my stepmother, said Gaspar after a while.

When, not long after (she had been ready for some time, just waiting for his call?) Malvina entered the room, Gaspar felt such a dreadful thud in his chest, his heart galloping, his hands moist and cold, then suddenly a wave of heat rise to his face (they might notice, take care, Gaspar, he thought rapidly, almost cleverly; since his last attack of anguish he was learning to control himself), he felt such a shudder that he instinctively reached for a chair to lean on. Like someone protecting himself from an unexpected vision, which he nevertheless – dread fear! – really expected. The stepmother he sent for was not the Malvina he expected and feared. The stepmother he sent for was just a word and a name, not a person.

The person who entered the room was as truly, diabolically marvellous (of this she herself was surely aware), as burningly, radiantly present as the one he saw in her on several occasions (sinuous and snakelike, mysterious) and who began to appear (at first mistily, with a thousand disguises) in his dreams, whom he afterwards consciously bore away to the solitude of his room: where, after some resistence and remorse, he reviewed her, trying to make her out from her smallest gestures, often certain he had understood the meaning of her semaphore, and suffered in his flesh the scourge of desire and torment. He who had crushed each and every sinful inclination of his heart: his heart must stay pure and chaste like his mother and sister.

Sunk in anguish, feelings and memories before the body of his dead father, he had, in fact, until now not thought of the real live, dazzling, disturbing Malvina. He had only thought, when at all, of names and words scattered here and there – Malvina, she, stepmother, without going into these names until he met the being they indicated. Knowing, nevertheless, that she existed, clamorously and scarlet, afraid (he pushed her away into the distant mists) that she would rise again live and red-hot from the ash-covered brazier (apparently extinguished and cold) at the slightest breath of wind, at a more dangerous curve of the memory.

Malvina entered the room. Though not meaning to, all eyes turned towards her, there was no need for anyone to announce her. Because they wanted to see, and in this their imagination was fully occupied, how she looked in mourning. What her charm and beauty looked like marked by grief; if she really felt anything. They suspected and wished that she did not suffer, everything in her should be pantomime, theatre, pretence. She so provoked the town with her different, brash manners, her filmy dresses and daring looks and laughter, her swaying gilded sedan-chair brought from Portugal. So self-assured and so free, the other women felt small and criticized her from a distance, while having already committed all those sins in their hearts. The Minas country and the gold, the blood and slavery, the crimes and greed brought upon themselves all the blame and punishments. This was what he suddenly thought now, reproaching them. Forgetting that often, not consciously and lucidly (his darker, more critical side was doing the thinking), he rebuked and punished her, by punishing and rebuking himself, not her, for his own memories and dangerous thoughts. This was now, not before; before he was not sure, he suspected. And he always covered his suspicion with increasingly heavy layers of soil. Because it pained him to admit, to think. He actually forgot.

She looked so beautiful it was impossible not to turn round. Even the few who had not been all smiles and laughter when the Captain-General arrived had their eyes turned towards the glittering black apparition. Only she existed: everything faded, went dead. The bells stopped tolling and the silence was a deserted beach reverberating with sun and sound waves of light. By the side of Malvina's rustling black silks and taffetas, everything else was picture frame, backcloth, blue sky.

She looked so beautiful, more beautiful than she really was, he thought, pierced by light and pain. More beautiful veiled by mourning, in the presence of death. In panic he saw her hovering above the clouds of the abyss. And suddenly, still in heightened panic, he saw: what had always fascinated him was not really death, it was beauty, a beauty which he did not allow himself even to think on. Out of fear, because he knew he lacked the strength, that he was defeated beforehand. So great was his desire, the silent sinister attraction, that he had to protect himself with the cloak of death, of whiteness, of colourless purity. He feared and loved women for what in them was warmest and most beautiful, strong and consuming. The heat, smell and blood of wild female animals in the late afternoon.

And the flash of lightning which revealed to him the truth so long hidden, submerged and feared, contradictorily gave him a lucid certainty. He had to avoid her, fantasies were impossible, sin existed, he had to overcome it and crush it, just as one crushes a viper under foot. He was stronger than he thought, a man always saves himself.

Strange how things alarm us before they happen, he said once more. And the sentence, from repetition, acquired a tone and a meaning it had not had before. He could vanquish her and overcome himself. Instead of avoiding her and running away, he must cloak himself in tranquillity, see what he had so far only allowed himself a furtive glance at: her in her dangerous entirety, excited and beautiful. It was a way of punishing and purging himself.

And he saw that he no longer had a childish or adolescent heart. Suddenly he grew old, he was even a very old man. He was a man who was taking his father's place. He saw himself with the cold, severe acceptance of fatality and resignation: his destiny in the past, the termination of life.

And without a blush, his heart open, without fearing her, he was then able to look at Malvina.

She had shrouded herself in mourning and the mourning did not drown her beauty, more beautiful still. The lace mantilla which covered her face, falling down over her dress, accentuated the quivering roundness of her shoulders and breasts. And in all that black, her breasts, deliberately compressed from beneath by the bodice, rose and fell, undulating; they were firm, free, white, scented. Her whiteness and beauty needed no jewel – although she was not white, but red-headed. And that harmonious blend of round, burning forms shone resplendent beneath the veils and the black lace. Her eyes, which were large and full, red with weeping or sleep, had a brilliance so strong such as no darkness or blackness could eclipse. And her red hair, polished copper, dark gold of the highest carat, shone with its own light, gleaming. Even in the dark, her hair and her eyes would shine and illuminate.

Malvina bent her knee, dropping her head in a curtsy to the Captain-General. He held her hand, raised her and prevented her completing the bow. As in a dance, in a brightly lit ballroom and to slow music, the two of them moved, in measured steps, in a minuet, towards the body of João Diogo Galvão. Silent and illuminated, a grand pageant of grief was in progress.

She on one side of the bier, he on the other. Malvina did not yet dare look straight at him. Her attention apparently turned towards the Captain-General. Gaspar knew that, from the moment she entered the room, Malvina's eyes had been searching for him. Once having found him, they would not leave him, though lowered and concealed. Their eyes had not yet met in a long, slow look. He thought he was tormentedly cool and calm. Even knowing his hands were trembling and his knees shaking, he was no longer concerned, he was resigned to it. What matters is the heart and the head, he tried to tell himself when he said once more how things alarm us before they happen. He was controlling himself. Though she was strong and bold, when they came face to face she would be the one to retreat. I am a different man, he said, seeking support from his recent certainty.

He could see her as he always wished and feared: motionless, facing one another. Malvina approached the bier and her hand, reaching out from under her mantilla, was about to touch the coffin. No, she was not going to touch João Diogo Galvão's body! Her free, live fingers would not endure the cold, waxen touch of death. She would not go so far, at least not in front of him. That hand attracted him, still more brilliant because of the black mantilla. And she, those cold, unyielding eyes on the skin, withdrew her hand; as quickly as if she had touched the frozen waters of a stream. Better so, he thought. Against the black of her dress and her mantilla, Malvina's hand looked like another hand. The severed white hand floated in the air, he saw it once in a dream.

Malvina sighed deeply, and the handkerchief under her mantilla dried her eyes, everyone saw. Cautiously, apparently respecting her recent widowhood, the Captain-General started to put his arm round her shoulders. He did not actually touch her, everyone was facing towards him, and he let his arm fall. So close to her, he must be breathing her warm smell, thought Gaspar. The smell of her breasts, the warm smell of her breath, of her repressed sobs, the smell of benjamin which she used. Even from a distance Gaspar could smell it. The Captain-General's eyes, pretending to rest on the damask cloth, slid covetously sideways to her breasts rising and falling in the frame of the daring décolletage, veiled by the mantilla. The Captain-General said something to her, Gaspar was unable to hear. To be closer to her, of course, and inhale more deeply of her warm, lascivious smell. Pig! thought Gaspar and, without knowing why, he suddenly felt a violent hatred towards the Captain-General.

And what he had been expecting so long happened: she is raising her eyes towards me, he says. And for the first time the two of them looked each other straight in the eyes, dangerously. Like two deadly enemies facing one another, probing, checking the sharpness and gleam of their daggers, each eyeing the smallest movement of the other. In a lengthy, silent challenge, each telling the other you will be the first to retreat.

But no, she was not his enemy, only he said that; she said something else: she begged and implored, her eyes really full of tears. She was imploring and begging what? He did not know, nor did he want to, his heart suspected from a long time back, he guessed in any case. And her eyes seemed to be saying well? What now? All this over his father's corpse, he thought trembling deep down inside.

But he did not divert his eyes, he was absolutely certain of overcoming her. It was a matter of time, at the moment he knew he was stronger than her. Malvina lowered her eyes, humble and sad like a rejected child, a dog driven off. And he saw that Malvina was really weeping now, hot tears, shaken by heavy sobs. He could lower his eyes.

Her weeping must be upsetting the Captain-General, he did not know what to do. He was no doubt thinking of his position, of the recent embarrassment when he had to remove the arm which was going to support her. The Captain-General signalled to him, calling him. Gaspar pretended not to understand and waited in dread. Another nod of the head, the eyes speaking, this time he was surprised, commanding imperiously. And Gaspar walked over to Malvina and the Captain-General. As his father would do, he thought, accepting the role of an invented João Diogo Galvão.

Malvina bent her head towards him, in grief. He made no movement to protect or support her. His arms hanging loosely, nerveless. Unable to move, he simply looked at those brilliant, full, weeping eyes which implored him desperately and impatiently. He would not respond. Not that he did not want to, but because he could not. A cold tingling ran through his numb arm from his neck to his fingertips. Even this time she was the active one, he had not overcome her.

Malvina bent forward a little more and, moving softly, grievingly towards him, laid her head on his shoulder. Prevented from any reaction, he did not move. Malvina's head heavy and warm on his shoulder. The crackling smell of her hair, the undulating smell of her breasts, the burning smell of her eyes and her nostrils. Her arm pressing against his its full length, her hand groping for something. Finding and squeezing his hand. Her hand was as cold, sweaty and tremulous as his. The house spun, the earth shook noiselessly, the bells tolled inside the drawing-room, his body vibrated – a vast diapason, the deafening waves, unending.

And anything could happen. Nothing happened.

2

Just as there was in Malvina a memory of the future and in Gaspar a memory of the past, one can say that there was for him a destiny in the past and for her a destiny in the future. Although these words, linked together like this, particularly memory of the future with destiny in the past, may seem contradictory and arbitrary, and indeed they are and their concepts and meanings clash and contradict each other (memory is normally concerned with the past and with absent, yet living things – or rather, dead, because they have happened – the substance of destiny is always the future and latent, livid things, yet to happen), only by recourse to an arbitrary, contradictory comparison, a simile or metaphor, shall we be able to understand and love two beings at once so different and so close, so difficult, if not impossible to unite other than through destruction, and everything that has happened and is yet to happen to them. For this reason we examine them, immersing ourselves in her memory of the future and his destiny in the past, in his memory of the past and her destiny in the future, and we accompany their anguish and despair, their desires and torments, and we witness the movement of the activated mechanism, and we keep watch and listen to the oracles, and for both of them we implore the cruel, vengeful gods, unmoved by or indifferent to our useless prayers and threats. So high above and so close to us are the gods.

If in Malvina's case it was not destiny but memory which governed, although she lived in and for the future, and for this reason she loved (when she turned to the past it was to justify her behaviour and to seek fresh strength for the upward journey) – because she, in her pride, relied on herself, on her strength, certainty and power, and therefore anticipated and calculated – the things which her imagination continually invented and dreamed of as a still unfulfilled, but pre-established destiny, acquired existence and reality, that immutability of things that have happened, and it was difficult for her afterwards to know if they had occurred or not, to such an extent she saturated them with the essence of love in the warmth of her heart.

She was not conscious of these things nor of the mechanism which controlled her, nor did she know what was yet to happen, but was happening or already happened in her heart, and therefore she could remember what she dreamed and desired as something in the past, thus having happened, and she sought refuge in this future transformed into memory and lived in it, trying to learn lessons, see the mistakes and accidents to be avoided, like someone looking at a map in the dark; she did not know that all this is a form of destiny and possesses the inevitability of fatal things. If only she had the simple, ancient knowledge that all is destiny and destiny lies with the gods who watch over human life, and that to think that way, even in moments of grief and torment, comforts and relieves the heart; that men's fortunes go up and down not in response to their actions and questioning, and changes follow one another with absurd, gratuitous inevitability, at least to us, perhaps not to others; that destiny is blind and only a blind man can see in the dark, though one can, after the events, examining causes and consequences, say that there were remote and even immediate reasons, and that things happened for this or for that reason (a perfectly acceptable mistake or accident, for example), in the very human desire we have of explaining and predicting everything.

O Tiresias, inwardly illuminated by the light of thy darkness, help us to uncover and understand, because that is our inquisitive human desire; though knowing that it is impossible for man to alter the intricate web. At times, Tiresias, we think so, and for this reason we look to thee, in Hades or when thou wert still alive, and even now, knowing beforehand that it cannot be avoided and nevertheless desperately wanting, illuding ourselves that thy words, so heavy with sorrows, omens and significance, might tell us something and direct us in our tasks and actions, the way the ancients, not as ancient as thee, navigated by the stars and the mere direction of the magnetic needle. We beg thee because thou art and wert human and not a divine being, and we know that to the Lord of the oracles, not to thee to whom it is given only to see, we can stammer only this ancient prayer: Deliver us, Lord, from pains and scars, and if that is impossible, give us the strength and courage to endure them.

If in Malvina's case it was memory, in his case it was destiny, destiny in the past. More lucid and tragic than she (he accepted that), from having delved so deeply into his heart in the attempt to know himself, from so avoiding dreaming and from advancing, not forwards like her to the future, but backwards, ever more, always in the direction of an increasingly misty, impenetrable past, as distant and fleeting as the future and, like the future, inevitable, he followed his road towards the past, with neither despair nor alarms (not that he did not suffer, he did, and this we have seen), lucidly anguished, with the silent, cold acceptance of irresolute beings who walk towards death – certain that he would inevitably find it, there was no point in running away. And he followed his destiny in the past, not as she did her memory of the future in order to discover the mistake and thus be able to avoid it, not in order to know where the past fault was, but to accept it as inevitable and irremediable. Just as he would accept every punishment, even if the blame was not his. Because, cold and aware, he knew that to return to the past simply to relive an old sin, real or not matters little if felt as such, and, by way of this going backwards with the intention of modifying things, to change the present and the future, the past itself, and therefore destiny, is magic and he did not have the keywords which exorcize, regenerate and redeem. Therefore, though knowing, contradictorily he returned, not in order to change anything, but to advance further and further into the darkness and the immutability, and to live in the past until he found death. Living, for him, thus became transformed almost into a silent, propitiatory ceremony, a mythic and cosmic act, which put his very existence at risk and whose end was the tomb. Unprotected and empty-handed, lacking the instruments and the magic words, in silence and solitude, it was towards her (death) that he travelled voluntarily.

From all that has been said about his living in the past, where he took pleasure in his memories of his mother and sister, one might deduce that he made concessions to crime and sin. No, on the contrary: he was severe with regard to sin and would punish crime rigorously if it were up to him to punish. As a man of a conscientious turn, it was himself, however, that he punished.

And as he travelled towards the past, she always went in the direction of the future. Two beings travelling in opposite directions, slowly at first, then, in time and with acceleration, reaching a paroxysm of dizzy speed. And ending up at the same destination, thou mightest say. Tiresias, with the clear, ringing voice of thy blindness.

Not that they did not meet, they did. But their encounter was merely the brief, passing moment when they saw and knew one another and which could have been quietly prolonged. Ah, Tiresias, they were not wise; although they had suffered, they had not yet suffered as much as they supposed, as they were yet to suffer, each in his own way and privately – alone – and therefore they could not predict: she less than him, despite her memory of the future, built of dreams – they could not see – to pursue, with dizzy speed, their opposite routes; he retreating and running away when he realized, she advancing in the illusion of finding him. Since happiness for them was a brief moment, an intersection in time, a point of encounter, it could only last in time itself, in the past, which was then his exclusive domain. Their joy (if one can call it that) was merely a crossing of ways and this brief crossing, thou knowest, Tiresias, is what men call a happy life. Submerged and lost – she in the inscrutable clarity of the future, he in the darkness of the past – they each followed their destiny. If it were possible to prolong, dilate, halt time's mechanism, this brief encounter, the present . . .

Neither of them knew, Tiresias, that the destiny of the future is the territory of the gods, where nothing can be done; and that the destiny of the past is the realm of the dead, which it is vain and impossible to inhabit. He, child of darkness; she, child of light. She was living, he dying. Dangerously.

3

Why did they not continue to enjoy the calm delights of those tranquil hours? Why did they not prolong much more, stretch out for ever those pleasant, peaceful days when they lived happily and without agitation? Why increase, with hasty hearts, the speed of time? Why not leave to time itself the unhurried pace of the hours? The silent happiness, the slow, restful sluggishness of time. When things did not happen or happened so slowly that one did not notice, it was as if they did not happen. When they had not yet begun to happen. Why hasten time's mechanism, the voracious well of its sands? Why not forget time and simply enjoy straightforward, unhurried love? Why even think and say the word love, when everything could have carried on namelessly in the silence of their hearts, eternally happy and carefree?

These were the questions he asked himself constantly when there was no longer anything he could do. When, delving into the past, his pasture and domain (not the way he formerly took pleasure in his recollections, trying to live in and on them without asking why things happened, merely seeing how they happened), in order to find and keep (not to correct what was left behind, make a neat copy of his life, change the present and the future: merely to find and keep), when it was that everything started. If it had perhaps been him (no, it was not me, he told himself, going against his tendency to blame himself for everything) and not her (yes, her, in her craving to live more and more, always wanting more, and to fulfil what the heart may only imagine) who had ruined everything, trying to speed up time's mechanism and collaborate with destiny, sanctioning not the immutable, unpredictable laws of the future, which he feared so, but the proud desire, the impetuous haste of the heart.

Now his indolent heart no longer ceased inquiring. And he strove to discover, in time, in the secret rooms of memory, when it was. It had not been in the first days. At least he did not notice, and even now, keen and meticulous as a watchmaker, he saw it was not. Definitely not on that distant first day.

Only very much later, months afterwards, he discovered that what he called silent maternal repose, pure affection and respect, leisurely friendship, everything that he wished to prolong infinitely, and she did not allow, could have another name, for example: for him be called love, for her – passion. When he still tried to turn back, because just by thinking that he loved Malvina he had committed the worst of sins against his father, whose wife, despite the great difference of age, she was. Because he could not, he must stifle that feeling, pure and chaste though he thought it was. And when, afterwards, he failed to, he tranquillized his conscience by telling himself that the mere enjoyment of those calm, peaceful, pleasant hours was not yet a sin, or if it was a crime it did not deserve punishment. And he began to mix the dreams in which he and she appeared in different guise (stripping the dreams the way he scaled his memories, he saw with horror that in them he satisfied, in disguise, desires and projects which his heart did not dare to confess to itself, and he at first accused himself, in imaginary dialogues, in his father's voice and through other darker, more terrible voices) with the day-dream fantasies woven with the scraps of those tiny events which in reality seemed not to exist, when he supposed that time had stopped and life in the house was a coagulated, timeless lake, cloudless and waveless, which could go on for ever without winds or storms. What he called silent maternal repose, pure and chaste, even then, from the outset, forgetting that no mother–son feeling was possible between them (madness, a sinful audacity of the heart merely to imagine it), she so much younger and so different from his mother, very much younger

162

and livelier, more impetuous and impatient than him, a sluggard at heart. And yet he continued, accepting the blame as long as nothing more happened, no gesture or word, beyond that pure love, beyond that nothing happening which filled his calm, secretly silent hours (because there was the music and the conversations, the poems and the myths, but everything in such a muted undertone that it was like a continuation of his inner silence), as long as she did not touch him, as he never touched her, only afterwards (the clatter of the horses, the fall, and anything might happen, nothing did), when things were unleashed. Completely oblivious of his hatred, his repugnance towards women. . . .

In his meditations he went from end to end of his memory, not down in the deep abyss of time, but very close, to the most recent layers of his sentimental geology. Not the cosmic, chaotic memory which escapes time and its laws, though being contradictorily substance of time, but the memory which he was trying to put in order as a cold, chronological succession of facts. From now back to that far-off day, in that same drawing-room where they later mounted his father's bier, the crackling candlesticks, the purple damask, the bloodstains. In order to discover and understand.

That far-off day, more distant than it was in reality (he believed it very close to the bottomless well of time), because things suddenly began to happen at too fast a rhythm for a sluggish heart, everything happened so quickly.

He had arrived tired from his journey. Those days he spent shut up in his bedroom, his weary body sunk in sleep, his eyes glazed and lacklustre, things far away, the figure of his father sneaking up to his bed, the voice which he could scarcely hear, not understanding anything of what his father was trying to say, not even sure where he was in time and space, if he was in the house in Padre Faria district and if his mother was still alive (as a boy he sometimes wanted now/then to ask his father where she was; this behind the mists, from the end of endless corridors), those heavy, misty days, as if he lay in fever in a room full of hot, moist steam, at times he suffocated, in a dull stupor which he occasionally thought was the effect of the fever (he must surely have caught malaria in the woods and wilds through which he passed in his endless flight, not so much from his father and his stepmother, whom he did not yet know, as from himself), only to say in his lucid moments (his body still heavy and numb) no, it is not fever, I'm not sick, it's exhaustion, my heart cannot stand up to the absurd, slow way I have chosen to die – because he was sure that his weak body would not withstand that way of life. Maybe he was dying and that tepid sensation of faintness, of falling into a void, into a dizzy, bottomless well, was the first step down to death, he wondered, even, and, not his consciousness, if anything else told him it cannot be, death is silence, opacity, nothingness, if a part of him thought this, it was because he was alive.

When he succeeded in emerging from that lassitude and torpor, he said I am alive and saw, remembered that he was in his father's new house in the Rua Direita, on the square, near the palace. He bathed, trimmed his beard and put on the change of clothes his slave had left on the chair.

Only at the door, when his hand turned the key, did he think about her. How would he face her for the first time? How would he control his displeasure in the presence of that young and, undoubtedly, beautiful woman his father had chosen to replace the mother whom he considered irreplaceable? That woman with whom he would have to live under the same roof, a stranger, reputedly an aristocrat into the bargain – a local aristocrat, and he found it difficult enough to stand Portuguese aristocrats. He could not be always running away, hiding in the woods, all his life, since that way he did not die. If he wished to kill himself, he had to find a quicker, more efficient method than that.

No longer accustomed to standing and walking, he felt a buzzing in his ears and his head whirled, but it only lasted a moment, then was over. Now, more certain of himself, clean and fresh, he could go out.

The drawing-room door was open, even so he stopped on the threshold. A curtain moved and he said it is the wind, he saw nobody. Alone like that he could see the room at his ease, get to know his stepmother's taste, the Vicentine aristocrat – he thought ironically, as a way of trying to protect himself. He could know and predict, assess what she was like. Predisposed against her, the portrait his father painted of his chosen bride had caused him some revulsion. She could not be much good, to want to marry an old man like that. With an eye on his great fortune, of course. The repulsive colours in which he viewed his father's senile passion and which made him hide away deep in the remotest bushlands. But since they had to live together and he respected his father, the best thing was to see her with his own eyes. He would put aside all his ill will. Wait, maybe she is very different from what he imagined. He did not really believe it, but he thought it.

He advanced a little farther and his astonished eyes slowly ran around the room. From the floor to the ceiling, the walls and windows, from the carpets to the curtains caught up with silk ribbons. All very costly, much more costly and tasteful than he would have imagined. The settee and the chairs of engraved wood, their seats upholstered with damask. Dressers, console tables and tables with fluted legs, locks and drawer handles in wrought-iron filigree, covered with brocade and damask cloths, he inspected meticulously. She excelled herself, he would never have imagined. Expenditure in excess. But he could not deny she knew how to live and to arrange a house. And the crystal chandelier glittering resonantly with every breath of air, the panelled ceiling. He could not believe it, his father must have spent a fortune. Costly paintings, they had even gone to the trouble of engaging a painter of allegories. On the ceiling panels the four seasons, around the chandelier flowers and garlands, Cupids and medallions. Painting in bright, flat colours, blue and red, deep green, the black to emphasize the outline of the figures. He smiled at the Cupids, they looked more like two church cherubs with saucy features. A naive, imperfect type of painting, a representation which departed from the artistic canons, a mingling of east and west, of Greek fable and local products, thought the uprooted colonial he could not cease being. His eyes accustomed to soft, blurred lines and outlines, to the nuances and pinkish tints of the fleshy parts, to half-tones, to the gradual passing from colour to shade in the way clothes are draped, to the perfection of the figures, to the painting now in fashion in the places he had visited, he smiled condescendingly at the work of the anonymous painter who lacked the art of other lands and did not know the places he knew. A colonial of the Enlightenment, he was not used to very warm, flat colours. And the letters on the scrolls, flowery and out of proportion. The painter no doubt could not read, otherwise he would not separate the syllables and letters like that. Even so, it doesn't matter, it must have cost a great deal of ready money. The old man was spending his money, so different from when his mother was alive. She did not need anything, she asked for so little, his mother. Linen, the best linen. The last time, when he said goodbye. My son a linen cloth of the best Galician. I shall not see you again. Something tells me. Don't think like that, Mother. First it was Leonor, white. The other begged, wanted, demanded. What was the other like? She couldn't be a good woman, the favourable image faded. Open-handed, spendthrift. One to save, the other to spend. For those paintings, the conceited creature. She wanted the sort of life that only capital cities, not those backwoods, could offer. A *paulista* aristocrat, vainglorious and pretentious! In Portugal they laughed at the American nobility. . . .

Then he saw the small piece of furniture covered with a damask cloth. Damask and brocade all over the place. No, it was not possible! An Italian-style harpsichord, a spinet there in the mining country! And from its legs, which were slender and delicate, in fact the body and the legs, it must be from Portugal, meticulously fashioned, in the French taste. He walked towards the spinet, lifted the cloth and saw an item that was all refinement. A real jewel, his father must have laid out a goodly sum in gold. My boy, she likes reading, said his father. So far so good, now he discovered she dabbled in music. Despite the ceiling painting, the good impression returned. And, as with other things, she must be very demanding. Could she play? He smiled again, his old self, the bad impression again. He did not take very seriously those mulatto musicians, her probable teachers, more or less players by ear, little versed in written music. While he was in his bedroom he did not remember hearing any music. Even when he was coming round.

A Bosten spinet, he said, lifting the lid and reading the maker's name. Yes, one of the costliest and most perfect makes. She had taste, he could not deny that. At least with regard to the spinet, a small spinet painted all in gold, with medallions, shells, lyres and mythological figures. All very meticulous, so different from the allegories on the ceiling. To *his* taste. He pushed back the lid: the soft colours, the delicate symmetry, the figures in relief, the languid musical grace, very much to his taste. A Greek landscape, Ionic columns, a blue lake, an abandoned boat mirrored in the waters. He recalled some arias and adagios, pastoral, Arcadic poetry. So long ago! Before she died, his mother.

And everything that, for some time, until now, he denied, came back to him. And he was an educated man, no longer a hunter and backwoodsman, to the rhythm of the minuet. Educated a noble, delicate soul, the refined and subtle colonial who lived in the capital, in other lands. The slanting chords, clavichord. With the purest, most splendid sound. His fingers rested lightly on one or other of the keys. He did not yet dare to press them. He merely felt the smooth white of the ivory. Leonor, the cold hardness, the blue of her face. The first time timidly, afterwards it was good to stroke the cold skin. All in white. Linen, the purest, my son. The best Galician. But the smoothness of ivory, the keys were different. No, he would not yet produce the first sound. A Bosten, so long ago! Would he still be able to play? He was a flautist but he could play the spinet a little. She might not like it. Let her, the house was his too! He could. He struck the first key and stood listening to the clean, metallic sound of the note pierce the silence of the drawing-room. Another note, louder, to test the quality of the sound, the condition of the spinet. Another, he stood following the trajectory of the sound, the bright, clean tone crossing the room like a crystal blade.

And he played the first chord. How awful, he was so out of practice! He would give up, and he was about to close the spinet furiously and go away. But he decided to try the chord again. Better, much better, he smiled with satisfaction. A question of practice, if he wanted to he could go back to playing. Not the spinet, the flute, so long abandoned. The same chord again. More self-assured, right now, if he so wished, he could play the adagio of a sonata. His eyes gradually became still, like lakes, a peacefulness, a vague feeling of tenderness in his soul.

Suddenly he felt divided. No, he could not allow himself those feelings, when what he wanted was to die. The red damask cloth fallen on the floor. The white cloth, of the best Galician. Linen, my son. The burial shroud, the passion of Veronica. White linen, the hymn. The hymn, whiteness, Leonor. In his ear, in his soul. A buzzing, a vague recollection, a pain deep in his breast, a hardness in his eyes. His mother, the linen, Leonor. Now that woman! A violent desire to destroy everything, abandon everything. An anguish, a painful aura. Everything became confused inside him. Destroy, destroy the spinet. Not the spinet, something altogether too painful deep in his breast, something which for a few moments, when his eyes became two silent lakes, had disappeared, now came back again. Dazed, numbed, an absence which could engulf him. And not caring where he was or what he was doing, he ran his closed hand violently over the keyboard. From one end to the other. He screwed up his eyes, he was coming to, he felt he might cry. A silent, long-drawn-out tremor.

Suddenly that shout. She said no! and her hand was gripping his arm, holding it fast. Without even turning, he shook his arm in order to free himself. To free himself he knew not from whom. The firm hand, the hard fingers digging the nails into his flesh, hurting. He was unable to free himself from the anteater's claws, the snout which sucks up ants. He turned round and saw her. Startled, his eyes glazed, he did not know who she was. Only after an enormous moment, during which the aura grew and the ground disappeared beneath his feet, did he realize it might be her. His arm was still held, the blood left him, his heart felt faint. He did not know what to do in the face to those staring, flashing eyes which wounded and laid bare. As if he were naked. You, she shouted again, and her strident, furious voice awoke him to the reality of its owner. And he felt her fingers (no longer hard, the nails) relaxed and warm. And the blood flowed back, warm, into his face. The quivering in his body stopped, only his hands still trembled. Her fingers continued to hold his arm, pressing it. The pressure of those female fingers bothered him terribly.

Don't do that, she said in a quieter, though still commanding voice. His face was burning, ashamed. A child, he had behaved like a child. He gently removed the hand that held and pressed him. Without a word, he walked away, over to the window. With his back to her, filling his chest with the cold morning air, he composed himself. He breathed with difficulty, his heart throbbing wildly in his throat and in his ears. His face moist, sticky. He wiped his hand vigorously across his face. A cold, sticky sweat.

He stayed like that for some time. Until he could turn and face her, more under control. Still insecure, he turned round, he could not stay that way any longer. Too awkward, he had to control himself. More lucid, his eyes clear, he turned round.

Forgive all this, he said and saw that she was looking at his hands which he had unintentionally held out to her. He pulled them back abruptly, hiding them behind his back. He protected himself instinctively. From those eyes, at first dark with anger, which were gradually returning to their natural colour: blue eyes, doll's eyes. And he, who had never dared look a woman straight in the eyes, kept staring into those blue eyes. A pair of large full eyes, they attracted. Oddly, he did not feel afraid. They were gentle eyes, no danger. Pale she was, probably because of the shock, he thought. Not being able to tear himself from those eyes and letting his linger longer than he should, he saw that she was defenceless. Like me just now, he thought. And pale, he had upset her badly.

Suddenly the eyes became more brilliant and fiery: she was no longer a weak, defenceless woman. From being gentle and motionless, her eyes were transformed and grew darker, such was their strength. Threatened, in danger again. The ground disappearing again. He diverted his gaze from those strong, blue, flaming, burning eyes. He bent his head and made a bow. If you will permit me, madam, he said and withdrew.

The days which followed were different in every way from what he had imagined in the seclusion of his room. Only on the following day, when she appeared, did he feel slightly embarrassed and confused. But it did not last long. She put him so at ease, her eyes were so gentle and kind, that he regretted the bad opinion he had formed. Despite the difference of age, his father had chosen a good wife. She was attentive, her voice serene and warm, her gestures calm and slow; he had no reason to be on his guard against her.

Malvina had a delicacy, a natural refinement, such as he had never encountered in any woman. She liked to serve him, she was always asking if he needed anything, if everything was to his liking. Forgive me if you are short of anything, I am not accustomed to being mistress of the house, she said. She actually had a specially affectionate way of serving. A maternal affection, a sweetness, a gentleness he had not seen for a long time. He ought not be afraid of her.

Malvina's maids looked after his clothes and saw to his food. Men do not know about these things, she said, when he pointed out to her that he had his own slave for that purpose. She insisted on looking after everything, seeing to everything. In no time she learned his tastes and habits. She was the one who attended, through Inacia or by herself, to his favourite dishes and titbits. Her solicitude was touching. Only his mother was able to divine his thoughts like that.

For the first time since his mother died, he felt that someone could be tender and pure towards him. That there was an affectionate relationship with no wantonness. That there was nothing evil in her, no ulterior motive: she was as clear and pure as a cool running brook. That he had no need to run away or to die, his heart was now joyful and happy.

So happy, so joyful and carefree, that he was no longer afraid of going to the drawing-room when he heard the first chords on the spinet. As soon as she sensed he was in the room (however lightly he trod, she always sensed it), she lowered the tone, then stopped playing. Go on, continue, he said. No, I am still learning, do not make me feel embarrassed, she said. I am one of the family, he said, do as you please. He must never forget that they were stepson and stepmother, related therefore.

Since she did not want to continue, he left it for another day. And the two had long conversations, for hours on end. He told her stories about Rio de Janeiro, Portugal, the capital cities he had visited. He talked about music and poetry, opened up a whole new world to her. A world for which her heart must yearn. So delicate was her heart and she so refined. Alive, aware. She listened enraptured, letting him talk. Her blue eyes open wide, she was sailing in a dream. He, always so quiet and reserved before, was the one who did most of the talking. She retained the smallest things she heard and showed such an interest in his past life that, without noticing, he opened his heart to her and made his confession. He even permitted himself to talk about his mother and sister. And to laugh, he even laughed when he was with her, he suddenly realized, surprised at the changes he was going through. He thought of drawing back, but saw it was not necessary. Those hours were calm and good, so pure that he now reproached himself for having thought ill of women.

After so long in the shadows and in the kingdom of the dead, Gaspar was reborn to life and light. Not a single sad thought, everything tranquil and pacified. Even silence, which disturbed him so much when he was in other people's presence, was good, he began to enjoy being silent when he was with her. A new man was being born.

And the new man spent hours on end shut in his room, trying to regain his old skill on the flute. His fingers hard at first, his mouth and tongue stiff, his blow wet and laborious. He went back to his sheet music, the dusty scores at the bottom of the wicker chest, so long forgotten. In a few days his fingering became correct, his blow regular. He could already play the most sophisticated octaves, the most difficult chromatic scales and the fastest passages and trills. He once more played with his former ease and precision. He was so pleased he even hummed the area 'Consolati e Spera!' by Scarlatti, of which he was so fond. And he searched in concertos, sonatas and operas the passages which could be played without voice, as a duet for spinet and flute. He made the necessary arrangements, consoling himself this way for the time he had to wait. He wanted serious, lofty music, none of your sentimental ditties which were all the rage, a proper fever, even in Portugal, whither they had been carried. Basically, as a cultured colonial he found them vulgar and obscene. Being of a refined nature, she would learn with him. And his father, who loved Malvina so much, would be doubly pleased hearing the two of them play together. They were now a happy family.

She was still reluctant to play in his presence. The moment she sensed he was in the room, she stopped. Gaspar left her at her ease, picked up a book and started reading. From the very beginning she would not let him call her madam. Such an old-fashioned form of address is unthinkable between us, she said. They both used the familiar form of address without any embarrassment. So intimate, so harmless, those afternoons in the drawing-room, after much pleading she condescended to play a little. Bashful, hiding her face, she asked if it was very bad. No, on the contrary, for the short period of time you have been studying, he said. You need more practice and to perfect your turns. She asked if it might not be her music teacher. No, he is good, keep on with him, said Gaspar, who wanted to leave the boring business of teaching her to read music to Master Estêvão.

Even though he did not mean to take the mulatto's place, he was in a sense her music teacher. Master Estêvão was left with the job of teaching her to read music, and the monotonous, tiring scales. His was the more pleasant side of her learning. Thinking ahead already, he taught her the slower passages of a sonata for flute and spinet. Every afternoon, the moment he heard the first notes he would come down to the drawing-room and stay by her side. At first she was still bashful, afterwards completely at her ease, although she still pretended to be embarrassed. He thought it was coyness, an attractive feminine vanity which suited her very well. Indeed, everything about her, now, was unadulterated attraction, beauty and charm. So understanding, kind and attentive was he.

With her always interested and keen, and him patient, tender and gentle, in a short time Malvina could already play a Spanish pavane by herself. She was so quick and diligent at learning, he was amazed to see the ease with which Malvina already played a tarantella which was too quick and lively for a beginner. With Master Estêvão in the mornings and with the assistance of Gaspar in the afternoons, she would sometimes play whole pieces without his needing to correct a single mistake.

Self-assured, with a clear silvery laugh which he found so enchanting (he too now laughed without shyness, for the slightest reason the two of them laughed and laughed), it was she who insisted they play a duet. Gaspar said a pretend no. Why not? she asked. I know you play very well. Don't I hear you every day playing in your room? He went bright red, as if he had been caught committing a serious offence. I don't want to, he said, not yet. Why not, if you play so well? she asked and he answered for no reason. Because of your promise to the Virgin? she said, and he was amused by that story that was spread around and she believed. It's not because of that, he said. If that is not the reason, then it is because of me, you don't think I can follow you, she said, pouting and making a face. All right, tomorrow, he eventually agreed.

Not satisfied with his agreeing, she then asked him to read some poetry. He laughed, pleased to see that she liked his way of reading.

Like his father (much less so, of course), everything she did, even her faces and affectations, enchanted him. Like that charming habit of running her tongue between her teeth and moistening her lips. In fact, her gleaming, sparkling red hair, her large, full blue eyes, her fleshy, prominent mouth, her prettily shaped nostrils, her round face, the gentle curves of her shoulder and bosom, even the fullness of her breasts which, supported by her bodice, floated quivering and sighing, her smell a mixture of tranquil flesh and benjamin or basilicon (he could not distinguish the essences, being unaccustomed to those odours, to being so close; he tried to remember afterwards, in his room), all her warm beauty (he could not remember ever before seeing so beautiful and pure a woman), her well-modulated way of speaking, its bright tone at times reminding him of a violin played quietly, so soft and melodious was her speech, none of this upset him any more. Quite the contrary: he let himself be dragged along, possessed by that beauty and grace which he saw as the purest gift from heaven. Without the least suspicion, with no wantonness in his heart.

Then came the flute. And with it the afternoons and evenings became fuller and gayer in João Diogo Galvão's house. His father came to the drawing-room and listened enraptured, his eyes languid and moist. That pair were the joy and happiness which God had reserved for his old age. Unaccustomed to these refinements and melodies, in a short while he was asleep, to the rhythm of that celestial music. The two smiled and continued on the waves of the music, blissfully oblivious, immersed in that soothing peace.

He did not limit himself merely to accompanying her (the reverse should really have happened, but he did not want it) and teaching her the sonatas and suites which he carefully chose and arranged for spinet and flute, with a knowledge that astonished her, but he also talked to her about what he had heard in Lisbon, in Venice, in Florence, in Naples, in Paris, in all the places he had visited. He talked about Pergolesi, Monteverdi, Alessandro and Domenico Scarlatti, Marcello. So changed that he even gave voice to some arias from operas and psalms. When the suite or sonata was more difficult and Malvina could not yet play it, he played solo versions of the passages which his flute could manage.

Gay and grateful, she always begged for more. Sometimes she gave the impression of a slight sadness, a hint of despair, a veiled impatience, but she quickly and cleverly corrected it and he thought it had been an illusion. That serene calm could never come to an end.

If he talked to her about theory and technique, she showed little interest. Sensitive as she was, with such a harmonious and melodious spirit, she was only interested in those things which spoke of sentiment and passions. She wanted the spirit, pure emotion, he thought. When he told her that Scarlatti took from the spinet almost everything the spinet could give in terms of harmony, of its great innovations, she showed little interest. When he told her that the Princess Maria Barbara was taught by Scarlatti, her interest in Scarlatti grew. When he spoke of the passionate, solemn feeling of his music, he saw the ecstasy in her brilliant eyes; Malvina was a chosen spirit, her homeland was heaven. If he said, look at this, and even solo played for her the accompaniment of a psalm by Marcello, she looked bored. No, Gaspar, it sounds like a church choir, a litany, let's play something else, she said once. What shall we play then, he asked and she said something more tender and warm. He smiled, he could not play those passionate, pathetic things on the flute, she would have to play alone. Why not, she asked. Because the flute will not, it isn't suitable for that. She became sad, she so wanted to! What is suitable for the flute are sweet, dreamy, poetic pastoral melodies, he said, master of his art. Then she gave him a gentle, misty smile. Her eyes were so dreamy and moist, her mind so far away, her features so pure and peaceful, it was as if she could already hear the flute, not in the drawing-room there, but in green fields, among groves of trees and dulcet, crystalline streams. And in thought he joined her in the airy meandering of his words. And mentally, a shepherd with a lyre, he was playing in a field of daisies lightly stirred by the soft fragrant breeze, in a distant valley, the rustling leaves like the veiled sound of wandering violas, of an Aeolian harp touched by the wind. If heaven existed, it must be like this, he thought, surrendering to a tenderness he had never before experienced. But heaven was not like that.

One day, when she arrived, she was agitated, tremulous and nervous, though she tried to disguise it and appear calm. But there was a different vibration in her gestures and her voice which she was unable to hide. She was inattentive and made mistakes one after the other. So distracted, her eyes so absent and far away: as if they passed right through the score, which was a mirror, an open window through which her thoughts took wing.

Here, he said, stretching his arm over Malvina's shoulder to point to the chord on the score. His arm brushed her bare, round shoulders and he did not know, at that moment, why he either would not or could not turn back, and his hand rested on the staves of the score longer than was necessary. His hand motionless for a time which afterwards, and even then, seemed to him excessively long. And without noticing that he had almost pressed his body against hers, he was contaminated by the heat of those round, burning shoulders, of that vibrant, odorous body. And Malvina (it could not be an illusion, afterwards he was certain, when a thousand times he recalled his feelings), instead of moving away (and he was accusing himself of being imprudent), sought to move closer to him, very gently, but so close, warm and odorous, that he could not fail to be aware – everything she did was deliberate. Even then he did not retreat, he was paralysed by the tremor of the emotion. A painful, burning pleasure ran through his whole body, making him shudder. His hand trembled more than usual, revealing the violence of the emotion. He was not innocent, the two of them knew that or suspected it. And she, ever more astute, sinuous, disturbing, advanced farther (here? she said) and seized his cold, trembling hand. She too was trembling, their cold, trembling hands warmed each other. It was as if they had spoken out all they were feeling and thinking, she more so than him. Now he could remove his hand, but he did not. He delayed longer than he needed.

But suddenly a feeling of dismay, of shame, a sense of sin, a crime against his father (she was his wife, she was in place of his mother) prevented him continuing. More self-controlled, even though with his face burning, he attempted to regain his equilibrium. She must never suspect that he was aware of everything, was participating covertly in that dangerous game. He must pretend: she could not become aware that they were experiencing the same harmony – the same wind at that moment was blowing them along. And he told her with his eyes this must never happen again. She let go of his hand.

And this minimal encounter brought him awake, changing his whole life, and marked him out a destiny for ever. Not only had she loved him for a long time, maybe since the first time they met; he too. Not just her, they both loved and their love was mutual. In different ways, according to the character and destiny of each, but they loved one another. Malvina ardently desiring (on the surface she concealed it, only communicating her passion by means of cabalistic signs and semaphores, which were only later, much much later, deciphered), he not. She, keen and quick, aware, abrupt and wild, seeking to control the events and the days, to take possession of the future: he, slow and sluggish, irresolute even, unaware of what was going on in the lower layers, not wishing to go into the future, but just to prolong those good, peaceful hours, the quiet togetherness, without the great moments – everything that can be called present happiness. A man of the past, he was now moving into the present.

That period of time suddenly became an eternity to him, since the day when he entered that room and saw the spinet for the first time, until when their hands met and through the cold, the tremor, the touch and the warmth, they spoke to one another and discovered that they were in love or could love one another (he at least; she, for her part, already knew that she loved and wanted him), that period of time was a short moment, a mere intersection in time, the crossing of two roads in search of opposite horizons.

And then, with horror, he knew it: he loved her, not just now, but furtively and covertly, on an imperceptible ascending scale, had loved her for a long time. He was unable to locate the moment in time when it all began, things happened so leisurely, she conquered him so slowly.

In the light of that minimal encounter of hands, everything took on a different appearance, acquired a new meaning, revealed itself clearly, naked and meaning what they really meant, those gestures and words, those looks and silences, what they said. The light retreated, and he, once again a man of the past, turned towards the past, pursuing the bright light. Not with the wish of living in it as formerly (he was now another person, the time he had lived in the present had changed him – so, at least, he thought), but to discover when it had all started, see the initial fault, follow the sequence of sins.

And he saw that all the communication was made by means of cabalistic signs, semaphoric channels. The signs were only now unveiled in his consciousness – like a seed underground they had swelled and grown, he simply did not notice. Without his suspecting it, she inseminated him, he had been possessed by her.

Malvina had lived and suffered, he had not. What for him was a present prolonged to its maximum duration, for her was already a past. Malvina lived and suffered her slow agony, he was beginning only now to live and suffer. All his happiness had been a brief intermezzo.

And all that, which he called peaceful, affectionate togetherness, without bad thoughts, good pure hours, maternal solicitude and attention (after all she had no children and she was his father's wife), veiled innocent tenderness, could have and did have another name. For him that name was love, for her passion. When he was able to give a name to everything he had felt in the secret, dark silence, there was nothing else he could do.

In his now unceasing return, in his journeying inside the past, until that first moment – the first time (disturbed and confused he ran his hand violently along the keyboard, then afterwards they looked at one another; at first, not knowing what he was doing, he looked forcefully deep into her surprised blue eyes and she blushed – like him she blushed too – perhaps wounded and astonished, confused, and she lowered her eyes, only to go back immediately to being the strong, aggressive woman she always was – and it was his turn to lower his eyes, and he moved away), and then to come back to the present, only to return once more. . . . He was complicated and tormented, the more so after happiness, without his noticing, passed him by.

In his suddenly cold, hard, lucid eyes, free of scales, things acquired their true real significance. He could no longer be in any doubt: all veiled language, artifices and traps, misunderstood and shady nuances. A language which he only now had ears and eyes to understand. Not only on her part, on his too. He too spoke and said things. And the, for him, most innocent conversations took on another significance.

He recalled the shadows in Malvina's eyes, her gently undulating and suddenly raised tone of voice, a more pronounced tremor of her hand, a deeper sigh, how she lingered over his name (at times she seemed to say Gaspar for the mere pleasure of saying, between the lines in the folds of the sounds – his ears then not capable of catching it – saying my love, my darling, my life), and later, always advancing one more step, over whole phrases, veritable pleas and confessions. My God, why had he not seen?

He recalled how certain lines of poetry acquired special, private meanings for her, as if he were (not the poem, but he himself) confessing, offering his strangled heart in his hand. Those lines had been written for her, they were missives. And even long after, he shuddered and blamed himself, felt ashamed of the arias he had hummed, the words he had spoken. How he had lost his good sense, his discretion!

He recalled her eyes lighting up (not with pure ecstasy but with passion) when he talked about the solemn, passionate sentiment of a sonata or an aria, and he was really talking about his own heart. When she said let's play something more tender and warm, it was a subtle, passionate invitation. And even he, at the time not realizing, wanted to speak out too, to confess his feelings. She, the eager, passionate spirit, seemed to hear and understand everything. When he said the flute is not suited to passionate, pathetic melodies, she no doubt understood I cannot accompany you in your desperate passion. Because Malvina's eyes saddened. And how they smiled at him when he consoled her: the flute can play only sweet, poetic, dreamy pastoral melodies. There he was warning her of the danger, inviting her to a pure, secret love. The love they had been enjoying for a long time, the fleeting happiness which Malvina suddenly, despairingly and thoughtlessly, interrupted. And it could all have continued. . . .

It did not. After that day things were different. Not that they had changed, they did not change. They appeared to be the same, but different. Nothing continued to happen, nothing happened. At least on the surface, as far as he was able to gather. Gaspar retreated, trying to recover his lost balance, his tranquillity and peace of mind. She went on ahead.

They were days of torment, silent suffering, veiled flagellation. Gaspar accused and punished himself: as penitence for his guilt, he imposed the obligation of enduring everything. He would not leave Malvina, his father's house. That was where everything had to take place.

His father's presence troubled him, at times he thought he would not be able to stand it. At mealtimes, and especially in the drawing-room when his father came to watch them. He felt guilty for loving Malvina, impossible to go on as if he did not. The old man might suspect something, see in his eyes the guilt he was now attempting to stifle.

And he wondered if his father had not understood everything, their love made them so careless. The two always together, the flute and spinet duets, and on the settee, almost joined together, the murmured conversations, the whispered poems, and even when they spoke aloud, the things they said, the extravagant confessions of love. Was it possible his father did not see, not suspect? He suspected, impossible not to see. Cunning old boy, he saw it all, he was just keeping watch. When his father left them, Gaspar said no, he did not see a thing, he suspected nothing. He had been saved, miraculously saved. Mad, that's what he was. Now he had to watch his step, be more cautious, he could not be protected twice.

Despite all he suffered in the afternoons and evenings, the two of them alone in the drawing-room, he would overcome the harsh penance he had given himself. But what about Malvina? he wondered. So different from him, she was moving steadily forward all the time. And he unable to speak, unable to alert her. He would have to struggle not only against himself, but against her as well. He had to restrain her, it was worth any price. They could not continue in their crime and sin, he told himself in his hours of penance.

He did not make any changes in his hours, the afternoons and evenings. He only, and that gradually, tried to keep a distance, not allowing their hands and bodies to touch, their eyes to meet and exchange messages. Without her noticing that he was retreating. Without her seeing that he loved her, now as before. Without her suspecting that he knew she loved him. If she noticed, saw or suspected, all would be lost.

Torture to keep on feigning an innocence, a pure, carefree togetherness, a peace and a naïve pleasure which he had long since ceased to enjoy. Little by little he succeeded, he conquered himself.

It was a superhuman struggle against blood and against the darkness within, against her and against himself too. He called up strength which he had never supposed he possessed. He used all his capability, all his experience of life: everything he had learned from his solitary way of life.

And he continued until he conquered himself. He mastered his voice, his gestures, even the tremor in his hands. He even managed to smile, painfully. Everything went into reverse, while continuing the same. At no time could she become aware that he loved her and knew it. Malvina never came to suspect that he ever received her pathetic, tormented appeals. She was talking into the wind, no voice came back.

He succeeded so well in dissembling and disguising, that he actually repeated the same gestures and words formerly so charged with meaning; he deceived and confused her. Just as, for so long, he deceived himself.

But while he was winning his battle (he paid a high price, shedding in the solitude of his bedroom – those moist, cold, sticky insomnias – tears of blood such as he never wept before) and Malvina was coming to realize that nothing had happened between them, was happening or could happen (at least as long as his father was alive), the sorrow, the resentment and the dense despair which she could no longer conceal began to be obvious. And he was aware of the acrimony and bitterness in her eyes and in her words. Just as before he had not noticed her desperate appeals, he continued now, but in pretence.

The hardest test was when João Diogo had to undertake the journey to see his land grants in the São Francisco area. He failed to prevent his father's departure. After he had gone, he realized that one half of him wanted his father to go: that way he could endure things better. But another thought, another sin grew in his heart.

Hardly had his father disappeared at the end of the street, when an idea began, darkly, slowly, to germinate. He was no longer innocent, he was aware of what was happening. If he brushed aside the sinister idea, it would return in the guise of a dream. And for the first time he had the dream which would be repeated from then on with enlargements and additions. A tormenting and premonitory nightmare, the hand advancing in the darkness. His father lying alone in the double bed, swamped in lace and embroidery, silks and tassels – the white mask, the rouge-painted mouth. The black shape approached, leaped on to the bed and the arm struck repeatedly with a dagger. His father, mouth open, tongue purple, the scream strangled in his throat. Once the scream was uttered (by him, not by his father), he woke up soaked in sweat.

Gradually, as the days went by, he began to entertain the thought: if his father died in the cattle country, the kinship would disappear. Then their love would be possible, anything might happen.

And having admitted this thought while he awaited his father's return, he gave access to another, even more dangerous thought and began to live on intimate terms with it. If he did nothing, if they did not touch one another and did not speak to one another about what each was thinking, he could love her in secret. There would be no evil, as nothing more than thought it was permitted. A thought which was, by itself, the actual concretization of the sin, as he saw afterwards.

He was already punishing himself for being affected by Malvina's beauty and her presence. He enjoyed, delicately savoured in silence, in apparent coldness and immobility, that shining melodious voice, those eyes which became dark and bright, grew smaller or larger, reflecting the most secret emotions, that warm, permanent smell – quivering flesh, benjamin, basilicon. All without Malvina noticing, he was sure she never noticed.

Swamped in sounds, colours, smells, warmth, beauty and presence, he would go to his room and drop on to his bed. His whole body was one single tremor in the darkness.

His father returned. Yet again, this time willingly, he saw that he had committed the greatest sin against his father. However, he neither took fright nor accused himself: he accepted his damnation as inevitable. He had once more to stifle the thought, the love he had allowed himself.

The very opposite of Gaspar, who was all silence and acceptance, surrendering to passivity and to the negation of all desire or thought, living in a state of somnambular indecision, ineffectual and non-existent, yet monstrously continuing to play the farce of tranquil, innocent, joyful togetherness, Malvina moved forward. No force could resist her. Even so, he would try, it was his obligation. Time was moving fast for both of them.

He was never able to discover what was happening to Malvina. He cnever succeeded in divining her hopes and plans. Day by day more bitter and desperate. Malvina did not even hide her despair. She was ironic and mysterious, at any moment she might not control herself and openly confess her desperate love.

Malvina was becoming more audacious and ironic. One step further and she would speak straight out. She got to the point of speaking. That time when she thought up the idea of going to Vila do Carmo. He did not wish to, he was afraid of what Malvina was planning and plotting, of what was yet to happen. She provoked him, challenged him boldly. Don't you want to? she said. Are you afraid of going into the town with me? Nobody will say anything. After all I am your stepmother. And he saw, in the corner of her mouth and in her eyes, a mocking little laugh. She caught him out, Gaspar blushed again.

Malvina went to his father and got what she wanted: now the two of them were going to Vila do Carmo. Malvina was more beautiful than ever, she took a lot of trouble. The small hat perched atop her flaming hair, which crackled and gleamed, her eyes afire, the lace and embroidery on her white blouse, on the cuffs protruding from the sleeves of her blue riding-jacket. She was a goddess, a goddess of the hunt, thought Gaspar with rhetorical exaggeration. Restless and nervous, Malvina tapped the silver whip against her riding-habit. But gay, a gaiety and brilliance which blinded him; he was afraid he would not stand it and would betray himself. To overcome his own nervousness, he asked her playfully if she was going to some ball. He was immediately sorry, when she, more boldly still, said yes. The two of them were going to be dance partners the whole night, waltzing together. He felt his face burn, he must be redder than the first time. And seeing him blush, she gave a loud, ringing laugh, she was gay and happy. She finally had the upper hand.

Gaspar recovered his calm and self-control. To get around his nervousness and awkwardness, he talked about things to do with the wilds and the backlands. He told her stories about Tripuí, about the people from Taubaté who were the first to come into the Minas country.

Then they met the half-breed and she (Gaspar saw it now, at the time he only noticed Januario's impudence) allowed the mestizo to admire her at length. Then she laughed out loud, gave a shout, whipped her horse and set off at a furious gallop. That Arab was not as gentle and firm of foot as he thought. She applied the whip and shouted, something would happen. Still astonished, he watched her race ahead. He whipped his roan and dug the spurs into its flanks, trying to catch up with her. In a cloud of dust she disappeared round a bend in the road. No longer accustomed, lashing the horse like that, she might fall. Lose control of the reins, the horse running free. He was afraid for her.

He caught sight of her. When he was close to catching up with her, he saw Malvina's horse rear up, its front legs pawing the air. No doubt she had tried to stop him by pulling sharply on the reins. It almost sat on the ground, she fell to one side, the horse to the other. Could have crushed her.

He reached her. Jumping down, he half lifted Malvina's body from the ground and raised her head, resting it against his chest. She was in a swoon, her face extremely white. Malvina's head rested on Gaspar's shoulder, her face against his neck. He felt the firmness and roundness of those shoulders, the heat of that body, the warmth of her breath, her snowy breasts rising and falling with her distressed breathing. The smell and the live softness of her hair close to his mouth and nose. He had never held a woman in his arms. Malvina's heart beat against his. The most dangerous, perilous temptation: he held her tight, pressed his face against hers, felt her against him to the depths of his being, melted into her. His lips timidly caressing her smooth skin, the skin of a peach which he was tempted to bite. With her unconscious, he could. But she stirred, seeking a more comfortable position in the arms which protected her, trying to reach him with her lips. Her breathing was hotter and more laboured, she was coming round. Maybe she had not fainted, was pretending, and he. . . . He shook her, fanned her with his hat. She began to wake up, opening her eyes. She had been saved, nothing happened.

After that insane ride, contrary to what he expected, Malvina withdrew. Something was happening to her, she seemed pacified, she had resigned herself to tranquillity. He did not know what it was and did not inquire. The tranquil afternoons returned, the nice tender togetherness. Going against his promise to himself, he now allowed himself the secret tenderness. That way they were happy and could go on in silence for a lifetime. If she wished, and she seemed to. In the purest love.

They did not continue, suddenly everything went so quickly. The mechanism in motion, things began to happen. The terrible night when it all happened. Strange how things alarm us before they happen. Like a refrain. His father dead, murdered. The bier mounted in the drawing-room, the crackling candlesticks, the smell of molten wax and flowers. The people, the movement, the aura, the anguish. His premonitory dream was finally becoming reality, it was real. It was his own hand which stabbed his father in the nightmare. The dream revealed itself, no mystery. He could have no further doubt, it had been him who killed his father.

Contrary to what he came to think when João Diogo travelled to the backlands, now his father was dead, he could no longer. Now his father was dead, he had to be a different person, take his place. Put on another mask, play another part. Not by her side, he would go away. In the presence of the others, the town, the Captain-General. In command of his possessions, his father's mines and estates. To save something from the general ruin, which was not evident. His father would have liked to see him like that. He was once more his much loved son. A different man, he would be a different man. A different man is born, he said again. Everything straightforward and cool, he now knew how to act.

Until the Captain-General asked for her. Malvina came, and then what he most feared happened. She squeezed his hand. Her hand was cold, perspiring and trembling. Like mine, he thought, unable to control the deep tremor echoing in his breast. The room went round, the bells tolled, the earth shook. He was a struck tuning-fork. But nothing happened.

When the Captain-General asked if, as a precautionary measure, he could send a trusted lieutenant to stay a few days with them, he felt that he had once more been miraculously saved. That way he would avoid Malvina, protect himself against her, nothing else could happen. During the lieutenant's stay he would have time to arrange the old house in the Padre Faria district. Which his father ought never have left. Once the days of mourning were over he would move there. Malvina stayed right there in Rua Direita, the mansion was hers after all. Him well away, free, happy.

That was how it all went. After the period of mourning, when the two of them returned from the mass, the lieutenant informed them that his presence in the mansion was no longer necessary. Captain-General's orders, they had discovered a plot, now the chief was going to take action.

The lieutenant left, the two of them suddenly alone together in the drawing-room. With flaming eyes, Malvina faced him once more. He was in no doubt, it was going to happen. He waited, now he actually wanted it to happen. So that he could finish everything once and for all.

She looked him straight in the eyes. Well, she said, and now? Now what? he said. The two of us, she said. I know about me, I've decided what I'm going to do, he said challengingly. Yes, what are you going to do? she asked and he replied that he was moving to Padre Faria that very day.

Malvina screamed and slumped forward until she fell to her knees on the floor. She embraced his legs. He stood motionless and stiff, he would not raise her. No, she said, in tears. Not after all that has happened. All for you. There is no more point in pretending, you know about my passion now. If you didn't know, I tell you now. I love you, Gaspar, I have always loved you. From the first time I saw you. From that time.

No, he said, and she began to get up without letting go of him, embracing him more tightly, leaning against him to lift herself. Once in a standing position, she took his head in her hands. Face to face, staring one another in the eyes. Why no? A cold terror gripped him. Certain however of what he was going to do. Because you are my father's wife. My father's wife was my mother. What? she screamed, shaking him, tears falling from her eyes. Your father is dead, we are free. And what have I to do with your mother? Everything and nothing, he said. I would not be able to, Malvina. You had better convince yourself of that. No, she said, screaming and sobbing. You would! You can! And she kissed him on the mouth. He did not move, he would not move. Of stone, of ice. His lips were cold and wet. Flushed, in despair, she kissed him, she bit him. She clutched him, she shook him.

Seeing him cold, seeing herself rejected, she pushed him away. Frigid failure! she said, in one last attack, to see if, by offending his manhood, she could at least force him to move. You are not a man! she said eventually.

Gaspar bowed his head and turned away without a word.

The Wheel of Time

1

One, said Malvina, hearing the first chime of the Carmo lead bell. Some committee member of the brotherhood, no doubt. She waited for the second, to confirm what she already knew. The first time she heard, very early in the morning, she asked Inacia what it was they were ringing. Inacia said for the dying. She, Malvina, shuddered. There was shadow and premonition in the hoarse black drawl. Once she prayed to Our Lady of the Conception not to let those bells wake him. It should be her, the harpsichord music silent for ever. The coffin covered with a purple damask cloth, the bloodstains. When he arrived from his journey, holed out in the woods, always running away (from her? when he did even not know her), and he would not come down to the drawing-room, shut away in his bedroom. In torment, she waited like now. Worse now, in despair. Then there was still hope, before. Now she was alone, abandoned, rejected. She looked at the street (and inside it was so dark): all so bright, the day promised to be brilliant. Not for her; the darkness for me, she said.

The second chime. Damned bells, before they only annoyed her, now they would drive a soul mad. What a fateful, idiotic idea to invent such a fashion. They were deafening. They rang inside the drawing-room, her head stuffed inside the bell, a huge, painful clapper. Dizzy, desperate. Felt like crying, screaming. Her eyes dry, just hatred. Hatred doesn't produce tears, it is hard and dry. It was a deep, long chime, hung in the air a long, long time, swelling. Prayers, they wanted prayers. Someone who was going to die but would not. Needed prayers, much praying. Not she, someone moribund. If only it was her, that way she would be sure of death, however long-drawn-out the agony. She would find the peace and silence of God. She did not deserve it. To hell, damned things! She was not going to pray, she had never prayed again since she was abandoned. When her first appeals were answered: only for her to end by suffering more. Even her fear of thinking that way had gone. At first she still struck her mouth thrice. Damnation, death. If she did not pray for herself, why pray for other people? And she said, perversely, no

longer afraid of any punishment from heaven, let the agony last! Like
hers, a year. Or was it more than a year? She had lost her notion of time,
from suffering so much. At times she seemed to have lived a vast amount
of time, she was really a wrinkled, finished old woman. Since that
night, the two of them: she in front lighting the dark corridor, her
trembling hand shielding the candle's flame, on the way to João Diogo's
bedroom. She was not certain what was going to happen, she was
confidently hopeful. Since that day, the bier mounted in this room, the
damask cloth stained with blood. When, in the presence of everyone (at
that moment she could, no one suspected), standing next to the
Captain-General, she slowly bowed her head towards him, her sore,
tearful eyes asking for support. Her head on his hard shoulder, she felt
protected. But how cold it was, that body sought for so long. And a
strange peace, never before achieved, overcame the months of weariness,
the tormented wait. And since he did not move, she went and pressed her
arm against his, her hand feeling for that hand so often dreamed of in
torment. And finding it, the other hand, cold and sweaty. He was
trembling more than she was. In a way, the beginning and end of the only
happiness she had known. Forgetting those days when she thought she
was happy, when she discovered she was in love. It lasted such a short time
and hurt so much. As she remembered, now, it hurt again.

Then came the third, she kept counting. The chimes vibrated on and
on in the air – endlessly, like waves in a lake without a shore. Damned
bells! Like that time so many years ago, so it seemed. Damned things!
she kept saying, as if the bells were to blame for everything that had
happened. When the bells only tolled after the event. Or maybe not?
Like now, for the dying. What if they rang before things happened, too
softly for our ears to hear them, like omens announcing what was to
come? That time it was worse. No, she discovered a moment later. Then
the bells were tolling the death-knell in all the churches by order of the
Captain-General. Melancholy, but not distressing like now. On account
of João Diogo, the King's friend. Now only in one church, Carmo
Church, right next door. The effect was worse, however, she had no
more hope, she was just waiting.

And the fourth, the fifth. Those chimes were endless. How such a
short time could last an eternity. She was afraid she would scream, if she
did Inacia would come straight away. She wanted nothing more to do
with Inacia. If she gave an order, the nigger woman obeyed, but it was no
longer the same. Inacia no doubt right there in the corridor. She wanted
to be alone. She obeyed, but Inacia was really in charge of the house and
of her. In Inacia's hands for ever, since then. Not for ever, today she
would end things. Without a word, Inacia obeyed. When she went to

184

take the letter to Gaspar. She took so many, before. He did not answer, he did not come nor would come. Him. She waited desperately. He would pay dearly. The old man and the young man, all the blame. Cold, like ice. Only towards her, she felt humiliated. Not the other woman, of course. Could crush her easily, she would. No, him. He was the one who deserved it. He had not come till now, he would not come any more. Yet she waited. She was waiting for the sixth (it came) and finally the last chime for the dying. It did not come, it was taking a long time. Afterwards it started all over again, the agony. Until the wretched person found peace. She would never find it, never.

And the lead bell struck the seventh chime. Longer than the others, it dissolved very round and slow in the air. Because it was the last. She sighed with relief. Until it started again, in a short while. Until the end. If the person died first it would not come again. Suddenly, contradictorily, a blank terror of the vast silence. The dying man finding his peace, she not. It would come again, she was sure. The bell.

Feeling relieved she went to the window again. The sky was clear, the mist had disappeared, only Itacolomi still covered for sure. A piece of blue sky, brighter than it should be. Because seen from within a well: she was immersed, drowned in the damp darkness. Silence and blue sky: relief, repose, peace. If only there were still a way out, she could see none. Now the mechanism was racing, the mechanism she never discovered how to stop. A clock mechanism gone wild. The clock rang the bells, brought the things. Things happening ceaselessly. Everything was slipping through her fingers.

Alone, she was completely alone. Even with Inacia waiting behind the door. Waiting for her final order, if she called she would come. Early that morning Inacia tried to keep her company, give her support. She did not let her, now it was all up to her alone. She had made up her mind, no one would make her turn back. But she did not know just what to do. When Inacia returned. Later she would know. When Inacia returned from Padre Faria, from Gaspar's house. No, why did she say his name? She didn't want to. Just saying his name made her feel bitterness in her heart, shame (for everything she did, that he let her do), an uncontrollable hatred. When Inacia returned from Padre Faria, from Gaspar's old and new house, saying that he would not come. Or rather: that he would later, depending, it depended on her. She still waited, it could be. In the face of her sufferings, after he read over her last letter when he was alone, he would feel sorry and return straight away. For one last word, she begged him humbly. Oh God, the shame of it! If at least he came, it would be worth it. Everything else was unimportant, her shame and humiliation would pass.

Letter after letter, she no longer remembered how many letters she had written. Since he abandoned her, after the mass. When she, the two of them alone at last in the drawing-room. The two of them alone, in this very place. When she confessed, her love so long stifled and hidden. Kneeling at his feet. Oh God, how humiliating! What he obliged her to do. That same day he was moving out, was what he said. Alone by herself in the suddenly enormous house. The maids, Inacia, were of no use. She did not need anyone else, only him. He did not come. Depending, it would depend on her.

A soldier went galloping past, on a pack horse. Then another soldier on horseback, and another. Like that since last night. Her door guarded by two soldiers. Like the day of João Diogo's.

He would not come, that was what he sent word by Inacia. For the time being, it depended on her. How was he, Inacia? What did he say? she asked. Inacia seemed to be afraid of speaking. Or she was deciding what to say. She always thought first. The two of them together now for ever, she could do nothing against Inacia. Nor Inacia against her. Together, wretchedly together! For ever! In the same boat, same river. Tell me, Inacia, you can speak. Missy won't have me beaten? Two-faced nigger, she never had, she wasn't going to start now. Inacia could do nothing against her. Missy won't have me beaten? Sly way of speaking, bad habits from the slave-quarters. From being beaten so often and seeing so many others beaten. If she could, she would have her beaten. Until she bled, then salt on the wounds. For the advice she gave her. No, she asked for advice. She only heard from Inacia's mouth what her own heart wanted to hear. Missy won't be angry if I tell? No, Inacia, you know I shan't. You know how fond I am of you, missy. If missy dies, I shall die as well. That's enough, Inacia, tell me straight away. If she could she would scream, she did not.

Inacia still played hard to get, she wanted a request, no doubt sick of orders. Tell me, Inacia, she said more gently, asking, almost imploring. Beneath the black woman's shiny face, behind her brown eyes (she never discovered what they were hiding) she thought she saw the gleam of a triumphant, happy smile. It was too much, so much humiliation.

I don't want to see missy suffer, you have suffered enough, said Inacia. If you don't want me to suffer, why are you making me wait? Why did you take the letter to Padre Faria? Oh, 'cause missy sent me. Your not telling me, Inacia, is what makes me suffer, she said, and suddenly believed she saw in those eyes: Inacia was not what she had been thinking, there was kindness and devotion in her eyes. Maybe in her agitation her head was confused. Inacia loved her, the two of them in grief for ever. Missy think I don't love her no more? said the Negress, guessing. It's not that, Inacia, today is just too much for me. There are times when I can't stand it, I think I shall burst. Don't make me suffer more by keeping me waiting.

Then Inacia told her. He was in the drawing-room, in the dark, only one window open, lying on the settee, his head on a pillow, seems he had spent the night there. His eyes were closed, was he asleep? She entered at the back of the house, told a black woman she knew that she wanted to talk to Massa Gaspar, she had a message for him from Missus Malvina. The black woman went away and returned with Bastião, the Negro who had served him since he was a boy. Bastião, without a word, he did not like her, made a sign with his head that said come, you can come in, he is waiting.

Gaspar still had his eyes closed, wasn't sleeping though, by the look of him. Bastião said master, the nigger woman is here. Even then he did not move. She had to clear her throat, she coughed. Then the young master got up and looked her straight in the eyes, those eyes of his that frightened her. Massa Gaspar don't like me, he never liked me, said Inacia. On account of missy.

Come on, said Malvina, tell me. What is it this time? he said. The usual, master, a letter for you. He looked the other way, said abruptly you can leave it there on the table. And since she stood waiting, he shouted, you can go. She waited, she was doing exactly what missy ordered. This time she had orders to wait, he was to read the letter first, send a reply. By word of mouth, or written, it doesn't matter.

Inacia could not read but she guessed everything that was in the letters. In the beginning Malvina used to tell her, recently she kept silent. More than just unhappy, she was alone and suspicious, fearful.

Massa Gaspar turned towards her again, stood looking at her for ages, he was surprised at the impudence of missy's favourite maid. What did missy say in the letter? Inacia asked her. I shan't say, Inacia, you shall know in the end. Because, missy, he went white like he was covered in flour.

Gaspar never used powder. He went whiter than he was, than he always was. And he felt for support, he might suddenly fall over. Those weak spells, those occasional absences, thought Malvina. So far away, at times, lost. In the beginning she thought it was his dreamy eyes, poetical haziness, his mind wandering pensively on a different plane. Afterwards she saw it was not. So far away, she had to call him back. While the black woman was speaking, Malvina seemed to see him. That aura, that whiteness, more like illness, no one was like that. No maternal feelings, like that other time. Gaspar leaning on the table so as not to fall. He looked at the black woman and did not see her. Massa Gaspar, Massa Gaspar, she shouted. Yes, what is it? he said, surprised at finding the black woman in front of him, as if he did not know her. Ah, it is you again, he said, recovering himself. All right, give it to me, he said, and his voice was hoarse and trembling. His hands trembled more still, when he took the letter.

His back to her again, he was reading. Like that, with his back to her, she could not see from his face what was going on inside him. His shoulders rose and fell with the panting of his breath. Him in that window here, his back to her. Exactly the same. She had to shout out, seize his arm. In his fury he might even break the spinet, so violently did he run his hand along the keyboard. He was reading her last confession, her final threat. She kept it for the very end. She never told him before, even in the worst unanswered letters. Now she told him. It had been she who had planned everything. Januario merely. . . . She was wrong to tell him. No, she was right. She contradicted herself, having doubts. She did not know what she was doing lately, she did not know what to do any more. When he turned back to her he was somewhat revived, though still pale. That time, the spinet. Januario was merely the hand that struck the first blow which killed your father. Now she wanted to see, now that he knew, what he would do. Very sickly, he might fall ill. But something would happen, had to happen today still. Januario, the soldiers. The town under occupation, the dragoons and orderlies riding through the streets, shouting, Januario was coming, he has come, that one, she was sure. He was kept from coming nearer only the soldiery placed everywhere. She was no longer interested in him, she wanted to hear about Gaspar.

What did he say, Inacia? she asked. He took a long time saying anything, missy. Rather eccentric, it was not fear. He was fearless even in his eyes. Don't make me wait, Inacia. For God's sake don't drag things out so much. I'm telling you the way I know how, said the black woman. If I don't tell you the way he was, you'll not understand what he meant. He said very little, but enough to understand what he meant. From that I guess what missy had the courage to write. Missy wouldn't tell me. . . . He spoke really very clear, I shall repeat exactly what he said. He said it was all right.

Gaspar said it was all right. So, he was not afraid, he would see. He would not take her grief seriously, he would see. Tell her that I read it and that I have already forgotten it, said Inacia. So, he was not taking any notice then, he would see!

And Inacia, not sure what Malvina might be musing, said that he seemed very concerned about her. He would do well to be concerned, thought Malvina. He said that missy was very upset, the best for her to do was calm down.

Yes, she should keep calm, while he was with the other woman. He with the other woman, and never coming to see her. Not even answering her. Not answering, while she was suffering. At least he could have written her a few words. Saying – wait, I am coming. Like the other times. No, he never said wait, I am coming. The first two or three times, when he still wrote. Then her letters stayed unanswered, her voice not returned, her shouting in the dark with no echo. When he left the mansion and went to the old house. At least a letter, for her to see his handwriting again. The other letters, from her kissing and weeping on them so much, had become stained and faded. The letters which one day in great despair she tore into a thousand pieces and threw away. And now she wanted to see again.

The best thing for missy to do was calm down, said the black woman. And the Carmo bell started to chime again. The same chime, the same toll, the same death agony. Malvina covered her ears and, with glassy eyes, shouted no, no, No? Don't missy want to hear me? Why did you have me speak then? As if Malvina could hear her.

Startled, Inacia did not understand what was happening. Had missy gone off her head altogether? Why was she shouting no, no. Enough, I don't want to hear it! I'm keeping quiet, I'm going away, said Inacia. Malvina did not hear, she closed her eyes, bent her head and pressed her ears so hard as if she wanted to go deaf.

No, missy hasn't gone off her head. Only a bit delirious, from all she has suffered. Because she said it's not you I don't want to hear. I don't want to hear the bells! Those damned bells! Who invented the idea?! As if she were listening to what Inacia was saying now.

Ah, the bells, said Inacia. She so concerned about missy, she only now appeared to hear. The same toll as a short while ago, she did not count. From the length of the chimes it was for the dying. Somebody who is dying, she said. Somebody is asking for prayers and forgiveness.

Someone is dying, Malvina said to herself, within her voluntary deafness. She said as if repeating Inacia. Her ears covered, she had not heard what the black woman said. She was dying, while he was alive. Dying, since she met him. A slow death, bit by bit. He would have a slower death, die very very slowly. The bells would toll for him, pity she would not be able to hear them. Those she would like to hear, she would not cover her ears. She would count the chimes one by one, enjoying them, savouring them. Just like that deep pleasure she once experienced.

The bells went silent. Malvina kept her ears covered as if she could

189

still hear. Inside she heard, she counted the slow chimes. It has stopped, missy, it has stopped, said the black woman, shaking her. She put her arms round Inacia, said Inacia I can't stand it, I think I'm going to die! Die, how, missy? We shall still win. Yes, she would win, she repeated, mentally. Alone she would win. Her eyes were sore and swollen, she could not cry any more. Stop those bells, Inacia. Try and make them stop. Stop, how, missy? They'll think I've gone mad, I'll probably get beaten. It's like that, missy, long and slow. The way to stop it is for the one who is dying to die. Pray for him, missy. No, said Malvina, hard and sharp. I don't even pray for myself any more. Strike your mouth thrice, missy, God will punish you. Haven't we done enough already?

We've done. She was not alone, Inacia was there, she did it too. What if the two of them found a way out? There must be one. Which, I don't know. Afterwards she would not ask Inacia's help, now she only wanted to know.

What else, Inacia? What else what? said Inacia, forgetting what she had been saying. What was it he said after you gave him the letter?

Now she remembered. In view of missy's anger, she was now afraid of what she was about to say. She wrapped up the sweeties, taking great care over what she was going to say. She kept a good deal to herself, but she had to say something. I think he is right about one thing, missy must first calm down. Calm down, me? said Malvina. For us to see what we are going to do, said Inacia.

Yes, she would see. And nervously she reviewed in a flash everything she had a thousand times thought of doing. The truth was she did not know what to do.

He put the letter inside his coat, right next to his heart, said the Negress and saw that the windows opened, missy's eyes lit up in a sort of smile. When he in front of her. Wickedness, damnation. He ought to have at least some pity for missy, missy was suffering so much, after so much she had already suffered. He could easily have put it inside his coat, the way she said. Right in front of her, he tore up the letter. You can tell your mistress I am not going, that was what he really said. Not the other times, Massa Gaspar, who never liked her, was being straight, he was speaking clearly for the first time. Not the day before yesterday, nor yesterday, nor today, he said. After all this complication, all this madness she got me into. Let her do what she pleases. After all she had done! No, there was no way she would tell missy that. Missy would lose her head, put an end to things once and for all. So she said, making it up, he sent word you were to calm down. You calm down and once all this confusion of soldiers back and forth is over he will come.

Malvina held her arms and shook her, looking her right in the eyes. Is that the truth, Inacia? Did he really say that? Just that, missy. Why should I lie at a moment like this? said Inacia, and saw that missy believed her, because she let go of her. Now you can go, she said.

When she was alone, her heart uplifted once more, the room looked clean again, the sky blue. But shadows insisted on coming back. By now she was regretting what she wrote to Gaspar. Now he knew everything about what she had done, she could not wait. Would he have the courage to accept her? Knowing how his father's death had really happened. No, not with a nature like his. Impossible to turn back, take back the letter, never have written it. Like the other letters she wrote. The one to Januario as well. Unless, maybe . . . No, if he did not show himself before already, he would not do so now. Maybe now, fear would bring him back? Oh God, maybe? I don't deserve so much. Maybe he always loved her. Maybe it wasn't true, what she sometimes glimpsed, as a result of wanting so much to see it. Maybe he had not received those desperate appeals and semaphores of hers, when she silently confessed her love to him. In that case he must be a stranger person still than she always supposed. And the two of them would live in sin, she was afraid. Not of the sin, but of what might happen.

But what about the other woman? What would he do about her? The other woman he had gone to. The other woman who had everything she did not have, perhaps just a dream. Felt like calling Inacia, sending her to look at the other. Ask Inacia again what she was like. Because she saw her once: sallow, ugly, stupid-looking. Maybe it was her eyes that were misted over with jealousy? Maybe Inacia saw things differently and the other was beautiful and charming. She knew her name, but so great was her hatred and jealousy that she did not dare say it. Beautiful and charming, the other had succeeded where she had not. No, he would not come, definitely. Maybe Inacia lied to her. She would call Inacia, verify everything in detail. She had only to shout, she would come.

No, she would not call Inacia. She was confused and restless, desperate. For that reason she got everything mixed up and doubted the ever faithful nigger. Forgetting what she thought earlier. He was right, he was always more sensible than her. What she should do was calm down. And wait calmly. Today still? Once all this confusion is over, the soldiers, was what Inacia said.

She went to the window, the soldiers were standing guard at the mansion door. She looked towards the square, more armed dragoons. Like that since yesterday. Everything so different from what she planned. Everything went wrong, it always did. Even when she thought she held the reins. When she thought she could dominate him and control the things that were to happen. She was never in control, she saw

191

that now. Even now, all wrong. Those soldiers, Januario would not succeed in getting to her. In the town, hidden, she was sure. Because he came, he heeded her letter. The other did not, he would not come. The wildest letters. What insane plans she concocted. Everything went the opposite to what she thought. Those soldiers, Captain-General's orders. But how had the Captain-General found out that Januario was coming? Unless Gaspar . . . did Gaspar know, had she said so in the letter she sent before? When she imagined she could bring the two of them together. The two would come, meet one another. Meet and decide things for her. That other time, too, on the way to João Diogo's bedroom, she did not altogether know what would happen. And everything happened better than she expected. Now the plan was not repeated, things were slipping from her control. And he did not come, the other could not come. She no longer wanted Januario to come, now that Gaspar might come. Her doubts, her pendular anxieties, returned in continuous waves. The bell might well delay. How long? She could not imagine. Gaspar would not come, how long. How did the Captain-General find out? He spread out his men to receive Januario. Januario would come, he was fearless. He has come, Inacia actually said a soldier had seen him somewhere. Inacia knew as well, Gaspar might still, Gaspar might still come. But if Inacia told her, why did Inacia tell her that? For the two, Januario and Gaspar, not to meet. To protect her, probably. She would call Inacia, she couldn't, without her order. Confused as she was she ought not to call her. Better to calm down, he was always sensible. Wait calmly, trust him. And when she was calmer she realized that it could not be Inacia. Nor Gaspar. Most likely someone saw Januario on his way and came to inform. Then the Captain-General set the trap, the snare – Januario would fall. Not against his wishes, wanting to. Tired of running away, fearless. Poor fellow, he had nothing to do with her passion, knew nothing about it. He acted as a hand for her. The hand was hers. She looked at her hand, her bloodstained hand. Januario's dark hand. No, her hand, quite clean now. But he was a mestizo accustomed to this business of killing and dying, he must know. If he did it, it was because he wanted to, again, like always, she justified herself. It could only be him, she had no other choice. Later, he must have spent the night waiting. But he would come later, he could have come already. Once again she began to want Januario to come. For it all to end once and for all, and then Gaspar. There was no danger of the two meeting. Gaspar said he would come afterwards. In any case Januario would never succeed in getting as far as her door. Let alone by the back entrance, in Rua das Flores, the way he came at night formerly. Because of the barracks behind the house.

She looked once more at the two entrances to the street: the square and the corner lower down. Full of armed soldiers. If he came from the square, it was certain death. From down below, if he came from Cabeças, it would be a miracle if he crossed the Ponte dos Contratos. She was protected, all she had to do was wait. That was what he said, he would come.

She went over to the settee and sat down. Her legs swinging restlessly in nervous irritation. The spinet covered with the purple damask cloth. He pulled the cloth forcefully, that first time. He stood looking at the spinet, that gem, Master Estêvão called it. All so far away, so distant, it had happened to someone else, another time, another place. The damask cloth on the floor, before. Then the damask cloth over João Diogo's body, to cover up the bloodstains. Did my hands get bloodstained? The other hand was useless, the damask too. The stains always appeared, came to the surface, she could see them even now, she saw them. Januario's bloodstained hands, her own hands. The bier mounted, the candlesticks crackling, the flames – those tongues of flame above the heads of the apostles, so they said. She remembered everything. She felt for the hand by her side, gripped his cold sweating hand. Like hers, it trembled. Facing João Diogo's body. Fortunately his face, his whole body was covered with damask. The sin no longer had a stopping-place, it deserved punishment. A sudden terror assailed her. Everything seeming to go back and João Diogo present. Herself alone, João Diogo's coffin. The dead leave their presence in things, he was there. Harder and more real than the spinet covered with the damask cloth, which she never again touched. João Diogo's white, waxen hand might appear from beneath the cloth, point at her, accusing her. He said you, you whore! For the first time, the only time in her life, someone said that to her. But that was what Januario must be thinking now, when he found himself surrounded by the soldiery. And Gaspar? Gaspar no, my God, he said he would come. You whore! pointing the pistol at her. She had the idea of blowing out the candle, that was what saved her. The flash and the bang, the room in darkness. All at the same time. In the drawing-room, now, suddenly in darkness, João Diogo might appear to accuse and punish her. A cold sweat on her forehead, the feeling that she might faint, die – for run away she could not.

She jumped up from the settee and ran to the window. Outside was bright and blue, she breathed deeply. When she felt better, she turned slowly round, João Diogo might still be there. But she saw with relief: the spinet was a spinet again, the damask cloth was quite clean – no dirt, no stain, no damp patch. It was all her distress, anguish, it went away.

But she found it impossible to keep calm. First calm down, was what he said. She must calm down, he would come. The soldiers at her door, from every window a thousand eyes watched her. A thousand fingers pointed at her. Whore, you! She drew back in fear and went back to the settee. On the settee, with her head resting on her knees, her eyes closed, she hoped to control herself. She must calm down, so that Gaspar could come.

After a very long time, she felt calmer. Calm, he could come. Calm, she could think. But she did not want to think, she had thought a thousand times and her mind was powerless in the face of the coldness and inevitability of things. Fortunately things were cold. If things were alive, if drawing-rooms and bedrooms retained people's presence after people have gone, then she would be done for, the way she thought just now. The pistol pointing at her, you, you whore!

Her things cold and lacking brilliance, their former brilliance. The crystal chandelier, its prisms, its faceted chimneys, formerly glittering. Fifty lights (it gave her so much pleasure!) unlit. The chandelier now merely silent and useless. The panelled ceiling, the paintings of the four seasons. Her choice. He stood looking at the paintings one by one. Spellbound, he approved certainly. The wicker chairs, the tables and console tables, the vases and decorations, the pictures and mirrors. Everything chosen by her, in the best of taste, absolute perfection. In earlier days, when she was a girl in Piratininga, she had such things. Lies, never like this. Hearsay. Her mother always wanted them, her father showed off. They took everything away from her, the river took it. She so wanted to be happy! Everything might go down-river again, her happiness did. Wealth, damnation. It was well said, what the waters gave the waters took away. After the gold the misfortunes. Other people's misfortunes did not bother her, hers did.

In the corners of the ceiling again, winter, autumn, summer. Even the spring flowers, which fell from a spiral urn, no longer had the colour and brightness they had at first. They were withering, fading. She had not noticed before, only now. Why not autumn, summer, winter? Why spring precisely? Time seemed to be playing a game with her. Her things held a message which was being revealed little by little, presence.

The spring was over, life at an end. A vast period of time had suddenly gone by, she was an old woman. The paint was fading, the outline of the figures becoming faint, the colours growing pale. An ugly old woman, very wrinkled, waiting for someone who did not come. Someone came to inform her, her hour had arrived. She would die slowly, falling gradually asleep, her eyes were heavy already, things were fading away. The colours disappeared not in years, but suddenly in a minute. As if one could see the flowers actually close, a rosebud open suddenly, not in the time they actually take to open and close.

Everything slow before, now racing. No, she would die very slowly, as if she were falling asleep. Without any struggle, without any agony, she would deliver up her soul. No, there was no need to ring any bells, she would say. And all was peace, a good soft peace.

But peace and silence were not made for her, she was coming back. It was the paintings that had the peace and silence of useless things. It was the paintings that, once so alive, were fading away coldly and quietly. Or was it her who thought so, did things vary according to a person's state of mind and the time of day? Time only existed a short while? No, time sped voraciously. The vortex of the hours, of life. Carnivorous flowers, dry spring. The paintings were the same and not so much time had gone by. The tempera was good, it could not have lost its colour. It was her, her eyes. Her eyes had changed, they devoured the colour. After all the tears she shed. Before, she had not really suffered, and she suffered. Maybe later on she would say the same thing. Suffering is at the time, afterwards one forgets it. Like no one can say how much somebody is suffering, we can only say so-and-so is suffering. If we knew – we only know our own, probably we wouldn't make others suffer. She did not know how much she was suffering. Her tears dimmed the light and the colours. Not her eyes, her eyes were the dwelling place of fire, brilliance and light. Now that her eyes were cold, and desperately blind and dumb, things acquired greater importance for her, they returned to their worthless indifference, existing in silence. From a distance, emptied of any burden, any aura, any meaning, one can actually see things. In the heat of the moment, in the haste of the heart, one does not see, one only feels. This was what she thought as she looked at the spinet. Its long, slender legs, gilded with art, so slender and long, so fragile and delicate, that she herself, if she so wished, could break them. Just like he once ran his closed fist so violently along the smooth, delicate ivory keys. A gem, the spinet. Before it seemed to radiate light, even when silent it played and sang. When she still believed in arias and lyrics, eclogues and sonatas, elegies and pavanes. In muses and flutes, violas, lyres and pan-pipes, pastoral songs. In shepherds and shepherdesses, Aeolian harps touched by the wind, the silvery plash of the streams. In Glauras and Anardas, Analias and Nises. How false it all was, she felt like laughing. Why did men do that, write that, think such things? Soulless and without fire, motionless like that and distant, for ever silent, the words and the things could only provoke laughter. But she was unable to laugh, a painful sneer at the corner of her tightly drawn mouth. The spinet was now just a silent box of gold-painted wood, time could come crashing down, she herself might suddenly destroy it. He would have destroyed it, luckily she was there and shouted no, startling him.

He did not come, how tardy he was. How tardy my love in Guarda, he said that old line of verse once. Verse, lie, reverse. It might all be a lie of Inacia's, to tranquillize her. He said nothing, he probably said something different, threw the letter away right in the nigger's face. Afraid of offending her, she might lose her head, do something foolish, Inacia hid the truth. She would call Inacia, now she had to tell the whole story, properly. Inacia, she shouted.

Inacia was keeping watch behind the door, she was there in a flash. What is it? What happened, missy? Malvina looked at her in amazement, she had shouted involuntarily, she did not really want to, it was her distress that had shouted. It's nothing, she said, feeling sorry, but not wanting to show weakness, now that she was thinking about things coldly. Nothing, missy? You called me, you don't want to tell me. Do you want me to stay close to my little lady? No, said Malvina, and, fearing the other might wonder if she was in her right mind: I only wanted to ask you one thing, then you can go, she said casting around for something to say. Even in her state it was not difficult for her to think of something. Tell me, I really wanted to know what the girl is like. Which girl? said the Negress in amazement. The two of them were playing hide-and-seek. You know, the little bride, she said, in an impossible attempt at irony, the sneer hurt her mouth. The bride, missy, don't worry about the bride, he will come. He will come and everything will be different. After they finally kill that mestizo they already hanged once in the square. He's the one who's upsetting everything, maybe Master Gaspar is suspicious, is afraid he will talk and ruin everything, said the Negress, inventing a really good reason, and she saw a light suddenly appear in missy's eyes, shine for a while, then gradually fade and die away. No, Inacia. What is the bride really like, the woman for whom he has rejected me? said Malvina, forgetting that it had not been like that. She must be a real beauty, she must have charms that no other ever had, he has always run away from women. I didn't have, I'm no good, she is! Come now, missy, said the Negress reproachfully. You know you are beautiful, beauty like yours only in heaven. In hell, Inacia, hell is the place for beauty.

Inacia did not want to take that desperate path, she said the bride is ugly, she don't come to missy's ankles even. She's sallow and dull, awkward, a scarecrow. She don't even know how to wear fashionable clothes and she plods like a mule, like this. And Inacia performed a pantomime, trying to imitate the other's gestures and her walk, making a picture she well knew was a long way from the truth. To see if she could disarm missy, see if she could make her laugh. Her eyes were dim, like a dead goat's, a bit slanting, and she has a button nose, she said, and saw that Malvina suddenly began to laugh. A hard laugh, like a sob. Sobs her laughter turned into afterwards. Thanks to Our Lady of the Rosary, friend of the black people, to whom she had addressed her pleas, missy was crying. Hard, swollen eyes, dry and glazed, that wasn't good. While we are crying we are getting saved, after we have cried comes the balm of salvation.

Malvina fell on her face on the settee and wept. The Negress stood watching from a distance, wanting to go close to missy, hug her, put her head on her shoulder and rock her, stroke her head, saying sleep, baby, until she was like a little girl again and went to sleep. But missy was confused and desperate, she might well reject her affection. When missy stopped crying she would see what she could do.

And after a time, the embarrassing silence between the two of them, Inacia herself felt that it was better to leave her, the confusion might return. I'm going to make a herb tea for missy to be able to wait. Go, Inacia, said Malvina, really wanting to be left alone.

Once alone, she fell into a nice gentle lethargy, it did one good to cry. Oblivious of everything, sunk in apathy. Her whole body seemed to float, as if it did not exist. The outside world and her inner world faded away and disappeared. Soft, distant music, so soft she could hardly hear it. Smooth, neutral music, emptied of any emotion. More like chords breathed by the breeze, music made by the wind: they meant nothing and she could not hear. Malvina was floating away.

After she started coming back from her apathy and lethargy that were like a dreamless sleep (how long did it last? Impossible to know and it was even difficult to get used to time, to the real world, to the place where she was, the room in which she would have to live), she began to see more clearly and precisely. The world was cold and colourless, grey or indifferent. Things had no importance, they merely had to happen. They would happen, she could now decide. As if, during the time she had been inert and dormant, without conscious life or feeling, a small barely discernible vein, a breeze, a breeze quivering in the dark, without any possibility of a seed, a mere scrap of a thought, something deep inside and beyond her, had thought on her behalf. Because suddenly, lucid and cold, she saw an articulate summary of all she had experienced, all she had lived through and suffered. And she understood life's intertwinement, her own reason for being. Everything made sense, now she knew what to do.

And without the slightest despair, like someone merely asking herself questions, she said what did I do, my God, for all this to happen? What did she do or what had they done for her? Before her? Her mother? Her father? A whole endless chain, which started nowhere and went on without ever stopping, a wheel. What was her sin, what the sin of all those before her, that in order to punish it the invisible black presence (that was what she said, or rather – felt) inspired and incited her, and she passed on, to Januario and Gaspar, all those diabolical ideas that were gradually born? Because that first meeting, the love which she thought was a gift fallen suddenly from heaven, was a destiny worked out long before, from which she could not escape. What she supposed a blessing and a gift was the punishment which her damnation was waiting for.

She said all this (in thought) without apparent sorrow and without remorse either. It was a cold assessment, an ascertainment of the past, as immutable as the future – as if spoken by an intrusive voice, a mysterious chorus and clairvoyant.

And she ascertained that it had all been useless, had gained her nothing. And when, before, she thought she controlled everything and that things happened as she wished, a powerful, concealed mechanism was working and she could do nothing against it. Just as Januario was the hand that served her, so she in turn served as someone's hand. All her plans useless, the lost hours useless. All happiness, all suffering, all love, useless. The dreams and the sins, the torments and desires, all useless. Her silent betrayal of Gaspar, useless. Useless, too, her frivolous yielding to the Captain-General, when she thought she might still win him with this last resort and actually told him, Gaspar, of it in one of the latest unanswered letters. The letters and semaphores, the magic thoughts and the premeditations, useless. Useless for her to go on living.

This suggestion of uselessness did not, however, blind or madden her. At least, so she thought. She saw with a clarity of which she never thought herself capable (she always followed her intuitions and premonitions, the conviction of those who believe they are the chosen of the gods and that nothing happened unless she wished it; because things belonged to her, and should belong by birthright, by nobility of lineage and sentiment), saw that Gaspar had loved her in secret, but no longer loved her. Despite loving her, he had betrayed her miserably, there was nothing more she could do to get him back. If she could not have him when he loved her, how could she now, when he feared her and no longer loved her? And even if he did come back, it would no longer be the same thing her heart had uselessly dreamed. He lacked the courage for great gestures, the courage to sin, to suffer and to feel pain. Had no fibre, no strength to desire, no spirit to really love. He was the harbinger of a dying world. With them the world would come to an end, just as the gold is going to dry up. Eternal damnation, never more.

And so, as she now had a fatal vision of the past, she saw what she must do. Future and past came together in her, materializing pain.

And almost with a smile on her lips (thought rather; inside, because she was not smiling), as if she wished to laugh at herself, at her naivety and innocence, she saw that even her black maidservant, an ignorant nobody, was capable of deceiving her and of lying outrageously to her. It might be out of devotion and love, little matter: she always and again just now deceived her. She would do nothing against her, she had a clear idea of what she must do. Cold, precise, lucid.

Inacia, she said aloud. Not too loud, no sharpness in her voice, no stridency or sharper tone; even so, at a distance, the nigger would hear. The way a dog hears its master call. Even if Inacia were farther away, at the back of the house; even if she were at the end of the world, she would come – she would hear in her soul. Such were the confidence, the certainty, the conviction and magic of her voice; such her confidence in the power of her words, of her soul, of her decision.

Once again Inacia was in front of her in a flash. The black woman's eyes opened wide, brown eyes glazed with astonishment. Malvina was not as agitated as before; she was actually serene and light, cool, unhurried. But terrible, and Inacia, open-mouthed with astonishment, saw in Mistress Malvina a strange figure. She was no longer the old missy, her darling missy. Had another one been born while she was dozing? Because Malvina's eyes were hard and icy. If they shone, it was with a shallow brilliance, the hard metallic brilliance of polished surfaces which reflect and terrify; the brilliance which keeps away, warns, repulses, puts to flight. She was no longer the broken, vanquished woman to whom she had advised tears as salvation. Far away was her accomplice, the lady who had stooped from her caste to make a sinful pact with her. She was now a proud lady who had buried deep inside her, in a cranny difficult to find or divine, all her weakness, all her grief. A queen, thought Inacia in her primitive, fabulous, magic mythology. And before a queen one falls down and kneels, kissing the outstretched hand, the blue cloak, of ermine royal embroidered with gold and silver thread. Before a queen, before the gods, the only thing one can do is obey and sacrifice.

And without realizing what she was doing, in obedience to an archaic fear and respect, she no longer thought of her as missy but as Mistress Malvina; not as that young madam who gave orders amiably, exchanged and permitted confidences, but as a lofty, noble lady. If it were in her capacity or habits, she would address Inacia differently, the loftiest manner she knew; majesty, perhaps.

Did you call, madam? she said, in a hoarse, fearful voice. For the first time she saw that lady who was suddenly growing and became older. Tall and lanky, thinner than she really was. Head held high, eyes aloft; she was not going to ask or to speak, her silence was an order. The black woman no longer had the strength to face the grandeur, the statue of gold and jewels, the soothed non-existent grief: that old story had completely disappeared, lost in the past.

Yes, I called, said Malvina, and her voice was silvery, crystal-clear and pure, of a non-existent whiteness, dewy, hard and cutting as a spinet note, the edge of a knife blade. Just now you told me a story, you told me certain things which I am now beginning to see better. And I can see that you were lying, that you have always lied to me, said Malvina, without changing her voice, with a smooth, horizontal modulation. No, madam, I never lied before. And just now? asked Malvina. He took the letter and put it inside his coat, next to his heart, did he not? No, madam, he did not, said Inacia. He tore the letter in a thousand pieces. Master Gaspar did well, that was exactly why I wrote, said Malvina, and she was so sure of what she said, that Inacia could not even remotely tell if she was lying, it was all the same to her now, lying or telling the truth. Tell me again, just for me to hear, she said.

The Negress was so afraid and amazed she could not even cry. She must speak, she would not be punished, she was a slave again. You can have me beaten, now I will tell. He told me to say he would not come, you were to do what you believe you must do. After everything you got him into, all the things you did. And I tell you for my part, Mistress Malvina, he had no fear at all in his eyes or in his manner.

She fell silent, bowed her head, not daring to face Dona Malvina's bright, dry eyes. And since Malvina said nothing she raised her eyes and asked can I go inside to where the other niggers are, and wait for the overseer? No, not yet, said Malvina. Wait for me outside the door, in a little while I shall call you to go out.

Malvina crossed to the dresser at the far end of the drawing-room. The lead bell once more started to chime the seven bells for the dying. The heavy waves of sound died away slowly, farther away than they were. No anguish, not a tremor, she seemed not even to hear.

Seated at the dresser, she lowered the lid of the escritoire. With her fingertips she lightly touched the white powder that had spilled from the pot of drying sand. She opened the ink-well and picked up the quill, checking to see that it was clean and well sharpened. All slowly measured, no vacillation. Hard and precise, she had time. She alone could tell if in her flesh, beneath the skin, in her hand on the blank paper, there was any tremor. But she was not concerned with that, she seemed not to see. Her eyes unblinking, she visualized meticulously the curve, the flourish of the first letter in the air. As meticulously and precisely as a clockmaker adjusting and rectifying the weights and the wheels of the mechanism on the glass surface of his work-table; the teeth of the escape wheel, the pallets of the balance wheel, the spindle and the anchor. The clockmaker oils, advances or retards the wheel of time, lord of the hours. At the top of the page she wrote: My Lord Captain-General.

2

Inacia left, Gaspar went back to the settee where he was lounging half asleep when the black woman arrived. He lay back to rest a while from his sleepless, agitated, restless night. While he awaited the day that lay ahead, the things he was sure were at last about to happen.

It was all happening so quickly, he did not know what to do, he had thought about it a thousand times, now he was simply waiting. However, he knew what he must not do. This certainty, like before (so long ago and yet in reality only a year had gone by) when he decided to return to the old, abandoned house, was a comfort in itself, it actually gave him a confidence he had never thought he possessed: unlike before, when he made a show of strength and certainty and it was nothing more than the defensive barrier of the weak. A confidence which would enable him to endure what was still to happen.

In his gestures and in the misty, far-away look in his eyes, there was a sort of premonition and resigned acceptance of that day of soldiers, shouting and horses' hoofs echoing outside, behind the closed windows, through which the morning filtered in slivers of light. The morning of a day which promised to be terrible, ominous and threatening.

That was when they came and woke him from his drowsy state. They came to tell him that Malvina's maid wished to speak to him. So early in the morning? Already? he thought. Like him, Malvina did not sleep; like him, she was waiting. Rather she had slept, that way she would give him a respite, stop her endless machinations. She never rested, the peace had been but temporary, her letters were now more frequent than ever, more terrible and more threatening. Her letters received no reply, he tore them up after reading them; he did not wish to leave any trace, any sign. That way he thought he could resist, she no doubt hoped that he would keep them. All in vain, he was defeated in advance.

No doubt another letter, he thought. If only it were the last. Her letters went from bad to worse with more stories and calamities. Had she not gone far enough with the one in which she told him she had news that Januario was coming back and asked him to return to the mansion in order to protect her? What senseless ideas, what contradictory machinations, Malvina was not at all well, she was not right in the head. But it might even be true, something was about to happen. How had she discovered? The half-breed had sent her a threatening letter, that was what her letter said. Why threatening? He could not make it out, her letters were so confused and nonsensical. And then he never really understood his father's murder. At first, he thought the motive really was theft, but the Captain-General made such use of his father's death (that farce of the death in effigy, produced with all the detail of a spectacular and important public hanging, in the square, merely to frighten the town), he so mixed up the facts, arrested so many people in the political stratagems in preparation of the levy tax, that Gaspar could no longer make sense of what had happened. Because he never believed that that bastard mestizo was capable of plotting against the state, or of any conspiracy.

Even though he knew it could not be true, he decided to go and see the Captain-General. Then came news from other sources, people had seen the murderer in the neighbourhood, they came with the information. People who knew nothing of Malvina's letter, of his denunciation, of the measures taken by the Captain-General.

What she wrote might be true then. Even so he would not go and see her, he had nothing to do at the mansion, he never wanted to meet her again. Since he had met Ana, he had done everything to forget Malvina, he really did forget her, he tore her from his memory by force. Malvina (he could even speak her name, what he felt now was fear and foreboding, not the pangs of love), she was very well guarded and protected by the Captain-General's men. Januario would never succeed in getting close to her. From whichever side of the town he attempted to enter, he would be taken. To be hanged for good. That way Gaspar would feel more at ease and tranquil, he did not want anything to happen to his stepmother – he was a true successor to his father.

But he was not at all tranquil and at ease when they came and told him that the black woman wanted to speak to him. He ordered her to be brought to him, but stayed just as he was, sprawled out limp with fatigue. His body heavy and worn out with tiredness, as if he had been fighting all night, he could hardly move. As if he had been beaten. His head in a turmoil and seething with the most confused ideas and the most absurd fantasies that his weary mind could concoct. Like that all night, pacing up and down the living-room, treading the same path over and over again, like a potter's ox. Only after he was overcome by tiredness did he collapse on to the settee, in the hope that the numbness would allow him to drop off for a while.

That heavy night, dragging on full of alarms and forebodings, and gloomy, ominous recollections. Immersed in a mist, in hot, moist steam. A night of endless agony which continued into the day. He had thought of all the ways out, of all that had happened and could still happen. As was always his habit, he always waited for things to happen. But this time was different, he knew: he was not waiting passively, he had done the right thing by deciding what he was not going to do.

So, when Inacia left, he, dazed and giddy, went back to the settee. His head whirled, he could no longer make sense of anything. Worn out with tiredness, inside and out, he gradually slipped into a lethargy, a haziness very similar to that heavy, mortal tiredness, that deep sickly sleep, experienced when he returned to his father's house from his escapade in the backlands. As if, even though he did not yet know her, a blind, secret voice within him was warning him of all that was to come, his doubting heart. Even though he did not know exactly what it was telling him, the advice being so masked and coded, before. Now it was the desire for the sickly sleep to be repeated, days on end without having to account for himself, sunk in the flesh and formless mush of time, barely existing, perhaps dying. The powerful death wish which he had always lived with, death always calling him, he lacking the courage to appear: death an ever-open door through which he could escape. Sleeping like that, in the pasty sleep of death, he would cease to think, would not have to act, would not see things happen and be unable to do anything about it. He was the same man as in former times, he was trying in vain to relive a situation buried in time.

Now he was very agitated, that torpor of waves dying away in the distance would not last long. Outwardly motionless, no apparent sign of life, as if he had fallen into the deepest sleep. Inside him, though, life was swarming, a life of a thousand ants, spiders and fretful anxieties. A confusion of phrases and voices, his whole life gone over again. New phrases and old phrases mingled together in a fantastic, hallucinated uproar. Phrases uttered by Malvina and his father, others spoken by his mother and Leonor like a soft breeze in the darkness, his own phrases and meditations. And suddenly the letters spoke aloud, the threatening words. He tried to reply, to see if he could calm Malvina and his father, if he could avoid further utterances and more letters, everything still might happen. This time his mind did not go along with his heavy eyelids, his exhausted formless body, it refused to depart.

And suddenly fear, the severed hand, the dagger gleaming in the dark, moving towards his father swamped in laces and silks, the severed hand

203

was his own. What she said was not true, Malvina had gone out of her mind and he too. But he needed to be lucid in order to wait and take precautions, there was something he could still do. The fear of the dream being repeated stirred him out of his desire to sink into a semi-death, a dreamless sleep in which the world temporarily ceased to exist and things happened without his seeing them. Nor was that torpor possible any longer, he would have to be alive. To avoid the dream when it came near again. A moist, sticky dream which threatened to bear him off in its heavy, suffocating mists, in its fleeting shadows, to a bottomless precipice. He knew what that hand meant. Anything, even the agony of waiting; anything except that bloody dream, that hand, that dagger which would be plunged into his father's chest. The dream pulled him, a voice calling.

And suddenly fear, the muffled noise. The voices, the phrases returned. The voices fell over one another in a single babble, a mush of wholly incoherent sounds and noises. They all spoke at the same time, the voices grew louder and deeper, then fell shrilly, rising again deafeningly. And they were no longer phrases and voices, but howls and screams echoing through the night, saws, hammers and anvils, clanking metal chains; disconnected sounds mingling in a terrible crescendo, a very loud, sharp sostenuto, deafening.

When the single, continuous, endless mush of sound into which the voices had been transformed reached its greatest intensity, the highest point that an eardrum can endure, he returned from the lethargy and the dark depths in which he had at first tried to immerse himself for ever and ever. At the edge of the abyss, he started coming back, he made a leap. He jumped up from the couch and his hands went groping in the air as if still in the night, in the most utter darkness. With glassy, blazing eyes he moved towards the one open window, like a plant or animal moved by tropism in search of light. His hands found the hard window-sill, he stopped blindly. The hardness of the wood returned his body to him, he began to feel a great blinding pain. The hardness of things and the brilliance of the pain had always saved him, now they saved him once more. And the pain receded, his eyes became clear. At first a luminous, far-off mist, the light came closer and closer. He could now see some confused shapes, some more marked and gleaming outlines, more consistent shadows and masses. And the pulpy shapes, the masses and shadows, now acquired body and firmness, formed volumes, edges, colours and protuberances – the world was coming back into focus.

And he could see that he was once more in the living-room. His eyes no longer clouded, he smiled at the day outside, at the light that was soft and gentle as the air. Light and air were one and the same thing, he

204

existed again. In his youthful joy at finding himself safe, he felt an irresistible and unreasonable desire to laugh and to thank the old, suddenly brilliant green of the windows, the crowns of the trees, the whiteness of the whitewash on the walls and that piece of clear blue sky. He opened and strained his eyes, ears and nostrils, letting himself be invaded by the soft new sensations, round and soothing like the distant waves of a bell that he started to hear.

The bell was ringing far away, so far away that he thought he must still be immersed in the time of dream and memory; lucid, strangely happy. Was the ripple of the bell inside him or far away? The far-off chime hung vibrating in the air until it found the tomb of silence. After a long silence another chime. The Rosario chapel? Antonio Dias, the cathedral church? St Francis? Perdões Church? If it was not in his memory, it was Carmo Church, so far away were the chimes of the lead bell. Speaking these names, being able to think, it all comforted him, he even felt happy.

He raised his hand to his cold moist forehead, felt his chest beneath his damp shirt, listening to the beat of his heart. It was good to feel alive again.

But this happy feeling of being alive did not last long, he started thinking again. Thinking, he remembered. He remembered that that accursed Inacia left just a short while ago. The letter, he tore up the letter in the black woman's face. He should not have done that, he should have controlled himself. He had revealed himself in front of the maid, he who was always restrained. Now she knew the secret of what had happened between him and Malvina. No, from his side there had been nothing, she could not know. She did, Malvina told her everything, of course. Told her what, if Malvina herself did not know? She must know about Malvina's side, the two of them were always whispering together. How could a lady who was formerly so refined put herself like that in the hands of an ignorant nigger who he suddenly saw had taken charge of his father's house? Inacia was going to tell Malvina everything, he had done quite the wrong thing. Who knows what Malvina might do now? She was capable of anything. Ana, what if Malvina wrote to her in despair? She might have written to Ana, someone else. No, she only wrote to him, she would not be so crazed as to write those mad things to anyone else. Lies, inventions, despairing fantasies, none of that happened. Impossible, it did not make sense. She only said she had slept with the Captain-General to make him jealous. No, it was probably true. He recalled the Captain-General's oily eyes. After she realized that he was not going back, she started to go to the palace; a scandal, she did not even observe mourning. She was talked about, but then these people talk about everyone who is above them. In one letter she said one thing, in another she contradicted herself. Like this time. That it had been her, with the help of the mestizo Januario, who had killed João Diogo. It could not possibly be. She scarcely knew Januario, she only saw him that once. The two of them on their way to Vila do Carmo, only that once. Only that once, never again. It was not possible, he would have noticed something, he did not remember going out at night, always with her, she never went out any more while his father was alive. The house was well guarded, the half-breed would not get inside, he would not have the courage. What if Inacia opened the door at night? It was too much, at that time she loved him. At least so she said, she confessed it. Her letters were contradictory, she was lying. With the Captain-General maybe, but not with that bastard mestizo. The letters, why did he not keep the letters? he almost shouted, suddenly realizing the danger he now was in. Might it not be better to go and see her? He would calm her down, then return. If he went there, he would be lost, he would never return. That was what she wanted. That was why she wrote to him, all lies. She wanted to provoke him, invented things to make him go back. None of that existed, neither Januario nor the Captain-General. Why did he not keep the letters? he thought with regret. He could compare, it would be easy to see that she was lying. A proof, he would have a proof. There was no way he could go back to the Rua Direita, to his father's house. But how could he find out if she had written to anybody? Ana, maybe Ana knew. She knew and was not telling him. No, Ana was good and pure, incapable of hiding things and lying. She would tell him everything. Even hiding, naive, a child, she would give herself away. He tried to remember his fiancée. Nothing to suggest that she had received any letters from Malvina. What if she had not received any, but received one today? She had never told him anything, she only wrote today in despair. As she wrote to him, she might well have written to her. For the first time, realizing that she had lost him for good, giving him up. Seeing her whole dream go down the drain. Who knows what she would be capable of making up to tell Ana? If she told him that. She and the half-breed, his father's murder. She might lie to Ana, seeing that he was now living peacefully, was going to belong to another, be happy. He would find out from Ana, the solution was to go there. If she wrote to Ana, she may have written to the Captain-General. If only he had the letters. He would go there, go there right now. Just as he was, he would not bother to change. Just wash his face, run a comb through his hair, adjust his clothing so that she would not be shocked by his appearance, a whole night without sleep, all untidy, agitated. Seeing him in that state, she might suspect something. If she had received a letter from Malvina, seeing him like that, it would all be confirmed. What would be confirmed, if he did not even know what Malvina might have written to Ana? If he was not even sure if she had written? If she wrote to Ana it was dreadful, but he could still explain. And if she made up something else? What might she have made up? Something else that happened between the two of them? But nothing did happen. With the letters, if he had not torn them up, he could prove it. Now what was he to do? He had to be quick, to get ready. Before Ana, having read the letter, had too much time to sleep on the matter. Afterwards it would be difficult to undo. However much Ana loved him, the seed might remain for ever. He might meet Inacia on the way. First she delivered the letter to him, Ana's was afterwards. It must have been like that, the contrary was impossible. No, he was not in time, too much time had passed, he had to fly. He would not catch her, he had to fly because of Ana, to undo the evil the letter had done.

He rushed to his room, changed his clothes, he was ready in a moment. He managed a look at the mirror, the dark rings under his eyes, his eyes sunken with tiredness and lack of sleep. Now he had to be calm, keep cool, lucid and calm. He could not let himself be overcome again by the anguish, the aura. He was prepared, he had a way of avoiding it, he simply had to want to, he told himself in order to gain strength and certainty. Now that he had left his irresoluteness behind and decided to act. Everything would depend on him once more.

Although he had given no orders, suspecting what might happen, the Negro Bastião had his horse harnessed and ready. He had only to mount and ride off.

He galloped past the Padre Faria chapel and into the Caminho das Lajes. In no time he would be in the Rua do Ouvidor, near the square with the first whipping post, where Ana lived.

As he was leaving the Caminho das Lajes in order to take the Rua dos Paulistas, he saw a soldier riding furiously behind him. Stop, shouted the soldier. In the King's name! He reined in his horse. More soldiers on the street corner. What is it? he asked the soldier. Ah, it is you, sir, said the soldier, recognizing him and saluting. You should not ride so fast, sir. I could have mistaken you for the criminal, fired at you. I did not think of that, Gaspar replied. I am in a hurry. Excuse me, sir, but I have to know where you are heading, said the coloured soldier. It's orders, since early this morning nobody must be on the streets. I did not know, said Gaspar, impatient at the delay. In your case, sir, being the deceased's son, I suppose we might allow you, said the mulatto, inquiring of an ensign who arrived with his armed men. It's all right, but you must tell us where you are going, said the ensign. I am going to the house of Colonel Bento Pires Cabral, said Gaspar. A matter of real importance. But ride slowly and be careful, said the ensign. In all this confusion you might be mistaken, be hit by a stray bullet. Gaspar thanked him and with difficulty restrained his fiery horse in his haste to arrive.

He reached the Largo do Pelourinho and immediately knocked the door of his fiancée's house. To his surprise, Colonel Bento Pires himself opened the door. You, at this hour, sir? said the colonel. Has something happened? You are as white as a corpse, not a drop of blood in your face. It is because I have come in a great hurry, at a gallop, said Gaspar. I have not slept well, he said, trying to reassure him, disguising his own nervousness. He wanted to speak to Ana straight away and there was the old man upsetting things with formalities, which was at odds with his casual slippers and short-sleeves.

What matter brings you here, sir? the colonel asked. What is all the haste about? I badly need to talk to Ana, said Gaspar. Talk to Ana, my young unmarried daughter, at such an early hour? said the colonel wide-eyed, astonished by such forwardness. She is at the back of the house, in domestic undress. I do not think she can receive you. Furthermore, if the matter is so urgent and important, I am the person to whom you should speak, sir. I am the head, the one who deliberates and decides the affairs of my family. I know, colonel, said Gaspar, annoyed at so many rules and formalities, so much delay. It was going to be very difficult to speak to Ana alone, her father was an old-fashioned man. But the matter concerns only the two of us, said Gaspar, scarcely able to check his irritation. Only the two of you? said the colonel, frowning. What fashions are these now? Forgive my forwardness, sir, but I badly need to speak to Ana, said Gaspar. Afterwards, I shall speak with you, if any decision has to be taken.

The colonel was very fond of Gaspar. Ana's marriage would be the saving of him. Caught up in debts, in arrears with the Royal Treasury, his fear of the levy tax making him lose his sleep, like everyone else, though he was aware of Gaspar's eccentric reputation, he badly wanted that marriage. Old João Diogo's contracts were still yielding profits, but what sharpened his interest most were the grant lands and the vast quantity of cattle in the São Francisco outback. Because the Jequitinhonha and the rivulet workings might also start drying up, the way the gold was obviously finishing, the gravel workings dying, the diggings abandoned. The news from there was not so good as at first. What the water gave, the water takes away, was all one heard from the distressed mouths.

For these reasons it was good to be attentive to Gaspar. I shall go inside and call the girl, I shall be straight back, he said eventually. Even so he went off grumbling about courtships these days.

Alone in the drawing-room, hat in hand, he could not keep still, not even sit down. To pass the time and take his mind off things, he began to notice how Bento Pires's house had been emptying recently, the white patches on the walls, where before there were pictures and mirrors, the costly, prized items of furniture. First was the clock brought entirely from Portugal, not only the works; then the crystal mirror with its gilt frame; the chased silver candlesticks, even the lacquered and wicker furniture, in the latest style, French taste, had disappeared, exchanged for quite poor ones, with leather seats with neither pattern nor tooling and the worse for wear. Even above the windows gashes where the plaster had come away. Colonel Bento Pires Cabral was not doing at all well. His slave-quarters were empty, with only three house slaves remaining, which he, shamefacedly, hired out for outdoor service. Gaspar recalled that Ana no longer used jewels, her dresses always the same. If everything ended well, if nothing happens today, he would hasten their wedding. The way things were going, Bento Pires would end up accepting the furnishings and the bride's trousseau from him, which would be vexing for a man formerly so well off.

Bento Pires returned, this time properly dressed, in tailcoat and waistcoat, knickerbockers and the rest. His clothes faded and worn, his stockings stitched and darned.

The girl is coming, she is getting ready, she was unaware of your visit, sir, said Bento Pires. We had better take a seat, you know how young ladies take their time, they always want to prettify themselves.

Gaspar seated himself in the chair next to the settee where the colonel took his place. At first an awkward silence hung between them interrupted by the hawking and wheezing of the old man's asthma. Bento Pires did not cross his legs, no doubt so as not to show the holes and patches on his shoes. He did not need to hide the soles, even the uppers, from which the silver buckles had already disappeared, showed the signs of wear and time. Gaspar felt sorry and somewhat embarrassed, he looked away. Other people's misfortunes are disturbing, they remind one, that could also happen to him. It would not, even with the gold disappearing and diamonds getting scarcer, he still had the grant lands in the blessed outback. He would move out there; in addition to the cattle, he would plant sugar cane in the fertile lands, erect mills. Already increasing mentally his father's work. If everything went all right today.

Well, said the colonel, interrupting Gaspar's reverie, breaking the silence which by now was getting stifling. How are things going, sir? Not well at all today, it seems, said Gaspar. You can see that from the window, sir. What? said Colonel Bento Pires, wide-eyed with astonishment. Bad news? The tax levy is coming after all? It is not that, Gaspar said soothingly, I am talking about the dragoons and orderlies, all this feast of muskets and quarter-staves which the Captain-General and Governor of Minas has prepared for receiving my father's murderer. Ah, Bento Pires sighed with relief. I was thinking about another matter. Anyway, you should not speak like that, sir, remember that walls have ears. These days we have to keep our lips sealed, be careful not even to think aloud. No, I was thinking about the mine-workings, the celebrated tax levy, the collection of tithes by force, that makes us tremble just at the thought.

And Colonel Bento Pires, wheezing asthmatically, choking with catarrh and emotion, his eyes smudgy and dismal like those of a whipped dog, asked his future son-in-law if he thought ruin was upon them, if it was all coming to an end. I don't know, one can never know, said Gaspar. It's like they are saying now, what the river brings, the river can take away. I am no Tiresias to foresee and divulge. Who? asked Bento Pires, still more alarmed. It does not matter, a very old soothsayer, said Gaspar. Did you speak to him, sir? What exactly did he say? asked the old man. Gaspar smiled, he was an old man who had died more than two thousand years ago, in ancient Greece. Greece! said the old man, disheartened. I thought you were talking about serious matters and here you come with poems and pan-pipes, soothsayers and shepherds, peridots and filigrees and the like!

Gaspar did not feel offended by Bento Pires's gruff talk, he even smiled. No one can know, father-in-law to be. There are people who say that the golden days, the happy times, can return. We just need to keep our heads, tea and patience – is that not the advice? – and things will improve. I believe it to be so.

He spoke more to calm the old man, in the depths of his pathetic, catastrophic heart he thought that Minas was really finished. What he said served only to distress further the colonel's tormented, humiliated heart. I am very old, in my dotage, I have no more time to wait, said Bento Pires. When the favourable winds blow again, if they do, I shall already be on the other side, in the Lord's peace. From what I could understand of what you said, it seems everything really is coming to an end, said the old colonel, bowing his head, hiding his smudgy eyes, dog's eyes.

It is best we be frank, after all I am going to be one of the family, said Gaspar, impatient with the uncomfortable conversation. Ana was taking a long time. He spoke, even thinking that the old man might start to cry. Tears no longer bothered him, that was what handkerchiefs were made for, he thought bitterly. And adding coarse irony to his bitterness: for asthmatic catarrh, tobacco phlegm. Impatient, distressed, he thought or said the worst things. The Minas country as we knew it, he said, the Minas country which you, sir, and my father made and I knew and enjoyed, that Minas I think will really come to an end. Maybe another will appear, he added, seeing the despair of old Colonel Bento Pires Cabral. But a pin-point, a prick of compassion, a sting of pity stirred inside him. Everything will change for the better, sir. Do you not have faith in God and the King?

The colonel seemed not to hear Gaspar's last words; he put his hand to his forehead and bowed his head. The embarrassment became greater and Gaspar, despite the bitter irony with which he had protected himself before, was afraid that that solemn, ceremonious man, formerly wealthy and highly regarded, might suddenly start crying in front of him. And there was nothing he could with the tears of a ragged, ruined old man. But he would not console him with lies, he preferred to encourage him a different way.

Let us be frank, Colonel Bento Pires, he said. There is no need, there is no necessity for you, sir, to ward off an unknown evil, to be torturing yourself, things will come right. When the inventory of my father's estate is complete and the shares have been made, I shall have more than I need. Mine-workings? asked the old man, his head still bowed, in a disconsolate voice. No, many, many leagues of grant lands, said Gaspar. Only land? And cattle? asked the old man, lifting his head, his eyes acquiring new life. But I do not have a single piece of grant land out there in the cattle country, said the old man, seeking a signal, a promise, a helping hand, in Gaspar's eyes. But I have, said Gaspar. When the possessions have been worked out, I shall have more grant land than I need. We, you and I, go into partnership, you go to the outback with me. But I have nothing to offer, no capital to put in, I do not want to be a dead weight, said the old man, feigning a diffidence and a delicacy that poverty had consumed. You have a daughter, sir, who is richly gifted, a genteel shepherdess, your finest possession, whom I love very much, said Gaspar, gallantly, in the Arcadic manner, and saw the old man's tired, dusty eyes open and fill with life and light. And as the shine increased, beginning to water, in a moment the old man's eyes filled with tears.

You must forgive my weakness, sir, I fear the emotion is too much for me at my age. In my family, you know yourself, I am not used to poverty, we have always had things easy, had everything of the very best, said Bento Pires, snuffling. He took from his pocket a large red cotton handkerchief, stained with snuff, and covered his face as an excuse for drying his tears.

It was very hard, that conversation, the humiliation of Colonel Bento Pires Cabral, formerly a proud man of great wealth. A ruined man, thought Gaspar, remembering the thin times of which his father, before his new marriage, spoke so often. Of the celebrated year of the great famine, years before, the weighty old shadows which the pomp and gold of Minas, the wealth from usury and the ore-bearing gravel, dissolved in thin air. It must have been like that, time promised, just like that, when, even though they were rolling in gold (gold was no longer worth anything, they had forgotten the planting, a plate of food cost a fortune; the savage Indians wreaking vengeance on them; when a carbine was worth the gold of a whole band), the gold sprouting on the surface, visible in the creeks, brooks and streams, the men had to abandon the shafts, mine-workings and diggings, to return only later, with their eyes once more sharpened by greed.

Like that no, thought Gaspar. Now it would be worse, those old-timers were harrd and hot-tempered, tough and strong, it was only in their old age that they became acquainted with wealth and magnificence, the extravagance that makes people go soft. They did not know the churches covered with gilt carvings, with stone tracery pediments, angels and saints carved in wood and stone, costly paintings, the palaces and mansions, the opera house. They did not the music and the poems about lyres and shepherds, pan-pipes and sighs, a thousand delicacies. They had not yet heard about orchestras and scales, spinets and chromatic harps, flutes and violas, resounding organs, all from Portugal or other countries. They only knew by hearsay about the academies and soirées and the genteel, aristocratic, amusing hours spent there. They were not familiar with them and they did not know why they had been the ones to pay for them and make them possible. The men of today were like him. He was pale and thin-blooded, all auras and anguish. He was the herald and signal of the ruin that was on its way, of the inevitable disaster. To start over again? Not with men like him. He was thinking of his anguish, of the despair with which the old man infected him. Marked by death since youth, decadent in the prime of life, already dead before he had even started to live. With people of his ilk nothing would be done: he, a colonial intellectual, pampered by life, suckled on gold, on diamond ear-rings, was the end of a race, of an ill-gotten nation, an unborn people. The crimes and the acts of injustice, he was thinking, oblivious of himself, suddenly remembering, the slaves and the rhetoric, the blood and the damnation. As if everything that was happening and threatened still to come about were punishment and expiation of old failings, incests and sodomies, thefts and usuries, torturing and abductions.

All this Gaspar was chewing over, with pain and disgust, while he waited for the old man to stop crying. Until Ana arrived.

His powdered face, from when he went inside, now furrowed and grooved by the trickle of tears, the old man tried to embrace Gaspar. My son! he said. Come, come, colonel, said Gaspar, pushing him away courteously. Do not upset yourself!

Colonel Bento Pires went back to his seat and settled back happily. Now that his tears were dried, his mask and his now bright eyes revealed a happiness he had never dreamed of. He was sailing, already gently riding the waves of a dream, wandering in a dream of green meadows, colourful riverbanks, cane fields swaying in the wind, cauldrons of steaming, aromatic syrup, the good, mournful lowing, the monotonous yet pleasant sound of the herding calls and the mooing, so very lovely of the cows in the corrals. And what were formerly excavations and gold-diggings, workings and shallow deposits (white gold, dark gold, rotten gold), rivers, streams, sandy soil washed and panned (pebbles and small stones, diamond chips and large gems), was transformed in the old man's idle happy imagination into pastures and woods, bulls, cows and calves which were almost real. In the old man's dream the Minas country moved to another place.

Though awkward and embarrassing the conversation had been good. Gaspar consciously directed it to that ending. That way he would be guaranteed against possible intrigue, with Malvina's letters flying around. The old man would accept everything, but what about Ana, who was taking so long to come?

The small bell at the gaolhouse began to ring the hours. Nine o'clock? said Gaspar when the bell's short shrill chimes finished. I came very early, forgive me, colonel. Never mind, my boy, you are one of the family now, said Bento Pires, all confidential and intimate. To take his mind off the old man who was dreaming about new-found wealth and to master the disquiet he was beginning to feel again, he began to roll and unroll round his finger, backwards and forwards, an old gold chain that had belonged to his father. Is she not coming? said Gaspar. Who? asked the old man; Ana, said Gaspar. Ah, I'll go and see, said the old man.

Bento Pires went out and after a short while Ana appeared. She was dressed in white, in a silk skirt and a linen blouse she had embroidered herself. Without jewels or ornaments, her jet-black hair caught at the back with a white ribbon: in her pure, artless, simple, ethereal beauty. Gaspar felt the soothing breath, the balm in his heart. So different from the other, without her fire and flashing brilliance, no danger. A slender, oval face; dreamy, gentle black eyes which would bring him only peace. The same eyes, the same gentle manner as his mother and sister. With

213

her he would be safe, his soul would find quiet and calm once more. He could not lose her, everything would depend on that day. But the other? What would he do to make her stop, disappear?

Ana was alone, her father allowed her. The two of them alone for the first time, without anyone hanging around them, watching. She came towards him, held out her hand. Lyrically, passionately, Gaspar raised her light, smooth, white hand to his lips, then to his heart. He would not let go of it, more than ever he needed that support.

But what has happened, Gaspar? she asked, trembling and startled. You here so early! Wait, let me look at you. How white and tired you look, my goodness! Tell me, has something bad happened?

Gaspar saw from her clear eyes, from her easy, unresentful words, from the way she spoke: Ana could know nothing. No letter, he should not have come, all excessive haste, foolishness on his part. But it was good to have come, if he had not come how would he know?

She lead him towards the couch. Hand in hand, very close to each other. Her sweet, tender presence, her good, soft smell; that delicate beauty, that sublime gentleness; it all enraptured him and struck him dumb. His soul returned to the subtle, ethereal, brittle world of poetry, to the lyres and pan-pipes, to the meadows and shepherds, to the quivering mirror of the waters, to the leafy springs. He relived the myths and the fables, a whole theory of love. Everything that he had lost with his mother's death, that had later revived and that Malvina's impatient fire had burned.

Tell me, speak, she said in distress. You don't need to be alarmed, be like that, he said. Nothing, it was nothing at all. I was wrong to have come. No, said Ana, you were not wrong. I am the one you should come to.

That I am the one you should come to startled him. Maybe she did know, maybe she did receive the letter. But there was nothing special in those clear silky eyes, no shadow, all innocence and childhood, flowering meadows.

That was why I came, he said. I was not feeling well. I had a bad night, I could not sleep. Unpleasant thoughts, something might have happened to you. To me? Why? she said. No, to me, my thoughts are all confused, I say meaningless things, I don't know what I am going to say. Then say nothing, she said. Rest your head on my shoulder, when you feel better you can speak.

What ease, what peace she gave him! He laid his head on Ana's shoulder, and it was all so pure and good, he did not even notice that he was embracing Ana for the first time, revealing himself, feeling at ease with a woman. Unable to contain himself, the tears fell from his eyes:

also for the first time he wept on a woman's shoulder. And she, with her free hand, took a handkerchief from her sleeve and while she dried his tears, she said weep, my darling, weeping does you good, my beloved.

In happiness time is brief, a long period of time went by. Happy and free, he wanted to forget everything. Without her, how would he manage?

The idea of losing her brought back his agitation. Agitation, fear and distress, the dreadful, dangerous thoughts. He must cut things short, Malvina might still. Gently and tactfully, so that she would not suspect. He moved a little way away, he wanted to look deep into Ana's eyes while he spoke. In her arms, in the peace of tears and tenderness, he was afraid to give too much away.

I came for something else too, Ana. To warn you. Warn me about what? she asked and he said I don't know, anything can happen. Don't look like that, she said, calm down, don't say anything. No, Ana, I need to speak and you are the only one I can speak to. If it helps you, if you need to, Gaspar, then speak. It is my stepmother, he began, she is not well, very confused and unbalanced since my father was killed. I am afraid that she might do something foolish. I can't fathom what, but I have a feeling that something dreadful is going to happen yet, I am so upset, all these things affect me a lot. At times I think I am having a bad dream, it is all a nightmare, I want to wake up, Ana. I still hold back, but my stepmother. . . . Since yesterday she has got worse, because of all this commotion in the town, this chaos of soldiers, this awful waiting. No one knows if the man is going to come or not.

So that's it, said Ana, all kindness and understanding. In Ana's eyes there was nothing, she did not receive any letter, did not even suspect anything. You are like this yourself because of this waiting, she said. After all the man killed your father. It stirs one up, churns us up inside. Me too, the whole town is on edge, I can imagine you, with your good gentle heart. All this will pass over, Gaspar. This tumult, all being well, will be over today. And everything will go back to the way it was before. Dona Malvina will calm down, you yourself will forget all this. Are you sure, Ana? he asked. My heart tells me so, she said.

Ana stopped talking. Though he was nervous, he kept himself under control so as not to say anything. He was afraid of revealing too much, he should leave. When it was all over, he would come back.

But suddenly the silence filled her with anxiety and distress, she asked if he thought the man was really in the vicinity of the town. Do you think he has come back? she said. I would come back, Ana. I shall not run away any more! I accept my death, my guilt, I shall not run away any more, he said pathetically. As if she had asked him a different question, the question he had been asking himself in his heart for a long time. I do not understand what you are talking about. I asked you about the half-breed, you tell me something else, she said.

And only then realizing his mistake, he said I, I confused things. I meant, if I were in his place I would come back. Because they already killed him a long time ago, at the time of that theatre in the square. But you are different, my darling. You are not like that heartless brute, you have a heart. Do you think so, he asked and for the first time she felt uncertain looking at Gaspar's mournful, pathetic eyes.

He moved away a little and leaned back on the couch. With his eyes closed, he tried to recover the tranquillity he had lost once more. He felt Ana's light, fearful fingers on his forehead, beard and dry lips. And that first caress of hers restored his peace once more. He felt all right, a wave of tenderness flooded over him. To stay like that all his life, silent and oblivious, his heart stilled. And he began to hear once again, closer now, the long chime of a bell. A long gap, then another chime. A long, long time, another one. He expected another, it did not come; the last chime hung in the air.

What are they ringing, Ana? he said. Don't you know, have you forgotten the local customs? No, I just didn't count, he said; I only heard it now. It is the seven tolls for the dying, she said. Between one toll and the next there is time to say a prayer, plead for the person who is about to die, said Ana. I did not pray before because I was occupied with you.

Even with his eyes closed, he could tell that she was now praying. Not praying between one toll and the next, according to the rule, she was praying at the end. She was praying silently, only her lips were moving. Even so he could hear the echo of the prayer she was saying within her heart.

I hardly remembered any more, he said. My mother knew the bell code, she always prayed like you must be praying now. Just like that, silently, just lips, no speech, just like you.

She said nothing and her feather-like silence did not disturb him any more. Such was the peace, the happiness, the lightness he felt. It is sad, the toll for the dying, she said, when she finished praying. Yes, it is sad, but it is very beautiful, Ana. You think so? she asked. Do you like death? I feel so sorry for someone who wants to die and cannot, someone who asks for clemency and prayers through the guild bell. They say it is some awful sin that prevents a person dying. The soul is afraid to deliver itself into God's hand. I don't think so, Ana, he said. However bad my sin, those tolls would be my freedom, I would die happy.

Ana began to cry. Seeing her tears, Gaspar said forgive me, my love. I should not have said that, I ought not to have come. I am going, farewell.

216

No, she said, not yet. Stay a little longer, stay with me until this is all over. I cannot, he said, getting up, I have to go back home. Stay, Gaspar, I beg you. I must go, Ana. I left without saying where I was going, my stepmother and the Captain-General may need me for something. After it is all over, I will come back.

She saw that it was useless to try and detain him. Go then, she said, I shall go on praying. And he smiled, because he had long since ceased to believe in prayers, he did not believe in anything. And he wiped away her tears with his fingers. He kissed her forehead and left.

In the street the dragoons and orderlies were more restless. He dug his spurs into his horse's flanks. He no longer took any notice of the advice the soldier had given him; he galloped. He did not worry about the bullets, about what might now happen. Something called him, he must go quickly. He dug his spurs deeper, now galloping furiously. Behind the shutters, windows and half-opened doors, astonished and curious eyes followed him. He did not see a thing, nothing else mattered. He flew home, he would not run away any more, that was all he could say.

When he arrived home a nigger boy ran to him saying that Aunt Inacia was waiting for him in the drawing-room. Again? he said, his heart racing. The boy stood watching, blanched and glassy-eyed, without understanding.

What is it this time? Give me the letter, he said to Inacia. There is no letter, master. The letter I had, I took to the Master Captain-General. For you, master, I have a message from Mistress Malvina, I am afraid even to speak. Speak at once, blasted nigger, Gaspar shouted impatiently. She said to say she told the whole story to the Master Captain-General. That the half-breed Januario is free of blame, she confessed. In the letter she said that it was her and you, master, who killed Master João Diogo.

Shot through with pain, Gaspar closed his eyes. He turned his back on the black woman, moved away from her and went over to the window. He fondled the chased silver pistol, the one that had belonged to his father. He was afraid of what he might do. Terror-stricken, Inacia sidled away and leaned against the wall, waiting. She was waiting for the punishment which, atavistically, she always expected. But nothing happened, he did not appear to notice her, or anyone else. Within him, none of what he always feared was happening: no despair, he would wait his time coldly and lucidly, he would not run away. Everything would really have to have its time. And with the implacable connecting logic of the vanquished he began to imagine that they had laid a terrible trap for him. She or someone on her behalf, invisible, arbitrary and inevitable.

The letters, why did he destroy the letters? Only the last letter she wrote remained – the letter to the Captain-General. Useless to defend himself. Even in the hour of his death he would not accuse her. For the honour of his father, because of his own desire to die.

Suddenly, without even asking permission, a nigger came running in, pale with fright. Master, something has happened, something very bad has happened at your late father's house, stammered the nigger, panting. Tell me at once what it was! said Gaspar, already guessing what had happened. Mistress Malvina, she killed herself, said the nigger.

Inacia screamed and fell on her knees. In a mixture of saliva, tears and sobs, she wept and wailed in a mixture of Yoruba and Portuguese, of saints and African gods. Take this damned nigger out of my sight, shouted Gaspar.

And, once alone, he sank heavily on to the couch. He had nothing more to do. Unlike the other, he would not die in effigy, it was impossible and useless to run away. There grew inside him the certainty that everything he had dreamed really did happen.

3

The cocks in their fretful challenge, to see which was first to announce the morning. A haggard dawn was on its way, brightening the sleepy valley. The mist now whiter and more luminous at the edges, gradually dispersing. The town buried under the cold ash of the mist, which had settled heavily during the night over the valleys of the Tripuí, the Caquende and the Funil. As the light and warmth increased, Isidoro, the black man, would see the spires of Carmo Church, the saw-edged profile of the mountain, the gentle curve of the hills inside the town, Hangman's Hill. The town lit up, reborn from the mists, only the peak would keep its crown of clouds.

Now, woken by the cocks' clarion, the morning advanced more rapidly, the sky a whitish grey. Five or six o'clock. In a moment the sun would drive the remains of night far away. And with it the tormented wait, the nightmares, the bad thoughts. Cold and inoffensive, the carbine now looked unprimed. Before, the temptation, he thought it would be easy, massa being asleep. The only way of really finding life, freedom from slavery. A life he had never known, having been born a slave. Not even this was possible now: the dark gold, the devil who thought for him, went away along with the darkness.

Massa sleeping, all doubled up with cold. The blanket and the skins were apparently not warm enough, the cold was from inner weariness.

Like trying to find a snug place for one's hands, a deeper protection, an impossible warmth. He was snuggled up, like a puppy all curled up. And doubled up like that, he looked even more like a boy. Even his face, of smooth bronze. Poor boy, there was nothing more he could do for massa. Only wait for daylight, when what massa had decided would be done. What they had decided for him. It was no longer possible to keep on waiting. He too would decide, he would go his own way at last. That was no life even for a nigger.

The sun himself is going to wake massa up. Overcome by tiredness, massa badly needed to sleep. He hadn't slept for a long time. Was he dreaming? Though close to death, he was dreaming. It's close to death that people dream most, old things come back, they say. You even recall things you never remembered. Really old things, swallowed up by that hungry animal time. Life you never even thought existed.

The light was breaking up the mist. First the cocks with emblazoned crow, all clarion and coloured feathers, now a bell calling people to mass. Six o'clock, he counted. Carmo's treble bell with its short, high-pitched chimes, abrupt and quick. Mass with a vicar, not any odd priest. Because of the longer gap between the last three chimes, after the usual short chimes. He knew the language of the bells, the tolls and chimes, the peals. What the small bells, the tenor and lead bells were saying. Since a boy, the bells. Though he was captive, a nigger errand boy, before he was sent to the excavations as punishment (the first fetters and neck irons), he used to go with Vindovino the bell-ringer at the cathedral church of Antonio Dias. It must be good to be a priest's slave, he would take charge of the towers and the bells. Even for a freed slave it was good to be a bell-ringer. Because of the music, the tolling and hallelujahs. Bells for everything, for every time of day. Vindovino taught him the rules of the tolls, the chimes and the peals. His fear of the great tower bells, their quebracho support bars. As they swung and wheeled, they could kill someone. The stories they told of someone who died like that in the double roll of the bar. The treble bells were cute: joyful and clear when they were rung. Bells for mass, bells for the souls. Bells for feast days, bells for the deceased. When it's a committee brother it goes in this order: first the treble, then the tenor bells; you finish with the guild's great bell. Vindovino taught him. You need to understand the language of the bells to know about life. The brotherhood bell, if the one who died is an important person. Two chimes three times, a short chime between each knell. When it is a child, it sounds quite gay, I like that, just peals. For me ringing for a dead child is fun. The funeral knell, now that is dismal, it goes on tolling grievous inside one. Of grown-ups, not of children. The Eucharist bells, the bells for the dying. The lesson learned from Vindovino. The bells, always, before, now.

Now it was morning, the mist was dissolving and breaking up. Carmo Church was gleaming, a light buried beneath the whitewash. The houses all white and gay, the window frames, the windows and doors, blue and green. In the Funil valley, behind Hangman's Hill, a stubborn, rheumy mist still prevailed. The day would be radiant, it was already bright, already morning.

His closed eyes were leaden, swollen, impossible to open. The sticky inbetween of sleeping and waking, the mushy gruel of dream and things beginning, coming out of the mist, reborn in pain, drowsy and sleepy. The certainty that if he lifted his head he would fall back into sleep, into the nightmares made up of real happenings. They were not inventions of the void, of the pregnant silence of darkness, of his drowned soul. Of his own body, slimy secretion, a suppurating sore. If he let go of his arms and legs, abandoning his body, he could sink once more into sleep, now he did not want to. He had to wake up, begin to live. To die, he almost said, beginning to think, no longer dreaming. The sunlight forced him to turn over instinctively, seeking protection and shade. Not his eyes, it was his body that was starting to see.

At first the light, the noises, the things. The world was beginning. The eternal reinvention, the unceasing recreation, the endless rebirth, the always return. Life, inauguration. Everything for death, he meant. Now he knew, he had really begun to think. Afterwards God would make the creatures. In the beginning God created heaven and earth. The flat voice, the readings in the dining-room at the seminary in Vila do Carmo. The mouths chewed silently, ravenously. The noise of the mouths. Feigned calm, silence, contemplation, meditation. The monastic rules of the seminary. The earth was unformed and empty. Light, there was light. God separated the light from the darkness. The waters, let the earth and the oceans appear. And the green grass and the trees and the fruits. God created time. The day and the night. For ever and ever. Or did time only come with man? He said let this be done, everything was done. And then came the great whales, the wild beasts and the other living things. Only on the sixth day, man. Later woman, taken from his deepest pain, from his rib. He did not feel anything, was asleep. While he slept, Malvina. Only on the seventh day did he rest. God needs rest as well. Man and woman, together they would inaugurate hell. They did not need the devil. And God's work would continue its course. For ever and ever, amen. The seminary, the forgotten lessons. The inaugural hell, the fear of blasphemies. Anathema, they were shouting all the time. They taught. Until death do come. In the first seed it already existed. Like the shape of a tree in its seed. The name itself was deathly –

Seminary of the Good Death.

Massa was waking up, Isidoro noticed. It's all going to start. He is stirring, stretching himself. It is going to start again, all over again. For the last time, he was sure. The two of them, free for ever. He had decided, but massa was likely to change his mind. In that case he would change too, being a slave. Always a hope. He would not change, he knew massa. Half-breed, mestizo. He wanted to be black, just imagine! He felt like laughing. Poor boy. She did what she wanted with him. Foolish massa, wee birdie kept going forward until it fell into the snake's mouth. That was how they did it. He had realized himself, often suspected. But massa was blind, there was no point in telling him. He wasn't sure either, just an idea, a suspicious mind. Used to sufferings, to betrayals, to wickedness. The fear that came with him from other worlds, crossed many seas. The vomiting, the pining niggers, the rotting corpses. The older ones told about it. Those who had come, those who still kept coming. Even if he told him, massa would not for a moment believe. People don't believe what others say, only their own experience. He really did suspect. Didn't he see Mistress Malvina the times massa had sent him to talk to her? White women! he said with hatred. Massa must be saying it half asleep. After he saw that he was betrayed. The two of them knew it, only they could not talk to one another about it. Leastwise, he couldn't, a nigger. Niggers can't speak, only when spoken to. He learned under the whip. Even massa didn't have the courage to talk about it. If he talked, he would realize that he had made a mistake, she wasn't worth it. Bitch! he said with hatred. His soul felt suddenly free, he could say that about a white lady. She had never been worth it, altogether worthless. Well, didn't he see, those times he came into town? The first time she still received him. After that she always sent word she could not, it was very dangerous, sheer madness to keep on sending him. When she could, she would send word at the time. She never did, only now, in the letter he got from Inacia. Trick letter, he tried to tell massa; his courage deserted him. Wasn't sure either. Massa had to come back. To put an end to it all. Massa might kill him in his fury, if he said anything. About the letter. At first he didn't suspect either. When massa fell into a really deep sleep it came to him in a flash. The letter was a trick letter, a trap. She was all trickery. Mistress Malvina. Could massa not see, did he never see? A trick letter to bring massa, the soldiery would see to the rest. They had fallen into the trap, the snare. Now, leopard caught, had to die. The soldiers in the square, massa would go down. He could see massa going down now. What use was it now telling him it was sheer lies? The lady's letter. Just like a whore, the bait. Even a nigger whore don't do that. False, the lady. Those gold ornaments, all powdered, her head-dress criss-crossed with pearls. Her face, some sorts of beauty is nearly always perdition. Shameless, white whore. Massa was better off when he slept with unselfish prostitutes, women without haughty airs. You got money, you pay, you go to bed. Any one, no choosing. They didn't play hide-and-seek, unlikely to get hitched to them. Some did, not massa. What enchanted massa was her fiery beauty, white woman. It was the airs and graces. White snake with open mouth, he went like the birdie. Chirpety-chirping, he went. Now there he was caught, stuck fast. He could never, never did, go far away from the town. Like a turkey on a line. Caught, stuck fast. In that house, in Santa Quiteria, in the shadow, sniffing the lady's trail. Massa would never go to the cattle country. Even if he told him the truth. Before he only suspected, in that flash he became sure. Massa was going to die, he was delivering his body. Like delivering a message. Only the body was missing, he was condemned. Mulungu the hangman pulled the rope with all his strength. The doll swaying backwards and forwards in the air, imitating a person. Dead a long time ago, all that was really left was to deliver the body. That was what he was going to do. Nobody able to stop him. Even if he himself, Isidoro, wanted to, damnation. When a man decides, condemned man wants to die, there's nothing more to be done. He could still try, a faint light of hope winked far away. A small bell scarcely heard in his soul, an agonizing desire to listen. The bells pealing. She still received him the first time. After that she sent word with Inacia. Even Inacia suddenly started avoiding him. A plague on you, nigger, go away. Like as if she was a white woman. Looked as if she would like to hit him, throw stones. Spit, that she did. Is it catching, arrogance and wickedness? Inacia got to be all airs as well. Took no notice of niggers, of him. Blasted race, deserves it. He began to tell massa lies. Said he had spoken to Mistress Malvina herself. He saw Mistress Malvina twice out in her sedan-chair, all jaunty, on the way to the palace. Like before, lounging at the window. With Master Gaspar, her stepson. Him very serious, she was doing the talking. That was before it all happened. Before massa got infatuated. After massa got infatuated, he, Isidoro, kept prowling round the house in the Rua Direita. He saw the lady and her stepson, always close together, their conversations on the balconies. Before massa did the killing. Was it with him? She wasn't deceiving only her husband. Was Januario getting a pair too? There was no stopping that woman. Like a prostitute, a black whore, but more wicked. They said he was engaged now, was going to get married. He was back living in Padre Faria, in the deceased's old house. Even so he was suspicious. Might be pretence, they were meeting in secret, like with massa. Inacia came and opened the door for massa. After massa went in she waited outside, keeping watch. Was it like that with the stepson? He couldn't find out. He suspected. Might be with others. No, just him. Others as well. Her laughter on the palace steps, at the Carmo Church door. Before it all happened. When massa was following her in her chair, like a dog sniffing its master's scent. Artful woman, tricky. The spell, massa's head turned. Gaspar always solemn, on the mansion balcony, before he moved to Padre Faria. But men are like that, they are more composed. A woman, when she's gone to bed with more than one, always gets loose. He never told massa he was suspicious. When massa went to her house every night. He only said he didn't know. The agonized look in massa's eyes, he never had the courage to tell him. Even had he known formerly. It was only today it came to him in a flash, he didn't know before. Now he was putting the pieces together, tying the ends together, he could see the pattern. All straightforward, clear water trickling from a spring. Why didn't he see it before? If he'd seen like he saw in the flash, he would've told. Even if massa beat him to death. Sometimes massa was furious, lost his head. Not with him. But in his great hatred of death, even with him. If he spoke. She had set it all up, careful embroideress she was. She was the one who shuffled the cards, he saw it clearly, Massa was not coarse like him, ignorant nigger as the white men said. Though of mixed blood, a natural son, not blessed by holy water, they'd sent him to the Boa Morte Seminary in Vila do Carmo. He should have learned, didn't they teach him? Or did they only teach litany, praying? Didn't they say it was priests that knew about souls, about exorcising sins? Even with massa not being a priest, only at the beginning of his studies. He should have suspected. You don't see, mad passion throws sand in your eyes. Like in the fog you don't see nothing, only shadows sometimes. If he himself, from outside, didn't see things clear, how could massa see, and him sunk in the mists? Him that didn't live in no mist, except the mistiness of his race. If he had heard the voice of his blood, the voice from a thousand years ago, from dead times. Being brought up among whites corrupts, blinds a man's hidden eye. White man's ears is stopped up, like as if they poured lead inside. He would've seen. Niggers know everything, just need to strain their ears, listen to the darkness. Our mothers, the protective gods. If we stick a pin in a doll and say that's the one we want to finish, he's going to feel it far away, even suffer the pains. Massa's body hanging there swinging on the gibbet, in the square that time. Now they were saying massa was dead, to the King. Was that killed massa, he felt it far away. A doll hanging. The blow on his throat, he must've felt it from far away. The shudder. From then he started to die. Till now when he was going to finish. In his death agony, his last agony. He could accompany massa too. Die with him. Deliver his condemned nigger's body.

223

Suddenly, as if he heard the nocturnal voice he thought was now dead and which had haunted him during the night, when his fingers played absently with the trigger, engaged in what might suddenly occur in a flash of the devil's eye, aiming, so easy, Isidoro said I'm not going to die with any white man! They are not worth it, all rubbish! I'm not even going to die with massa. I shall fight, he answered, for fear that the devil might reappear in full daylight, urging him to kill. He was no longer a slave, he was there because he wanted. His slavery was different. He would try, there was no harm in trying. He began to hear the first stroke of a bell. A fairly lengthy, round chime. Just from the first he knew already, he waited for the others before speaking. He would try, for the last time.

Though awake, Januario kept his eyes closed, protecting himself against the light. He did not want to see the light of day, he was afraid of going out into the light. In the full light of day he would see everything he had started to see in his half-waking state. Things were now beginning to make sense. The connections, the sunken roots were coming to the surface. Everything that he could not, would not see. Everything now so clear, instantaneously. Only he, the fool, did not see. So easy now, before he could not see. Even Isidoro must have noticed. Damned clever nigger. A Sudan nigger, my son, his father put a high value on the slave he had presented him with. Isidoro just didn't have the courage to say anything. Afraid of being beaten, the ancestral fear. Even knowing he had never been punished by him, only by his father. Afraid of his hatred.

Emerging from the mists, now he was beginning to see more clearly. The truth only germinates in the darkness of the earth, a watered seed. All those dreams and recollections. When he could not distinguish whether he was dreaming or merely remembering. Whether he was already inventing what was going to happen, might happen. The tiny seed began to swell in the at times sticky darkness of those dreams. A seed already carries in itself the whole tree it is going to be afterwards. For ever and ever, amen. The same as, before it is fulfilled, a man's destiny is blind. But exists hidden in the first seed. Suddenly he could see in reverse, unwinding. And it all made sense. A game, the pieces of which he was only now, after the blinding revelation, able to put together. So easy, why didn't he see it?

Now he could see it clearly, the set-up of the game. He saw it suddenly. Now he remembered what he had suddenly seen. Everything that had happened without his being able to understand was being unveiled. A design, a plan made just for him. Why had he not understood?

Malvina had the ends of the threads and the needle, he was a toy in her hands. Even when he thought he was making the decision, Malvina's idea was in charge. He merely did things, she made the plans. In league with the devil, that woman was in league with the devil, he realized suddenly and was afraid. The schemes, the demon in human clothing, in a woman's skin. So the devil did exist, he saw that. Otherwise, how to explain it all, the sequences from the beginning, from the first seed, fitting together? All that he did not understand before and that was now as clear as the sun in his eyes? He preferred to believe in the devil rather than see evil stamped on Malvina's face. How she made him womanish. What she had done to the mighty potentate. João Diogo under lace-embroidered sheets, coverlets and pillow-slips. Those clothes, in the bed he looked like a coquettish old woman. That woman castrated, destroyed everyone who came close to her. A curse weighing on her, from the very beginning, written down the better to come to pass, not be forgotten. He himself felt like a woman, his gestures become effeminate, musical. He was becoming mellifluous, sugary. He hated what she did to him. To him and to João Diogo Galvão. The glories of a dread name, his dark past, all this she dandified. They had all been toys in Malvina's diabolical hands. Only by thinking of the devil was he able to understand. By oneself it would not work, the scheme became obscure. With an intelligence, a player, behind it, he could understand.

And now that he could see everything so clearly, he hated himself even more than her. Himself small, a little girl by the side of her. Like João Diogo, a sweet little old lady dressed all in lace. Why didn't he understand? From the first day, she must have thought it all out, worked it out. A doll in her hands. All the initiative was hers, even when he did the thinking. She controlled him from a distance. Like him trying, from a distance, with his breathing, to control João Diogo's sleep. He merely did things, a well-taught boy. Even the dagger, she gave it to him. She had never mentioned the dagger. Concealed in her skirt no doubt. All following her scheme, the devil's machination. She only said that the old man would die with shock, if he woke up. They would have very little to do. He could hear her voice, see her eyes suddenly turn dark. He would only need to choke him with the pillow. If João Diogo came round. Even if he didn't come round, to be sure the old man had died. She thought of everything, left nothing out. Even what he still did not know, what only she knew. What would only be known later, at the resurrection. At the time of reckoning. She saw to the smallest things. João Diogo would die of shock, his heart was weak. But she carried the weapon, she handed him the dagger. Like that it was quite clear, murder. Murder was what she wanted, not just death. Just João Diogo's death did not interest her, hers was a different plan. If she had only wanted her husband dead, she would have set things up in a very different way. She said nothing to him about the pistol near the bed, within reach. She must have known, she knew. Maybe she wanted him also, the two of them, to die. She would be free of both of them at one go. Without soiling her hands. Or had she engineered the two outcomes, leaving it to chance, either one would do? Because she did not warn him she was going to put out the candle. She would let the two decide. Or the devil? Not God anyway. God's plans are more secret, you only see with your heart, before or after they have happened. With the devil it's intelligence, head work, when everything makes sense. The way he could see it now, quite clear. Every man is male–female. Male in the head, female in the heart. It is in man's heart, in his hidden female side, that God deposits his seed. A man all head is the devil, an aberration. She is an aberration, all that thinking, chewing over, scheming. Not two outcomes, maybe three or more. In the first João Diogo would kill him, afterwards she would explain, no one like her for explaining. She would once more find peace in her husband's arms. Or did she hope that, after her husband killed him, he would faint away with the emotion and she would then kill João Diogo? No, she would not do it, others on her behalf, without her lifting a straw? Only blowing out the candle. That second shot he thought he heard. Then the other, he was sure. There was a great deal only she must know. With her anything was possible, he could see that now.

Everything just as she planned. She must have thought through and through the whole scheme she afterwards unleashed. Things made more sense, now anyone could understand. The jewel casket, for them to think it had been theft. The casket ready beforehand, like the dagger. It didn't have her best jewels in it, he saw that now, afterwards. The coral silver choker, that time. No one would believe there could be anything between her and him. No one knew of anything between the two of them.

Again the suspicion that maybe she wanted João Diogo to kill him. Anything was possible with her, how did he not see it? Surely not. She knew he was done for. Blinded by passion, he saw nothing. He jumped from the window, she screamed. All the appearance of a theft. Malvina's shadow in the lighted window, the last vision. She must have stopped at that point, all that conspiracy business was the Captain-General's invention. Blindly he did not see that Malvina only loved him with her body, her soul was not his. The other's, of course.

Which other? And a name rose out of the dark depths pregnant with menacing silence. The same name that his jealousy sometimes whispered to him. Not before, after he fled, when he recalled things. Like now, foaming with rage, he was sure. And he did not want to hear.

226

Because he knew it was true. Now, that is, not before. Before he was not at all sure, everything was still very hazy. Now it suddenly took shape. The name announced itself. Gaspar, he was the one she loved passionately. Gaspar was like her, he was not – a mestizo and a bastard. Wasn't it obvious? She always loved him, even before he, Januario, came into her life, the two on horseback that time. Malvina was capable of anything, he could see that now, he kept repeating, monotonously, in his anguish and loneliness. Everything would come in good time, she planned everything. The devil bides his time. The devil knows that the world is round and that if a man keeps going straight ahead he will end up at the same place. He only had to wait at the door, the devil was biding his time. A matter of time, even if she had stopped scheming. Gaspar and Malvina could even get married. There was an impediment, but what could not be bought with money! A papal brief, he knew some cases of even closer kinship. It would come, it was a matter of time, of biding one's time. She could bide her time, she never got flustered. Even at the moment. Any other woman would probably have trembled and failed. Not her, she waited.

At times he again could not understand some points, he did not suspect all of Malvina's secret intentions. It was said that Gaspar was a virgin, must be wicked talk. Was it before that day, she was on horseback, when they first saw each other, devoured one another with their eyes? Even long before that, she loved Gaspar? Now, he no longer had any doubt. Malvina's soul was his, Gaspar's. That first time, the two of them on horseback. The way Gaspar looked at him. Who is it? she asked with interest, or so it seemed. It was just some half-breed, nobody. There was something more than hatred in Gaspar's eyes. It hurt, then and now. A look of scorn, the look of someone who knows he is superior, master of the situation. How small he, Januario, was next to the other. Next to her. He had cut a sorry figure. Gentry, they were, made for one another. White people understand one another, Isidoro said. Now he felt like the lowest of men, almost a nigger. He should have seen from the first day, the two of them on horseback. Now she was galloping, laughing. Her laughter began to hurt him deep inside. Some half-breed, nobody. How could he have believed that she could love him, a half-breed? A bastard, a whoreson. That was all Gaspar needed to say. Thought it no doubt, everyone knew. But all he said was nobody. A bastard is nobody. He didn't have the courage to say it. They didn't say redskin in his presence. Let alone whoreson, son of a bitch. Not even in jest. Red rag to a bull. They reckoned he was wild, plucky. Nobody like him with a knife, in brawls and disorders. But he was really more of an overgrown boy. Maybe that was why the Captain-General thought. . . .

227

Suddenly things became entangled, he ceased to understand, in some places the plot became confused. Did Gaspar know about everything? No, that would be too much. The evil was all in her. Like she did with him. On the quiet, soft-footed, a clever, velvety she-cat. Not that he was trying to make out he was innocent of the old man's death. He felt deceived, the idea had been hers, his the hand. Gaspar could not have known about his affair with Malvina. No one knew. If he had known things would have been different. Gaspar definitely did not know. He came across Gaspar several times. Gaspar did not even notice the impudent way he looked at him, just to test him. To see if the other knew anything. Playing with fire, could ruin everything. Even so he looked at him offensively. Gaspar seemed not even to notice. Or was he covering up, pretending not to? No man can manage to be so crafty. He reacts eventually, reveals himself. Only a woman or a hermaphrodite. She was all shrouded, a thousand leaves. An onion, a periwinkle. A woman, a she-cat, many cloaks. Child of the sun, queen. Child of fire, damnation. She purred and bit. A hybrid, a monster. Like the damned angels, monstrous. Like her brothers in flesh. Her goat's feet hidden. No doubt that was why she didn't get pregnant, didn't have children. Not from the old man, maybe, but what about him? He already had children round and about, had passed on the destiny he inherited. Whoreson, son of a bitch. Waiting, she was, to spawn monsters. She-cat, claws, queen. She taught him and he learned the hard way that nobody loves a queen. Why didn't he see that before? Now he had learned, in his guts. Nobody loves a queen without paying with his own death. If not of the body, of the soul. A drone whose purpose in life is to fertilize the queen, then die. They kill, they murder. If she had become pregnant he would have been killed. He was killed in any case. In his soul, in effigy. Wasn't he now going merely to deliver his body? The way a child is taken to be baptized, in order to live. After she was pregnant, he should be killed, she set up the trap. Maybe she was pregnant. No, unless she disguised it. Madness, she used to be naked, he stroked her flat, empty belly. That way his death made sense. Only the males, only the drone is killed. A strong, plucky male, now he saw he was a child, a small animal. A fly in the syrup, he couldn't escape. He would have to wait for a slow death. He had been the victim, not the murderer he supposed himself. Now it was coming, his death agony.

That first time, on horseback. She must have thought that savage had turned up at the right moment. He merely obeyed everything exactly as she planned, he came back to his monotonous repetition. He fell into the trap, the snare. A child, a mere boy next to her wickedness. A drone, she was a queen. The woman and her philtres. All false, lies. Even that letter summoning him. A fake letter, deceiving woman. There are people who like using them. Like a cat hiding its paw after the evil is done. She-cat and queen. Her hot purring breath on his neck, when she was all on fire, without her queen's clothes. Her naked body gleaming in the semi-darkness. Her claws in his flesh, she dug them in. After her letter no doubt she sent word to the Captain-General that he was coming back. The trap was laid, he would not run away any more. It was not impossible, but because he made up his mind. It was fate, coming to take what was hers, his body. Once he was told about a man making a contract with death. Or was it with the devil? A deceptive contract, simply to gain wealth. Man is always evil, they said. At the end of some years he would come for him and take him away. They set the date, he pushed it out as far as he could, she didn't bother at all, she had all the time in the world. She fulfilled her part, the man became wealthy. One day the allotted time came, he was sure she would not fail to come. She did not, she came. The man went and hid at the back of the house and blackened his face, his hands, his feet, everything that showed, with coal. She would think he was a nigger, instead of himself. She arrived and said where is the one I said I would come for? He's gone, run away, said the man, now all black, in the hearth. What about you, nigger? she said with a laugh. Me, nothing, he said. Doesn't matter, said she. So's not to lose my journey, I'll take you instead. And she did. He would give himself up, deliver his body. Wearied, already nearly dead. Or was it she herself talking to the Captain-General? He could hear Malvina's voice. Her hot words in his ear. Maybe it was with the Captain-General. They said he was in love with her. Madness, impossible. The condemned angels, the darkness. He would never be able to understand the hidden side of that woman, her thousand leaves. Anything possible. No, not the Captain-General. A foolish notion, born of a heavy soul. She had never talked about the Captain-General, except by chance. When she was boasting about going to the palace on special occasions. Gaspar was more likely. She only mentioned Gaspar occasionally and then her voice seemed to quaver, now. Now he noticed how she went out of her way just to mention her stepson. He remembered it jealously, with impotent hatred. Castrated, he could do nothing. Yes, undoubtedly, Gaspar. So obvious, why didn't he see it? he repeated. Now he could see. His circular, labyrinthine, tormented thought. Now Gaspar could enjoy Malvina's body, its secrets. If he had not been enjoying them already for a long time, since long before.

Before he could sink back again into his mists, into his lethargy, into his ruminations, into the blackness of time's endless pit, only memory, his body transmuted into the flesh of anarchic time, slipping down the ravine, until the final agony (when he would be lost, prevented from doing what he had already decided to do), he opened his eyes and saw Isidoro staring at him glassy-eyed. The hard, inscrutable gleam in the eyes of a captive nigger, which can hide everything, from tenderness to fierce hatred, death. If detected, the eyes opened for an instant, allowed themselves to be penetrated, became two lakes. And their hardness softened into a moist glitter. Which might as well be the verge of a permanently checked tear as mere tiredness, he did not know, lack of sleep. Even so, they did not let themselves be seen, did not show what was behind them. The black man's eyes seemed to question, they did not surrender again, recovering from the momentary weakness which had made them moist. The white of the eyes was browner and more brilliant than ever, all streaked with blood. The eyes velvety from so much lack of sleep.

You let me sleep, said Januario, and you did not sleep. A shadow of hatred passed over Isidoro's eyes, a cloud hiding the sun, growing dark. I am not the owner of anyone's sleep, said the black man. There was something strange about Isidoro, the black man had been like that since last night. He frequently surprised him with his eyes motionless, opaque, hard. If you were dead tired, what was I supposed to do? said the black man. I didn't close my eyes this night, I was keeping watch. Wasn't that what I promised? It's the last time I shall keep watch.

Yes, he promised. For the last time. He remembered that Isidoro had in fact promised. His softly spoken words last night, the voice he knew. Today it had a strange hardness, a rough tone, almost an animal snarling. The whole of last night, all that business the previous day, their conversation. Very blurred, something very old. Going back in time. Many many years ago the two of them had arrived last night at the town. He wanted to tell the black man I'm not expecting anything from you, but he felt enormously weary at having to speak, after what he had decided to do.

You didn't sleep. What time do you think it is? he asked. Long past eight already, in a little while the gaolhouse bell will strike nine, said the black man. Right, in a little while I shall go, said Januario. D'you have a fixed time? asked Isidoro, provoking him. He looked slowly at the black man, he was beginning to understand those changes in the gleam in his eyes. He suddenly realized: Isidoro was no longer his slave, he was there because he wanted to. An equal, a companion. Yes, I fixed it, he said. Neither you nor they know it. And can a body know at what time it'll be? asked the black man and there was a taunting smile on his lips. But Januario did not respond, he would not respond any more. He would merely take the first step, everything would be as it had to happen.

You can go away, I'm not keeping you, he said gently to the black man, without the slightest resentment. A dreadful weariness, a deathly sadness choking his soul. No, said the black man, I shall wait and see. Maybe when the time comes you'll change your mind, go back on it. What I've been saying still stands. You can give up, said Januario. I'm not going back any more.

Isidoro knew it was true, it was all going to finish there. They would separate, two branches of a river. Each one seeking other rivers on the way to the sea. There was still something missing, that was why he was waiting. Something might still happen, he neither knew nor suspected what it was. He was just waiting, with that silent, apparently docile fatality of coloured people.

Tell me something, Isidoro. Just to check on something I was thinking a little way back, said Januario, once again overcoming his tiredness. He needed to know, the nigger would surely not refuse to tell him now. Did you see Malvina all the times you said?

Without knowing why, he began to say Malvina, not Mistress Malvina, as if they were equals.

Isidoro stayed dumber than before, than ever. That dark, heavy, sticky dumbness that only black people can put on. Tell me, man, for God's sake! It's the last thing I shall ask you, said Januario with that doglike, shamefaced humility that only mestizos can put on.

The nigger was going to talk, he felt it. No, he said. I only saw her once, that first time, after we ran away. Why didn't you tell me? Why did you lie to me? said Januario. Not to hurt you, foreboding, fear, I dunno, said the black man. To be frank, even Inacia wouldn't see me any more. If you had told me (Januario was turning over past possibilities), things might have been different. No (Isidoro confirmed the fateful immutability of the past), nothing would be different. Everything had to be the way it was. (And Tiresias reaffirmed, reconsidered and foresaw the impossibility of changing the past, as if to say the past is as immutable as the future, except that the future is concealed, only the blind, immersed in the darkness of time, being able to see the pieces of an absurd, inconsistent game played, in its cruel glory, by heedless, vengeful gods.) What's done is done, said Isidoro, and we can't change it. Only what's ahead, what's still to come. So's after it happens we can say it had to be like that. The future can't be changed either.

Probably the nigger was right, thought Januario, accepting and, unknowingly, answering the queries of the blind, the soothsayers, the messengers, and the mournful warnings of the invisible chorus, the wish of the gods. Why keep tormenting his heart still more? He wasn't going to decide anything, what was done was done.

He began to hear a bell ringing far away, with long, dark, unhurried chimes. The chimes finishing, they had been ringing for a long time, he only now became aware. He could not tell what they were announcing, though he sensed, from the sad resonance of the chimes. You know about bells, what are they ringing, Isidoro?

The black man was increasingly loath to answer, supposing his eyes alone were enough. Speech was losing its use for him, silence was all that mattered. Didn't you hear it before? he said. No, it's the first time, said Januario reluctantly. The black man looks as if he is going to laugh, his eyes are already laughing. Didn't you really hear it before? Or did you hear it and not count? Likely I did hear it before, Januario replied. He could not remember. It isn't the first time, said the black man unwillingly, still not wishing to answer. It'll probably go on like that all day.

After a time the black man said here comes the last. Listen carefully. You don't know what it is, you didn't count, I counted, I count even without meaning to. It's the seven long chimes, very long drawn out, like usual. Even with me telling you, you don't know what it is? Seems you're playing with me, white master, but they really are tolling for the dying.

(And Tiresias smiled triumphantly behind his blindness.)

My death, thought Januario with a shudder. A tremor ran all the way down his spine, from the nape of his neck. No, it was not his death. Someone else's. Someone else also needed to surrender his weary soul and could not do it.

Somebody is dying, said Isidoro. The tolls are asking for a helping prayer. It costs nothing to say a prayer, that's what white people teach us. I used to pray myself, don't any more now. So's the poor wretch don't suffer a lot dying, the bitch's fingers.

Not suffer a lot, sink into God's endless silence. Everything that comes from down there, before them comes silence. Like blindness with soothsayers. Silence is God's speech. You keep wanting to hear God's voice, you don't listen to the silence. Before he said let there be light, there was God's breath, silence consecrating the earth. Even today, if people try, just before they die, they can hear the silent breath of God. And the spirit of God moved on the waters. Once again the toneless voice of the reader at the seminary. And the spirit of God was silence, Januario realized in the deepest, most heartfelt humility. And he began to see, filled with a sudden peace, a very bright light inside and outside him. A peace that was like a soft, scented breeze.

He got up and looked at Isidoro, already standing. Are you coming? he asked more for the sake of asking. As he might ask what time it was, though he had already heard it strike nine. Now it was indifferent, he

232

knew that when the time came he would be alone. He asked as a sort of farewell, instead of saying goodbye.

No, said the black man. From now on I'm on my own. I shall go to earth somewhere in the wilds, there's no shortage of backlands. God knows where I'll go. You're going to meet your death at last, white man's world is finished for me. I'm pulling out for good.

And Januario felt a strange happiness, all his weariness disappeared. On his face the fresh air of the breeze that was licking the foliage, blowing on the flowers. He breathed deeply and his chest was all a field of light and flowers, with the coloured silence of the butterflies flying over it. All soft, he could die. And a great tenderness, a light of happiness, began to gush from inside him; a processional hymn, God's epiphany. He felt like kissing Isidoro's hand and, for some reason, asking his pardon.

Shall you make for a slave settlement? Shall you become an escapee slave?

In the tone of his voice, in his questions, all the gentle, glowing tenderness he was unable to put into words. Maybe the Great Settlement, he said, a piece of advice which was meant as a caress. Because he was unable to say what he really meant.

The black man was silent for a long time. His silences were becoming longer and heavier all the time, they were Isidoro's only way of speaking. His eyes glowed enormously.

There is no Great Settlement any more, said Isidoro. If anyone says there is, he's dreaming of souls from the other world, talking to the other side, in the darkness. Papa Ambrosio has been dead these many years. Time for everything belongs to everybody, there's no mine and thine, that's finished, won't come back.

But there are people who still talk about him, said Januario, not very convinced. He did not want to leave the nigger alone in the silent void of solitude. They say Ambrosio isn't dead, he went on, hoping to see a different glow in the nigger's tormented eyes. They say one day he will come back with an army of centurions, more than a thousand, that he is busy freeing and gathering together all over this God-forsaken place.

What, said Isidoro, with a forced laugh. You only have to count on your fingers. Nobody lives that long. Ain't no Ambrosio any more!

They say Ambrosio doesn't grow old, that his death was a lie, a white man's invention, said Januario, repeating what he had heard in his father's slave-quarters.

Only if there's another Ambrosio, that one is dead, said Isidoro, beginning to want to believe. No, it's all a story, smoke, invented! We need that, better that and suffer than nothing and no pain. We need smoke, air, blueness. To be able to endure the pain of living. It's like that King Sebastian that many white people are still waiting for today. If you think there's still slave settlements. . . . he said, wanting to believe, almost believing.

There are, you know yourself there are, said Januario.

The black man was chewing on his heavy silence. An ox was grazing in the distance, outlined against the sunlit blue sky.

There's always some stray runaways hiding out in these forests, said Isidoro. That never stopped. Yes, you may be right. I shall look for a slave settlement somewhere around, there must still be some. Till that bitch death comes looking for what's hers since I was born.

That's the best you can do, said Januario. You've got a race waiting for you, a night to shelter you. I don't have a race, I'm like a mule, stained at birth. They call me redskin sometimes, you know that. I'm not even that. I'm more of a whitened half-breed on account of my father. Neither white nor Indian. I'm not anything. I'm going to meet up with this nothing that is me.

The black man's silence was now quite enormous, greater than the previous night, the night which awaited him. The odd miserly word, small, painful words torn from the depths of silence, that was all Januario could get. From what I can see, you don't want to talk to me any more, Januario gasped.

The black man was more reluctant still to answer, as if he had to tear the words from his very flesh. It's not that at all, he said. What is it then, Januario asked. Nothing, said the black man, looking at the sky. Nothing, shouted Januario, and his shout went echoing into the distance. Isidoro looked at him, a long look and deeper than ever, in the eyes. The black man's gaze pierced his soul. He only wanted to speak with his eyes.

And Januario saw that a terrible thing, a deafening silence, was growing behind the black man's eyes. Speak, Januario begged, despite the fear inside him of what the other might say.

I'm going to speak now for the last time, Isidoro began, speaking slowly and firmly, as if dictating a letter. (And Januario realized: for a long time he had ceased to be a slave, the two of them were equals.) From now on I shall never again speak in white man's tongue. I shall only speak Yoruba, the language of my colour. No white man will understand me. They can beat me to death, lash my back, feet and arms on the whipping-post, but I shall not speak white man's language any more, Portuguese or *paulista*! If there are no more slave settlements, I shall gather together some like me and make one. A settlement bigger even than Ambrosio's, as big as my whole people. Only niggers like me will understand me! They'll only take me dead. I shall die with a blunderbuss in my hand!

And when Januario tried to ask another question, the black man started a mixture of howls, moans and a savage gibberish of guttural sounds. Goodbye, anyway, said Januario, aware that the other would not answer any more.

And he set out down the hill, almost sliding. When he turned round, he saw the black man motionless and silent. The carbine in both hands, in front of his body. His whole figure was hewn out of black stone against the pale blue of the sky. Head held high, chest bared, his eyes staring into the distance, he looked more like the guardian of a temple, the keeper of the gate and silent guide of his people. He went on a little and turned round again. Isidoro had disappeared altogether in the light. Now he went on alone, almost running. He did not turn back any more. He reached the street and passed the Mercês Church.

The square opened into a lake of luminosity. The air sparkled in waves of sound, full of streaks of light. And in long waves the bells of Carmo Church began once more to toll the first of the seven mournful chimes. But he did not hear, he could not hear. Immersed within and without in the brightness, blinded by a column of light, he was walking towards death.

The square full of blue jackets, the sleepy soldiers in small groups, sitting on the ground or leaning on their muskets. A boy recognized and shouted aloud look at him here. Right next to him, then ran away.

Januario kept coming down, slowly now. The soldiers looked at him as if they could not believe their eyes. Yet no one moved, all eyes fascinated by the sinister apparition.

Come on, yelled an ensign, breaking the lethargy. Seize the man! It's him all right!

Januario makes as if to run, or is really going to run. He wanted to be killed outright, he was not going to be arrested. For a more impulsive soldier to shoot. The soldier runs towards him, shouts stop. Januario did not stop. The soldiers stops, he fired. Amost at the same time: the explosion, the blow on the back of his neck. Januario fell face down on the ground.

The soldiers ran towards the fallen body. Another shot, this time at point-blank range. Another. Enough, said the ensign, turning the body over with his boot so that they could all see the face. And as a coloured soldier was about to fire another shot, I said enough, no more shooting! He's dead, look how his eyes are sticking out, his mouth foaming with blood!

From the four corners of the square soldiers came running to the throng that formed around the body. Move back, shouted the ensign, opening a passage. You two there, carry the body. A soldier asked if he should go on ahead and give the news that the man was dead. The ensign glowered at him furiously. Nonsense, he said. We have to take the body for them to see. He's been dead for a long time. Long before we fired a shot.

METROPOLITAN BOROUGH OF WIRRAL

DEPARTMENT OF LEISURE SERVICES

LIBRARIES AND ARTS

WITHDRAWN FROM STOCK